Praise for
Eight Girls Taking Pictures

"Thoughtful, nuanced depictions of the complexity of women's lives . . . *Eight Girls* is a moving read about the pleasures and pangs that define the lives of women."

—*USA Today*

"[A] rich ensemble novel . . . full of glamour and grit."

—*T, The New York Times Style Magazine*

"[A] tour de force . . . This exquisitely written novel-as-linked-stories is an impressive ode to feminism. . . . Spanning several decades and various romantic settings . . . Otto's novel highlights the challenges these women face as they attempt to balance career with family life. . . . Like a master portraitist, Otto focuses on the details, describing studio settings as if she were staging a photograph herself."

—*BookPage*

"Otto's photographers battle society's denunciations and personal demons as they seek love, acceptance, success, and harmony. A visionary and distinctive look at the sacrifices and triumphs of daring women."

—*Booklist*

"Otto skillfully develops each character and draws the reader in with rich detail that must be the result of careful and extensive research. Highly recommended; those with an interest in photography, women's history, or feminist literature should particularly enjoy."

—*Library Journal*

"Blending Otto's saturated yet accessible prose with her talent for stitching together stories of multiple characters with a steady, glittering needle, the novel pays homage to a number of 20th-century photographers whose lives inspired its eight interwoven tales. . . . Otto's vivid narratives of these women's lives—often bohemian, occasionally luxurious, always richly intellectual and full of love—render them as complete, complicated mediums between their cameras and a world that treats them so ambivalently."

—*Portland Monthly*

"A fascinating portrait of 20th-century women exploring and establishing their artistic vision. Writing with vivid detail and finely tuned sensibility . . . Otto's ability to capture and corral [these women's] lives . . . is laudable for shedding light on this sisterhood of pioneering artists."

—*San Jose Mercury News*

"The reader is captivated and transported on several levels with a book that rings with universal truths as it pays homage to eight very real groundbreaking photographers. . . . You don't have to be an art historian nor even like photography to love this deeply soul-satisfying work. . . . [E]ach work is a gem to be savored and appreciated like a fine work of visual art."

—*BookTrib*

EIGHT GIRLS TAKING PICTURES

A Novel

Whitney Otto

Scribner
New York   Toronto   London   Sydney   New Delhi

Scribner
A Division of Simon & Schuster, Inc.
1230 Avenue of the Americas
New York, NY 10020

Copyright © 2012 by Whitney Otto

First Scribner paperback edition June 2013

For information about special discounts for bulk purchases,
please contact Simon & Schuster Special Sales at
1-866-506-1949 or business@simonandschuster.com.

The Simon & Schuster Speakers Bureau can bring authors to your live event. For more information or to book an event, contact the Simon & Schuster Speakers Bureau at 1-866-248-3049 or visit our website at www.simonspeakers.com.

Designed by Carla Jayne Jones

Manufactured in the United States of America

1 3 5 7 9 10 8 6 4 2

Library of Congress Control Number: 2012009167

ISBN 978-1-4516-8269-4
ISBN 978-1-4516-8272-4 (pbk)
ISBN 978-1-4516-8273-1 (ebook)

Photo credits and text permissions appear on pages 341–42.

CONTENTS

Contents

For Joy Harris, Jan Novotny, and Simone Seydoux

EIGHT
GIRLS
TAKING
PICTURES

CYMBELINE IN LOVE
OR
THE UNMADE BED

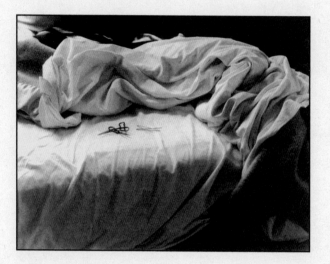

PART 1: AMERICA

The Third Fire Lit by Mary Doyle, 1917

The kitchen smelled like burnt wood and water. Cymbeline closed her eyes and imagined that she and Leroy were breaking camp on a cool morning in the Olympics, the carried river water flooding the remains of the breakfast fire before they set out for a day of photography and painting, and sometimes simply lying back in the sweetness of the grass, doing nothing. Their first year of marriage had been marked by these small journeys into the empty beauty that surrounded early-twentieth-century Seattle; Cymbeline and Leroy—a naked husband modeling in nature for his pregnant wife—making good on their promise to each other to not be like everyone else. In fact, that was the very argument he had used to urge her into marriage when he first wrote to her four years ago, in 1913, while he was still in Paris.

Nineteen thirteen was the year Leroy began traveling and painting, falling so in love with his new life in Europe that when a mutual friend put him in touch with Cymbeline—a working Seattle photographer with her own rather well-received studio that allowed her to support herself if she cut all luxury from her life—he fell in love with her as well.

The original purpose of Leroy and Cymbeline's correspondence was the organization of a small American exhibition of his work, until their letters moved easily from the logistics of the exhibition into something more personal. It was inevitable that the painter and the photographer who saw photography as a fine art would quickly find common ground, each excited by an ongoing paper conversation that seemed so warm, so effortless. All those months of shared ideas and enthusiasms were intoxicating; it was flattering to be told that she understood him so well. She was an artist, he said. He said, You are my kind.

3

She loved his paintings. He loved her pictures.

Still, she was thrown when he wrote, *Ever since the thrill that your first letter gave me, you have continued to move me. Yes, I confess it, I set out months ago with the deliberate intention of winning your affections because I wanted them, oh, I wanted them so much!!! Underlying all this, however, is that want, that emptiness, that completeness.*

She remembered the heat of her studio as she read those words, one hand holding Leroy's letter and the other a glass of iced tea, which she pressed to her forehead. It was as if Leroy's confession of emptiness and want had amplified the heat in the room as it touched upon her own hunger. It wasn't safe, she knew, to feel so much need.

He wrote, *You are the ideal woman for me, and fearing no longer, in all hope, tranquillity, and happiness. I ask you if you will be my friend and companion for life—if you will be my wife—Love and time in Italy!* She must come to him, he said, they would live in Italy and, he added, *Let's not be like anyone else.*

A million images of Italy flipped though her mind: ruins and churches; olive trees, fountains, rolling hills, and the sea. Wading in wildflowers up to her waist. The country in shades of oyster white, smoke, dusty green, brilliant New World gold, blood red, and that blue, blue sea lazing beneath the azure sky. The whimsy of Venetian palaces, and Michelangelo's slaves straining against the stone; the unrealized dream machines of Leonardo. Leroy wrote, *There are such wondrous lands to explore—*

Let's not be like anyone else.

She weighed his proposal against her studio. She weighed it against her tiny foothold in American art, having recently had her first exhibition even though the patronizing tone of the male critics who said her pictures were "pleasing" cut her a little. She balanced her present against her future; she thought about marriage (something she seldom thought about) and children (something she often thought about). She weighed out her education (the first in her family with a university degree, in chemistry and German).

She weighed out her physical aspect (she was small, with unruly red curls, metal-framed glasses, a good, if slightly pear-shaped figure), her looks enhanced by her intelligence and curiosity and willingness to accept the complexity in most things. But as to beauty, the best she could claim was a kind of specialized beauty, the sort that someone may feel happy to have stumbled upon. She weighed out her professional possibilities and the knowledge that America had not yet caught up with a woman's ambition. She weighed out the fact that she and Leroy had yet to meet, face-to-face.

She was twenty-nine years old.

Along with the doused campfire scent, the kitchen carried the aroma of torched cotton and paint—a kind of nervy, toxic smell. The glass windows appeared slightly altered, as if the high temperature had softened them.

The damage to this room was nothing when compared to the room with which it shared a wall: Cymbeline's darkroom and studio. The wooden floor and bits of debris crackled under her boots, though the place wasn't completely destroyed; the damage was sweeping yet selective, the overall effect was of the room's entire contents seeming unsalvageable, until her eyes grew accustomed to its shocking appearance. The urge to slide to the floor in the middle of the mess while surrendering to tears had to be resisted since she knew she would have a hard time getting back up, both figuratively and literally—she was eight months into what had been, and still was, a difficult pregnancy.

All this while Leroy was off painting in Yosemite, Cymbeline no longer able to comfortably accompany him as she had in the first year of their marriage. Even when she was pregnant with Bosco, their first child, now a two-year-old, she could still keep up with Leroy. She could take nude pictures of him as he posed in the forest or near a lake (she was said to have "invented the male nude" in reference to those honeymoon photographs). One of the most successful was of him as Narcissus, seduced by his beautiful reflection. This was during her Pictorial phase, when she believed that photographs could be made to imitate paintings.

Her approach to photography eventually changed, but Leroy stayed the same. The self-involvement that had masqueraded as charm when they were new was now just an accepted fact of their marriage.

When Bosco was a baby (she had gotten pregnant so quickly!), Leroy left on a monthlong trip in the spring, followed by a two-month trip in the summer, "the only time to work in the San Juans," he insisted. She understood and complied, staying behind to manage Bosco, the house, her photography, and to pen love letters to Leroy.

And so life went on with Leroy needing to "get away" for his art (Leroy already talking about ten weeks making seascapes along the Northern California coast in late August) while she stayed behind with Bosco, her troublesome pregnancy, the even more troublesome Mary Doyle, and their now partially burned house.

On her good days, Cymbeline took pictures of Bosco as he investigated the flowers in the marginally tended garden (which she had no time for). He spilled water on the cat. He pinched a pill bug between his strong little fingers, an old discarded shoe lay nearby. There was Bosco eating a sandwich that had recently fallen in the dirt. Sometimes he slept naked in the sun, and she took pictures of that too. Bosco held her fast with his love, and his practical needs; her photographs of him were not so much a mother's desire to record her son's life as a consequence of all that endless togetherness.

Someone sent her a magazine with pictures by Elliot and Andrs; photographs by men she knew, had worked with; men who had mistresses, muses, studio assistants, and wives—a wealth of women to do for them—pictures that she had no time to study because Bosco was crying. Bosco wanted lunch. Maybe Bosco didn't nap today because he was coming down with a cold that would keep him up all night.

Then there were the few clients she still saw, who felt like another demand: Could she arrange a sitting? Could she touch up the negative to, you know, fix things a bit? When could she drop off the prints, or when could someone pick them up? And yet she still loved her work so much that it almost killed her, loving it so much. The chemical stains on her fingers meant more to her than diamonds.

She wrote to Leroy, *I have spent so much time in the darkroom. My mother came at 3 & took B. for a little walk. I hardly had time to speak to her because I had to get 2 of my morning prints dry & flat & spotted & get the others finished before an expected caller at 4. I'm still sick as a dog.* She didn't write, *I can't do this alone,* because they had hired a young woman, Mary Doyle, to help her. He wondered why they needed the extra expense when they already lived so close to the wire. Housemaids, he announced as he finished packing, were nothing more than a luxury.

Mary Doyle, Cymbeline wanted to write, steals small, inconsequential things that become important only when they're missing. But she couldn't complain to Leroy about Mary Doyle ("nothing more than a luxury") because Mary made it possible for Cymbeline to keep what was left of her photography. *Mary Doyle is careless when she lights the evening candles. Once I watched her light each taper before holding the flame to the hem of a curtain. When I called out to her, it was as if I had awakened her from a trance, leaving me to rush in and slap out the sparks.*

On the days when Cymbeline was too weak and worn to leave her bed before noon, Mary Doyle hustled around the house, softly singing to Bosco, baking bread, and cheerfully sweeping the floors.

No one would listen if Cymbeline tried to describe Mary Doyle setting a small, smoldering log from the fireplace onto the hearth rug, then strolling out the front door to retrieve the mail. Cymbeline smelled the burning material almost immediately as it began to catch, and she rushed to stamp out the embers, singeing the hem of her dress. She was torn between what she believed to be true about the girl (that she could not be trusted) and her need for help around the house.

So she told herself that Mary Doyle got distracted, and no wonder with all she had to do all day to allow Cymbeline the time to do as she pleased; who in 1917 would sympathize with a married woman who chose to work? Wasn't Mary Doyle exactly like someone she deserved?

So when Leroy was off painting *El Capitan*, Cymbeline spent her days in the little Seattle cottage with their two-year-old son, Bosco, while

Mary Doyle set Cymbeline's darkroom and studio on fire, igniting the kitchen only as an afterthought. Cymbeline berated herself for taking her eye off that sweet, angel-faced girl whom the police gently escorted to jail.

She simply couldn't take the pressure of More Things Going Wrong. There was never a rest from the sense of the unpredictable, and often the unaffordable, pressing in on her. The Lives of Artists, she thought wryly, and what did she expect? She had been old enough (no child at age thirty) when she married Leroy to understand that the creative life was often one of constant hustling; her naïveté had surfaced when she thought she could do it with children. How could she have known how much space a child takes up in one's thoughts and in one's heart? Her first thought following this last fire was Thank God Bosco was with me, his safety always on her mind. Her second was, had anything, anything at all happened to that little boy, there was nothing that could save Mary Doyle. How close motherhood could bring her to dark fantasies of murder.

Yet listening to Leroy, one would think that he was under so much more pressure than she, which was why he absolutely had to be able to nip off to Nature to paint. So he could come home rejuvenated and inspired.

Cymbeline couldn't remember the last time she'd felt inspired. And if she did feel the familiar elation of creative possibility, it was almost instantly crushed by Bosco calling her to play with him or to feed him. Or it was Leroy who wanted supper and could she please quiet the baby? Oh, and where was that paintbrush he had so recently bought? Then furious to see Bosco loading it with mud in the garden.

This was the sort of thing that would cause Leroy to rant about the lack of order in their household and how was he supposed to paint if she wouldn't do her part? He would accuse her of indifference to him, of professional jealousy (hers toward him), of caring more about domestic matters than she did art, you see, then pronounce her "happy with her little home life but he needed more." This contradictory line of reasoning would sometimes segue into "I don't even know who you are!"

Under her breath she would say, "I don't know who I am either."

———————————

In the wreckage of the studio, Cymbeline sorted through the ashes of film stock, prints, the burnt barrel that housed her stored glass negatives, those pictures of another life. The baby kicked. Bosco sat with his grandmother in the other room. Across the studio was a black leather carrying case, miraculously spared, that held six exposed glass plates Cymbeline told herself she would print one of these days, when she had the time. Not allowing herself to think too much about why she "never had the time" to make prints of *Waiting Room, Anhalter Bahnhof* or *Mathematics & Love* or *Tulips*; or *Late at Night, the Brandenburg Gate* or *Something to Want* or *The Unmade Bed*. Or *Julius*.

She picked up her old folding camera, a Seneca No. 9, the one she had bought before she went to Dresden, that she wouldn't have left out of the black leather carrying case had she known the fate of her studio. Though it was miraculously intact, on closer inspection she could make out slight damage to the lens, a couple of minuscule holes in the bellows where it looked as if sparks may have landed. She carefully set it back down, walked into the kitchen, took paper from a drawer, and sent yet another letter to Leroy: *By the time you get this we will be packed and on our way to California. We'll be staying with your parents until I find all of us a new place to live. With love, C.*

But what she wanted to write was *You were wrong. We're exactly like everyone else.*

PART 2: GERMANY

Her Dresden Year, 1909–1910

Seven years before the kitchen fire, through luck and hard work Cymbeline was awarded a scholarship to study at the Technische Hochschule in Dresden with Julius Weisz, the most famous professor of photochemistry in the world. The personal time line that had brought Cymbeline to this point went something like this: reading the classics, summers spent painting and drawing, her first year of university, when she decided to become a photographer, six months to determine exactly what that meant, a love of art and the belief that taking photographs could be like painting with light; the good advice she took to major in chemistry (photography as an academic discipline? A degree in art? It did not exist); college employment making lantern slides for the botany department, her still indulgent father building her a shed-darkroom where she worked by the light of a candle in a red box ("I can't see what all that studying at the university will do if you're just going to be a dirty photographer," said the man who confused the matter by doing without so his daughter could have art classes). A self-photographed nude taken in a field of uncut grass surrounding the campus, in which Cymbeline looked more playful than sexual. Then graduation, a job with a famous photographer who "took" famous pictures of Native Americans even though he was arrogant and absent, leaving so much of the work to his assistant, who, in turn, instructed Cymbeline. Then the scholarship, the black leather–covered Seneca folding-bed camera that, when closed into a relatively small box (seven by seven by four and a quarter), weighed all of three and a half pounds if not loaded with a pair of dry glass plates; everything, camera and a handful of plates, fitting into a compact black leather suitcase that was part of her prize.

She took the Seneca, packed several boxes of Eastman dry-plate glass slides, and her few belongings aboard a train barreling across the country to catch a steamer bound for Liverpool. It was during that trip that Cymbeline met someone, and, in the time it took to span the Atlantic, the affair had run its course. Neither partner mourned its brevity; when Cymbeline and the man said good-bye in Liverpool, she was already past their encounter, excited for the next new thing.

With every traveled mile taking her farther and farther from Seattle, Cymbeline could feel herself opening. Everything was new and marvelous and confounding and curious. She had suddenly, miraculously, caught up to her own life. The future stopped eluding her grasp long enough for her to enter it, breathless and happy. Even the shipboard romance was perfect in that it was nothing more than a soufflé.

Then she arrived in Dresden, a colossal confection of a city, where she enrolled in a studio art class, found a teacher to improve her German, and became the sole woman accepted into the photochemistry seminar of the renowned Julius Weisz, which was when all her best intentions to leave love alone left her.

The first day of her photochemistry class at the Technische Hochschule, Cymbeline realized that not only was she the lone woman in the room but, at age twenty-seven, she was quite possibly the oldest student in there as well. Her American smile, nervous and reflexive, was met with indifference when it was met at all.

Her solitude forced her out into the Dresden streets—curiosity too, laced with loneliness—pushed her out into this place that felt as insubstantial as an invented story with its impossibly romantic architecture, grand concourses, perfectly arranged gardens, and fountains. There were churches and palaces. And all of it as elaborate as expensive pastry. While she was in transit, being unattached was exhilarating, but the moment she stopped, so did the high.

Seattle was raw, unfinished and barely begun; surely no one could miss Cymbeline's hayseed aspect as she wandered the gardens and city squares and wide boulevards, alternately fixated on her environment while unaware of the people within it. There was something fabulous about walking along the Elbe River instead of gazing out across Elliott Bay, or spending her days going largely unnoticed in a college class of men, or hearing only German and no one talking to her in class or on the street, leaving her unsure about her conversational skills. It was as if she had willed this dream into being then forgot to make herself visible.

Additionally, she was now cursed with all the time alone she never felt she could get enough of back in her stateside life. So novel was this situation that she barely knew what to do with herself. She tried to list the advantages of being overlooked, chief among them having to be concerned only with herself; then she would see something funny or provocative or puzzling, and, without someone with whom to share the funny/provocative/puzzling thing, her aloneness would come to her all over again.

The Advantages to Being Alone list had a single entry—that of having to be concerned only with her own desires, which pretty much exhausted the upside.

As a photographer, Cymbeline was drawn to the pictorial photograph. She loved the softness of Käsebier, the manifesto of Stieglitz, the dreamy, blurred beauty of Baron de Meyer—these pictures that could be paintings. She believed, as others did, that a camera was good for more than recording the world. A photograph wasn't a response to something; it was something. (After Berlin, after marriage, she would say that she "shifted her own artistic expressions along less sentimental lines.")

There was no one in Dresden she knew well enough to pose for her. No friends or models to arrange in biblical allegories, or tableaux of Greek gods and goddesses. So, on a dry autumn day, Cymbeline stowed her boxy camera in the little black leather suitcase, along with a handful of dry plates, and went into the street. If she was to be invisible, then she may as well use that invisibility.

It wasn't long before Cymbeline came to a massive mural made of tile. Even if it was placed at street level and not well above the sidewalk, and below a bank of windows on what looked to be an important building, the thirty-foot-high picture would still dwarf whoever stood beside it. The illustration was a parade of theatrically dressed men, some on horseback, others on foot, all resembling finely drawn ink etchings on white, with a yellow background. There had to be a hundred figures, many with names written below and just above the bottom of the ornate border that framed the entire scene.

There was no way to photograph the whole mural; the building across the street threw shadows, and photographing straight up, or when standing at one end of the hundreds-feet-long mural, caused distortion.

Cymbeline, the open suitcase beside her, camera in hand, was trying to gauge the shadows and distance when a voice said in faintly accented English, "Why don't you photograph real people instead of drawings of people?" She was so accustomed to being unseen, it didn't occur to her that she was being addressed, even in English. "It isn't the original mural, you know."

This time Cymbeline turned to see Julius Weisz, her photochemistry professor.

"*Fürstenzug, The Procession of Princes*—a history of local royalty— was first carved into the wall about three hundred years ago. When the years faded it to almost nothing, a nineteenth-century artist named Wilhelm Walther decided to carve it back in."

"Wilhelm Walther?" asked Cymbeline.

"I suspect many people wondered who he was, so he etched himself as the last man in the procession. Like a 'hanging on,' yes? A hundred years later his painting was replaced with tiles," he said as he was already reaching for her camera. "May I?"

He held the camera for a moment, then opened the hinged flap that protected the ground-glass viewfinder, which he turned vertically and horizontally before adjusting the bellows. "It's a good weight for street pictures," he said.

"You know, I do photograph real people, not lately because . . . That is, I did work in a portrait studio for the last two years. Mostly, I made prints and negatives."

"Is that how you came to be interested in your platinum paper experiments?"

"I think there's a way to use lead to increase the printing speed. The whites will be sharper, and the result, I think, will be more beautiful." She stopped. "Anyway, I came to that on my own. Not from the man who ran the studio."

"You didn't like this man?"

"No." She sighed. "Being well-known made him arrogant. My lessons came from his assistant, who did everything."

"And what did you learn about people when you worked there?"

"You mean about portraiture?"

He said nothing as he studied her from behind the wire-rimmed glasses that were exactly like hers. "This bad man influenced you to stop taking portraits?" His hair was longer on top and close on the sides, and he had a small beard. His informal attire was pretty par for a scholar; her discerning eye caught the quiet money in the cut and fabric, and something else: an unexpectedly stylish quality. His face and figure were pleasing; funny how she had never really noticed that he was, well, rather handsome. For someone in his early forties, anyway.

"I don't know anyone here," and in that moment she could have sworn that he understood the isolation of being an American girl walking around Dresden, on a day off from class but without the company of a single classmate.

"And I'm to be somewhere."

"Oh, sure, of course," said Cymbeline, "I didn't mean to keep you."

"But you didn't keep me."

He seemed genuinely reluctant to leave. "May I take your picture? A souvenir of this great bathroom wall of German princes and their shameless friend, Wilhelm Walther."

The suggestion itself was enough to make Cymbeline feel better than she had in weeks as she stood there, posing against a backdrop of blond brick, well below the image of Mr. Walther, the mural almost too high on the building to capture anything but the decorative border, boots, and horses' hooves that hovered above Cymbeline, even with Julius Weisz standing across the narrow street. She imagined how the pair appeared to those walking by: two tourists, maybe lovers, spending an afternoon together.

"I really do have to go now, but I will see you again." He returned her camera.

Was he asking to see her again? Was he interested in her? Her experience with men was so thin that she couldn't quite read him.

"At school?"

"At school," she agreed a little too enthusiastically in an attempt to hide her misunderstanding of his words.

As he walked away she realized that during the train trip from Seattle to New York; the week spent in New York City; the Atlantic crossing to Liverpool; her five days in London and the following three in Paris before arriving in Dresden, she had taken pictures of prairie and farmland, country train stations, monuments, museums, cathedrals and gardens, fellow travelers and other strangers, rivers and boats, and zoo animals, but not one photograph of herself. She was a kind of nonpresence in her own adventure. Her absence didn't occur to her until Julius Weisz suggested taking her picture. It was as if he knew what it was to be apart and on one's own, as if he knew her. Much later, she wondered if all love begins with these sorts of simple understandings, you know, just one person seeing another.

———————

The encounter with Julius Weisz at *The Procession of Princes* changed everything. Having that a casual meeting on a random street meant that Cymbeline was someone living in a city where she could have a casual meeting on a random street—only that street was in Dresden and not in Seattle. This ordinary thing made Dresden more of a home to her than anything else ever could. Which set her to thinking about home and familiarity and belonging. It also had her studying Julius Weisz, if only to convince herself that she hadn't imagined she'd once had his undivided attention. She tried to ignore the reasons why this mattered.

When she was growing up, Cymbeline's father, a forward-thinking man enamored of the spirit world, vegetarianism, and his daughter's education, named his daughter for a Shakespearean king—"Not a queen," he said, "not a girl" (years later it was Leroy who delighted in the coincidence of his name translating to "king" in French and hers being the name of a king, just more evidence that they were meant to be)—instructed her in Dante, Theosophy, American Transcendentalism, Latin, and the *Encyclopaedia Britannica,* since it offered a "foundation for everything." He made sure she had art classes in the summer though her large family could barely afford them.

But it was when she recited Homer that she realized she wouldn't want to return once she had left, a thought that had more to do with watching her mother labor in a home where she barely had enough time to sleep, let alone pick up a book or meditate on the spiritual beliefs of Madame Blavatsky. Life on their Seattle farm was so very hard in all the ways that a rural life, where the money seemed to come and go in proportions so exact that growth and debt canceled each other out, is hard. She loved her parents and her brothers and sisters, but, for now, in Dresden, she loved being away more.

Everyone in Julius Weisz's class was expected to attend the International Photographic Exposition. Cymbeline had been twice already, looking again at Stieglitz's work—his pictures taking on a more personal meaning now that she herself was studying in Germany, much as he had twenty years before—but the work that really held her belonged to Baron de Meyer: all that glamour, all those elegant dreams embodied in still lifes and portraits.

Julius Weisz said, "There is an arrogance in the demand for the viewer's attention." He went on to say that if the photographer isn't going to pay attention to the picture he is making, that if he thinks the camera is just a machine and not an avenue of expression, then he has no business asking anyone for anything, let alone their time and interest. Don't show the world, he said, invent the world.

In this regard, the soft-edged beauty of the de Meyers was extreme. His graceful universe was like seeing life on a star. The fashions worn by the models always went one luxurious step, one extravagant diamond and pearl necklace, one highly stylized headdress or sleeve further. Her favorite picture was of two hydrangea blossoms, their stems suspended in a drinking glass, bending over the side as if they meant to fall: the glass, the water, the table, the wall ethereal. At first glance, the photograph was as simple in its subject and composition as his pictures with people were baroque.

It was at this very photograph at the exposition where Cymbeline and Julius Weisz caught up with each other.

"What do you think about photographing flowers?" she asked.

"It depends if you're talking about living flowers or cut flowers."

She was about to ask him about the difference when he said, "One is memento mori, so to speak. Its life is ended, its appearance in rapid decline. As a photographer you have a completely different set of problems to solve when you photograph cut flowers."

"Like this picture with the reflection of the water and the table and wall?" she asked. They were looking at de Meyer's hydrangea blossoms.

"Sure, okay. Let's take this picture. There is the problem of the light bouncing on the reflection of the water, the glass, the tabletop, and the wall. But any picture could deal with the problem of light. The problem with this picture is greater than that of reflective surfaces—it's one of death. You invite a profound theme into your work when you choose cut flowers. You are talking about mortality and time moving forward. You are saying that everything, everything we see and experience and love happens uniquely and happens only once. When you take a picture of a flower in a glass you are, paradoxically, capturing evanescence. You are also showing the indifference of Nature. There is no mourning in a flower photograph, only a shrugging of the shoulders."

"I think it's beautiful."

"That would make de Meyer very happy to hear."

Across from the de Meyers were some photographs of gypsies, dressed in a kind of exotic finery, though Cymbeline's practiced eye could still make out their scratch living. Next were pictures of New York, so beautiful they could break your heart. Except Cymbeline had been to New York, walking herself to exhaustion during her five days there, and all its beauty could not blind her to the immigrant slums she saw, the overcrowded darkness of some parts of the city. It was her habit, as a photographer, to constantly observe the light, natural or artificial. The poor in these neighborhoods were so crammed together that one of the luxuries they were forced to forgo was sunlight. Strange to think that money bought the sun, which rightfully belonged to no one. Cymbeline slightly amazed that the wealthy would find ways to keep and control something that shouldn't have been anyone's to control.

Maybe it was because she had grown up from a poor girl into a young woman who had to watch every penny that things like this often crossed her mind.

"What are you thinking?" asked Julius.

"I'm thinking, Did the photographer set up the shots of the gypsies or were they allowed to be themselves?" She had not forgotten some of the artificial poses the famous portrait photographer in Seattle imposed on his Native American sitters, not to mention the antiquated costumes he forced them to wear.

"Ah, the bad man you worked for at home."

"I'm uncomfortable with the artifice. It feels condescending."

"You prefer the unartful de Meyers. The flowers in the crystal bowl, the grown woman in a tiara wearing a cloud of tulle, the man with kohl eyeliner dancing in the costume of a pasha?"

She wandered back to de Meyer's pictures of his moneyed, arty society, which were pure artifice. She sighed, aware of the contradiction. "I love these. I just do."

Julius, who had followed her, nodded.

She turned to him. "Perhaps my taste lies somewhere between reality and dreamland."

"Why not meet me tomorrow at the Himmlisch Garten? We'll talk about people and life."

"People and life?"

"I mean portraits and flowers."

She laughed. She liked his teasing.

A young man, somewhere in age between Cymbeline and Julius, and whom she thought she recognized, hurried over. As he slid his body between them, addressing Julius, he subtly forced Cymbeline out. "Julius, *Sie müssen kommen und sehen*," pulling him by the hand toward the adjacent gallery with Cymbeline hesitantly tagging along.

The trio entered the high-ceilinged room to find a large crowd gathered in the far corner. From their vantage point they had to keep readjusting their sight line to see the man speaking.

"This little camera is affixed like so—" said the man speaking, holding a pigeon firmly, though not unkindly, in his hands. He held it aloft so everyone could see the tiny camera that was part of the harness buckled to the bird's breast. There was a sound of birds cooing.

"The Bavarian Pigeon Corps, whom we are happy to introduce to you today, has been taking aerial photos for us since 1903. This camera takes automatic exposures at thirty-second intervals during the bird's travel. On the wall behind me, you can see the results." Through the interstices of the crowd, Cymbeline could see the photographs hung on the walls without being able to make out their contents.

The pigeon man, a Herr Neubronner, who, as it happened, was the inventor of the avian camera harness, began handing out penny postcards of the bird-shot aerial photographs.

One of the cards made it all the way back to Cymbeline, Julius, and the young man who stood near the arched doorway of the gallery. As she studied the picture, she marveled at the wonder of seeing the earth from the clouds. The closest she'd ever come to something like that was when she had hiked up a very tall mountain, though it didn't seem anywhere close to peering down with nothing but sky below your feet. For a fleeting moment she thought about what her father, the animal lover, would have said about these birds being pressed into service wearing this ridiculous apparatus.

As she went to hand the postcard back to Julius, she noticed the young man whispering something in German to him, his hand resting lightly on the back of Julius's jacket. This single, unremarkable gesture struck her as unbearably intimate; she could neither stand it, nor walk away.

He was saying something that made Julius laugh. Now she remembered: She had seen him once, in profile, when she was passing Julius's office. He was sitting across from Julius's desk, laughing and talking. Another time he was drinking coffee in a student café near the school. She had a hard time determining his age, something she attributed to his having the curly hair of a Renaissance angel.

"I am rude. I am sorry," said the young man to Cymbeline, as if he'd only just now noticed her. "I am Otto Girondi. I teach maths at the school, and I think I may have seen you there."

"I think I've seen you—" The loud, collective ooohhh of the crowd interrupted her. The small flock of pigeons had been released in the room and were diving and climbing as they swept about the gallery. It was difficult to count the number of birds because of their intersecting flight patterns, but there seemed to be at least a dozen.

Herr Neubronner announced in a loud, excited voice that these birds were, at this very moment, taking aerial photos of everyone below! Cymbeline stepped back, taking refuge under the archway, having lived among animals long enough to know that a bird doesn't care if it's inside or outside when it comes to its droppings. Julius and Otto crowded in next to her at the first cry of someone on the receiving end of earthbound waste. It was from this vantage point that the three watched a crowd first entranced, then panicked at the amount of scat falling upon them.

One bird landed on a woman's hat, another on a man's bare head, his hair worse for the experience; mostly they swooped and made a mess as amazement turned to chaos, with Herr Neubronner alternately trying to redirect the birds and regain the crowd's attention. No one listened as they fled the room in their now white-flecked clothing, Cymbeline, Julius, and Otto pressing themselves against the outside wall of the adjacent room.

Cymbeline caught somewhere between amusement and disbelief. "Just when I was worried that taking a decent picture required no greater skill than having a camera strapped to my chest."

"You don't need a class," said Otto, "you need a dovecote."

"And a raincoat," said Julius, laughing along with the other two. He barely touched Cymbeline on her shoulder, his hand almost hovering. "The Himmlisch on Saturday," he reminded her. "Bring your camera. Buckled to your body."

And just as quickly as she felt the three of them united in their luck at missing the Wrath of the Bavarian Pigeon Corps, she again felt excluded from the company of the men. She couldn't say why, or how, this happened; she was accustomed to feeling outside the groups of her male classmates, but this was different. This was a puzzle she couldn't quite put together.

———————

"I want you to see the difference when photographing flowers in the garden." Julius was coaching Cymbeline as he set up to take pictures of the few flowers still in bloom in the Himmlisch Garten before the season finally changed. She was more interested in the shrubs and the trees, with their variety of leaves and branches.

She sighed.

"What?"

"I can't attach any meaning to any of this," she said. "That is, I don't know why I would want to take these pictures." Nor could she attach any meaning to his interest in instructing her outside of class, an interaction that left her unable to completely get her bearings.

"We can't always photograph that which engages us—unless you are a rich girl prowling around for a hobby. Something that you can tell your friends about. Some sort of Kodak Girl," he said in reference to the advertising posters of a well-to-do girl with a Kodak camera. A pretty amateur. The ad campaign encouraged photography as a harmless hobby, something to do before marriage.

She told herself, He is teaching me. He is a teacher. Not a friend. Not a lover. Yet the tone of his voice and his implication that she was unserious in her pursuit of photography cut her. It was unlike her to be so sensitive to something some man said—she had spent enough time with men in chemistry class and botany labs and working for the famous, awful photographer to disregard their remarks as they often disregarded her. Even an internationally established photographer like Alfred Stieglitz (something of a guiding light for her), whom she'd met when passing through New York, could barely hide his impatience as she confessed her ambition to have a picture appear in *Camera Work*.

She had wondered at times why her father bought her art lessons or encouraged her to attend the university. It wasn't lost on Cymbeline that everyone loved and admired the eccentric heiress, the rich girl who defied societal expectations. It was the rebellious working-class girl they mistrusted; not only should she be working but she should be working

21

for *them*. Cymbeline had learned from a very early age that money buys things that people with money never even realize they've bought, like time and freedom. Because their privilege came to them so naturally, it was unimaginable that others didn't have it too; that is to say, if others didn't have it, perhaps that was because it would be wasted on them, the rich always seeming to believe themselves meant for better things.

There was something tough at her core, Cymbeline knew. Was it being singled out by her father, who'd named her for a king, or was it wanting to be a photographer, so much so that she would suffer anything to have it?

After months in Julius's class, she was seldom invited to study sessions or included in coffee-fueled discussions with her male classmates. They weren't rude to her; she didn't count enough for rudeness. True, she was older than most of them, but not by much. And she knew that she wasn't a common beauty, something that shouldn't matter yet always does.

The closest she came to any sort of professional camaraderie was when one of her classmates—perhaps the most talented—asked if she would sit for him. He explained that he needed the practice since he planned to open the best studio in Berlin, then said that he'd heard she had some skill in printing, so it was possible that he would *allow* her to print something for him. And, he added, if all went well, maybe she could do even more work for him. No pay, of course, but what a great opportunity for her to hone her darkroom skills, and besides it would free him up to take more pictures.

Cymbeline said, "Maybe," while thinking about the rustic darkroom her father had built for her during her college years, where she printed by candlelight coming from a red paper box. There were all those botanical slides, not to mention the conceited Seattle photographer and the sheer luck of being able to work with his German assistant, who'd taught her so well and so patiently. There never seemed to be enough hours in the day for her own photography, especially when she was diligent enough to try to get it right.

She thought about the way the men in her class went on and on about their ambitions, philosophies, and ideas without ever asking her a single question. She thought about the confidence it took to believe that only what you did was important, that a man's artistic perspective of the world was the only perspective.

It was a funny place for women photographers where they were accepted into the profession (usually taking soft-focus Pictorialist scenes of domesticity)—some were quite well-known—and they were always a half step behind their male counterparts.

So when Julius Weisz made his remark about her work as a hobby, it wasn't anything she hadn't heard before. What was new was hearing it from him.

Julius sighed. "You should understand that I'm not asking you to find the thing in a subject that engages you—rather I am suggesting you see that subject in a whole new way—as photographer, see it so that everything will interest you." He said, "You can do this, Cymbeline."

Here was the strange thing: She understood absolutely that he believed in her ability, yet his belief had the effect of suddenly making her doubt herself. And something else, too; she had a moment of hard clarity that her life, her woman's life, would be full of choices—ordinary ones a man might not even see as choices but as "life"—that would constantly be canceling each other out.

"These plants may not mean anything to you because you aren't ready to understand them. Listen, we are not always meant to get everything all at once. And what I mean is that they may not have any complexity for you right now—not like the cut flowers with their combination of beauty and decay, right? Like trying to hold on to nothing. You need to see that everything has something underneath. The seen and the hidden. Nothing is what it seems to be—the underneath. Do you understand?

"It's okay," he said. "Come. I have someplace else to show you."

Julius explained that the palace rooms where they stood were called *Wunderkammern*, or wonder rooms. Souvenirs of nature, of travels across continents and seas; jewels and skulls. A show of wealth, intellect, power.

23

The first room had rose-colored glass walls, with rubies and garnets and bloodred drapes of damask. Bowls of blush quartz; semiprecious stone roses running the spectrum of red down to pink, a hard, glittering garden. The vaulted ceiling, a feature of all of the ten rooms Julius and Cymbeline visited, was a trompe l'oeil of a rosy sky at dawn, golden light edging the morning clouds.

The next room was of sapphire and sea and sky; lapis lazuli, turquoise and gold and silver. A silver mermaid lounged on the edge of a lapis lazuli bowl fashioned in the shape of an ocean. Venus stood aloft on the waves draped in pearls. There were gold fish and diamond fish and faceted sterling silver starfish. Silvered mirrors edged in silvered mirror. There were opals and aquamarines and tanzanite and amethyst. Seaweed bloomed in shades of blue-green marble. The ceiling was a dome of endless, pale blue.

A jungle room of mica and marble followed, with its rain forest of cats made from tiger's-eye, yellow topaz birds, tortoiseshell giraffes with stubby horns of spun gold. Carved clouds of smoky quartz hovered over a herd of obsidian and ivory zebras. Javelinas of spotted pony hide charged tiny, life-size dik-diks with velvet hides, and dazzling diamond antlers mingled with miniature stuffed sable minks. Agate columns painted a medley of dark greens were strung with faceted ropes of green gold.

A room of ivory: bone, teeth, skulls, and velvet.

A room crowded with columns all sheathed in mirrors, reflecting world maps and globes and atlases inlaid with silver, platinum, and white gold; the rubies and diamonds that were sometimes set to mark the location of a city or a town of conquest resembled blood and tears.

A room dominated by a fireplace large enough to hold several people, upholstered in velvets and silks the colors of flame. Snakes of gold with orange sapphire and yellow topaz eyes coiled around the room's columns.

Statues of smiling black men in turbans offering trays of every gem imaginable—emerald, sapphire, ruby, topaz, diamond—stood at the entrance to a room upholstered in pistachio velvet, accented with malachite, called the Green Vault. Peridot wood nymphs attended to a Diana carved from a single pure crystal of quartz studded with tiny tourmalines. Jade tables, and jade lanterns. The royal jewels, blinding in their sparkling excess: crowns, tiaras, coronets, diadems, heavy ceremonial necklaces, rings, and bracelets that could span a forearm, surrounding the world's largest and most perfect green diamond.

Above it all was a night sky of painted stars, with inlaid cut crystal set in a series of constellations.

Cymbeline had to sit down once they were outside the palace because she felt that she had just been miniaturized and trapped in a box of heat and light. It was if she had narrowly escaped a place meant to be astonishing and unworldly and desirable where all she felt was anxiety.

As she slowly recovered from this fever dream of opulence, she turned to Julius and said, "You've made your point. Something so glittering like—"

"—Grünes Gewölbe or, in English, Green Vault—"

"—could be heaven for someone like—" She looked to him.

"—August the Strong, who built it in the early eighteenth century—"

"—but it's unbearable to me, even though I can see the appeal for someone else. What should be thought of as beautiful is really a show of power, though it could be thought to be merely beautiful. But it isn't— it's intimidating. I understand now: There's always an underneath."

"No, no, Cymbeline." He laughed. "I only took you there because I thought you might like to see it. Not as a student—as a tourist. So when you went home you could tell your friends that you saw the famous Dresden Green Diamond. This was not meant to scare you." Now they were both laughing.

———————————

Winter came and went, with spring appearing and everything coming back to itself. The air was cool and sweet. Cymbeline was still on her own much of the time, except when she was with Julius Weisz. It wasn't difficult to see how they formed the friendship that began with taking photo journeys around Dresden, with Julius as tour guide. They would meet somewhere—a garden, a church, a palace, a neighborhood, a platz, a riverside—she with her five-by-seven camera and extra dry plates in her small black leather suitcase, and he with his Kodak roll-film camera.

Eventually the time spent together lengthened, and they would linger over coffee and a pastry. On other days, they would dine together at lunch, occasionally dinner. They talked about photography, and chemistry. Cymbeline explained her experiments that had led to a paper that spring called "About the Direct Development of Platinum Paper for Brown Tones." They talked about the use of color, of how to use a romantic blur without being sentimental—"I abhor sentimentality," she told him. They found more aerial photos, pictures taken from tethered hot-air balloons, kites, even small rockets. Maybe it was the fact of Cymbeline's time in Dresden drawing to a close that edged their many conversations into more personal topics.

"Cymbeline, Cymbeline," Julius said, "is that a common name for American girls?"

"My father has some interesting ideas about women, like giving them men's names. He once made us live in a spiritual commune on the Strait of Juan de Fuca in Washington."

"A spiritual commune? Like a place of ghosts?"

"No, but he believes in those too."

"I would like to meet this father of yours."

Then there were times when Cymbeline felt they were speaking in code; she would offer an opinion, say, about the recent hunger strikes of the jailed militant British suffragettes, and the increasing violence toward women, and Julius's ambiguous response about being "allowed to be who you are" would leave her to wonder what, exactly, they were talking about. It was similar to when her family members would have loud, lively and slightly aggressive political discussions that seemed to have little to do with politics and everything to do with the friction between certain family members. All those unresolved disagreements that cannot be addressed directly lest the confrontation cause permanent damage, the unkind words and frustrations laid bare. Much better to dress it up in something like politics.

Her confusion was that Julius sought her out, seeming to enjoy her company, but in what way she wasn't entirely sure. There were times when she felt nothing but the warmth of friendship and professional camaraderie. It was the other times that threw her, when she was aware of a spark much like the little flash from the day they ran into each other at *The Procession of Princes.* Most likely she was simply one more temporary student-friend in a long line of temporary student-friends. It seemed so unsurprising, that students and professors sharing the same interests would share a friendship. Then the students grew up, moved on, or went home (like Cymbeline) while Julius remained in place. And maybe he was a little lonely too?

Cymbeline also noticed him "giving her the once-over twice," as her sister Ruby would say. Cymbeline was shy around men; she was not shy around Julius.

Then there were the times when he seemed to disappear outside of class and she wouldn't see him for days. And other times when he was with her—yet not with her—and she knew enough not to ask where he was when his attention was so clearly elsewhere.

She told herself it was a German thing, something cultural that she didn't understand. She told herself that she didn't ask because she didn't want to be rude, when, in truth, she didn't want to know. It had occurred to her that he might be married; no one wants to be in love with a married man. There. She admitted it. She was in love with Julius Weisz.

Berlin, 1910

The trip to Berlin came about because Julius told her, "You really should see Berlin before you leave." Though she very much wanted to visit Berlin, if for no other reason than that it was the city of Alfred Stieglitz, she demurred. "What would be your hesitation?" he asked.

Going away with you, she wanted to say, because I have no idea what it means to go away with you. Instead she said, "I'm not sure I have the money for it."

They would take the train, he said, spend the day and return that evening. "You will be my guest," he said. "Cymbeline, you have never seen anything like Berlin. It's one of those cities that can't be mistaken for someplace else."

So this is how Cymbeline ended up disembarking from a train at the Anhalter Bahnhof, a vast cathedral of a train station flooded with light and possessing four separate waiting rooms, including one used exclusively by the Hohenzollerns. They stepped out of the station and into a crazy intersection of five converging boulevards ("Potsdamer Platz," said Julius). The sheer volume of pedestrians, trolleys, horse-drawn carts, bicycles, pushcarts, motorcars, and carriages was exhilarating. There were newsboys and flower sellers. Tram bells and horses' hooves and car horns. There were men in elaborate uniforms escorting elegant women. It was a jolt: the noise, the smells, the buying and selling and rushing and strolling and conversing and meeting and parting amid all the enormous buildings housing offices, stores and shops, cafés, theaters, and packed restaurants, spilling people into the streets. It was the thrill of being in the congested center of such a metropolitan city, populated by shopgirls, workmen, noblemen with their formal manners and air of entitlement; students, local and foreign. Scientists, artists, musicians. Poets. Factory owners, department store owners, bankers, and purveyors of fine goods. People passing through, people without the means to move on.

On this unseasonably warm spring day, Cymbeline knew happiness. And when Julius took her arm, she thought, Yes, this is where I was always meant to be.

"I thought we would wander and see what we find," said Julius, as they threaded through the throng, passing a rather garish and massive establishment claiming an entire street corner, its name emblazoned across the facade.

"Piccadilly?" asked Cymbeline, coming to a stop.

Julius tried to pull her away.

"Let's go to the Tiergarten," he said. The Tiergarten was Berlin's wildly lush city park.

But she wouldn't budge, watching patrons come and go from the Piccadilly. "It isn't as if we *have* to be somewhere," she said.

"You won't like it."

"How do you know?"

"It isn't what you expect."

"Now you've just convinced me."

"Well, then, if you insist," said Julius, reluctantly escorting her toward the door. He stopped her from entering by placing his hands on her shoulders. "Yes," he said as they stood face-to-face, "you really should see all that Berlin has to offer."

"You think I'll be shocked."

"What's the American expression? 'It's your death.' Yes?"

"*Funeral.* 'It's your funeral.'"

In truth, there was a line for Cymbeline, despite her practice of free love and her unorthodox upbringing, so called for the collision of her father's progressive and traditional beliefs, and, to a certain extent, the bohemian life she was choosing. When sex was too raw, too divorced from feeling, it displaced her. However, her knee-jerk response to someone predicting her preferences, combined with her persistent natural desire for experience, pulled her through the oversize doors.

Her eyes had to adjust from the simple sunlight of the day to being in a theatrically lit, multistory space that rivaled the train station in scale and seemed almost as populated and diverse as the platz outside. There was a grand common space, ringed with myriad rooms, whose entrances were gathered velvet drapes, or swaths of see-through silk, or strings of colored-glass beads. There were privacy booths and standing floor screens. Swan boats floated on a lake in a lobby large enough to prevent the boats from colliding.

It wasn't just the chaos and cut-crystal chandeliers, the painted murals and ceiling of copper stars, or the four gracefully turned staircases carved with mermaids and sea monsters; it was the clash of costumes, decor, and music in many languages. All of which fractured Cymbeline's focus into a dozen directions, everything in competition with everything else. "What is this place?" she whispered, though Julius could not hear her.

"Welcome to the poor man's European tour."

"Ah, this is clearly the Bavarian Room, and located, as it should be, next to the Viennese Room through the archway there, so noted for its own overblown operatic bluster. But first, let's step out onto the Moorish terrace."

She followed him in a daze, taking in the abundant national clichés that decorated the rooms (Bavarian, Viennese, Spanish) where patrons dined, drank, gambled, or all three at once. The serving staff were clothed according to their assigned countries, serving the German interpretation of each location's cuisine.

Cymbeline and Julius leaned on the carved balcony of Black Forest hunting scenes that divided the Moorish terrace from the main floor. Along the man-made lake was a replica of a Paris quay.

"And I thought you were going to corrupt me," said Cymbeline.

"I said you'd be shocked."

"Shall we see what's upstairs?"

As they mounted one of the curved stairways, Cymbeline said, "It's a kitsch palace."

"No!" Julius exclaimed as they arrived on the second floor. "It's France! Next to Vienna!"

The third floor revealed a Budapest ballroom, with champagne, caviar, dancing, and cabaret. Tucked off in the far corner was a café festooned with enough draping to mimic a Bedouin tent, where harem girls served Turkish coffee.

The American Wild West Bar, located on the fourth floor, had patrons dancing to a black jazz band.

"Chicago jazz? In the Old West?" she said.

"What were they thinking?" He sighed. "It was all so perfect until the jazz. What do you say we return to the Rhineland and I'll buy you a beer?"

Back on the main floor they settled into a swan boat, with a Japanese parasol resting against the upholstered bench. They floated on the indoor lake, under the imitation night sky studded with tiny lights, watching boys in lederhosen serve steins of beer to patrons sitting on blankets along the "shore." Italian opera played in the background.

Cymbeline opened the oversize parasol, saying, "Do you think someone left this here?" Then she was startled by the sudden clap of thunder and a traveling crack of fake lightning that illuminated the fake night sky, followed by a brief downpour. She laughed as she pulled in close to Julius, who was laughing too. "That was like a one-sided conversation with God," said Julius.

"I rather like their interpretation of the Old West as Indians waiting on cowboys. You think it's a government land issue when it was about tipping all along."

The stars twinkled above them in a field of indigo as Julius rowed over to the bank to receive more beer from one of the lederhosen boys. Cymbeline, who rarely drank, was feeling the alcohol. She reclined in the swan boat, relaxed, her eyes closed. Julius trailed his hand in the water. They didn't speak, but it was a silence of contentment.

"Aren't you glad you made me bring you in here?"

"Oh, my God," said Cymbeline. "I love this place."

"I was being sarcastic."

"I know. But I love it anyway."

Then she did something a little out of the ordinary; she picked up her camera, saying, "I want to take your picture." The thing that made the moment unusual was her desire to capture something she never, ever wanted to forget. Her photography was by turns pragmatic and struggling for art, not for memories, not an attempt to record a moment.

Maneuvering around in the swan boat, given the beer, made her sloppy and apologetic. When she'd finally positioned herself across from Julius, she said, "You'll have to put down the parasol," allowing the light from the ersatz moon to catch the planes of his face.

But the first shot was wrong. She knew it even as she took it. She knew it wouldn't look like him. "I'm a little drunk," she confessed.

"Let me offer a suggestion," he said. "I'm going to do a mathematical problem in my mind, and when you think I've come to the point of the greatest intensity of thought, take the picture."

It turned out to be an excellent portrait. But he didn't look like he was thinking about mathematics; he looked like he was thinking about love.

When they went back into the searing light of day, Cymbeline, shielding her eyes, asked, "Why did you let me drink?"

Without thinking, she reached for his watch. It was 2:00 in the afternoon. She moaned a little, to which he said, "It seems I corrupted you after all. Come on, we'll get you something to eat."

The Tiergarten was less like a city garden and more like a garden city, with its wide boulevards, meadows, woods, flower beds, gazebos, outdoor theaters and café. Like those of the train station and the Piccadilly, the dimensions were impressive. "Does everything in Berlin have to be so excessive in size?" asked Cymbeline.

"Only when you have a kaiser with a child's arm," answered Julius. Kaiser Wilhelm, the German emperor and King of Prussia, had been born with a withered arm that, it was rumored, emotionally ruled his life, and not in a good way.

Rows of tulips bloomed in the plots next to them. When Cymbeline looked at Julius as he was telling her a story from his own student days, she noticed that it appeared as if the flowers were arranged on his head, like a strange sort of floral crown. Asking him to hold very still, she took another picture.

She didn't know what she expected the night she shared a room with Julius. He meant to sleep on whatever furniture there was in the room to allow Cymbeline the bed, but there was nothing usable. No sofa. One armchair. One small dresser. A rug on a floor that was mostly wood. He was almost apologetic about the whole thing, as if it were his fault.

They were fortunate to have any room at all, since the train derailment had stranded so many passengers. There would be no trains until the early morning; there had been two casualties and many more injuries. "I'm trustworthy," said Julius. And Cymbeline found herself thinking, I hope not.

Julius said he was going to walk to the drugstore to buy them toothbrushes.

As soon as he left, Cymbeline unfolded her camera and waited until he appeared, four stories down, on the street below.

"Julius!" she called, causing him to look up, his hand shading his eyes. "Think of an impossible chemical compound," she called. As he was posing, people passed all around him, so that he was only another face in the crowd. She took the shot anyway, knowing that he would be the clearest figure since he wasn't moving.

The awkwardness of their situation, made more awkward by their being unable to speak of its awkwardness, had them avoiding the room. In response, they stayed out as late as possible, which was how Cymbeline ended up seeing her first operetta, an entertainment that reminded her of the Piccadilly in that it wasn't quite a musical, and not quite an opera, and less entertaining than advertised.

Afterward they walked down a street of beautiful homes. Then a street of businesses. A street of bars and cabarets. A street of immigrants. They stopped beneath the Brandenburg Gate, huge, Neoclassical, with Victoria, the Roman goddess of victory, being pulled in a chariot by four horses. As Cymbeline stood between two of the Doric columns, running her hand on one of them, she asked, "This isn't about the child-arm again, is it?"

Julius laughed. "Someone else beat him to it."

"I think I saw one of these in the Piccadilly."

"Was it made of strudel?"

"No, it was schnitzel."

The lights from the avenue of linden trees that stretched behind the gate created a ghostly effect. She stepped back from the gate. She unlocked her camera case. "Can you stand in the central arch? Under the horses?"

"It's not allowed actually. I'm not royal, so I must use the spaces at either end." He positioned himself, without posing in the slightest, between two columns near the end.

"Think about being allowed to walk through the center of the gate but choosing not to, and when you get to the most ridiculous part of that edict, I'll take the picture."

As it happened, he was smiling.

———————————

Julius gallantly tried to sleep on the floor, but his tossing and turning distracted Cymbeline from sleep, and, for the tenth time, she asked him to sleep beside her. On the eleventh time, he said yes.

They arranged the sheets so that he was on top, and she was underneath, and the blanket covered them both. They kept on as many clothes as they could without looking too rumpled in the morning.

Cymbeline must have dozed off because she awoke within that strange consciousness where you are awake enough to know that you aren't in your own bed but can't for the life of you figure out whose bed you are in. She must know the man beside her, she told herself, as she struggled for understanding. Her eyes scanned the room, fixating on the light from the window to adjust to the darkness. The sounds of the city, muted in the very early morning hours, were unfamiliar. Her heart knocking against her chest as the adrenaline surged through her so that she was suddenly fully awake. The calm aftermath was like recovering from a sprint, full of relief and exhaustion. The man beside her was Julius. Without shifting her position as she lay on her back, she slipped her hand into his.

"You're okay," he said. "It was just a bad dream."

Later, she could not say how it started, but the way it ended was unforgettable. She remembered her fingers threaded through his hair and his kisses in places that made her long for him years later.

Then everything wound down to nothing, Julius quiet as he lay beside her, his fingers lightly resting on her arm.

"What are we doing here?" she asked.

"I thought you would understand Berlin."

"No. *Here.*"

"Waiting for the morning."

They were silent.

"Do I mean anything to you?"

He said nothing.

"I love you, you know." Then, because she couldn't take back what she hadn't intended to say, she added, "I love you." And that was when she felt the rearrangement of every molecule in the room.

"Scheisse, schiesse, scheisse," he said so softly she almost couldn't hear it. He said, "I wanted to have Berlin to remember you by, you know, so maybe I would miss you a little less."

But I can stay! she wanted to cry out. *I want to stay!*

"I'm sorry," he said finally.

His apology scraped across her heart, leaving her angry and confused and in love and angry and confused.

She once read that the sea will silently pull a mile back into itself before returning to the shore as a tsunami. In the stillness of this moment, she fought against being overwhelmed by a violent surge of truth and loss that felt imminent. She said, "How could I have been so stupid." She said, "Of all the girls in the city you pick me? *Scheisse.*"

"You're not the other girls."

Now she was sitting up. "And what about your wife? Is she 'not the other girls'?" (No response.) "Or is it a girlfriend?" (No response.) "How not the other girls is she?"

He turned his back to her as he sat on the edge of the bed, his head in his hands. In the morning light she could see his hair, mussed and ungroomed, his undershirt, his slim, square shoulders, so perfect to her, exposed. She loved him she loved him she loved him—every other thought obliterated but that one.

"I don't have a woman." He turned toward her. "Do you see now?" He rose and began to dress. She watched him. He paused to tell her that their train left in an hour and did she want to meet at the station?

The sun was up, flooding the room.

She crossed to the window and saw him disappear down the street.

35

It all came back to her: the advance and retreat of their relationship; the genuine camaraderie and shared interests. The warmth between them that never quite caught. The comment about the suffragettes, and people being allowed to be who they are. The young man, Otto Girondi, at the Photographic Exposition—the same young man who had been laughing in Julius's office. ("I teach maths," he had said.) The look of love on Julius's face in the picture where he was thinking of a mathematical equation.

It was so needlessly trusting, she thought, to see something every day and not for one minute consider that there is an underneath.

Before she dressed, Cymbeline unfolded her camera, slid in a plate, and took a picture of a bed with rumpled sheets, and a pair of hairpins.

PICTURES OF BERLIN, 1910 BY CYMBELINE KELLEY

1. *Waiting Room, Anhalter Bahnhof*
   (A cavernous train station of four waiting rooms, including one used exclusively by the Hohenzollerns)
2. *Mathematics & Love*
   ("I'm going to do a mathematical problem in my mind, and when you think I've come to the point of the greatest intensity of thought, take the picture.")
3. *Tulips*
   (A crown of tulips in his hair)
4. *Late at Night, the Brandenburg Gate*
   (Avoiding the awkwardness of a shared room)
5. *Something to Want*
   (Julius looking up at Cymbeline from the crowded Berlin sidewalk where all she could see was him)
6. *The Unmade Bed*
   (Two confessions of love)

There was one more photograph from Dresden that she always kept with those Berlin pictures. A seventh picture. It was the one Julius took of her that first time they ran into each other at *The Procession of Princes*. It was called *Julius,* though no one but Cymbeline ever knew exactly why.

PART 3: AMERICA

The Third Fire Lit by Mary Doyle, 1917

Cymbeline sifted through the rubble that used to be her darkroom. She opened a charred barrel that stored a number of glass-plate negatives from her old portrait studio, the one she'd closed when she married Leroy; her attachment to many of the images wasn't to the pictures themselves but to the life she'd left behind. She thought about her first photo exhibition. Then she thought about Bosco and how she would gladly give up anything for him.

But there are all kinds of love in the world. So when she came across the six spared glass-plate negatives in the black leather case from a day and a night in Berlin, and the seventh glass plate from Dresden from 1910, she felt her heart break all over again. *Berlin,* she told herself, *was a door and a prison.*

After she and Julius returned to Dresden, their friendship left them and was replaced by a professional association. They experimented with less expensive printing materials. They continued to play with ideas of color. He was Professor Weisz, she Miss Kelley, and the people they were before and during Berlin turned to dust.

Cymbeline returned to the States by way of London, where she attended a massive women's rights rally in Hyde Park on July 23, 1910, which was largely peaceful though with an undercurrent of menace. She opened her Seattle portrait studio, telling her sitters "to think of the nicest thing you know," because if they emptied their minds it was impossible to get a good picture. She told them this as well.

Then Leroy wooed her, telling her that her being named for a king and his name meaning "king" in French was kismet, and she believed herself in love again. Then Bosco. Then Mary Doyle. Then the third fire.

Thoughts of Mary continually crossed her mind as she did her best to pack up her household, with the occasional helpful presence of her mother, and the burden of her pregnancy.

They'd first met when Cymbeline, driven to tears by Bosco as she was shopping for groceries, was helped by Mary Doyle, resulting in her hire. Cymbeline thought about how Mary was pretty in a way that Cymbeline was not, her black hair, pale, pale skin accented with roses, and her blue eyes straight out of Manet's palette. Cymbeline thought about how Leroy, so frequently cranky and complaining, was never impatient with Mary Doyle, and how solicitous she was with him.

She thought about how Leroy had never been in town when the fires started, or had any of his personal belongings been scorched.

And though Leroy, for all his bluster, always made Cymbeline feel beautiful, even when pregnant and pale and green about the gills, she wasn't young and their marriage wasn't a honeymoon; they were deep into it now, and they both knew they were deep into it. It was so easy to forget that he'd once courted her.

It was disconcerting to see Mary Doyle outside the context of the house, and her complete lack of concern at either being in custody or seeing Cymbeline. Cymbeline considered the idea that a simple girl could covet her position as wife to an artist.

Except that Mary Doyle's usual uncomplicated sweetness had shifted. Her relaxed aspect seemed less like a lack of awareness and more like that of someone who had stepped out from behind the curtain.

"How could you?" cried Cymbeline, despite her determination to remain cool and guarded as she faced Mary Doyle, not even knowing if she meant possibly being the Other Woman, or torching the place.

Mary Doyle, her manner calm, her tone conversational, as if arson had been just one more domestic chore, said, "I hated being in the house so much that all I ever wanted to do was raze it to the ground."

Cymbeline didn't know what to say.

So they sat in silence, with Cymbeline wondering if the conversation was over, until Mary said, "I know that King Cymbeline's daughter is Imogen. I'm also familiar with Linnaeus's biological classifications. My Latin is fairly good, but your German is far better than mine." She stopped, then began again. "Descartes's wax argument says that, though the characteristics of wax may be altered by heat or cold, wax remains essentially wax. You probably learned that at university," she said, "as I did when I was in Dublin, at Trinity."

"But . . . then, why . . . work as a housemaid?"

"What else is an immigrant girl to do?" She leaned in close to Cymbeline and whispered, "You hated it as much as I did. Aren't you glad I got us out?"

In between sifting through the charred mess of the darkroom, salvaging what could be salvaged—small stacks of glass-plate negatives, the black leather carrying case (with the undeveloped Berlin glass plates), the Seneca No. 9, which had sustained some damage, prints, the singed wooden barrel of yet more glass plates, the film gone, her trays gone, her few props gone; so many things gone—Cymbeline wrote to Leroy about the move to California, where his parents could help her with Bosco and the new baby.

With no possibility of opening a studio and no established clients, tethered to the little home outside San Francisco with her boys while Leroy taught or was off on one of his painting vacations, Cymbeline would begin spending time in her garden—a crazy riot of flowers, bromeliads, cacti, dusty green ground cover, and fruit trees. She would photograph the leaves and blossoms and branches found just behind her house, while her children played in the California sun. One day she would fill a museum with all her gorgeous black-and-white botanical photographs, rich and lovely and strange.

Eventually she would write that with "one hand in the dishpan, the other in the darkroom," she began to photograph the things around her. Her pictures would be of plants, but their true subject would be domesticity; every flower one of her children, every tree Leroy. The late-nineteenth-century female Pictorialist photographers made pictures of wives and mothers as if they were saints. And the men thought them pretty before returning to their talk about Important Things. Cymbeline was never sentimental enough for saints.

No one had ever photographed domesticity as a garden, plant by plant, flower by flower, tree by tree.

Two weeks after Cymbeline had left Dresden, when she was spending a week in Paris, she got word that Julius Weisz had been killed by a tram as she crossed the street.

If she could've written to him about the photographs from her California life, she would've said that even living flowers have an underneath, and he would've understood.

After Cymbeline sent the letter to Leroy, the one in which she told him that her darkroom was beyond repair, her old Seneca camera ruined, and that she had packed his paints, palettes, easels, his printing press, knives, and brushes, along with the rest of their household belongings (almost impossible without Mary Doyle's help, paradoxically, since Mary Doyle was the reason for the move), that she was moving everyone and everything to a house outside San Francisco to be closer to his parents, a necessity with her late state of pregnancy, expressing her doubt at being able to take care of things when he was gone, but that he shouldn't worry, Leroy wrote back to say that he was *perturbed . . . that you would so arbitrarily, capriciously give up our little home seems a great misfortune to me . . . you have no consideration—as usual—for where I come in.*

The day before the movers were due, Cymbeline was in her darkroom to collect the random glass plates that still sat, pristine and perched on her desk, her worktables, the seat of an old chair with the back burned off, waiting to be placed in an empty barrel.

When she reached for the first plate, her stomach seized in a false contraction, causing the muscle to flex to the hardness of stone and the plate to drop from her hand. It was nothing, just the usual late-pregnancy occurrence, though it still left her breathless as she waited for the moment to pass. Looking at the broken glass that actually didn't seem out of place in the mess of her darkroom, she suddenly felt the crushing weight of everything coming down on her. Instead of reaching for the broom, she carefully, deliberately edged yet another glass plate off the table. And another, then another, then another, then another, then another. She took her time as she moved from table to counter, gently sliding more plates to shatter on the floor. Another, then another, then another, then another, then another. Like fallen stars, smashed into a billion little pieces.

A LITTLE DOG IN PEARLS
OR
MACHINE WORKER IN SUMMER

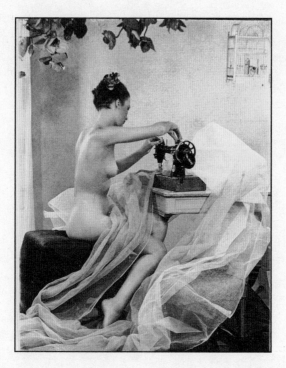

Amadora Penelope Allesbury was born to very comfortable circumstances in an English home that valued tradition (but only to a point), moderate adventure, a good laugh at the world and at oneself, and independence for girls. To that end, Amadora's parents gave her a family name (Penelope) and a first name (an Italian name having to do with "love") that people often suspected she chose for herself (she didn't). Frankly, it sounded as if *Amadora* should be *Isadora,* and it would be just like a girl trying to be different to change the *Is* to an *Am*. It was also true of Amadora's upbringing that, while her father favored independence and individuality in girls, he was less forthcoming on the subject of it in women.

Maybe it would be more to the point to say that he wasn't sure how he felt about female suffrage in general, but when he thought about his two daughters, Amadora and her younger sister, Violette, he wanted them to be happy.

Both girls had a series of governesses who they tormented out of boredom. Eventually, the girls were sent to a very modern all-female school that placed more emphasis on a girl's physical well-being than on her intellectual development, based on the philosophy that exercise and fresh air were all a scholar required.

Their sojourn at that school ended when the students were divided into Girl Scout–type patrols, learning all manner of outdoor skills (campfire cooking, fishing, animal tracking, shelter fabrication), which quickly devolved into something less arcadian and more sinister. Warring patrols started stealing each other's water, knives, and compasses before moving on to pulling hair and throwing a punch or two.

When asked later about it, Amadora would say it was actually fairly exciting, though she declined to get involved. She watched, she said, from the vantage point of a nearby tree. To which her father said, "Clever girl."

From there it was a school in Switzerland. More boredom. Then a two-month stop in Paris, which led to a very brief flirtation with cigarettes, a boy whose name she forgot within a month, and an introduction to the women's rights movement. When she returned to London as a suffragette, a family friend informed her that she was "too well-adjusted, too happy and attractive" for a movement that belonged to women who were "disillusioned and disappointed."

It was true that Amadora was raised with parties, social engagements, games, theater, museums, and music. There were friends, parents' friends, friends of friends, and pets. She would regularly visit her father at work, where his company made superior-quality inks of unusual colors, like London fog, pale pink peonies gone brown about the edges, black pearl, the green of a summer field, imported coffee, roses, fiery sunset, and shades of blue resembling a variety of skies and seas, all with their impossibly French names: *saphir, améthyste, topaze-jaune, rubis, émeraude.* Ink that glowed like stars; invisible ink that turned blue in the light; inks of silver, gold, copper, and platinum. There was something alchemical about so many hues deriving from three primary colors. Her father not only instructed her in the principles of color but encouraged her education in color and chemicals.

Amadora was as far from "disillusioned and disappointed" as one could get, and the whole concept angered her. Why would anyone believe that a happy, privileged life was incompatible with political participation? Even more shocking was when this attitude came from other women. She was too young to think it all through, but she did know that denigrating women—in this case, Amadora—because they (she) wanted the vote only made her more committed to the fight. From an early age she rebelled against other people telling her what she should or should not want. Nerve.

Amadora's response was standing on a corner at Piccadilly Circus two days a week, passing out suffragette literature. At seventeen and finished with school, she had the time and energy to face the weather, and the indifference, real or feigned, of passersby. Then, in July 1910, about the time the women were told by Prime Minister Asquith that they couldn't expect to receive the vote any time soon, Amadora attended a massive Hyde Park political rally (the same event Cymbeline described to Julius, prompting him to say people should be allowed to be who they are) where tempers began to flare. Unrest—and not the polite, ladylike kind—violence, impatience, and menace were in the air. In the same way that Amadora had taken to her tree in school when the Girl Guides came to blows, she had to rethink her commitment to the suffragette movement.

She later wrote, "I would gladly have embarked on a career of wickedness and violence to obtain political freedom, but I was frightened. The leaders of the Women's Social and Political Union conducted the campaign of violence like a war, to destroy property but not endanger life. If you signed on, you signed on for the lot. You couldn't say, 'I don't mind smashing windows but I draw the line at setting fire to a church.' I could not face prison and forcible feeding, which often entailed having a twenty-inch tube shoved up your nostril after being held down by half a dozen people. The prison matrons and doctors broke teeth, damaged esophagi, and left women seriously hurt, sometimes lying in their own vomit. My fear was not unfounded."

She was as uninterested in marriage as she was in pursuing a university education, or in going to jail for the political beliefs that she still held dear. She could take a lover and "go to the bad," as she said, or she could work.

She did what she always did at moments of indecision. She made a list:

(a) *Being a Doctor: Exams too difficult. Training too expensive though rather fancy myself as the "healing physician."*

(b) *Being an Architect: Exams too difficult.*

(c) *Being a Farmer: Very interested. Hanker after wide open spaces. Family hostile.*

(d) *Being an Author: Have an itch to write. Don't know how to set about it.*

(e) *Being an Actress: Ditto. Ditto. Not particularly stagestruck but have written and acted in plays since the age of seven.*

(f) Being a Hospital Nurse: Not sufficiently self-sacrificing. Hate the thought of bedpans, night-duty, and smells.

(g) Devoting myself to the Suffragette cause: Tempting. Would not solve economic problem.

The economic problem was making money of her own. Money, she knew, was freedom.

Amadora Allesbury had never been in a room with so much pink. The persistence of pink throughout the furnishings of the house was impressive, but it was the interior of the photographer's studio that really made this woman's commitment to the color explicit. There were pink velvet drapes, pink silk roses, pink damask on the upholstered chairs. The white bearskin rug wore a wide satin ribbon of pink around its furry neck. There were vases of rose quartz, Japanese statues of pink jade, and a series of white porcelain snow leopards, all with pink sapphire eyes. Even the photographs taken by the photographer had a pink hue.

Lallie Charles was forty years old but didn't look any age in particular. Amadora noticed that this wasn't unusual with women who had chosen not to marry, or to be taken care of by anyone. It was as if, by taking themselves out of the conventional life, they interrupted their own aging, and there were no children's ages by which to judge them, no graying husband or pensioned-off father with which to gauge the years.

As would be the case for Amadora in the future, she didn't use her observations as precursors to judgment; they were simply observations. Though she wouldn't have said this of herself at seventeen, it was as true then as it was at seventy: Amadora was more interested in watching, and in listening to, the lives of others than she was in making moral pronouncements. And it wasn't because she felt life was a free-for-all that she held her tongue—it was because she liked to be entertained, and people are so much more forthcoming when they sense an engaged audience. This, it could be said, was the source for her natural optimism. Her open mind. Her open heart. Her tendency to find the humor in most things.

She did not reserve this last bit only for others; she was quick to laugh at her own flaws. The idea of everyone being "only human" was good news, she would say. Most of the time anyway.

There was no more popular photographer in London in 1911 than Lallie Charles. Her portraits were everywhere: in newspapers, magazines, people's homes. The women she photographed were feminine and soft and pink. They came to her studio with changes of clothes and maids to help them dress and undress. They sat in demure poses.

It was Lallie Charles's popularity that prompted Amadora to contact her once Amadora decided that the best way for her to go about making a living was to become a photographer.

"So," said Lallie Charles, "tell me why you are here."

Amadora hesitated, wondering how ill-mannered it would be to remind Miss Charles that she had written to her about a position as a pupil-assistant and that Miss Charles had answered she thought *it would be a fascinating proposition, why not come by, say, on Thursday at 4:00.* Amadora didn't exactly understand what Lallie Charles meant by "fascinating" unless she would find it fascinating that Amadora's presence in her parlor was the result of a whim, an impulse not unlike that of a child proclaiming her intention to be a circus acrobat. She considered confessing that she had never taken a single picture in her life but instead said, "I'm interested in becoming a photographer," resisting the urge to end the statement as a question.

A butler came in with tea and cakes.

Amadora wanted to reach for a cake but thought better of it when Lallie Charles made no move toward the tray. She also said nothing, just watched Amadora.

"I admire you. I admire the way you've made your own way, having your own business. Everyone knows you and your work."

Lallie Charles waited.

Amadora could feel herself starting to falter. She couldn't tell if Lallie Charles liked her, didn't like her, wanted her, didn't want her, or was even listening. Though she was a young girl with a young girl's bravado, her respect for her elders led to a certain restraint.

"I know how much I can learn from you, Miss Charles. I'm a hard worker—you can ask anyone—and I tend to have a pleasant disposition—something for which I cannot take any credit, but it's true nonetheless." As more words tumbled from Amadora's lips, she realized how very much she wanted to work for the photographer. What had begun as a place to start in the work world was, in the course of this interview, becoming something more urgent. Amadora was thinking of income but also thinking, This may be something I would love. "I know any number of girls would clamor for this opportunity, but I'm hoping you'll offer it to me."

The butler returned, took away the tray of still untouched tea and cakes. He also whispered to Lallie Charles that Mrs. Willoughby-Cole was due at 5:30. She nodded to him, then called out, "Chang!"

The volume of her voice contrasted with the stillness of the room. As Amadora waited, she began to question everything in the interview, including her outfit, which, at first glance, seemed fashionable enough, until closer inspection revealed the elegance of the material combined with the playful, slightly bohemian details of the pleating of her white and red pin-striped skirt, and the vaguely sailor-style of her gunmetal gray blouse, pinned with a sparkling diamond brooch, handed down from her grandmother (and representative of that era), where the tie would normally be. Her hat was a black straw boater, trimmed with black velvet ribbon and another diamond brooch. A silver Victorian buckle bracelet on her left wrist. Her attire was neither purely feminine nor in the more masculine suit-and-tie style of the day for young women. Everything together sartorially stranded her; she was dressed neither for tea nor for a job as a working London girl.

In the midst of Amadora's second-guessing, in pranced a beautifully groomed Pomeranian. The hairy little dog wore a collar of three strands of pink pearls. It glanced over at Amadora before sitting down in front of its mistress, its back to Amadora.

"Dear Chang," said Lallie Charles to the Pomeranian, "what are your thoughts about Miss Allesbury?"

Amadora could not have said what act of Providence silenced her laughter (though she was already rehearsing the story she would tell at dinner that night), but she was grateful, because it became evident that Miss Charles was serious.

"Go on," said Lallie Charles.

The little dog with the pink pearls walked over to Amadora, gave her a sniff or two, then returned to its previous position in front of its mistress.

"Well?" said Miss Charles. "If you don't tell me soon I will take it as a no."

The dog wagged its tail.

"I'm not entirely convinced," she said.

The dog then got to its feet, wagged its tail with more vigor, and delivered one, quick yap.

"It's settled then!" Miss Charles said, facing Amadora (now torn between giving her attention to the dog or to the photographer), and slapped her hands down on the arms of her chair. The dog danced out of the room. "My fee is thirty guineas, covering your three-year tuition, paying you back at a wage of five shillings the first year, doubling in the second, and tripling in the third. We start at nine every morning."

Amadora liked the novelty of work. The first year she learned how to load dark slides, prepare, then rock the exposed glass plates in chemical baths, and how to book and interview clients; she learned about people as much as about portrait making. She also learned about money and society.

Being a modern working girl in 1912 made her feel that she was becoming the sort of woman the suffragette movement was all about; in this way she felt she was making good on her promise to fight the good fight, only from a different perspective.

On the other hand, she also became much closer to Chang, since it was her job to walk him every day in the nearby park. When he promenaded in front of her on his lead, she was sure she looked like a lady of leisure. This made her want to tell passersby that the picture they presented, lady and dog, was inaccurate. She wanted to say, I'm actually a photographer—except that she wasn't, not yet, even if her fingers were stained from chemicals—which made her more impatient when she spent time with Chang.

One day when she was in the park, trying to soothe the fractious Chang, she stepped into yet another dog mess, an ongoing hazard of dealing with the Pomeranian. As she looked around for a way to clean her shoe, while wrestling with Chang's leash, her long skirt, and the soiled shoe, she overheard a male voice say, "What sort of person dresses her dog in pearls anyway?"

And another male voice answered, "The pretentious sort."

She glanced over to see two men, not much older than she, seated side by side on a bench. It was obvious they were unaware of their carried voices.

"She looks like she bosses him around, and he looks as though he likes it," said one of the men, who, Amadora saw, was handsome in a kind of cold, unstudied, and therefore probably completely orchestrated way. At first, she thought he was referring to Chang, until she followed their eyes to see the object of the comment—a nicely dressed couple strolling in the park. She had to admit, the woman did look a bit stern and appeared to be pulling her smaller husband along, with her hand resting on the inside of his arm, and he did look a bit cowed.

The handsome man's friend, also nice looking but not as arresting, said in an affected accent, "Why yes, I am Fabian Socialist!" Amadora looked in another direction to see an obviously well-to-do man being trailed by what seemed to be a manservant of some sort while the well-to-do man was trying to impress a very pretty woman dressed in the style of a Pre-Raphaelite bohemian muse, or model.

As Amadora began laughing, having caught on to the men's game, she saw that the handsome man realized she had heard everything they said. Instead of looking apologetic, he offered the most minimal of acknowledgments by giving a little wave, his arm draped across the back of the bench, as if he couldn't be bothered.

While a little dog wearing pearls wasn't her idea, she could see the humor in it. She could also see an arrogance in the handsome man that was absent in his friend, who, once he knew she had heard everything, seemed noticeably embarrassed.

One day, feeling slightly oppressed by all the pink, as monochromatic as the use of no color in Amadora's opinion, she asked Miss Charles if it were completely possible, would she choose to do color portraits? Lallie Charles looked at Amadora as if she had suggested that Chang were merely a dog and answered, "No reputable portrait artist would take color pictures."

"Why not? If it were possible?"

"It isn't done," said Miss Charles.

"Why isn't it done?" Amadora insisted.

"No one would want it."

"What if someone wanted a color portrait?" asked Amadora. "Shouldn't she have what she wants?"

Miss Charles said, "Either you are serious about this work or you are not, Miss Allesbury."

"My father manufactures colored ink. He would have no clients if people didn't want color."

"But they don't want it."

"Why don't they want it?"

"Because it isn't beautiful. It is too much like life," said Miss Charles, punctuating the end of their conversation by handing Amadora Chang's leash.

It was called The Works, and it was where Amadora asked Lallie Charles to send her after a year spent arranging pink silk roses, pink silk draperies, pink velvet chairs. By this time Miss Charles had three other assistants doing what Amadora was doing, with the exception of walking Chang, who behaved as if Amadora belonged to *him*. The Works was the place where Miss Charles sent her negatives to be "improved"; Amadora made her case not just that she wanted to expand her photographic education but that Miss Charles would benefit from her new skills when she returned to complete the third year of her apprenticeship.

Lallie Charles was always a soft touch.

Amadora explained to her parents one evening, her father rapt, her mother less so:

"It's called The Works, and you can all but invent people. A retoucher rids the sitter of all manner of physical imperfection: jowls, thick ankles, unfortunate jaws, and midsections. Bodies become svelte and young again. Then the retoucher—which will now be me—applies a liquid known as 'medium,' picks up a pencil, and all wrinkles, lines, and other blemishes disappear!"

"Perhaps I'll come by your 'Works,'" said her father.

"Please no," said Amadora. "I love you as you are."

"I'd rather be as I was."

"That's the rub, you see. One must be very skilled when erasing warts and moles and furrows or you will be as you never were. Utterly unrecognizable."

"Dorrie," said her mother, "this *erasing* will be your new work? Won't you tire of it?"

"Once I master retouching, I shall be sent on to learn trimming, mounting, finishing, and spotting."

"Finishing?" asked her mother.

"A sharp knife applied to the mouth can make the sitter a villian, a sensualist, or a nun. Eyes can be darkened, made expressive, given the look of someone keeping a secret, or holding back a laugh, or tears. One can resemble a poet. Anything can be made bigger or smaller, happy or thoughtful, straightened or softened. Eyelashes, eyebrows, hairlines, nose hair, chin hair."

"And how do you work this alchemy?" asked her father.

"With a sharp knife, a paintbrush, watercolors, pumice powder, gum, and chalks."

"I'm a bit concerned about your knowing the look of a sensualist," said her mother.

Her father said, "This is where you want to work?"

"Without a doubt," answered Amadora.

Amadora was happier at The Works than she had ever been at Lallie Charles's studio. There was so much to learn, so much to master, whereas the studio was just more of the same—the same society ladies, with the same ladies' maids who helped them in and out of the same structured, intricate, corseted clothing. The same pose by the lattice window. The same pink glow.

It wasn't that Amadora thought less of the photographer; as theatrically eccentric as she could be, Lallie Charles was dedicated to her art, which, in turn, defined something of an era. But Amadora, not even out of her teens, was too young for nostalgia. She had all kinds of electric dreams propelling her forward. The ennui she had experienced when she returned from Paris (before her time with Miss Charles) was again upon her during her time with the photographer.

Even more disturbingly, before she left Lallie Charles's studio, Amadora sometimes searched for the haughty, handsome young man from the park. She worked for a woman, worked with three other female assistants much like herself, and the clients, with their maids, were nearly all women. No wonder, she said to herself, that I should be thinking about a man like that. He wasn't even nice.

"Girls," said Lallie Charles to Amadora and the three other assistants, "changes afoot!"

The four young women held their breath as they sat, side by side, on the parlor sofa. Business had been decidedly off for the past several months. No one knew if it was due to a decline in Lallie Charles's popularity or an increase in the interest in amateur photography, made simple by the Kodak roll-film cameras; or maybe it was the spate of complaints about the portraits themselves, which were prone to fading. Sitters would return unhappy about the quality of their photographs, asking her to retake the pictures.

"*Il faut cultiver notre jardin,* kittens, so we are relocating—home, studio, everything!—to a fabulous house, *la maison la plus exquise* just down the street. It will make all the difference!"

But the only difference it made was that Miss Charles went bankrupt.

Before the court determination of her insolvency, Miss Charles ordered a resisting Amadora back from her job at The Works ("Chang needs you," she said, clearly believing that Amadora should feel flattered); she undertook extensive renovations on her new house and studio, then gave an elegant, expensive opening, which was almost entirely unattended.

It was at this event that the cold, handsome young man from the park, all those months ago, arrived. Amadora was standing toward the back of the room, charged with keeping an eye on Chang, when she looked up to see the young man. She watched as he walked into the largely empty room, a puzzled expression as his eyes swept the space until they rested on Amadora. She was almost tempted to wave to him, as if he were an old friend.

"Excuse me," he said when he reached her, "am I early or am I late?"

"Neither, I'm afraid," said Amadora.

"Naturally," he muttered, mostly to himself as he walked away, "why should I ever rate a decent assignment?"

She had begun to follow when he ran into someone he knew.

"Clifton!" called the second man, who seemed relieved to have run into a familiar face, "what the devil are you doing here?"

"Being punished," the young man answered. While he didn't raise his voice for all to hear, he didn't take pains to lower it either. "This place is like death."

"Poor old girl," said the friend, tipping his head toward Lallie

Charles, who was genuinely charming the few people in her circle. Of course, Amadora was grateful to Miss Charles for all she'd done for her—the studio work and her experience at The Works. But it was more than that; it was having the chance to work for a woman who was making her own way in the world, to observe how she ran her business, how she dealt with her high-society clientele (always with grace and patience), and learning the business of the studio in the process. Art was Amadora's desire, but business was the way to achieve it. Amadora admired Lallie Charles, despite the photographer's repetitive approach to her work and her resistance to changing or pushing herself as an artist.

Lallie Charles took nothing for granted. Underneath all the pink, romantic glow was a woman as tough as any suffragette. Though Amadora was naturally inclined toward a kind of flirtatious charm, something more playful, hiding her truest self, her artist self, behind her quick sense of humor, none of this was so different from Lallie Charles using her sophistication and culture when dealing with people. Women, Amadora knew, were not admired when they showed how much they cared about their careers; no one wanted to see what it took to do everything yourself. Everyone preferred the illusion of effortless ease, and in some ways this was the most important lesson Amadora learned from Lallie Charles.

So it infuriated Amadora to hear the older man refer to the photographer as "poor old girl." She wanted to confront the speaker, asking what he had accomplished that placed him in a position to condescend to this woman. She had decided to say something—not that Miss Charles would approve of such an outburst, something that Amadora knew from months of observation—when she heard the handsome young man say, "How can I be expected to write anything for the paper when there isn't a single person here who seems even remotely interesting?"

At that moment, the young man turned to see Amadora, almost by his side, remembering her from when he'd first arrived.

"Pardon," he said, "I'm writing a piece for *The Guardian* on Miss Charles's studio change. I'm wondering if you can direct me to someone who may work for Miss Charles." With that, he handed his empty glass to Amadora, thinking her the help, and she accepted it because she wasn't quite sure what else to do. "Apologies," he said, noting the look on her face. "I mean someone who works for Miss Charles in a professional capacity."

"That would be me," said Amadora.

Now it was the young man's turn to look confused. "Oh, dear," he said. "Sorry." He took his glass back. "I didn't realize."

"Why would you when you came in and decided who everyone was without even speaking to them? How would you know the difference between a serving girl and a photographer? But, then, I know what a burden it must be to be the smartest, most captivating person in the room." Amadora snatched the glass back from the young man and made her way to the kitchen.

"Please," he said, following closely behind. "Allow me an honest mistake and to apologize once again. I'm not usually this boorish."

"Yes, you are," said Amadora. She stopped and turned so abruptly they nearly collided.

"Pardon?"

"I saw you—with your friend—one day in the park. I was the girl with the little dog in pearls—you know, me and my pretensions."

"I do seem to remember something like a dog in pearls . . . but I don't recall you—"

"You don't even remember those you insult? Well, if I'm not mistaken, that's even *more* insulting."

"I—" He took a deep breath, then shut his mouth.

As they stood in the kitchen, Amadora could see from the way he held his body and his struggle to say the right thing that his awkwardness was a result of trying not to compound his gaffes. His confusion at attempting to remember her was sincere. It crossed her mind that his proud, difficult demeanor masked a social discomfort, that is, she thought she could detect his decency despite everything.

She burst out laughing.

"Oh, God, it is more insulting, isn't it?" he said, laughing along. "It seems my pomposity knows no bounds. Look, may we begin again? Would you like to join me for supper tonight? You can tell me all about dogs in pearls and Miss Charles." He offered his hand. "George Clifton."

"Amadora Allesbury."

"Amadora."

"George."

"Like a cheerful young rat deserting, I departed, but I felt sorrow, regret, and love for the sinking ship." This is what Amadora said to George as she gave him the cut-rate tour of her modest Victoria Street studio. "I actually left just before Miss Charles's studio closed, and have not yet quite come to terms with my departure, inevitable though it was to be."

He walked around, taking in the camera with the Dallmeyer portrait lens (all brass and glass), lamps, chemicals, developing trays, and fixing tanks. Hypo tanks large enough for twelve-by-fifteen plates took up floor space. There was a old stove and ratty curtains and a darkroom with the dimensions of a phone booth. There were bottles of liquid, a dry-mounting machine, a desk, and a pink velvet sofa as a prop, along with a brass floor lamp, its shade made of opalescent glass sculpted to resemble fish scales.

He stopped at the sofa. "I see you've decided to continue on with the decorating theme of pink."

"It was left over from the previous owner—a photographer. I bought everything."

"You did well under Miss Charles."

"My father," she said as financial shorthand. Though Amadora had done a pair of pictures at Miss Charles's, she had knowledge in lieu of practical experience, and the sort of confidence that is really only possible in a twenty-one-year-old girl who has not yet known failure. It was this fearlessness that convinced her father to stake his daughter in the winter of 1914, when she was the youngest female photographer in London.

"How long have you been here?" asked George Clifton, making himself at home on the pink sofa, unaware that his position was almost identical to the one on the park bench the first time he had waved to Amadora.

"Since the week after we went to supper. Three months, four days, and two hours," she said, "if I were keeping track."

"I wasn't aware that you thought enough of our supper to keep track," he said, his body losing the relaxed, expansive pose as it closed in on itself.

"You would've known if you'd rung me."

George got up and crossed over to a number of black-and-white photographs hung from a thin rope, like laundry. She could see the awkwardness again, the discomfort. He said, "You've been busy."

"Not yet," she said, standing beside him. "I have to appear as if I have clients in order to attract clients."

"Who's this?" George pointed to a portrait of a girl, maybe sixteen, posing with a large, long-haired dog wearing a wreath of hand-tinted flowers.

"That's Violette. My sister."

"And this?" He pointed to a picture of a young woman in a sparkling ball gown, her hair done up in an elaborate style.

"That would be Violette."

"Hmm. Quite different," he said, comparing the two photographs.

"That's the point," said Amadora.

It was then he stared harder at the remaining pictures, all of young women or girls, hair down or pinned back; in casual clothes, formal clothes, even a beautiful robe; one sat primly on the pink velvet sofa, another played with a parrot, while another clasped a rose in her mouth, or held a glass orb, or rested a hand on a large library globe. They were smiling, thoughtful, serious, laughing. "Violette?" he said.

"One must be resourceful."

"And your sign outside—*Madame Amadora—Portrait Photographer*— more resourcefulness?"

"I wanted to stand apart. I'm not the only one taking pictures in London."

"If the photography doesn't work out, perhaps you can tell futures."

"Or run a house of ill repute."

"You have more imagination than that."

"More than you know."

"Actually, I quite like the new name. Doesn't truly suit you at the moment, but I suspect one day it will."

"I suppose it's by great good luck I've adopted an art-trade-profession-science that, like myself, is not properly grown-up."

"Amadora," he began, "I wanted—I wanted to bring you something—to wish you well—" He shyly handed her a narrow box.

When they had gone to dinner ("Three months, four days, and two hours"), they had had a wonderful time. George Clifton was twenty-four years old; a reporter for *The Guardian*, he was assigned all manner of random stories, covering a variety of topics, many of them, to him, pure fluff. He didn't want to be a features reporter as much as he wanted to write a serious, political column. One of the weightier subjects he had been allowed to write about was the recent conflict over women's rights. He absolutely supported the vote and thought the government's dealings with many of the suffragettes were despicable. Saying as much was the very thing that had forced him back onto light human interest stories.

But he told none of this to Amadora, saying only that he was a reporter who longed to be a playwright.

When he began telling her stories about his job, his subjects, and his life, she noticed a self-deprecation that had been absent in their previous encounters. He asked her questions, encouraged her opinions. He himself was an easier laugh than she had imagined. He kidded her. He was, in short, one thing and another and Amadora found herself completely charmed by him.

But when he didn't get in touch after their dinner, she supposed that what she'd felt must have been one-sided, though she could've sworn he enjoyed her company as much as she enjoyed his. She kept her disappointment to herself, reminding herself of her decision never to marry, to make her own way, and quickly became distracted by leaving Miss Charles. And, shortly after that, laying the foundation for her own business. George Clifton became someone she thought about in the odd moment, sometimes dreamt about and sighed for without truly allowing herself to want him. How it was possible to feel the absence of someone she barely knew was a mystery.

Now here he was, in her little studio, offering her a gift.

Inside the slim box was a string of fairly gorgeous pearls. She took them out, held them aloft as they tangled in her fingers.

"In case you decide to get a dog."

She threw herself on him, her arms around him as she pressed her face into his jacket, holding him as tight as she could, hoping he hadn't heard the small sob that she tried to hide.

———

Within months—months that Amadora spent taking pictures for free of well-known figures, mostly in entertainment, which the local papers ran, and which Amadora believed George had influenced, though he claimed otherwise—the Great War broke out. With the assassination of Archduke Franz Ferdinand and his wife in Sarajevo that June, every European country began to line up, each with its own established political alliance.

As a consequence, Madame Amadora's primary clientele went from stage stars to soldiers and sweethearts, young wives and mothers. Fathers. All those pictures that found their way into rucksacks, helmets, shirt pockets. And their counterparts, the photographs of the soldiers themselves, which ended up in purses, and on mantels and dressers, so serious, so young.

Amadora had worked hard in the preceding months to shake off the romantic techniques she had learned from Lallie Charles, as well as to teach herself to use materials that allowed her images to remain fixed. Her lighting made people look like themselves, instead of some dreamy versions of themselves, and this was the best thing she could've mastered for all those wartime separation pictures, in which the thing most needed was the real face of someone you loved.

———

The war was supposed to be over by Christmas.

Then Christmas came and went and the fighting went on.

Amadora and George were falling in love over lunches and dinners and park walks, and engaging in lively discussions that sometimes bordered on arguments in the way that two opinionated people discuss. However, they laughed together more than they argued, each discovering that they shared a similar worldview, George with his dry wit and Amadora with her playful remarks. Life, in general, still delighted her, and because of that she could coax George out of a mood when necessary. If he was a little less forgiving than she about the world and its frailties, he found humor in most things. She knew he wasn't perfect, but, since she didn't expect perfection from anyone, except maybe sometimes herself, his shortcomings didn't bother her. She would much rather have life with all it flaws and unpredictability.

If she were asked the secret to her love affair with George, she would answer that they let each other be who they were. Also that most things were actually quite funny if you only allowed yourself to see them that way.

George, being of imperfect health (a touch of asthma), was allowed into the reserves, which in his case meant staying home to write articles about the war. These articles would have been written by his colleagues had they not been pressed into service. Once or twice a prowar suffragette marched up to George, dramatically handing him a white feather. The women still had their own grievances against the government, and now they were divided on the war. Those who supported it took it upon themselves to present a white feather of cowardice to any man out of uniform who seemed to them perfectly able to serve. It was only at Amadora's insistence that George began wearing his uniform. "If only to keep me from pulling these women apart," she said.

"In the interest of saving lives at home, I will do as you ask," he said.

"I'm very protective of you," she said.

"I'll never know why," he said, gently touching her face.

It wasn't until 1916, when everyone was being drafted, that George Clifton was informed that he too would be sent to the front, as a correspondent.

"How does a German know that you're a writer and not a soldier!" demanded a tearful Amadora.

"Perhaps by the obvious insecurity," said George. Amadora playfully hit him even as she tried not to cry.

He told her that he'd be back. He said he was too cranky to kill. She insisted they marry. He said, "Timing is everything." And it was his refusal of her request that frightened her most of all.

No one really survived the Great War. No person, no place. It was too far-reaching, too catastrophic, too unimaginable. Those who made it home weren't the same, and those who waited at home were also changed. Everyone became a stranger of the most dislocating sort because everyone became, once again, unknown. Unknown yet looking familiar, everyone resembling someone he or she used to know. Sweethearts, young marrieds, parents and children, children and parents all had to relearn each other. This didn't even take into account those who returned yet never seemed to come back at all. Gertrude Stein coined the expression "a lost generation," but isn't every generation following any war a little lost?

After George Clifton went off to war, Madame Amadora was too distracted to continue to be Madame Amadora. While he flew in planes and sent his dispatches to *The Guardian, The Times,* and *The New York Sun,* writing his more personal dispatches to Amadora, she answered the call of the country asking its young women to work the land while the men were away.

She was assigned to a farm in Essex that was cold and the work dirty; the day began too early and ended too late, and in between she mucked stalls, milked cows, cleaned buckets, sheared sheep, took animals to and from pastures, fed them, and worked the garden. She lost weight, lost her good humor for the first time in her life, lost her health, lost sleep.

When she saw German planes flying overhead, bound for London, she fell to her knees in the muddy field, angry and weeping. Then she would pick herself up and go inside.

Then George came home, and again Amadora found herself on the ground, crying again but this time they were tears of relief.

But George's changes were deep. In the same way that his physical infirmities weren't visible to the women with the white feathers, his interior had been, as he once told Amadora while they lay awake in the dark, in the middle of the night, "rearranged."

He said this in response to her asking him to (finally!) marry her.

"I will give up my work for you if you ask," she said.

He gave her the sort of smile that scared her a little because she could detect a kind of pity in it, as if all her efforts would never, ever really be able to reach him. "I wouldn't ask," he said.

And because she so much wanted to offer him something, anything, so he would know how much she loved him, how scared she had been for him, every day, all day and all night; because the thought of handing over her independence before the war had been unthinkable, but if he was to be changed by the war, then so would she; because of all this, when he said the one thing he didn't want, should they marry, was children, she agreed.

It was an unthinking pact she had made because the war had driven home the possibility of losing him (and she couldn't lose him), and it was then that she realized she had always imagined having children.

George quoted Stephen Crane, "'You can depend upon it that I have told you nothing at all, nothing at all, nothing at all.'" He said, "Amadora, for all that I have said about the war, I have told you nothing at all."

By 1930 Amadora and George had been married for ten years. In that time, Amadora had reopened her studio as Madame Amadora and was so successful that, only four years into her new business, she was invited to speak at the Congress of the Professional Photographers' Association. Her lecture, titled "Photographic Portraiture from a Woman's Point of View," was smart, witty, and theatrical, and everyone was charmed.

Among the things she said: "Women seem to possess all the natural gifts essential to a good portraitist . . . such as personality, patience and intuition. The sitter ought to be the predominating factor in a successful portrait. Male portraitists are apt to forget this; they are inclined to lose the sitter in a maze of technique luxuriating in the cleverness and beauty of their own medium."

She went on to discuss the dangers of repeating oneself, of having "won fame by some special style or thought; to repeat ourselves is not only noncreative and purely mechanical." Then she declared that one must always reach higher, want more. She said, "Here I am talking about myself; the complacency that comes with success."

Her clients were all manner of famous people—politicians, actors, actresses, writers, aristocrats. She took a picture of a lord in his coffin, and another of an ancient duchess who arrived in Amadora's studio with her young male "assistant," then proceeded to strip naked to the waist. She wore diamond earrings, and a diamond brooch in her unnatural red hair. "Her enormous breasts, with large purple nipples, hung below her waist like gourds. She smiled with the utmost self-possession and asked if I liked the idea of the jewel in her hair . . . 'I suppose you only want a head?' I said, doubtfully glancing at the extraordinary effect below the waist. 'Head and shoulders,' she said with a simper, 'I have always been complimented on the whiteness of my neck . . .'"

George said, "You do get only the best people."

She did advertising work.

Amadora met Amelia Earhart and was befriended by Charlie Chaplin. Her cousin became a famous race car driver, once inviting George to accompany him to the South of France.

"How was it?" asked Amadora.

"Fast," said George. "Very fast."

"Was it exciting?"

"You know, it's such a fine line between excitement and sheer terror, don't you think? I think I may pass on Miss Earhart should any invitations come my way."

The self-portraits she made were as whimsical as her worldview: She dressed herself as a harlequin and a modified eighteenth-century noblewoman in a tricorn hat; she created an optical illusion in which she was tiny, like something that could be held in the palm of someone's hand, standing beside her camera, which now loomed like a five-story building. In her hand was a shutter-release cable, making her camera look as if it were on a leash.

Her black cat sat on a table against a white background, wearing on its collar a framed oval portrait of its mistress.

The studio too had gone upscale, to a new, more stylish address, with more space, more lighting and staff.

George quit his job when his first play was produced with moderate success, then adapted as a failed movie. He wrote other plays, which found audiences without making him a household name. He seemed unconcerned with a career that was one step forward and two steps back, but she knew that wasn't all of it. Amadora could see that, regardless of their individual accomplishments and their brisk social life, the war was in him. Nightmares interrupted his sleep and his waking life, since it took more than merely waking up to pull him back to the present day and their fancy address.

They would still laugh; the part of George that was prone to judgment still appeared on occasion, usually following some dinner party or opening, Amadora often enjoying the quick, humorous remark later, in private, that deflated some deserving guest.

What she did not like, and did not tolerate, was his lashing out just to lash out, which he did at times and not always in private. It was moments like these that had people wondering what the lovable Amadora saw in this mercurial man. She didn't care what they thought; she was never a believer in perfection. She knew his goodness and she knew his nightmares and she never explained anything to anyone.

Three things happened in 1930 for Amadora. The first was her boredom with black-and-white photography. She couldn't understand "everyone being in love with beautiful shadows," when all she wanted to do was work with color. Her father's livelihood was color. Painters worked with color. They knew that reality didn't lie solely in line and form, contrasts of dark and light; life was color.

A new photographic development process, the Vivex process, invented only a few years before by Dr. D. A. Spencer, a color chemist, joined with Colour Photographs Ltd. of Willesden. In it there was none of the delicacy of hand tinting; these colors were saturated, wild, pushed to that point where dreams begin, with the resulting images on large glass plates fixed at a processing plant. Amadora went out and bought a Vivex Tri-Colour Camera, an automatic repeating back camera that held three glass plates, which pulled behind filters of green, red, and blue, and weighed twelve pounds.

Colored cellophanes on the studio lights created even more color effects.

So, boredom with black-and-white was the first thing, and the Vivex process (the perfect mode of expression for Amadora's passion for color and whimsy and the visual kick of life) was the second thing.

The third thing, which was really the first, was George Clifton and her love for him, and the trip to Paris that she arranged, in the heart of spring, when everything was brilliant and in bloom, and the sky that perfect shade of blue that is never taken for granted. There were roses and women wearing lipstick. Amadora and George didn't talk about all his lost earnings in the recent stock market crash. Nor did they mention that Madame Amadora's studio was seemingly immune to the downturn. Paris was a distraction, not quite a vacation.

At Deyrolle, the taxidermy shop that was over one hundred years old, they saw a pair of gazelles, standing on their hind legs and dressed like shopkeepers. Upstairs they found glassed drawers and cases of butterflies—thousands of butterflies in every color: shimmering, iridescent blues, fiery oranges, a shock of red, a shot of green, a spark of yellow, the cool touch of purple. Two polar bears standing on a counter faced off over a pair of relaxing deer, while a lioness stretched on top of a chest of drawers, ignoring a nearby fox and geese and a flamingo.

Another lion with an impressive mane stalked between the cases, accompanied by a tiger and an Arctic wolf.

Sheep wandered around with badgers. Elands, dik-diks, and a wildebeest had a tea party with four zebras, one of whom sat on the table among the china. A llama looked out the window on the rue du Bac, while a horse poked its head through an interior oval opening over the stairwell.

"The butterflies," said Amadora. "The stuffed animals."

The place was provocative. Like a beautiful, disturbing masquerade ball.

They walked by the Seine. They had dinner, then walked the boulevards at night, listening to the sounds of cafés and bars and taking in the lights.

They walked the Galerie des Glaces, and Marie Antoinette's hamlet at Versailles. They strolled the gardens, circled the fountains, their shoes crunching gravel.

Amadora loved the eighteenth-century palette of the clothes, upholstery, wall coverings, and clothing; of Watteau and Boucher: powder blue, eggshell white, pale pink, light dusty green, the faintest trace of yellow.

They visited the Palais des Mirages, where they stood among a small crowd in an exotic mirrored room, in which they would be plunged into darkness only to find a new location in the mirrors each time the lights came on. They were in an Indian palace; they were lost in the forest. The mirrors provided depth and repetition and the effect of being held within an enormous, tumbling kaleidoscope.

They went to the Bois du Boulogne, the Tuileries, and the Luxembourg Gardens. Along with the writers and artists they knew, they visited Gertrude Stein and Alice B. Toklas's painting-filled atelier.

"I rather liked Miss Stein," said George, who could barely hide his disdain for the rich in the beautiful apartment where they had been dinner guests the night before, no one there the least affected by the ruined economy.

"That's because you're a man."

Amadora spent the entire evening in the humorless company of Alice B. Toklas, and the other wives of the writers and painters. When Amadora tried to move away from the clutch of women, to speak to one of the men, an old friend, her attempt was met with such icy disapproval that she immediately retreated, only to be shunned by Alice for the remainder of the evening.

The rest of the trip, however, Amadora was thrilled by the theatricality of these worlds against worlds.

They visited the American Surrealist photographer Tin Type and his muse-lover-assistant, Lenny Van Pelt, by whom they were told that Surrealism was art that accessed dreams, either producing art that resembled dreams or simply tapping into one's own subconscious.

As they made their way home after their Paris sojourn, George took Amadora's hand, pressed his lips to the palm before pressing it to his face. "Everything was perfect, darling, like a dream. Those animals and butterflies and Miss Stein's home and that Surrealist couple and Paris. A dream. I wish we could live there."

Amadora knew that he wasn't talking about Paris. And when he kissed her hand once more, told her that he loved her, George said that Van Gogh had told his brother he sometimes felt a terrible need of religion. He said, "Then I go out and paint the stars."

"You are that to me. You are the stars I paint," George said.

By the time they arrived home, she knew what she would do: She would make him a world.

———————————

Sometimes George was present when he was with her and sometimes he was elsewhere. She preferred it when he would say "I'm stepping out for a smoke," only to return a day or two later with oversize mixed bouquets of flowers. It went without saying that George didn't smoke.

He was restless in sleep and in consciousness, with breaks of contentment in between.

She woke to him crying in the kitchen one night, gripping his hair and saying, "I'm blind to all beauty." Then he allowed her to pull up a chair beside him and cradle him as best she could. He said he couldn't bear the loneliness of his memories. He said it was like living nowhere.

———————————

It didn't matter to Amadora that so few photographers worked in color because they found it "unacceptable," or that no "serious photographer would use it."

Amadora was never far from her understanding of women, glamour, or the fine line between elegant and camp, vulgar and vibrant, life and dreams. She never moved away from her suffragette beliefs; instead she brought them into her work with her usual whimsical eye, that sense of amusement. Color, she believed, was feminine. She said that women were masters of color, evidenced in changing their hair color, using eye shadow, mascara, powder, rouge, lipstick. You could see it in their jewelry—silvers and gold, gems, stones, pearls of every hue. It was in their clothing, from what they slept in to what they danced in. Their shoes. Their purses. Ribbons, barrettes, clips, and tiaras. Veils.

All this color to enhance their sex appeal, while men, she felt, were ill-equipped to handle color with the same ease.

This is why she felt that to truly portray women realistically one must free them from the shadows of black-and-white photography. She wanted the men to stop telling them that they were beautiful only if photographed in a series of grays; color simply made them stand out. Made them unmissable, even if it was all in fun. (Paradoxically, Madame Amadora's women, once they were portrayed in all those electric levels of color, were later thought to be extraordinary creatures of the imagination.)

Now Amadora didn't just want color, she wanted amplified color, crazy color, layers of red on red on red, or blues taken with blue cellophaned lights. Color filters. She wanted definition, sharp contrast; none of the gentle blurring of the traditional portrait. She wanted surrealism, whimsy, and Paris. She wanted color as it had never been seen in a photograph—no gentle hues, no heavenly glow, no delicate hand-tinted pictures. She wanted it as a painter may crave color. As an artist.

―――――――――――

"You did it," said George as he and Amadora kicked off their fancy shoes in the wee hours of the morning following her gallery show featuring her color portraits.

"I did, didn't I?" Amadora stretched and smiled, lying the length of the sofa.

The pictures on display were of her usual stage, movie, and literary stars, the same stiff nobles and their wives. Only this time they were in gowns of every hue, and dark uniforms festooned with gold braid and multicolored medals, red and blue floor-length capes about the shoulders. They stood before backgrounds of tiny gold stars against a field of white drapes.

There was a woman with red hair, red lips, wearing a red dress in front of a red wall.

Another woman appeared lost in thought as she sat before a pale blue sky hung with large, white cutout paper stars as she contemplated an enormous world globe.

All of Madame Amadora's props were here: the clouds of butterflies in iridescent blues and greens; the stuffed birds and a bull's head; the schools of glass fish; the masks; the fake flowers; the stars, small and golden, large and white; the tiny songbirds. It was as if she had raided Deyrolles on rue du Bac.

The centerpiece of the show was her series of twenty-four Greek and Roman goddesses. The models were all titled Englishwomen only too delighted to dress up as the immortals of Madame Amadora's dreamy firmament without understanding her sly, extravagant feminist view. She had learned to charm and flatter years ago, at Lallie Charles's studio, without ever changing her politics; her pictures were all about equality for women, whether it was a glamorous "housewife" hanging laundry that consisted only of French silk lingerie or a nude woman, plastic flowers in her hair, hard at her sewing machine, running through yards and yards of tulle.

But these women of means missed the humor and wit because they were beguiled by the glamour of Madame Amadora's interpretation of Andromeda, chained to a rock in a three-thousand-dollar Fortuny gown, girdled with a belt of cheap seashells. They couldn't see beyond Europa embracing a stuffed bull's head wearing a crown of silk flowers. Arethusa's hair was tangled in glossy green metal seaweed as she bent to a bouquet of tiger lilies, a parade of glass fish passing by.

Ceres was a fantasy in orange and gold; Hecate, Dido, Helen of Troy were cold and lifeless statues under blue filtered lights.

Venus was pink tulle and pearls, while Daphne was ladies-who-lunch pearls and lost within a laurel tree.

The Queen of the Amazons was clad in an off-the-shoulder spotted fur bathing suit, with a fur necklace that held a deadly arrow in her neck.

Medusa, the showpiece, was an arresting beauty with unnaturally dark lavender eyes, who stared out from the picture, her hair a mass of painted rubber snakes, studded with the occasional rhinestone, with more snakes coiling around her slender, stunning neck. The background was a hot pink. The model's measured gaze made the picture alluring and alarming by turns.

"Did you hear the critics?" said Madame Amadora.

"They marveled, I believe it was, at your 'take on classical figures,'" said George.

"It was a very good take, if I may say so," said Amadora.

They further praised her composition, use of color, and imagination, all of which were clever, unorthodox, and daring. "These pictures," they said, "change everything."

George sat in the chair across from his wife.

"I'm doing the zodiac next," said Amadora. "Then perhaps the tarot—"

"You put in everything," said George, "the trip to Paris, I mean. The stuffed animals, the lipstick—even that picture of the sewing machine, the one with the naked woman sewing—"

"Machine Worker in Summer, 1937."

"—what was the material? It reminded me of clouds—"

"Tulle."

"—all that billowing tulle in those Marie Antoinette colors. The only picture where you used them." George smiled. "Madame Amadora."

He rose, went to her as she raised her arms to be lifted up. A happy, sleepy middle-aged couple who believed that maybe it was possible to change one's world. If the war could refigure his worldview, then so could she. The Surrealists said that no one had ever seen the atrocities like the atrocities in the Great War; it was a place none of them had ever known. The only response was to harness these nightmares and call them dreams.

Maybe one could forget the war and reinvent a place where it had never happened. Madame Amadora directed all her talents, all her imagination, all her love for her troubled husband into her work. And on this August night in 1939, they both believed that she had succeeded. Their feelings of possibility and well-being about this world would last until September, when they would be completely, and permanently, forgotten.

THE SENTIMENTAL PROBLEM OF CLARA
ARGENTO
OR
MELLA'S TYPEWRITER

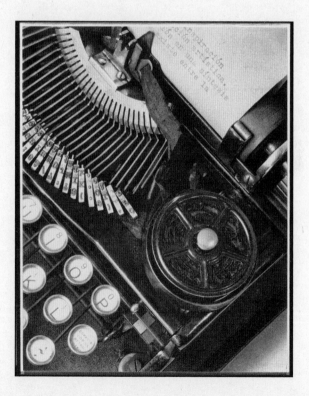

I hoped, M., that you would enjoy a good laugh when you heard I was accused of participating in the attempt to shoot Ortiz Rubio—"Who would have thought it, eh? Such a gentle looking girl who made such nice photographs of flowers and babies."

These were the words Clara Argento wrote to her former lover, Morris Elliot, in 1929 while incarcerated in the Penitenciaría in Mexico City just before her deportation by the Mexican government, before they loaded her onto a Dutch cargo ship bound for Rotterdam as if she herself were just so much cargo. The first port of call was in the Caribbean, where the ship delivered six crates rumored to contain artifacts of New World gold purchased by an island dictator with the usual monarchical aspirations. Clara was confined to her quarters for the time it took to unload the boxes. The second port was New Orleans, where the ship docked for five days to empty and reload its cargo. Clara was detained in a holding cell, which she described in another letter to Morris Elliot as a cross between a jail and a hospital with its long row of empty beds.

The good news, she wrote, was that New Orleans was nothing like the horror of the Mexican prison where she had been held for two weeks, with its iron bed and filthy toilet and endless darkness, which had taxed her inner resources, leaving her to wrestle with her own sanity. The window of this latest location looked out on what she said was an American lawn, complete with flag and flagpole and, she wrote, *a sight which should—were I not such a hopeless rebel—remind me constantly of the empire of "law & order" and other inspiring thoughts of that kind.*

She was reticent to write about how a rather exquisite thirty-four-year-old Italian woman, finely built, sophisticated, and full of grace, who'd first sailed to America from Italy in 1913 as another hopeful immigrant at age seventeen—could end up in a New Orleans prison, in the midst of her deportation from Mexico. She, a woman who had been an actress and a model and a muse, an elusive beauty, a successful photographer, willed herself not to think about where she was being taken—to Mussolini (more imprisonment, possible execution)—because she was thought to be behind the assassination attempt on the new Mexican president. And why, with her family having lived in San Francisco for the past twenty-three years, wouldn't she use her American passport, sidestepping the terrible fate awaiting her in Fascist Italy?

The sentimental problem of Clara Argento began with her father, Gian Antonio Argento, who was, at various times, a mechanical engineer, a machinist, a marble cutter, a photographer, and an inventor.

The photography studio was the first thing Gian Antonio attempted once he settled into San Francisco, and the only thing to fail, which was all for the best since it motivated him to establish his own machinist shop. It was located not too far from the Italian district of North Beach, where he lived with his two eldest daughters. In his shop he invented useful objects to his heart's content and made enough money to send for Clara, her two younger brothers, and his adored wife—one or two at a time—their eventual arrival making him the happiest man alive.

Not bad for a man who, back home, had been involved with the Socialists, protesting working conditions and eventually joining a radical group encouraging strikes and walkouts, until he was unable to find another factory job and was forced to emigrate to Austria, where he and his family had lived the lives of barely tolerated immigrants. There Clara had learned firsthand what it meant for someone to want your labor yet not want *you*.

It was also in Austria, while working at the factory, that Gian Antonio Argento invented the bamboo bicycle frame, giving the bike a lightness that helped in hilly terrain. However, when a worker does not own the means of production, then all patents and profits go to the owner of the business and not to the worker. Even when everyone was riding Gian Antonio's bamboo bicycle and thanking him whenever they saw him on the street.

This state of affairs—a large family with declining fortunes combined with having to surrender his dream machine ideas to someone with less imagination but more capital—resulted in a return to Italy, where Gian Antonio rejoined his hometown's Socialist Circle. Gian Antonio believed in fairness for the worker. He believed in the righteousness of a socialist system. He understood that, without significant political change, his five children would be factory labor before the end of their childhood. Clara Argento remembered being held high on her father's shoulders as he attended workers' rallies with their calls to arms and holiday atmosphere.

Not long after returning to Italy, Gian Antonio traveled to San Francisco, settling in North Beach. In 1911 North Beach was a crowded district of Italian bakeries, Italian cafés, Italian theaters, Italian tailors, Italian laundries, Italian markets, Italian coffee roasters, and Italian ice cream parlors, scenting the air with melted sugar, coffee, garlic in oil, cigarettes, engine exhaust, the sea, and the sweat of workers. An impressive Catholic church dominated the central square.

The transatlantic move did nothing to curtail Gian Antonio's involvement with radical politics. "This is the land of the free," he told Clara. "Freedom of speech. Freedom of worship. What good are these freedoms if they're only talk?" He would joke and say that he was "doing the country a favor by accepting what they are offering."

Clara Argento, seventeen and newly arrived in California, enjoyed the political meetings that were held in her father's house. "Later, the people who came were called "anarcho-syndicalists." There was always talk about workers and organizing and property." The meetings reminded her of Italy, with their high spirits and festive feeling. When asked if his New World successes—his shop, his inventions, his house—didn't make Gian Antonio rethink his political leanings, Clara answered that, because he had known enough of economic hardship, there were no circumstances—no matter how fortunate—that made it possible to think any other way.

Though Clara was comfortable discussing her father's politics, she did not talk about having worked in a silk factory at age fourteen, when there wasn't enough money to allow her to remain in school. Nor did she mention the family's time in Austria, so many years that she spoke

German with greater fluency than she did Italian. How strange it was to think that traveling to another country, speaking the language, and doing the jobs that they think only you are fit to do can carry such a lack of respect. You are a mule, a coal miner's pickax, the most unbeautiful, the most necessary machine.

———————

Clara sat on the enormous low-lying branch of a California oak that grew parallel to the ground. She wore a vaguely ethnic dress, printed in batik; silver bracelets adorned her wrists. The costume belonged to her (had been sewn by her and batiked by her "husband," Laurent Cluzet), as was frequently the custom in the era of silent movies. The smudges of smoky eyeliner, combined with the dark, wavy hair framing her flawless face, gave her an almost exaggerated sexuality. She looked predatory and world-weary. Clara tried to angle her face away from the sun, using the canopy of leaves while waiting for the film crew to set up the next shot. A disagreement between the director, the cinematographer, and her leading man was becoming more heated.

As she sat, she thought about nothing more important than what she and Laurent would have for dinner, guessing at who would be dropping by their large studio apartment, which had become a kind of ongoing impromptu salon for many of the painters, writers, poets, philosophers, and parlor radicals in the inner Los Angeles area. These daily parties were occasions for laughter and music and a shifting of partners that went beyond dancing. Some discussions blew like storms, and others were softer, more intimate. The apartment usually attracted friends, and acquaintances of friends, just after the dinner hour.

Clara and Laurent liked it that way, Clara because she was from Italy and a large family and unable to remember a life without political debates. Having people passing through the house, looking for company and conversation, a little food and drink, was the only home life she had ever really known.

Hers was unlike the childhood of her husband, an American by way of Quebec, whose quiet family homesteaded small farms in the Pacific

Northwest. Farm life can be tough and isolating, so Laurent decided at an early age that, while he loved his family, he wanted, as he said, "to cast my lot in with beauty." He said, "I conceived of a beautiful life, which I knew had to be somewhere because it wasn't where I was." With that in mind, he settled in San Francisco, changed his name from Lawrence to Laurent, wrote poetry and sketched, and later designed fabrics.

And, eventually, met Clara Argento, at the Panama-Pacific International Exposition being held in San Francisco in 1915 to commemorate the opening of the Panama Canal.

The exposition was a fabulous world's fair, a fantasy city within a city where it bordered the San Francisco Bay. The Liberty Bell was there. There was a promenade of mature palms called the Avenue of Palms; the Court of the Four Seasons; an Italian Pavilion with a court-yard recalling the Renaissance. An impressive, small-scale version of the Panama Canal offered boat rides with a piped-in recording of statistics. The Court of the Sun and Stars had an Arch of the Rising Sun. Visitors strolled the colonnade in the Palace of Fine Arts, and ate sweets at a fair within a fair called Toyland, which featured colorful flags creating an arched entrance. There were fountains and pools, and statues mourning "a life without art." There were paintings, murals, souvenir stalls, and food from every continent.

Nothing, however, outshone the Tower of Jewels: a 435-foot-tall structure with a ground-floor archway resembling the Arc de Triomphe—that is, if the arc had held a stack of progressively smaller round tiers like a collection of fancy hatboxes. Each level was adorned with smooth Italianate columns, carved Japanese eaves, Moorish arches, or a wrap-around terrace that held an assembly of gold statues, star maidens in diamond diadems. An enormous sphere rested upon another enormous sphere at the top.

It wasn't the star maidens and architectural details that made the tower extraordinary—it was that each tier was wrapped in imported cut-crystal "gems" of ruby, emerald, sapphire, aquamarine, citrine, and diamond, backed with tiny mirrors and hung from individual brass hooks that allowed them to shimmer and knock against each other when caught in the bay breezes, eventually causing the smallest, most inconsequential damage to the gems. It was the way the sunlight refracted through the jewels, and the way the fifty-four searchlights took over for the sun each night.

On her day off from I. Magnin's luxury department store, where she was both seamstress and model, Clara sat on the edge of the large reflecting pool that faced the tower. The pool, an exaggerated affair with its stone globe in the center, accurately depicting the land and water masses of Earth with a mythical rider bearing two angels blowing trumpets and spewing water upon his shoulders, was crowded around its perimiter with exhibition visitors having a rest. Clara sat among them, flanked on one side by one of the dozen fish statues situated around the perimeter and, on the other, by a young man.

Though Clara never cared for jewelry—her ideas of beauty would always lie elsewhere—nor would she ever be tempted to spend her money on such expensive accessories (all her money would go to living, helping friends, the Communist Party, and buying a pair of cameras—not necessarily in that order but close to it), she loved the Tower of Jewels. Which is how, as she sat on the edge of the pool, she came to say what she said aloud, without thinking that anyone was listening: "This building makes me think that anything is possible."

"Yes," said the man beside her.

The surprise of someone not only listening but responding to her comment made her turn her full attention to Laurent Cluzet, noticing the narrow mustache running the length of his lips; the small bit of beard on his chin; his tall, slender, long-legged frame. Having partially folded himself up, he possessed an almost frail quality, as if he were the male version of a model in a Pre-Raphaelite painting. He wasn't so much androgynous as slightly asexual; his rather formal, fussy clothing, a study in late-nineteenth-century aesthete styling, bordered on the theatrical. None of which bothered Clara, who was becoming a popular Italian theater actress and was therefore used to everything being a little larger than life.

It may be possible to measure a life by the times, places, and circumstances where you hear the word *yes*. Sometimes there is nothing so terrible as hearing "yes" when asking a question to which you don't really want to hear an answer ("Do you love her?"). But other times, "yes" is the perfect answer ("Do you love me?" "Do you want to come with me?" "Shall we meet here again tomorrow?" "*Yes*.").

"Clara," Laurent later asked, "shall we meet here again tomorrow?"

"Yes."

They met by the tower during the day. They strolled the nearby Avenue of Palms, and the Court of the Sun and Stars. Laurent bought Clara lemon ice and sailed with her through the Tunnel of Love in Toyland. They climbed a hill above the Marina to watch the fifty-four searchlights hitting the jewels as they moved in the night breezes, their little mirrors and facets bending the light back into the sky.

The closing of the Panama-Pacific International Exposition, coinciding with the end of 1915, saw a dismantling of all those fabulous pavilions and halls.

On the day the tower was to come down, Clara told Laurent that she had to rehearse a new musical, which wasn't true; she didn't want anyone to see how unbearable it was for her to see it go. Maybe she was attached to the tower because she attached it to Laurent, whose ideas of art and beauty and a bohemian life coincided with her own. The association was so strong that it seemed likely that, when the tower disappeared, so would he.

But Laurent didn't go away, and, three years later, he handed Clara a box the size of the palm of her hand. Inside was one of the rubies, nicked in two places, from the Tower of Jewels, with a note that read, *I know you would rather have this than an engagement ring. Come with me to Los Angeles and be my wife.*

In the six years since they'd met, and three years since they'd moved to Los Angeles, Clara had been working in the movies while Laurent drew, and designed fabric. They were content with their lives and each other. They had their bohemian friends, their fashionable address, their unconventional marriage, which was unconventional in that they never legally married yet considered themselves wed. Clara took Laurent's name to convince his family, to whom marriage mattered.

As Clara sat on the low oak branch thinking about dinner, a rather small, slight man caught her eye. He was leaning against a tree not far from where Clara sat. He looked to be on the young side of thirty, despite his deeply receded hairline and funny little mustache. As she studied him, she noticed an expression of deep interest in the goings-on of the film set, as well as a touch of coldness about the mouth. This combination of curiosity and a bit of a chill pulled her attention; it was so different from Laurent, who was so sweet that it was sometimes challenging to think of him as a lover and not a brother.

Who wouldn't be fascinated by the forty-acre movie lot, which consisted of scenery flats, mocked-up locations, prop rooms, wardrobe rooms, carpenters putting up this and taking down that? And then there were the animal actors that lived there full-time: lions, leopards, elephants, bears, parrots, chimpanzees, three zebras, and a few dogs. Plus, the mustachioed man appeared very taken with the director's increasingly excited conversation.

When the participants in the dispute finally stomped off in opposite directions, the small man disengaged his attention to notice Clara, who meant to look away but instead smiled. He returned the smile, igniting a low-level heat. Like many pretty girls, Clara had seldom been bold because she never really had to be. But she now found herself moving off the low branch with the intention of introducing herself to this man whose smile had caused such an inner disturbance, only to be intercepted by one of the movie assistants telling her they were ready to begin.

And when she had finished with her scene—the one where she, the beautiful Mexican maid, is mistaken by the hero for the lady of the house—the small, slight man was gone.

The Afternoon of the Leopard was Clara's second starring role and her fourth film. Her previous acting experience had been in the popular Italian theater of North Beach in San Francisco, where she had been in melodramas, operettas, and vaudevilles—many of them overwrought and mediocre to terrible. Clara was already feeling the constraints of sentimentality in the scripts, much in the same way that, as a model, she was beginning to chafe at pictorialism in photographs.

A famous woman photographer, Jane Reece, had traveled to California on a vacation from her Ohio portrait studio. Upon meeting Clara and Laurent, she immediately asked if they would be willing to pose for her. Clara was dressed like the sort of California Indian being repressively, unendingly converted by the Franciscan fathers who dotted the length of the state with their missions.

With Laurent, Miss Reece went straight to the source, depicting the tall, lean young man as Jesus.

"Jesus," said Clara under her breath when she saw the print. All that soft-focus, painterly nonsense with the camera; Clara hated it from the start. In the same way she had grown tired of Hollywood's insistence that she play the Exotic Girl in her harem costume or a traditional Oaxacan blouse and skirt, the fiery señorita in a mantilla, the shoeless Greek island girl.

She was always the siren, the sex goddess, the vamp, the temptation, the poor choice, the thief of every man's morality. At least when she was acting in the Italian theater she was seen as an actress, someone with the skill to portray a range of characters, and she did such a fine job that the North Beach audiences loved her.

In San Francisco, Clara modeled for a controversial statue of a naked woman. Then she posed nude for another photographer. And, like many beautiful women who want more than admiration, she was conflicted about her beauty. She devoured books and ideas; was a playful conversationalist; wore imaginative, stylized clothing sewn by her own hand. People lined up to buy the little fabric dolls she made as a lark. The attention her looks brought was intoxicating because it made so many things so much easier, except for the knowledge that it could not last.

Men were drawn to Clara because of her appearance, but they fell for her because of her goodness and her mind.

As far as movies went, she didn't want only to be the one who made someone's pulse race: She wanted to make art.

When she was on the set, she often observed the camera operators, the way they counted to themselves to time their shots, the way they adjusted the lighting or studied the angles of her face. Her father had been a mechanical engineer and a machinist and an inventor, and she was her father's daughter.

Which is why the man with the mustache, more intrigued by the makers of the movies than by the actors, had caught her eye.

The Cluzet apartment was in the Bryson Building, one of the newest and most elegant apartment buildings in Los Angeles. Their sizable studio was on the sixth floor, four stories below the baroque ballroom that Mr. Bryson had built for sixty thousand dollars, and six marble stairways up from the lobby of potted palms where "Blue Ali Baba oil jars were dotted around, big enough to keep tigers in," as Raymond Chandler wrote. There were Moorish archways, stone lions, a blue carpet, a birdcage elevator.

Laurent, with his dogged devotion to all things "beautiful," including Clara, often chose her clothes to complement the romantic apartment. Everything for Laurent was stage dressing; in this way, he was perfect for Hollywood. Clara shimmered in ocean colors, her upswept hair dotted with tiny rhinestones, bits of sparkle that made it appear as if a constellation were tangled in the strands.

Since the door of the studio always stood open on these evenings, there was no sound of it opening or closing to announce the arrival or departure of guests. Someone once asked the Cluzets if they were ever worried about someone walking off with their belongings, and they replied that they didn't believe in possessions.

Actually, this was what Laurent said in answer to a newcomer to that night's party—a prematurely bald man with a funny little mustache who entered the apartment accompanied by a second man, and a very pretty woman named Marguerite.

The mustachioed man, whom Clara recognized from that day at the studio three weeks ago, said, "Oh, are possessions now a religion?"

"Only if you live in America," said another guest, a foreign-looking man dressed like a banker.

"Now, see, this is what I don't understand," said the mustachioed man to his female companion. "Everyone acts as if there's no wealth anywhere but in the United States, as if we're the only people on Earth who enjoy it."

Marguerite smiled a knowing smile. "I wasn't even born here," she said, "and I think I understand your own country better than you." She removed her hat, handing it to Laurent as she smoothed down her hair. Clara admired the cut and quality of the woman's clothing, the beauty of the embroidery along the hem of her long jacket and her sleeves.

"You should listen to Marguerite," said Laurent to the mustachioed man of his female companion. "Not only is she sophisticated, magnificent, well-read, and well-lived"—he lightly tapped her hat on the chest of the mustachioed man—"but she is the most terribly spiritual genius."

"Listen to you," said Marguerite, laughing. Clara loved Marguerite's laugh, which always sounded to her like tiny Christmas bells.

The women kissed in a belated greeting, Clara turning toward the second man, who had come in with the small mustachioed man and Marguerite, extending her hand and saying, "I'm Clara Cluzet."

"Madame Cluzet," said the man without the mustache, "Jack Hartmann. Visiting from Berkeley."

"My family lives in San Francisco," said Clara. "North Beach."

"That's how I know you!" said Jack Hartmann. "You were with *La Moderna*, weren't you?"

"You know Italian theater?" said Clara.

"A little."

"Are you an actor?" asked Clara, though she was thinking that Jack was really too tall to be anything but a character actor, in the same way that she was too Italian, too darkly beautiful to be anything but someone's mistress, the one who ruins but seldom wins the leading man.

Jack laughed. "No, no. I'm a photographer."

"I should've guessed," said Laurent, "since you came here with Marguerite."

"Really," Marguerite said, "you think because I take pictures I consort only with other photographers? I like to think my social life is a bit broader than that."

"And you are?" Clara asked the mustachioed man.

"Morris Elliot," he said.

"I remember you from the movie studio. I was sitting on the branch of a tree."

"And I remember you, Madame Cluzet. *The Afternoon of the Leopard*," said Morris Elliot.

"Yes, *The Afternoon of the Leopard*. So what is it that you do when you aren't visiting film sets?"

"What made you think I was visiting?" asked Morris.

Clara laughed. "I work there, and *I* feel like *I'm* visiting. It's that sort of profession, you know, where your job lasts only as long as the movie."

"I'm a photographer," said Morris.

Laurent laughed. "Of course you are!"

Marguerite rolled her eyes, smiled. "Morris has a portrait studio in Tropico—a very good one in fact."

"Well," said Laurent, threading his arm through Marguerite's and simultaneously pressing Clara's inner wrist to his mouth, delivering a light kiss, "why don't we go and find something very good to drink? And you"—to Marguerite—"can tell me more about all the nonphotographer friends you supposedly have." He dropped Clara's hand as he, Marguerite, and Jack Hartmann ("It's all good to drink, if you ask me") went to the rolling bar cart near the window.

Once they were left alone, Morris said to Clara, "I take it you don't like acting in the pictures."

"No," she said.

Morris said nothing but kept his eyes on Clara. Though he seemed to lack a kind of natural warmth, he didn't come across as unfriendly. Clara recognized the same engaged curiosity that she had noticed on the set; he appeared intelligent. Perhaps it was the way he studied her that undid her. The look, the intelligence; there was no prurience in his questions, no searching for a nugget of gossip or the unintentional confession.

"I don't think that I'm expected to act."

"What do you think you're expected to do?"

"Be beautiful and exotic and dangerous." Clara took a sip of her drink. "It isn't interesting."

Morris took the glass from her hand, sipping before returning it. There was no presumption in the act; in fact, it was so intimate, and natural, so provocative that Clara's pulse sped up.

"Why not come by my studio sometime? I'll let you rescue me from the hell of baby photographs and Los Angeles matrons in soft focus." Now he did smile. It was a lovely smile. "Please say you'll help a modern man imprisoned in all that romantic dreck. I could be mistaken, but I think you need rescuing too."

Though he stepped no closer, Clara felt as if he were whispering in her ear when he said, "You are no more a creature of an Edenic past than I am. Men are confounded by your figure and your face, and decide that you aren't a modern woman but someone more primitive, more elemental. It must make you feel as if you aren't there at all, waiting for them to see you."

"Yes," she whispered.

She thought of Laurent and his endless pursuit of what he called "absolute beauty," something he demanded from all things in their lives. It didn't matter if it was Clara's clothing or the furnishings of their studio in their very beautiful building. His wardrobe, his sketches, his poems, their love. It all must be romantic. It must be Beauty and Art. Her fleeting thought was how long it had been since she was with a man who wanted her, not his idealized version of her. Theirs was an almost sexless love, but she seemed to be the only one who knew it.

"My husband has an 'intentional disregard for the modern spirit of this age.'"

"My wife is impossible."

She said to Morris, "I'm not sentimental."

Morris said to her, "Neither am I."

"Mexico," said Laurent one night in the aftermath of one of their parties—months following the party where Clara and Morris first spoke. "I plan to leave next month," Laurent said. "Then, when Clara finishes this last movie, she will join me. Can you imagine an art school where everything is free, for Mexicans and foreigners alike—tuition, board, room, paint, canvas, models, all free—no entrance exam. One must study, that is the only requirement. After ten years of war and unrest, it is wonderful."

The little group of remaining guests—Morris Elliot, Marguerite Mahler, Pablo Martín, Xavier de Sica, and Erik Norman—reclined in various positions atop the thick Persian area rug in the nearly empty studio. Because of the lack of furniture, Laurent and Clara had splurged on the "good" rug and an assortment of large pillows. Those encrusted with tiny mirrors were really for show, as anyone who ever tried to use one quickly discovered.

"Tell me about your movie, Madame Cluzet," said Morris, leaning a little too close to Clara, a little too drunk, with Clara not moving away.

"Let me see. Ah, yes, I play a Mexican. A *sultry* Mexican," she said.

"With a knife behind your back and a rose between your teeth? How original! And it seems . . . almost prescient," said Morris, clumsily holding his hand to his chest before having to steady himself. He smiled; she smiled.

Marguerite paled, just slightly. She had been looking a bit drawn lately.

(When Clara had asked Morris if Marguerite were ill, he simply answered, "She's unhappily in love."

"Do you know the woman?" Marguerite was a lover of women.

"It's not a woman this time—hence the unhappiness. Men make her more miserable because she doesn't really like them in that way."

Clara wasn't surprised when someone with a defined preference made the occasional sexual detour.)

"Why not take me with you, Laurent?" said Marguerite in a voice meant to sound flirtatious, but which succeeded only in sounding plaintive.

"Marguerite, you *should* come with Pablo and me. We should all go!" said Laurent. "To Obregón's paradise."

"Excuse me if I'm skeptical about anyone's president," said Morris.

"Vasconcelos has promised literacy and art to the people. He has thrown the library doors wide open. I'm sorry for your cynicism," said Pablo.

"Just because the United States doesn't have a minister of public education, like Vasconcelos, someone who cares about the arts—"

"—and the *people*," said Morris.

"Yes, and the *people*," said Pablo.

"I'm just wondering why the people are always being told what to want," said Morris.

"You don't know how bad it gets," said Clara quietly, "when no one cares about you."

Then, with a lightness, she said, "Having played a Mexican in not one but three movies, I would like to say, Viva la Revolución. And to Señor Martín, and to my wonderful husband, even to my friend Morris, may you never understand what you don't understand."

Morris leaned over to Clara, hovering for a moment before kissing her on the mouth, then pulling away slightly, saying, "Back at you, kid," before struggling a little to his feet. "The wife awaits. Marguerite, shall you take me home?"

Marguerite didn't move. She had been looking at the floor while everyone was talking, and now a single tear made its way down her pretty face. She nodded as she rose, picked up her cape and one of her original little hats, and walked over to the door, which Morris held open.

The other guests heard Morris say to her in the quiet voice of the drunk (which is to say a voice more audible than the drinker realizes),

"You don't really care about me, M. It's only something you've talked yourself into," before closing the door behind them.

―――――――――

For ten years Marguerite Mahler had been the photographer–business partner–object of a slight sexual obsession for Morris Elliot. For those ten years, she had also been his on-again-off-again mistress. He was inspired by her photographs—of fans, flowers, kimonos, shadows, seashells, showers, opera gloves, birds' wings, and waves of sand—as much as he was by her sunny personality, and her past as a prostitute. It was a spark that ignited in both directions, despite her preference for women. The fact that Morris was an exception for her made the sexual tension deeper and more mysterious.

A photograph taken by Cymbeline Kelley, on the occasion of Morris and Marguerite visiting Cymbeline and Leroy in San Francisco, shows the pair in profile; Marguerite's back is against Morris's chest, her head thrown back in a posture of surrender. He holds her as if to support her. It is an elegant portrait by any measure. Their intimacy is unmistakable.

Morris would say that it was Marguerite's intelligence, artistic brilliance, her original way of seeing and being in the world, that was the polar opposite of the domestic life he lived with his wife and five children; it was her eccentricity, her habit of disappearing for a few days at a time and returning to him like an exhausted, satisfied adventurer that made him see the possibilities of a life he was not living. For Morris, Marguerite was the life he longed for, the life that lived inside himself as he listened to his wife talk about the house and the garden and the children, whom he loved but could not, as hard as he tried, make the center of everything.

It could be said that Marguerite opened the door for him, but Clara was the one who made him decide finally to step through. This was the reason for Marguerite's tears at Clara and Laurent's Bryson studio. That evening she knew, as Laurent did not, that Clara and Morris had been lovers for several months.

―――――――――

By the time Morris and Clara moved to Mexico City, in 1923, Clara had been his sometime model and muse for just over two years. It was an off-and-on thing, fueled by the permissiveness of the times, when politics and relationships were in flux, largely due to the calamity that had been the Great War. The sheer scope and barbarism of the four-year war, not to mention the Spanish flu epidemic that took hold as it was winding down, made an entire generation rethink the expectations that had preceded the war.

Artists, writers, and wanderers gravitated toward Paris. Political idealists found their calling in the newly revolutionized Russia. Everyone else who felt unfit for or undesirous of "regular life" went to Mexico City. Some thought of them as a lost generation; others, like Clara, would say that they were found.

The Mexican Revolution had barely ended when the new president, Álvaro Obregón, who dreamt of a literate, artistic epoch for all Mexicans, enlisted José Vasconcelos to implement his programs, including hiring artists wearing workmen's overalls to paint the most fabulous murals for the same pay scale as the masons they resembled. This, thought Clara, when she had lived in Mexico only a short while, is surely paradise.

Clara and Morris sailed to Mexico, bringing with them Morris's eldest child, fourteen-year-old Bryce. If Morris's wife had thought to foist child-rearing duties on the lovers, she had miscalculated: Morris and Clara were very happy to have Bryce along. This may have been because Clara couldn't have children of her own and missed her large family, or because she was only now recovering from the tragedy of Laurent's death from smallpox.

As had been their plan, Laurent had gone ahead to Mexico while she finished her final movie. Then came the telegram of his illness, then his death while she was en route. She never fully forgave herself for letting him die alone, despite the disease having moved faster than the telegraph service and the public transportation of the time.

But Laurent's death did not deter Clara from moving to Mexico.

When Morris heard the news, he had the splendid idea of the two of them opening a photography studio. She would run the business while learning photography. "I will be your apprentice," she said, "for room and board."

Seldom has the word *apprentice* been so true and so euphemistic.

———————————

It didn't take long for discontentment to enter their household. In the beginning, Morris and Clara were caught up in the energy of the city: fiestas, shops, trams, flowers, music, dancing, cooking, fruit, and toys. The clothes. The cathedral. The zócalo. The holidays. The surreal gardens of Xochimilco, floating islands of flowers and willows.

Their business did well enough, though it didn't allow them much breathing room; no matter, their new life in the Colonia Juárez was exhilarating. Their new friends were some of the most famous artists, writers, poets, and radicals of the city. There was no one they wished to know whom they didn't know. Whereas Clara had once given nightly parties in Los Angeles with Laurent, she now gave them in Mexico City with Morris.

And the days Clara spent running the studio, taking photographs (portraits and flowers, including one of white roses, all crushed together, overripe and erotic), printing, and discovering that she not only loved the work of making pictures but had a talent for it. People began requesting her services.

All of this was punctuated by her nude modeling for Morris, usually on their rooftop, where Clara would pose as pleased and as natural and, to Morris's way of thinking, as unknowable as a cat in the sun.

It was not Clara's enthusiasm and talents that bred discontent in Morris; it was the insecurity brought on by her beauty. He once grumbled that "next time I'll get an ugly mistress." It didn't help that, when his nudes of Clara were exhibited, they brought her more attention (and notoriety) than they brought him. This was all the more galling since they also eclipsed his gorgeous experiments in modernism, as he had finally come into his own as a photographer.

"I don't believe in marriage or anything resembling marriage," said

Clara quietly when he complained of her casual lovers. "You knew how it was in Los Angeles. You were part of how it was in Los Angeles."

"This isn't the same thing," he said.

"It is exactly the same thing."

"Well, I don't like it."

"You said you didn't care about fidelity. You said if you did, you may as well stay with your wife."

He said nothing.

She could've explained that her sexual freedom wasn't simply a product of her time and bohemian choices; it was the tradition of her family. The Argentos were no strangers to common-law marriages, or the child of one man, born outside marriage, being raised by another. Her own parents didn't marry until three weeks before her oldest sister was born. No one gave much thought to whether a relationship was bound by law or love or both. What she said instead was "I didn't grow up in some midwestern America. I don't believe in possessions."

"Really? Then explain your marriage to me, because my hopeless midwestern mind seems confused, Madame Cluzet."

She was silent. Then, "Laurent and I were 'married' because we chose to be married. We lived together, we worked side by side—what else could marriage be?"

"Then what am I to you?"

"I'm with you now. No one else exists for me." Clara placed her hands on either side of his face and said, her voice kind and loving, "We only live in a single moment anyway."

Though Morris was uncomforted, he was more than willing when she took his hand and led him upstairs to her room.

———————————

For Clara in Mexico the smells of oil, spices, animals, machine exhaust, cooked sugar, pastries, cigarettes, and the sweat of workers took her back to North Beach, and further back to Italy. Mostly Italy. She belonged to Mexico. She said, "I feel Mexican when I'm in Mexico, unlike the United States, where I feel I'm in a foreign country."

On their one-year anniversary in Mexico, as a lark, Morris and Clara went to a traditional photography studio with corny backdrops, and, as they posed like man and wife, Clara said, "El señor is very religious, perhaps you can put a church in the background; and I should like to hold these lovely flowers. But you will have better ideas than we—your pictures are so artistic!"

They came out into the street laughing, with the promise to pick up the three different wedding portrait prints next week.

"Are you happy now?" she said, trying to catch her breath.

"Very," he said, pulling her into a happy embrace.

When Clara had her first exhibition, it was a success. Patrons were impressed by the modernism of her composition of glass-paned doors, telegraph wires, rows of concrete stadium seats, convent passageways. Then there were the plants and flowers that, like the architectural details, looked to be pure form.

The portraits were different. Elegant, expressive, compassionate.

And the pictures were well-received, even if they were always overshadowed by Morris's previous two exhibitions of Clara in the nude.

There was admiration for her intelligence, her generosity, her glamour, her leftist leanings, her peaceful nature, her skill behind the camera, her (eventually) storied, almost mythical love affair with Morris, with its hazy domesticity and creative synergy. Her beauty. Always her beauty. Her image appeared in more than one Diego Rivera mural, including the murals of Chapingo—"the Sistine Chapel of the Americas"—showing her in a languorous pose similar to that in the photographs Morris took on the azotea. For nearly a year she posed; for nearly a year she was Rivera's lover.

The men who were given her favors could not keep them.

Not to mention a certain man who could not garner her favor when he wanted it—that undid her in the end.

Cymbeline and Leroy went to Mexico to see their old friend Morris Elliot during a break in Leroy's teaching at his Bay Area college. Cymbeline later said of Clara, "To me she was a performer of real interest. . . . I was never critical of her, never noticed her accent if she had one, just took in her beauty."

Before Cymbeline and Leroy returned home, they purchased one of Clara's photographs, *Wineglasses,* which had the same modernist aesthetic as the telegraph wires and endless doors, eventually donating it to the Mallory College art gallery.

There was no photograph of Morris and Clara that even hinted at the swooning closeness shown in Cymbeline's photograph of Morris and Marguerite; for them the truth would look more like their separate photographs, hung side by side, but always in the same room.

———————

"Clara Argento—profession: men!"

She said jokingly at a party where the guests assembled to play a game where you tell something true about yourself, choosing questions from a hat. Only Morris wasn't laughing. This was the same party where another guest took a photograph of Clara seated between two men, their backs to the camera, their three faces in synchronized three-quarter profile, as one of the men drew pictures on her exposed shoulder and upper back.

In his refusal to seem "midwestern," as Clara had said, Morris took to turning a blind eye to her male guests. Fortunately, her room—the couple had never shared a room, partly to keep an element of truth about their master-apprentice relationship, and partly because of Morris's boy Bryce, who was too old to be fooled and too young to care—was on the rooftop azotea. In this way, Morris could almost, almost avoid knowing of her "little romances."

Morris tried sleeping with women in their social circle and traveling American girls who saw him as one more way to be daring until they returned home to respectability. The women in their circle talked too much about art and about politics; he was particularly sensitive to anything involving the Communist Party (Bullshit politics, as he thought of it), since Clara had become more and more entrenched in it.

She had begun doing translations for *El Machete,* since her spoken languages included Italian, German, English, Spanish, French, and a smattering of Russian. Her pictures ran regularly in the paper, and she held editorial and political meetings at the house.

Morris had no interest in politics, particularly in the Communist Party, to whose rhetoric he was subjected daily by their friends. Who was allowed in, who was thrown out, who allowed their individual, bourgeois needs to come before the collective. And always the Revolution.

Clara's pictures reflected her changes. She was no longer interested in studio work, unless you counted her still lifes of a hammer and sickle; or sombrero, hammer, and sickle, or guitar neck, dried corn, and bandolier, its rows of bullets like strung jewels. Instead she took street pictures of workers on strike, rural women nursing their babies, a homeless man sleeping on a curb. People carried flags and banners. And everyone looked weathered and tired.

Since the women they knew socially wouldn't stop talking long enough to allow Morris to at least distract himself for a while, he decided to take up with their housekeeper. His Spanish was never any good, and she spoke no English, making them, he thought, a perfect match. Clara paid so little attention to what he did that she said nothing, but he could imagine that, if she did know, he would get a lecture not on infidelity but on the exploitation of the working class.

He could almost recite it. Which, he thought, may have been the reason he did it.

His next transgression was when he crept into Clara's room while she was out photographing a puppeteer as a "visual critique on the current puppet government of Mexico." He lingered next to her bed, unable to ignore the sense of sexual excitement it provoked, along with the terrible imaginings of her other men, her bed almost chaste, like that of an ordinary girl. The modest iron frame, the simple coverlet. A tiny, sterling silver cross hung from a deep red velvet ribbon on the wall next to where he stood. He had been present when her admirer gave it to her; he remembered the pleasure in her expression as she held it in her hand, and he remembered how much he loved the touch of that hand.

Without thinking, he pulled the little cross from the nail on the wall, sliding it up inside his nostril until it hurt. He would pollute this new love affair, give it the disrespect it deserved. He would transfer the warmth of her palm to somewhere deep inside him. Feelings of tenderness tossed him back into feelings of anger, which pitched him back to tenderness.

He thought about Marguerite back in the States and how she made him feel found, and how all Clara was doing was making him feel lost. And how his unmanageable longing for Clara had him violating her privacy, and making him a stranger within his own heart.

When she came home that night, Clara was alarmed by his demeanor. He seemed disturbed and defeated. He said, "I have to go home for a while. You're good enough to manage the studio without me."

"Of course," she said, kneeling by his side, feeling his forehead.

He gently took her hand from his face, though he didn't let go. "I'm not sick, but I'm not myself." He couldn't tell her about the cross. Nor could he tell her that that action alone made him understand that, on some level, he knew their love affair had shifted completely. "Bryce and I will go, then I'll be back."

She knew that he missed his children. Eighteen months was a long time to be away.

———————————

Clara almost couldn't get out of bed the day after Morris and Bryce left. The house was hard, but the studio was unbearable. There was no way not to recall the daily conversations, the parties where she could see that Morris was being driven to irritation by talk of "the masses" and "the godless rich" and revolution this and revolution that, the muralists and their Syndicate of Revolutionary Painters, Sculptors, and Technical Workers, and ideas about accessible art for everyone, and equal pay, with Morris ranting later about their "sentimentalizing the people."

But then there were the evenings spinning her out onto the dance floor, or the time she and Morris exchanged clothes, everyone being entertained and a little shocked by his spot-on success as a vamp.

Mostly, she found herself in bed at night whispering, "Come back, come back, please come back."

———————————

Morris returned ten months later with his second son, Langston, to a Clara who seemed more beautiful and more inaccessible and still as sweet and serene as ever.

An American expatriate who had come to Mexico to paint and fell wildly in love with Clara said, "She impressed me immediately as a beautiful woman. I mean beautiful—not trying to be beautiful— but born beautiful." The American painted a dozen pictures of Clara before trading it all in to join the Communist Party. Clara had joined the Party, and if he couldn't have her then he would adore what she adored.

The photography studio had fared well in Morris's absence, and Clara had arranged for a show of his work to keep him in the public eye.

They were overjoyed to see each other; Clara equally happy to have a child again, but everything had changed. If Clara had become more breathtaking, she had also become more political.

Morris still believed in art for its own sake, while Clara wanted her pictures to serve as political statements, underscoring her radical beliefs. It was the "perfect antidote to playfulness," he once yelled at her. He missed her playfulness.

Gone were the lazy, hot days of a naked Clara posing on a striped Indian blanket. No more would Morris photograph her reciting Shake-speare and Whitman. No casual shots of her standing with her Graflex waiting for a sitter to arrive, or of her laughing at Bryce's (now Langs-ton's) antics.

Morris's final picture of Clara was of her in her Japanese kimono, walking up the stairs to her room as she briefly looked back at him over her shoulder.

Neither one knew at the time that it was the last picture. And nine months later he was gone for good.

Morris, Morris—for your peace I should not perhaps—and yet—for my outlet I must tell you that I am lonesome—lonesome—and that I am overwhelmed by tenderness as I think of you—dearest—surely I have always appreciated and have before tonight realized how much you mean to me and yet why is it that since you left I have been suffering and accusing myself of not being worthy of all that you are—tell me, please, mi amor—*that perhaps I have not been as bad as I imagine for really Morris I am suffering too much tonight—and missing you—I miss you—*

This letter was the written equivalent of Morris's photograph of Clara on the stairs in her Japanese kimono: another way of saying good-bye.

Clara's father was ill and wanted Clara. Without hesitation, she packed her bags, closed the studio for three months, and journeyed home to San Francisco, tamping down the worry that, by the time she arrived, her father, like Laurent before him, would be dead.

Instead, she was greeted by a recovering father who grew more robust every day. She hadn't counted on the pleasure of being with her parents and sisters and brothers. Even San Francisco was lovelier than she remembered, and it wasn't long before she went round to friends and colleagues, including Cymbeline Kelley, and the photographer who had come to her Los Angeles apartment with Morris that first time, many of them known through Morris, to see about putting together a show of her pictures. She wrote to Morris, now living back in Southern California: *You know what they say about a prophet in one's own country? Well, it works that way for me too:—you see—this might*

*be called my hometown—well all of the old friends and acquaintances
not one takes me seriously as a photographer—no one has asked to see
or to show my work. I never knew until I came here how much my work
meant to me.*

———————————

Clara returned to Mexico with renewed purpose as she took to the
streets of the city and surrounding villages. She traveled to other parts of
the country, always photographing the people, or their churches, or their
idols. But mostly the people.

She increased her commitment and time to the publication *El
Machete* and to the Communist Party. She promised herself not to fall
in love easily, not to be casual with her heart (or anyone else's), to allow
a new kind of gravity into her life. It was hard to write all this to Morris, who, she imagined, wouldn't be pleased that she had effected these
changes once he had gone.

It didn't matter because, before she could find the time to sit down
and tell Morris about the New Clara, she met two men: One was Italian . . .

His name was Vittorio Vidali. His name was Enea Sormenti. His
name was Jacobo Hurwitz Zender. His name was Carlos Conteras, aka
Comandante Carlos.

He said, when introduced to her at a gathering where Clara lectured
on the absolute dangers of Mussolini and Fascism ("Present-day Italy has
transformed into an immense prison and a vast cemetery," an informer
quoted her, taking down her every word), "My name is Vittorio Vidali
and I believe you and I are from two Italian towns barely five kilometers
apart," taking her hand. Then he told her the name of the town. Vidali
was not much taller than Clara, who stood just under five foot one. His
face was open and friendly, though the eyes were watchful and, if Clara
was honest, a little cunning. And while he had a pleasant enough appearance, there was something mutable about him, as if he could come and
go and no one would be able to accurately recall what he looked like.
He claimed to be a refugee, "like yourself," he said, then was interrupted

before she could correct him. He suggested having coffee some afternoon; Vidali still held her hand.

The other was Cuban . . .

"Oh, sorry, so sorry," said a man interrupting them to speak with Vidali. "I can see that you're busy."

Vidali reluctantly dropped Clara's hand. "Comrade Argento, Comrade Cruz."

One could hardly call oneself a radical in the late 1920s Americas if one didn't know the name of Juan Cristian Cruz, the Cuban Marxist revolutionary. Though he was twenty-five years old, six years younger than Clara, he was already something of a legend. He had swum with sharks in order to organize the crew of a Soviet freighter, had planned the hunger strike that followed a failed attempt to rid Cuba of its current president (and Mussolini sympathizer). Once out of jail, Juan Cristian thought it best to emigrate while regrouping.

Given his romantic past, almost as entangled as Clara's, as well as physical gifts and a charisma to match her own, it was almost inevitable that they would combust as a couple. They would eventually become an example of too much love, too much sex, too much beauty, but there was nothing memorable in this first introduction at the Party meeting.

The other thing of note is that, if Clara hadn't been so blinded by her love for Juan Cristian, she would've paid closer attention to Vittorio Vidali, her fellow Italian and comrade, a man of a thousand names and not one memorable face.

––––––––––––––––

After Clara met Vidali, a man she had been seeing very casually was suddenly called to Moscow for two years.

Vidali happened by Clara's desk where she did translations for *El Machete* and, noticing her staring distractedly out the window, asked if she was okay. She sighed. He insisted on taking her to coffee.

A man who was also hired as a translator for *El Machete* worked at a desk situated across from, but flush with, Clara's. One day, when Vidali was in the office, he saw them laughing. The next day, the translator's desk was cleared; he'd been transferred to Berlin, where "his skills could be better utilized."

Vidali offered a sympathy lunch to cheer her up. Clara gratefully accepted.

A man living on the ground floor of Clara's apartment building, the one she'd once shared with Morris Elliot, had dinner with Clara once a week in exchange for taking care of the potted plants on the rooftop and fixing things around the place. Twice Clara had run into Vidali near her neighborhood when she was walking home. Surprised to see him, she allowed him to take her to her door, where he met the man who was living in the apartment below hers.

About a month later the man lost his balance and fell from the roof to the street, dying upon impact.

The flowers that Vidali sent were spectacular.

———————————

Clara took pictures of Juan Cristian with the same artistic eye and fervor that Morris had lavished upon her. Everything felt new with Juan Cristian; Mexico itself was reborn in her eyes. She had loved Laurent (his gentle worship of her, more religious brotherhood than lover), then Morris (a flash of sexual attraction that flared, then warmed into close friendship), but the thing she felt for Juan Cristian was so different she began to doubt that it was love at all and thought it was instead some other as yet unexperienced emotion.

Everything she felt for him came through in two photographs especially: one of his manual typewriter and the other a portrait, taken from below, with his handsome head framed by the endless blue sky.

In the animal kingdom, it is considered aggressive to stare. In the human gaze there is aggression but there is also sexual invitation (women, however, are encouraged to avert their eyes). But the photographer is expected to stare, to study, to gaze upon her subject.

Juan Cristian was lounging on a *trajinera,* drifting through the Floating Gardens of Xochimilco. He opened one eye, squinting at Clara, who was watching him. "You will tire of me quicker if you keep looking so much, *mi amor,*" he told her.

"I'm only working out the light," she said, shy to be caught, her finger on her Graflex camera.

"Oh, so this is for your work."

"Of course. Why else would I be watching?"

"I'm quite handsome."

"Really."

"So I've heard."

"And what else have you heard?"

"That I'm a gentleman."

She laughed. "And?"

"And that you shouldn't love me because I will only break your heart, *amor.*"

"Unless I break yours first?"

"I'm only repeating rumor."

She sat at his feet.

"They also say you should come to me, so I can place my head on your heartbreaking thighs."

She was conflicted, wanting to touch him and wanting to gaze upon him, his beautiful arms now behind his head as he closed his eyes and lay back.

"You should know that if you keep watching me," he said, eyes closed, "I will become so familiar that you will have me memorized and will no longer want me around, leaving my wet bath towel on the floor, and never closing the cupboards in the kitchen."

On her hands and knees, she moved across the boat to him like a house cat. As she nuzzled and stretched into him, he pulled her close, whispering words of love in her hair.

———————————

In the darkest, quietest, gentlest part of the city night, as they lay in their bed, Juan Christian said to Clara, "I adore you. I love you tempestuously."

Other days he would call her "my sky." She would refer to him as "my earth." Lifted and grounded.

105

Their money came from Juan Cristian's well-to-do biological father (his mother had been the man's mistress) and Clara's work taking pictures of the murals of Rivera, Orozco, and Siqueiros, as well as other artists, for international museums. It all went out as fast as it came in, due to their political causes and struggling friends. They carried on with their Saturday parties, Clara less involved with the guests than she had been at her parties with Laurent and Morris. More involved with Juan Cristian.

All those Other Men who had driven Morris to distraction had disappeared from her life; she could only be with Juan Cristian. Juan Cristian could not bear to be apart from her either, but he still had the revolution to consider. Despite his adherence to the Communist Party, it was whispered that he was too independent, too much of an unpredictable radical. Too charismatic. And by the way, hadn't he been the least bit critical of Stalin, all the while championing Trotsky?

No matter. Clara thought, I have everything.

One man who hadn't left Clara's life completely besides Morris Elliot, with whom she still corresponded, was Vittorio Vidali. As two Italian expatriates, they shared a language and a culture. As two comrades, they shared a commitment to a political ideology.

He would stop by her desk at *El Machete,* tell her a joke in Italian for the pleasure of her laughter. He pushed through her membership in the Party, explaining her value to the cause. He would say, "Ah, Clara Clarissima, we believers must stick together."

At Party meetings he usually sat with Juan Cristian and Clara, the two men with their heads together, lost in conversation. Vidali always greeted Juan Cristian with a handshake and an embrace.

Vidali was a frequent guest in their home for parties, or for Clara's more intimate dinners of buttered spaghetti. The three expatriate friends stayed up late into the night, smoking, planning, discussing.

Vittorio Vidali moved about Mexico like a ghost. He was here, then he was there. He was in some pueblo in the south, then he was out of the country, then he showed up at *El Machete,* the Party offices, or Clara's soirees. Sometimes he came bearing gifts, other times he seemed a little worn, as if he had been not on any sort of vacation but on some other type of excursion altogether.

Had Clara been inclined to keep in touch with the world beyond Juan Cristian, she would've seen what hid in plain sight: that Vidali—for all his seeming goodwill and thoughtfulness—was in love with her. Even more, she would've recognized that foxy look she'd noticed the first time they met, a look that said he was waiting.

———————————

Diego Rivera wanted Clara to pose for yet another mural. "I should think that you know me by heart by now," she said. It was called *Distributing Arms*. And it was to depict the workers, with Frida Kahlo in the center, her work shirt embroidered with a red star, giving out weapons. Off in the lower right-hand corner was Clara, holding a bandolier full of bullets, gazing up into the eyes of Juan Cristian, their likenesses so taken with each other it was as if they were in another picture altogether.

Clara never truly forgave Diego for exposing their affection for all the world to see. However, it was her mistake to see only herself and Juan Cristian when she should've been looking over her shoulder—for there, with only his hat, eyes, and nose visible, stood Vittorio Vidali, close and studying something that he seemed decided to have.

Diego painted the picture as a warning to Clara, his ex-lover, model, and comrade. He explained that Vidali was dangerous, a Party assassin. "So what?" asked Clara, who was angry with Diego—all of them were because he was anti-Stalin and soon to be expelled from the Party, which led her to decide that his feelings about Vidali were tainted by his feelings about the Party.

"It wouldn't matter anyway," said Clara. "He knows how committed we are to the revolution."

And so January 1929 came, and on that cold night, Clara waited for Juan Cristian to return from a meeting with a man who claimed that a gunman had been sent from Cuba (by the same president Cruz had so angered) to murder him. Of course, Juan Cristian was suspicious, though not enough to stand him up, as Clara had suggested.

"Let's go," she said, tugging Juan Cristian's sleeve as they stood before the doors of La China café. "We don't know this man, so how can we know if what he says is true?"

Juan Cristian put his hands on Clara's slim shoulders. "Trust me," he said.

And in that moment she thought that if someone were to demand she make a choice between politics and Juan Cristian, she would choose Juan Cristian. She would, in a fit of individualism, turn her back on the collective and live her life as an artist in love.

But that wasn't her choice; her choice was to let him do what he had to do, and that, she knew, was no choice at all.

They agreed that Juan Cristian would meet Clara at the nearby telegraph office at 9:00 in the evening. She waited, on the sidewalk, pulling her sweater around her, pacing. Stopping. She went inside, then outside, then back inside. She refused to succumb to tears because crying would mean that she believed him to have stepped into a trap. It would mean surrender. She should've insisted that he cancel; this was her fault. Or at least made him wait for Vidali, who had promised to go with him.

"He said I should come alone," said Juan Cristian.

"All the more reason for me to go with you," said Vidali. "You don't know political operatives like I do," he said.

"Please listen to him, *amor de mi vida*," said Clara.

"I can make myself unseen," said Vidali.

And when Juan Cristian insisted that he was no innocent when it came to spies and subversion—wasn't he already on the bad side of the Cuban president for a failed coup?—Vidali only placed his hand on Juan

Cristian's shoulder and said, "You think danger looks like danger. That's your mistake, comrade."

Vidali turned to Clara before he left and said, under his breath, "Clarissima, I'll be there." Diego was wrong; Vidali would save him.

Stupid, stupid, said Clara to herself. Why didn't I go with him? Why did I listen to him? The only hope she had was that it wasn't an ambush or, if it was, that Vidali had met Juan Cristian at La China after all.

She kept her terror at bay until, at 9:25, Juan Cristian hurried inside.

"That man came to warn me that they want me dead," he told her and shrugged. "They're trying to scare me, that's all."

She wanted to throw herself on him and never let him go. Instead, she slid her arms around him, resting her cheek on his coat, which was scented with the winter night. They stayed in this position for several seconds. "Hey," he said softly, laying a casual kiss in her hair. "We should go," he said.

They walked the short distance to their home, down the empty street, Clara's arm through his and pulling so close that her stride synchronized with his. Her breathing relaxed; she closed her eyes for a moment, relying on his guidance. They passed the bakery with its one lone light.

She heard the shots before they registered, then tasted the gun smoke. Later, she remembered heat and a flash, and then Juan Cristian falling from her arm, pulling her down with him. She scrambled to her knees, crouched on the stones of the street, yanking and tearing at his coat, as if to bunch it up across his chest and stomach to staunch the bleeding.

"Everyone hear this well," he gasped. "The Cuban government ordered my death."

And then Clara was screaming for help.

She sat, bloodstained, in one of the hard hospital chairs, waiting as she had waited for him in the telegraph office an hour and a half earlier. He's young, she said to herself. He will come through the door. Love matters more than death. He will survive this.

Diego came, and journalists, and her friends, and Vidali ("When I arrived at the café, he was already gone" he told Clara), into whose arms she fell when the doctor emerged with the news that Juan Cristian had passed.

This time, Clara was as reluctant to leave Vidali's embrace as he was to let her go. But he had to release her because the police had come and Clara Argento was under arrest for the murder of Juan Cristian Cruz.

The police held her for hours. Her clothes, stained with Juan Cristian's blood, were unchanged. "Tell us again what happened," the police insisted. "And again," they said, until an exhausted, broken Clara finally said, "I can tell it twenty times and it will still be the same. If I could change this story, I would."

The authorities responded by contacting the press and running the nude photographs that Morris Elliot had taken of her when they were first in Mexico and still lovers. She was nothing but an immoral Communist without a shred of modesty or fine Mexican virtues, they said. Whore. Femme fatale. Libertine. It was as if she were starring in one of her old Hollywood movies again.

Next they ransacked her house, claiming it was a legal search. They cried that this was clearly a crime of passion! Much was made again of her beauty. Perhaps it was a love triangle! Clara was in shock from the death of Juan Christian, having lucid dreams that she would return from the market to him sitting at his typewriter saying, "Clara, you must listen" and "Where have you been, *mi amor*?"—only for them to transform into endless interrogations. She would wake up to their repeated questions, their terrible scenarios of the murder, her cell, her filthy clothing, her wrecked home.

Another paper ran her picture of Juan Christian lying in the grass with a caption that read "Photographic study made by Clara Argento of Juan Cristian Cruz while alive, in order to give them both an idea of what he would look like after he was dead." They called the case "The Sentimental Problem of Clara Argento."

Diego and his well-connected friends got her out after five days. The truth was that no one cared about one dead Marxist revolutionary. *Basura.* Trash. There would be no real effort to find the murderer, something the murderer was experienced enough to know.

And Clara never, ever cried until she found the photograph that she had taken of Cruz's manuel typewriter, upside down and kicked under a dresser, and then she wept.

———————————

Vittorio Vidali remained close at hand, in his here-and-gone way. Clara, no longer distracted by happiness, grew wary of Vidali; her belief in their three-way friendship had been compromised. Where was he that night? She remembered his saying to Juan Cristian that he thought "danger looks like danger" and the way he could appear and disappear. She read in the paper, and listened to the whispers at Party headquarters, about "activities" that often seemed to occur in places Vidali had recently visited. All this was complicated by rumors of the Communist Party's displeasure with Juan Cristian's popularity, and wasn't the assassination attempt on the Cuban president an example of rogue, individualistic behavior?

Clara chose to handle Juan Cristian's death by increasing her devotion to the Party, telling herself that her politics were inextricable from her love, and love was Juan Cristian. Loyalty to Communism was loyalty to Juan Cristian. And Vidali? The Party would never order the death of someone as true to its principles as Juan Cristian, and Vidali would never act against the Party. It was the vengeful Cuban president, she told herself, a man afraid of a better man.

Morris used to shake his head over her attachment to the Communists, reminding her that she was an artist, not a radical, to which she wondered if there was such a difference.

"Yes!" he said. "Me, for example."

She laughed and said, "You, for example, are living in Mexico with a woman who is not your wife, for example, while your wife stays at home with your children, one of whom lives with us. For example."

"True," he said. "But socialism, Clara?"

"I know it may not be perfect, but at least the socialists seem to actually care about others, which is more than I can say for the capitalists, who only care about themselves."

Now socialism was all she had left. And for this reason she refused to listen to rumors that the Party had hired an assassin to kill Juan Cristian, which meant she had to refuse to ask herself how Vidali knew to find her at the hospital that night.

The politics of Mexico shifted once again. The "good" president was out, and the "not as good" president was in. They were all the same to Clara, who spent her days taking pictures. Some for hire, and others of workers, rural women, bandoliers, corn, and scythes. She had more time to do so since the government had shut down *El Machete*.

Communists were so undesirable that if you weren't a citizen you were always under threat of deportation, a fate that would be particularly dire in Clara's case because, in 1930, she still carried an Italian passport. Mussolini's agents in Mexico never missed one of her anti-Fascist lectures.

Though Vidali came and went, Clara had no man in her life.

A few days into his administration, shots were fired at the new president. The police decided to revisit the file of that alleged Red assassin, the glamorous, mysterious sexual predator Clara Argento, who thought nothing of gunning down her lover on a darkened Mexican street. This time they kept her in prison for two weeks with murderers and other criminals in for life. Clara constantly tried to talk herself out of her fear, though it seldom worked.

No one could save her, not even Diego.

When they released her, they informed her that she had two days to get her things together and say good-bye before being put on a beat-up Dutch ship, where she would be treated like the rest of the cargo. In each of their ports-of-call she would be put in jail, and when they arrived in Rotterdam she would be delivered to the Italian authorities, who would pass her on to Il Duce. Bon voyage, Clara.

———————————

A man came to see her in her New Orleans cell.

"Hello, Clara Clarissima," he said.

"Hello." She knew better than to say any of his many names. She didn't question Vidali's presence.

He leaned toward her. "You know they'll be waiting for you as soon as the ship docks. Italy will be no good for the scandalous *communista* Clara Argento." He laughed softly as he gazed at this tiny woman with her worn beauty. "I can help you, you know, but I'm unwilling to share you. Those days are over."

Diego's mural came to mind: her love for Juan Cristian and his for her as Vidali edged into the picture, waiting. She could be so right about the wrong thing: There was betrayal in *Distributing Arms*, but not where she had thought it lay. In the same way, her passion for a revolutionary had become inseparable from the revolution.

So unsentimental in love, Clara saved her sentimentality for politics.

She wrote to Morris one last time in 1930, before leaving her American holding cell. *Speaking of my personal self—I cannot—as you once proposed to me—solve the problem of my life by losing myself in the problem of art—not only I cannot do that but I even feel the problem of my life hinders the problem of my art.*

In Rotterdam, she slipped away with Vidali, taking her single suitcase but leaving her Graflex behind. Those days, as he had said, were over.

THE ARTIST OF HER OWN BEAUTY
OR
OBSERVATORY TIME—THE LOVERS

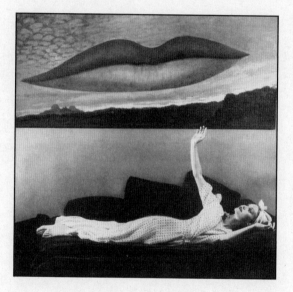

The Girl in the Snow, 1915

After Alexander Van Pelt purchased a stereoscopic camera, no one in the family was safe. His wife and his twin boy and girl, already accustomed to his usual picture taking, now prepared to see their likenesses captured and printed in lifelike 3-D. They generally enjoyed his inclination for novelty, whether in gifts or in his own inventions. For example:

The downhill skis he brought back from one of his many business trips to Switzerland, unusual objects for provincial Elysium, New York, located seventy miles north of Manhattan.

The perfect steam engine train (large enough for an adult to ride) that ran ribbons around a good portion of the one-hundred-acre Van Pelt farm.

When Joseph, Ellen's brother, decided that he wanted to build planes, his father designed a toy biplane with an engine powerful enough to get it airborne.

There were mechanical toys from Sweden, kinetic sculptures from Zurich, fabulous photographic lenses from Germany. The chemistry set from Berlin was seven year-old Ellen Van Pelt's favorite present; from the minute her father brought it home, she was in love with all those perfect little bottles. The set was liquids, powders, smells, reactions. Life and combustion and color and vapor. Alexander Van Pelt told his daughter that he had met with a famous photochemist in Berlin, a professor who had taught the American photographer Alfred Stieglitz, as if the name Stieglitz would mean anything to a little girl, but that was how her father always talked to her. It was almost as if he refused to believe that she was child.

Mr. Van Pelt, an affluent candy manufacturer, designed candy molds full of stars and the emblazoned names of his children, and chocolate elephants and chimpanzees. He created a process to make dark-and-white-chocolate zebras, butterscotch tigers with thin stripes of licorice, and peanut butter giraffes. Mr. Van Pelt, never short on ideas, was always experimenting with machinery, taste, and efficiency at Saint Chocolat.

Both of Alexander Van Pelt's children at one time or another followed their father into his darkroom (built in a converted bathroom, much to his wife's dismay) to watch him turn blank sheets of paper into images of them. He gave Ellen a simple box camera (more magic! Light making pictures? Fantastic!). And his myriad inventions around the house furthered their belief that he was their own personal illusionist.

A can opener, a toaster, lights that came on in a room when a door was opened; a series of four cables stretched from tall tree to tall tree and fitted with a harnessed pulley, allowing the children to sail high above the ground, landing on mattress-padded platforms built in the cruxes of tree branches. The children were blessed with freedom on the farm, their very physical play punctuated by all the tinkering with machines (the train, the biplane), construction (a rather detailed wooden clubhouse), and chemistry experiments (Ellen).

Mrs. Van Pelt's failed contribution to her daughter's life was to try to encourage an equestrian hobby, with Ellen refusing to "ride on any animal's back," protesting to her mother than she found it "cruel." She would add "demeaning" when her mother broached the subject again during Ellen's early teen years. In the interim, Mrs. Van Pelt purchased a palomino pony, an animal that Ellen never once attempted to ride but treated like a rather large dog, allowing it to follow her around the farm, including the solarium of the house.

This rejection was hard for Mrs. Van Pelt to understand: All the best girls rode, and wasn't Ellen enough of a wild thing to want to race around on horseback? If you asked Ellen about the girls who rode, she would shake the question off, saying that it was just more traditional female behavior masquerading as something "less girl." She would say, "You can't get more girl than riding horses." Ellen was endlessly empathetic with animals forced into the service of other animals. The whole arrangement disturbed her deeply.

On the other hand, Mr. Van Pelt adored the contrarian in his daughter. The success of the candy-making company was the reason for his triyearly trips to Europe, primarily Switzerland, once or twice taking the family along. It was unusual for someone in his position to do so much business travel, but then Alexander Van Pelt was an unusual man; his willingness to cross the Atlantic and the European Continent had as much to do with an interest in nearly everything as it did with an attraction to the more "sophisticated" cultures of Europe. It wasn't just sex, though sex was a part of it. America, he felt, was a bit provincial for a man like him. His wife knew it; in fact, that had been part of their initial connection, though once the family became one of the most prominent in Elysium, Mrs. Van Pelt distanced herself more and more from her husband's "interests."

These interests included taking nude photographs: first, when they were engaged, of Mrs. Van Pelt, then of their daughter. It began innocently enough, when Ellen was a toddler running around the farm, swimming topless like her brother and his friends. And the pictures were occasional and without fanfare.

What he mostly captured on film during her early childhood was Ellen dressed in dungarees and a shirt or sweater belonging to her brother, usually with a satin ribbon knotted and hanging lank in her bobbed blond hair—more evidence of her mother's failed attempt to feminize her.

Joseph was another story. If Alexander Van Pelt seemed much closer to his daughter, Mrs. Van Pelt spent all her energy on her son. It wasn't until he was six years old that she cut his curls, took the ribbons from his hair, and finally put him in boys' clothes. Though dressing a son like a daughter wasn't uncommon for a mother with the time and the financial means, it was unusual when the mother actually had a daughter.

Neither parent commented on the particular attention that each lavished on the two children: Mrs. Van Pelt with her son in lace; Mr. Van Pelt with his tomboy girl.

Everything changed a month before Ellen turned eight years old. Alexander Van Pelt took his first stereoscopic photograph of his daughter, naked except for her shoes, standing in the April snow on the farm. Her smile belied the discomfort she must have felt, along with her determination to tough it out, staying as still as she could. Anyone looking on would question the parenting of a man who photographed a little girl in the snow, then developed the pictures to be viewed in three dimensions, as if she was right before you.

What the uninformed onlooker wouldn't know was that this photo session occurred around the time Ellen's father decided to take her to see a progressive psychiatrist in New York City, a doctor who believed in the benefit of teaching the girl to separate love and sex. "We will work to see that one has nothing to do with the other," he said.

Someone may ask, Where was this girl's mother during these sessions? When her daughter was photographed naked in the snow?

And the answer would be: by the side of her husband, taking it all in and trying to hold it all together.

The Girl in Italy, 1926

Ellen Van Pelt, nineteen years old, had been in and out of a number of boarding schools and day schools, unable to obey the rules. "They bore me" was all she would say. Mrs. Van Pelt had turned from the frantic mother of Ellen's life before she turned eight years old (before the naked picture in the snow, in 1915) into an indulgent parent who had clearly lost her way in raising her daughter.

Town gossip chalked Mrs. Van Pelt's relationship with her daughter up to the fact that, while Ellen had been a beautiful child, she had grown into an extraordinary young woman. It was impossible not to stare at her, with her lithe figure, her shining blond hair cut short and male, parted on one side and tucked behind her perfect ears. Her sky blue eyes, with their slightly heavy lids, were watchful and amused, which always made her seem as if she had just come from some very satisfying erotic experience. More to the point, Ellen was aware of her physical gifts and made no move to hide her awareness of their effect on others.

And there were the rumors about her father and their relationship.

Mr. and Mrs. Van Pelt seemed to live separate lives. One would see

Mr. Van Pelt with his daughter more than with his wife; or sometimes with other women—employees, young and powerless, though it wouldn't be said that way in those days. It was known that he still took nude pictures of his comely daughter—in three dimensions—as if she was there for the touching. Sometimes of her friends too. He would speak seductively to Ellen's high school friends, daring them to pose without ever explicitly asking or changing his tone of voice. His persuasion was in what they perceived as his objectivity, his distance from them as people, a reassuring lack of intimacy. He didn't act like one of them; he was solidly adult, and this was the very thing that made them trust him enough to doff their clothes and intertwine with his daughter. Though, in truth, no girl even came close to Ellen's shimmer.

There are photographs of an eighteen-year-old Ellen seated on the arm of a living room chair, the sheer curtains drawn behind her allowing in a kind of celestial light, though her pose—one arm behind her back, the other stretched and draped across the back of the chair—suggests nothing of angels. Her head, with its boyish haircut, is in profile, gazing toward the floor. In another, similar picture, she has her hands behind her back, as if bound by rope.

What was she thinking as her father photographed her, her naked body open to the lens, knowing that her portrait would be in multiple dimensions?

Ellen Van Pelt told her parents that she wanted to study art in Italy. She added that she wasn't planning on college unless it was art school. She didn't tell them that she was happiest when the family traveled to Europe the summer before that first nude portrait her father took of her, an eight-year-old shivering in the snow, trying to act as if the cold didn't touch her. Before her father took her to the doctor who told her that it was possible to separate sex and love. Before, as her parents well knew, her life changed forever.

In Europe she could return to that state of grace.

But between the time of the nude photo and her request to spend the summer in Italy, painting, her life was one that had people talking. There was her appearance, dazzling even by metropolitan standards, and her wardrobe sense, which allowed her to clip her hair and dress in trousers with the effect of being more female and more desirable than if she had worn the current dropped-waist dress fashions. There were the schools that threw her out, and the smoking, and the sneaking off to New York City every chance she got and not even bothering to hide these frequent day trips.

And those boys she slept with and didn't care if they courted her or not. Nor did she care if they talked about the experience.

Some she liked more than others—one in particular, her "first love"—but she always liked the ones she slept with (otherwise she wouldn't sleep with them). They were fun. They would boat on the lake in the middle of the night, under the stars and the moon. Or drink in someone's empty summer home. There were car rides, and lying on a beach somewhere, listening to the lapping of the water. There were dances at clubs, coffee in cafés.

Sometimes she laughed off their suggestions, while other times she would cut them off, midsentence, and suggest they "go lie down somewhere."

"I feel there is an angel in me," she'd say, "whom I am constantly shocking."

———————————

It took a lot of convincing, cajoling, and playing on her father's favoritism to finally be allowed to travel with a chaperone, a Miss MacMurray, to spend the summer visiting museums and painting. Miss MacMurray was a single woman who taught at a local girls' school. She came across as prematurely mature, a spinster of a certain stripe who believed that when she was ferrying girls to Italy to gaze at art she was fulfilling her own destiny. She thought that offering up Michelangelo's *David* for the girls' viewing pleasure was transgressive and daring. She relished telling them that, in London, there existed a detachable plaster fig leaf that had been used to cover David's genitalia when the queen arrived, the anecdote making clear that Miss MacMurray would have no need for such modesty.

And parents trusted her. And she was, at heart, a trusting person, a nice woman who genuinely cared about art and about the girls.

It was on the ship, as it crossed the Atlantic to dock in Genoa, that Ellen decided to go by her father's nickname for her: Lenny. The androgyny of the name suited her.

Then, having arrived in Florence, along with the other seven girls in the group, she decided, standing in the Uffizi Gallery, that everything great to be painted had already been painted. She would have to find another art form.

Lenny snuck out of the museum into the piazza to smoke. As she stood watching the activity of the public space—vendors hawking their souvenirs, people drinking coffee as they sat at tiny tables, crowds spilling out onto the adjacent streets—she noticed a man was noticing her.

He was attractive, maybe thirty years old.

She threw her cigarette to the pavement, crushing it as she walked over to the man, who was sitting on a step in the shade, a small crowd of statues behind him, under one of the arches of the Loggia dei Lanzi, a camera in his hands. He smiled.

"*Che tipo di fotocamera e . . . e . . .*" Lenny allowed her poor Italian to lapse into hand gestures as she pointed toward the man's camera.

"Leica."

"Leica? In *inglese*?"

"It's Leica in English too."

As she stood there, she realized that she had misjudged the man's age; he was probably closer to forty. "You don't have an Italian accent, by the way."

"That's because I'm from Scotland. Though, to be fair, I don't have a Scots accents when I speak Italian because my mother's from Florence. You know, in case you're writing a personal history."

"May I see it?" Lenny extended her hand to take the Leica. It was the smallest camera she had ever seen, and surprisingly light. "What is this?" There was a metal piece that attached to the top of the body like a submarine's periscope.

He took the camera from her, removing the metal piece. "It's a removable range finder. And look." Here he collapsed the lens. Then he handed the camera back to her.

"My father would love this," she said. Then, "Where did you get it?"

"In Germany. They're very new and not inexpensive."

Lenny held the camera up to her eye, panning the piazza, taking in the arches that shaded the café tables, the tourists, the *fiorentini*, the vendors of souvenirs and sweets, and when the facade of the Uffizi was in the viewfinder, she saw her fellow students and Miss MacMurray newly emerged from the museum.

"Oh, *merde*," she said, quickly returning the camera to its owner as she hurried back to the group.

"Wait!" called the man, now standing.

Lenny kept going.

"American girl!" he called again. Now he was following her.

Lenny stopped, waving at Miss MacMurray as the man caught up. She half turned around without taking her eyes off the chaperoned group, which was advancing toward her. "Boboli Gardens. Tomorrow at eleven. I'll find you—" This last she said as she rushed to join the others.

Lenny didn't think anyone would blame her for allowing herself to be romanced by the man from the Piazza della Signoria. Though she understood that no one she knew would consider a sexual encounter in an allée in the Boboli Gardens (while the other girls were touring the sculptures) to be any sort of courtship. Flushed and still slightly out of breath, she caught the scent of his perspiration on the shoulder of her blouse.

"I thought adventurous American girls were a myth," said Alessandro, a little out of breath himself.

"I've had a tendency to bore easily since I was seven years old."

"What happened when you were seven?"

She said nothing as she studied his face. "How old are you?"

"How about, 'How old are you, Alessandro Ross?'" he said, pretending to be her and introducing himself at the same time. "Thanks for asking," he replied as himself, gesturing toward her to offer her name.

She sighed. "Lenny."

"Lenny," he said. He smiled. "Lenny, I'm forty-two years old."

"We're going to Fiesole tomorrow."

"I'm not sure I can make it tomorrow."

"Bring the Leica."

And then she was gone.

———————————

Fiesole is a few miles north of Florence. It has a piazza (Mino), a cathedral (di San Romolo), an archaeological area (*zona archeologica*) with an Etruscan temple, medieval artifacts, and an amphitheater and Roman baths. There is a convent (di San Francesco) and, in nearby Monte Ceceri, a hilltop where a stone commemorates Leonardo da Vinci's 1505 experiments with flight. It was in Monte Ceceri that Lenny and Alessandro arranged to meet, and Lenny posed naked for Alessandro, before the view and the blue sky and the whitest clouds. She stood with her back against the stone honoring da Vinci's flying machine, her face in profile, gazing downward, her hands behind her as if bound by rope.

When Alessandro was on his knees before Lenny—her very coolness and startlingly beauty causing him to tremble at her feet—he said, "You are so different. I can't believe my luck in meeting you."

Lenny said, "Jesus. Luck."

As Alessandro returned to Florence on the train that night, to his wife and child, he remembered thinking that having photographs of her, naked and shining and looking like something purely chimerical, was perhaps a bad idea. But then, when he thought about destroying the film, he couldn't bring himself to do it, if for no other reason than to prove to himself that she really had happened.

———————————

"You think you won't get sent home, but I assure you, Miss Van Pelt, you think incorrectly."

Miss MacMurray believed that when Lenny had stepped outside during the trip to Santa Croce she had snuck off for something more than a smoke. Not that she could prove it; call it intuition. And when she discovered Lenny sitting, alone, at a small café with an empty cup of espresso and the remnants of cigarettes, she knew her suspicions to be true.

"I'm so sorry that I can't provide anything to your liking," said Miss MacMurray.

In truth, the church was Lenny's favorite place of all their stops in Florence: She loved the high contrast of the black-and-white facade, which reminded her of a photograph, and the incongruous Star of David. She loved the simplicity of the interior, the Giotto frescoes, the sixteen chapels, and Michelangelo's tomb with its three statues, which were meant to represent painting, architecture, and sculpture but which looked to her like a weird little dinner party.

"You think," said Miss MacMurray, "you're so much smarter than everyone else."

Lenny took a last sip of her coffee. "It's funny that for someone so interested in what I think you get it so wrong." She dropped some coins in a dish as she picked up her bag.

"Where do you think you're going?" asked Miss MacMurray.

"With you. Right? Isn't that what you want?"

"Don't patronize me," said Miss MacMurray.

"I wasn't."

"You must think I was born yesterday."

Lenny sighed. "Can we stop talking about what I think?"

"I am wiring your parents today to tell them they can expect you home on the first ship to New York."

Lenny began walking away.

"Stop!"

"Look," Lenny said, "do you want me on the first ship to New York or not? Because if you do, then I have to pack. And if not, then I need to get back with the other girls."

Miss MacMurray was startled to see the seven girls watching them, which made her self-conscious and angry. Lenny's patiently waiting to be told what to do made her even angrier. "Fine!" she said. "Now I have your attention!" Then, instead of elaborating on what she wanted to say to Lenny, whose attention she now possessed, Miss MacMurray stormed off in what she hoped was an attitude of power: She was leaving Lenny, not the other way around. Only to realize that, because she was their chaperone, it really wasn't in her best interests to leave any student to her own devices. In fact, wasn't that the very essence of the problem with Lenny Van Pelt in the first place?

Why was that girl so maddening? Miss MacMurray thought it was because she turned heads with her slender figure, her boyish haircut, parted on the side, so neatly tucked behind her perfect ears. Or maybe it was the blue eyes, with their slightly heavy lids, which showed intelligence and amusement and seemed to be a little secretive, and more than a little seductive.

Some would say that she resented Lenny for her moneyed family, her exquisite aspect, her youth, her lack of concern, but it wouldn't be true. What Miss MacMurray envied, like any teacher on a teacher's salary who has watched her own extravagant dreams diminish with each passing year (and those students who never seem to age), was Lenny's freedom. The freedom that beauty (yes) affords but, more than that, that money can buy. This was the reason Lenny didn't get upset when Miss MacMurray threatened to send her home.

Miss MacMurray was aware of how Alexander Van Pelt indulged his daughter, and somehow she knew that sending her home would actually brighten his world instead of throwing it into a tailspin over what to do about Lenny.

For all these reasons, Lenny was not on the next ship home to New York.

And so, for the remainder of the trip, Lenny continued slipping away from the arranged tours of museums, gardens, and monuments to meet Alessandro. Then sometimes disappearing quickly after her sexual encounters to stand before a painting, a fresco, a statue, a sculpture, a door, an altar to take in alone what she was supposed to be learning about in the moving classroom led by Miss MacMurray. Not only had Lenny decided on her first day at the Uffizi Gallery to eschew painting but she had realized that she enjoyed looking at the various artworks only if she could do so in silence and solitude. Miss MacMurray's voice, no matter how informed the lesson, grated and distracted.

In this way, Lenny had visited the Uffizi (meeting Alessandro in the Piazza della Signoria); the Boboli Gardens (Alessandro in a copse near the allée); Santa Croce (Alessandro in an alley); the Ponte Vecchio (where a shopkeeper argued with a customer and Alessandro and Lenny slipped into the back room); the Duomo (behind a rather large pile of seemingly forgotten building materials on the upper platform, near the roof, as tourists trudged by, unaware of the lovers); the Gallerie dell'Accademia (in a janitor's closet); and the Battistero, with Ghiberti's gorgeous *Gates of Paradise*, so named by Michelangelo (very late at night, against a wall, where they were sure they were seen but didn't care).

When it came time to leave Florence, Alessandro casually brought up the possibility of returning with Lenny, who caressed his face—the only tender gesture she had ever displayed toward him, which made their parting even more fraught. He watched her board the train, saw her sit down next to a boy who looked about her own age. And when she smiled at the boy without even a glance out the window at him, he saw himself as just one more thing she did on her summer vacation; he was a memory that would last only as long as the Atlantic crossing. This realization made him understand that he would be slow to forget her no matter how hard he tried, and he would try.

The Girl in New York, 1927

Lenny Van Pelt spent the rest of the summer on her parents' farm; her pet pony had changed its alliance and now favored her twin brother. Boredom read in her face, her figure, and her short conversations with her mother and father. Mrs. Van Pelt, frustrated from trying to spend a day with her daughter, shopping and having lunch in the city, blurted out, "What is it you want, Ellen Van Pelt?"

At first Lenny thought that taking classes at the Art Students League and working on theater design would somehow quell the restlessness and dissatisfaction within her. New York wasn't Paris, but it wasn't Elysium either, and that was something to be grateful for.

The times when she felt both agitated and at rest were times spent with her father. When she posed for him, or when she stood next to him in the red-hued, intimate space of the little darkroom, or maybe when they discussed something one of them had read, or when he was explaining his latest health interest, such as having the gardener put in an organic garden ("no chemicals," he said, "getting into the plants and the soil and us").

They would repair the miniature train together, with Alexander replacing parts and tightening bolts as Lenny handed him the tools. She had been trained to be by his side, and, in exchange, he shared all his knowledge, enthusiasms, and worldview with her. They, as her mother often said—a statement that would be bemused or wistful or a little sad, depending on to whom she was speaking—were a world of two.

If asked, Lenny would say the only person who understood her was her father. She trusted him. How else to explain her willingness to remove her clothing and place her hands behind her beautiful back while he made her image on film in three dimensions?

Still, she longed to get back to Europe. In Europe, she believed she could relax. She could calm that restlessness that propelled her from place to place, person to person. She needed to put miles between her and her home, because home for her wasn't like home for other people; home for her was the reason for her flight and her rebellion. As long as she remained in New York, she believed, she would never be free.

It was an exceptional spring day in the city. Lenny had been dutifully painting the stage flat of a play set in Heaven (which, in this case, resembled a room in Versailles) when her thoughts were so far from where she sat painting that each stroke slowed, slowed, slowed until she stopped. There she stood, no longer seeing the wall in front of her, her hand poised over the tray of paint.

Her memories and dreams were crowding in, including the one thing that she didn't want to think about; that one encounter, undiminished by all the years, that she always had to keep at bay.

She dropped the brush into the tray. As she fished for her cigarettes in the pocket of her paint-spattered overalls, she was already rushing out the door of the art school. Someone called her name, but all she could respond to was that one thought, that one moment that had shaped her life, and from which she was so often running.

Outside, the warm day had her unzipping her overalls, letting them drop to her waist, revealing the fitted, sleeveless white cotton undershirt that left little to the imagination. She smoothed her hair, tucking it behind her ears, exposing her long, elegant neck to the sun.

It was when she briefly closed her eyes (inhaling the passing scent of someone's expensive perfume, so expensive it was barely in the breeze at all) that she was bumped in a way that caused her to lose her footing and sent her into the gutter.

Pitching into the street wasn't such a momentous occurrence in sleepy Elysium, but in New York, finding yourself flailing into traffic could be fatal. And with Lenny's usual luck, someone threw an arm across her upper chest, hauling her back to the safety of the sidewalk as if she were a mythical creature drawn from the deep.

"God, I'm sorry," said Lenny, who was face-to-face with a man dressed with the precision of someone who had a valet; that is, his appearance was too elegant and too extravagant to look like the result of one person's efforts. He was tall, and had a face that resembled a drinker's, with a slightly enlarged nose and the faintest broken capillaries. Or maybe what she was seeing was the gourmand in him, the results of a life of fine dining and drinking for the past (she guessed) sixty years, if his midsection were any indication.

"Don't be. No reason, actually."

As she tried to collect herself, she was suddenly aware of her dirty, multicolored overalls hanging from her hips, revealing her skinny white undershirt. Without a word, she yanked the overalls up over her body.

"I wish you wouldn't," said the distinguished gentleman.

Pedestrians moved around the stationary couple as if they were water rushing around jutting river stones.

Lenny hesitated.

"I love the hair—very gamine—and your neck, well, I'm sure you're very aware of its length and perfection. Small bustline—a nice echo with your hair—and your height is rather ideal. Five eight?"

She nodded.

"Can't quite make out the legs, but with a face and figure like yours, one can work with the legs. Don't you think?"

The man's familiar appraisal of her physical self was nearly devoid of sexual interest, an aspect that threw her off a little.

"I'm not wrong in assuming that you're a model, am I? That is to say when you aren't—what?—painting houses?"

"Scenery."

"The blond looks natural. I can already see you in print."

"Do you see me in print for money?"

He laughed. "Not for love, though I'm always open to suggestion."

"I'll just bet," she said.

"Is it a wager if you know you'll win?" The man checked his pocket watch—a small, jeweled miracle as expensive as the rest of his attire—before handing her a business card that said "Kristof Nash." Even ordinary people who never even read any of Nash's several high-end magazines knew his name.

As Lenny read it, she smiled. "I guess it's lucky that I still smoke, Mr. Nash."

"You will use it, won't you?"

Amazing to think that her life could completely change course in the space of a single encounter; then again, the impact of chance encounters was something that she had known about for a very long time.

Her first modeling assignment involved a silk dress as light and airy as a butterfly's wing, in a shade of pink so pale it was scarcely a color at all. The back of the dress dipped low enough that a fabulous brooch of winter white diamonds was strategically placed, obscuring the cleavage at the base of her spine.

Eder, the highest-paid fashion photographer in New York, believed himself to be akin to the common man. He was a champion of all things modern, including photography over painting (Lenny said, "A man after my own art") and declared that everything must be aesthetically pleasing and useful. The machinery of the camera was far more twentieth-century than a pigment-loaded sable brush.

Lenny arrived at the thirty-room penthouse belonging to Kristof Nash, currently in Capri with a young brunette, to find a small army of assistants waiting to make up her face, fasten her into the tissue of a dress, and try to do something with her short, side-parted hair until the photographer barked "Leave it alone," calling it "modern and sexually undecided." There were people in charge of the lights, the props, and the drapes of the floor-to-ceiling windows. Distant sounds could be heard from behind the doors of the formal dining room, where the table remained set for whenever "the emperor" (as they called Eder behind his back, this man who aligned himself with "the people") demanded his meal.

The rooms of the penthouse resembled imagined historical wealth. That is, there was nothing surprising in the Renaissance *cassoni*, the Louis XVI furniture, the indoor pool with Grecian fish plated in gold, whose mouths served as fountains. There were the Victorian velvets in shades of ruby, sapphire, saffron, and emerald in one study contrasting with the Versailles silks in the parlor. A conservatory's garden competed with the exterior garden, a wild English affair on the terraces arranged as if it had been lifted directly from Dorset. And the windows, miles of windows with nothing beyond them but the glittering city below and the blue sky above, were the truest luxury—all that open air.

Eder had Lenny lean against a wall next to a modernist sculpture that echoed the slim curve of her body. Lenny, a slightly bored beauty at the wrong party.

He asked for jeweled bracelets and placed them himself snaking up her arm. The lights hit the gems and exploded.

He shook his head and had an assistant slide them off.

He tried flowers, pearls, and fur. All of it he declared wrong. "I'm hungry," Eder said as he strode from the room.

The chef had prepared a meal as elaborate and fabulous as the penthouse, but everyone had only had a few bites before Eder leapt from his chair, nearly knocking it over, to say, "Now!" leaving the room with the same determined stride with which he had entered it only ten minutes before.

Every finger of Lenny's hands wore a diamond ring. "Lean on the wall, but face me—no, turn more toward me—no, too much—yes, there—and"—here he took his own hands, crisscrossed them over his chest, his fingers resting on his shoulders—"you see? Like so."

The modernist statue was less prominent in the frame as Lenny filled more of it; and the diamonds on her fingers caught and threw light, the explosions smaller than before and more precise.

It was perfect.

It wasn't long before other photographers at *BelleFille* magazine wanted Lenny, even though she was most often photographed by Eder. She liked Eder. Though twenty years separated their ages, neither one felt attached to the past, leveling the field of their friendship. Eder occasionally instructed her, or allowed her into the darkroom along with his assistant. Once or twice, when he was feeling less imperial, he allowed her to sit in on a shoot and take a picture or two.

"This is what makes the camera a perfect machine," he said, "anyone can operate it."

"Yes, but not everyone can take a good picture," she said.

"No," he said, " not everyone can make an Eder, it's true, but that's because they see the process all wrong. The picture isn't a result of who-ever releases the shutter—it's in the vision. That's why I can have you take all the pictures today, if I want, because I decide. And because I decide, they will still be my pictures."

Sometimes he tried to talk to her about the "equality" of photography, the "democracy" of the camera, but she had worked with him enough to know that what he truly loved, what he always depicted, was glamour. All his bluff and workman's clothing could never hide his love of the rich.

He liked to think that Kristof Nash paid him more than anyone else to shoot models—all those expensively attired, louche girls, alone at parties, or just arriving back at their posh homes, dropping an emerald cuff into an ashtray by the front door with as much concern as they dropped their keys—because of Eder's modern, workingman ethos, when the opposite was true. Kristof Nash valued Eder because no one lavished as much affection on all the trappings of wealth as he, nearly to the point of pornography. Kristof Nash knew, as Lenny came to know, that for a high-fashion magazine that trades in all the things money can buy, there was no better man than Eder.

———————————

On weekends home, she still posed for her father.

———————————

The other photographers, nearly all foreign-born, lower-royalty immigrants, made genetically fortunate American girls look worldly and sophisticated and of indeterminate origins. And no one was easier to transform than Lenny. It was as if her dream of living in other places showed in her face, dominated her posture.

With each photographer, she presented herself to the camera, unafraid.

Count Almeida, with his melodic Hungarian accent and his refinement, took a different approach. Whereas all the other photographers predictably portrayed Lenny as the Modern Girl, with her short hair, vogue figure, and romantic independence, Count Almeida saw some-thing else. Even Eder, with whom Lenny shared a progressive sensibility, gave his New Girls a poetic twist, as they emerged from chauffeur-driven cars, shedding mink wraps and floating toward their palatial dressing rooms; all that surrounding luxury, of which they took no more notice than they would of a bathroom sink, was essentially romantic and much less modern than Eder realized.

The count was not a handsome man by conventional standards, but he had a quiet charm and lovely manners; one felt that he had lived the sort of eventful life that gave him grace. There was a formality about him that was comfortable, as if one always knew where one stood, though that mannered quality never dampened the bit of sparkle that flashed when he was amused, which was often. He was seventy years old. His work was more fundamentally modern than that of the other photographers, including Eder.

Lenny, wearing a wide-legged, soft cotton jumpsuit, with straps that crossed over her bare back, was posing for him.

"Miss Van Pelt," said Count Almeida, "while your bosom is exceptionally fine, we need for you to keep it within the garment," for one breast kept finding its way out the side of the loose bib.

She smiled and made a show of tucking it back in.

"Ah, let's hope it doesn't make a second run for freedom," said the count.

But when Lenny bent her back, she was again exposed. She shifted her pose. "Not that I care," she added, referring to her partial nudity.

"It isn't only that," said the count. "Perhaps—" and he made a gesture to direct her into another position.

And so the afternoon went on, with Lenny and the count subtly at cross-purposes about how Lenny should model. It didn't matter if it was the shirtless jumpsuit or a small bathing garment of thin material and no structure that was all slack and straps, or a short sundress with no back and not much front.

The count sighed. "I think that if they would dress a grown woman like a grown woman and not like a little girl on holiday we would have better luck."

"It doesn't bother me," said Lenny.

———————

The count wasn't satisfied with the pictures. "We'll try again," he said. And at the end of the next day something still troubled him, though he didn't say what it was.

On the third morning, at a much earlier hour than Lenny was used to, her phone rang.

It was the count inviting her for coffee and sweet rolls, in about an hour?

When she arrived at his studio, he greeted her at the door. He kissed her hello, then guided her to the table set with coffee and crème-filled pastries. "Miss Van Pelt," he began. Lenny didn't ask him to call her Lenny, as everyone else did, because she liked the way he said "Miss Van Pelt." She also liked the trace affection in it; he had the strangest way of making her feel genuinely liked even though they hadn't spent but a pair of days together, albeit twelve-hour days. "We must retake yesterday's pictures." He reached for a small folder next to his chair.

"It's the breast, isn't it?"

The count smiled. "They are lovely."

He came to where she sat, standing behind her and to the side. "If you don't mind," he said as he leaned over to show her the pictures from their session the day before.

Being invited to look at herself was an infrequent occurrence. It was different from opening the magazine and seeing herself wearing dresses she couldn't afford, in locations she also couldn't afford. Even with her father's dimensional nudes, she mainly glanced at them as they sat on a table instead of peering through the stereoscopic viewer. And what she saw this day, on this table set with silver and china, coffee and sweets, was a gorgeous girl who knew she was gorgeous. Funny how seldom she revealed just how aware she was of her physical affect.

"It's modern," she said.

"It's modern, yes, this bold girl who dares one to stare at her. But there is something else." He was patient, polite, and Lenny sensed what he was seeing—what he wanted her to see—what made him slightly uncomfortable.

She picked up the photographs and examined them carefully. She wanted to say, "I look like me," and toss them back onto the table. When she had studied them without speaking for several minutes, Count Almeida sat in a chair next to her, pulled it away from the table and faced her. He hesitated, then said, "I'm not your lover."

This made Lenny laugh. "Good that we've settled that." When he said nothing, she again looked at the pictures, more as a way to stall before asking the count what he meant by "I'm not your lover."

It was then that she saw it: She wasn't naked, but it was in her eyes, her expression, her posture; it was all over the picture. She was her father's model, and it was there to see, only no one, even Lenny, had ever seen it, until now.

This girl in the picture was brave, brazen. All the other photographers picked up on her bravado as modern, so au courant, so young and fresh and bold. She was beautiful and a little tough and a touch androgynous, and they liked that. And maybe, just maybe, they liked the way she looked at them through the lens.

Lenny knew that the count knew that she knew. He gently took the pictures from her hands, then said, "We'll begin again, yes?"

There were always men in Lenny's life, the number increasing tenfold once she began modeling and attending all those New York parties where she understood that often she and her model friend, Claire, were part of the decor. The best parties were the ones held at Kristof Nash's penthouse, since he was, as Frank Crowninshield once called him "the man who knows more celebrities than anyone else in New York." The irony was Nash's lack of ease when in attendance at his own soirees.

The men in Lenny's life were publishers, lawyers, trust funders, aviators, physicians, painters, college boys, writers, department store magnates, titans of industry, and a man who made ice cream.

But there was no one she'd rather spend time with than the seventy-year-old, well-mannered Count Almeida.

After that morning when he showed her the photographs, after they retook the shots, he asked if he could take some pictures for himself. The result was Lenny as a girl. Not the fast, fearless girl indulging almost every impulse. There was a softness, a sweetness to these pictures, as if she was again Ellen, with her heart on her sleeve. The boyishness was still there, but infused with an openness that was rarely present in her pictures or her life.

It was like seeing herself for the first time—or like someone finding some essential part of her that she thought never showed.

It was like being known.

This was the start of their New York friendship. He photographed her not for her neoteric image but for her timelessness; not for the boy but for the girl in her. It was the most avant-garde act of all.

———————————

The count and Lenny sat together in her apartment, small and spare but wholly hers in decor. A bouquet of tulips, bent over and beautiful in creamy shades of white, pink, yellow, and the palest orange imaginable, sat on the table in front of them. For two years Count Almeida and Lenny had been friends and photographer and model. Though she was never his muse; he didn't take any more private pictures of her after that first time.

"I will miss you terribly," she said as she took his hand in hers, there, side by side on the secondhand sofa.

In this moment, she wondered how she would get by without his friendship. Many afternoons and evenings he would visit, and she would get food from a little Italian place down the street, and they would talk about art and Europe and music and photography. On warm summer mornings, when neither had slept well due to the heat, they would walk for miles, impressive for a man of his age.

"I know," he said.

"I love you," she said.

"I know."

It occurred to her that this was the only pure affection she had ever experienced, this old man who knew her more intimately than anyone had ever known her. And the love was innocent, chaste. Love had often felt constricting to her; there was too much want on one side or the other, too much bartering. There was pleasure as well, but everything felt glancing, as if it touched the surface of her skin, electrifying her without ever leaving a mark.

"Will you miss me too?" she asked.

He smiled. "Paris is a marvelous place. I remember my second visit there, when I was about your age, and I remember that it was where I most felt like myself."

"Why not come with me?" she said. "We could travel together and maybe find a place together. How grand would that be?"

"I must work."

"You can work there. I'll work with you."

"No. I think this is my New York time of life. But you'll write to me, and we can compare our respective Parises."

"I hate this," she said, starting to cry.

"Some people say the only thing worse than not getting what one wants is getting what one wants. How long have we talked about Europe?"

"Will you see me off at the ship tomorrow?"

"Can't. I have a job tomorrow: 'Every Woman Can Be the Artist of Her Own Beauty.' Cosmetics advert."

She wanted to plead—Postpone it, get out of it, oh, please, please don't let me go—but she knew that his having an assignment on the day she was to sail to France was no accident.

He took her hands in his, turning them over, at first saying nothing, then reciting:

> *(i do not know what it is about you that closes*
> *and opens;only something in me understands*
> *the voice of your eyes is deeper than all roses)*
> *nobody,not even the rain,has such small hands*

At the pier were four of Lenny's lovers, who had all argued over who was to escort her onto the ocean liner. As they went back and forth, Lenny's attention was taken by a biplane flying low overhead. She followed the path of the plane, leaving behind her lovers, so immersed in attaining the prize of saying farewell to Lenny that none of them noticed her quietly walking up the gangplank.

As the ship pulled away, away from the well-wishers on the pier, away from her lovers, who now all felt cheated and would agree to get a drink together in commiseration, Lenny wandered to the uppermost deck, gazing out at the open sea, still watching the little biplane as it appeared to follow the ship.

Just as the liner was a distance from the dock but still not too much into the open sea, the plane seemed to catch sight of her, standing alone on the deck, and it dipped, then dropped a shower of red roses at her feet. *The voice of your eyes is deeper than all roses.*

She plucked a rose from among those that landed on the deck and said good-bye.

The Girl in Paris, 1929

"Ideally you would apprentice with a famous photographer whose name begins with *St*," said Eder with a smile. "You know, Steichen, Stieglitz, Steiner, Strand. But failing that, here's someone interesting and, I believe, right up your alley, as they say."

The studio of the Paris-famous Surrealist photographer Tin Type was located on the rue Campagne-Première, next to the Hôtel Istria, where she had taken a room. The room was barely bigger than a closet, though the child-size bathroom still had a bidet and a toilet and a shower. The view was nothing much, just a mirror-image hotel (multistoried, narrow mansard roof) across the street, but Lenny was happier than she had been in years. She felt it in every relaxed breath.

She had barely settled in when she slicked her hair and lined her eyes with kohl and bruised blue shadow, increasing their usual heavy-lidded drama. Her lips were painted deep red. Her makeup was almost exaggeratedly feminine, because she wore a fitted man's cotton shirt and men's cut trousers, enjoying the play of the eyeliner and lipstick with her masculine attire. Then she went next door.

Armed with her letter of introduction from Eder, Lenny stood at Tin Type's studio door, reading the sign, *I do not photograph nature. I photograph my visions,* before ringing the bell.

She waited. She listened. Then rang again. This time she thought she heard someone inside.

If someone was there, he certainly didn't care to answer the door. As reluctant as she was to walk away, that is what she did, wandering until she came to the tall gates of the Luxembourg Garden. The day wasn't terribly warm, but it was sunny, and mild enough to wear a sweater. Lenny strolled the broad gravel paths, lined by pristine lawns of new grass. Later she left the paths to thread through the area of widely spaced trees, the grass replaced by dirt; Lenny had never seen anything like this strange grove in any American park.

As the sun heated up the day, Lenny noticed a grouping of little tables and slated chairs, with a refreshment stand nearby. As she went to buy a drink and consider her next step, she noticed two men, playing chess. One of the players, a rather compact man with thick dark hair, said something in French to his opponent, as he shook his hand, then leaned to kiss his cheek. The other man kissed him in kind, as they parted, the dark-haired man pausing to stretch.

In the midst of reaching his arms straight above his head, he caught Lenny watching him. He had the most intense, intelligent eyes as he watched her get up and walk toward him. She told him her name, as she handed him Eder's letter.

"I don't take students," said Tin Type. "And I'm leaving on holiday."

Lenny smiled. "I'm already packed."

———————————

The first picture was of Lenny naked, except for a velvet ribbon choker. She stood behind a printing press, the palms of her hands and the undersides of her forearms smudged with ink.

In another, she was half-naked, a corset folded down on her hips, her head cropped out of the frame.

In another, she was again naked, with shadows slashing the light that striped her as it came through the window blinds.

He painted a picture of her lips the length of the sky, above an empty landscape, the trees dwarfed below. He called it *Observatory Time—The Lovers*.

For three years, she was his muse, his mistress, his assistant, his apprentice.

He taught her how to carefully photograph silver objects, "because you think a silver object is very bright when it actually isn't, it's just reflecting what's in the room."

She assisted him when he photographed a black-and-white ball where all the guests had words projected on them as they spun around the dance floor.

Together they discovered solarization. He made a profile picture of Lenny so beautiful and breathtaking that she looked like the shocking angel she always believed herself to be. This Surrealist darling, this eighteen-karat muse. Everyone marveled at the small, dark celebrity photographer with a modernist eye, living with his shining girl who stood many inches taller than he, and their almost theatrical manner of dress, including strolling down the boulevard tethered by a thin gold chain, which had the effect of binding him to her rather than her to him.

Tin Type photographed Lenny kissing another woman, then cropped it so that all that remained in the frame was the kiss. He made sketches of the cropped kiss, then scribbled over the pictures, *Ellen, Ellen, Ellen*.

In another picture she was powdered white, naked from the waist up and posed as the Louvre's *Venus de Milo*. While he was arranging the shot, he confessed that as a teen, he tried, once or twice, to sleep with American girls so young they were barely out of childhood. "But that was back home," he said as he tied her hands behind her back to mimic the absence of the goddess's arms, "when I was someone else."

Through Lenny Van Pelt, Tin Type learned what it meant to be "hopelessly in love." Equal emphasis on the lack of hope and the abundance of love.

Paris was full of Surrealist girls, eccentric and inspiring and creative. For example, one showed up at tea dressed in a cardinal's red robe saying, "I wanted to dress in clothing never meant for a woman, worn by a man who's never meant to have a woman." Another peed in someone's hat on a café terrace in fit of pique. There were balls where everyone was naked from the chest to the knees, clad in costumes of winged sandals, thigh-high leather boots, and feathered headdresses, spikes and chains of silver. Someone fled Paris with someone else's lover, clad in a fur coat with nothing underneath. Someone else made a cup and saucer of fur. Someone wore a dress of "mother-of-pearl buttons engraved with tiny human footprints."

For the first time, Tin knew pitch-black jealousy, unable to live with Lenny's sexual impulses. She tried to explain that love and sex were separate countries in her personal atlas. He countered with possessiveness, fury, threats of violence to her, to himself. He made an assemblage of a photograph of Lenny's seductive, heavy-lidded eye affixed to a metronome accompanied by a hammer and called it *Object of Destruction*. A self-portrait had him seated with a noose around his neck, a gun to his head, and a bottle of poison on the table before him.

And still their love stumbled on.

"What is it?" Tin said as he gripped the groceries that he'd been carrying. "What's happened?"

Lenny was on the floor, holding a telegram now tearstained. "My father will be here on Thursday," she said. "On his way to Zurich. He'll want me to join him."

"Well," said Tin, relaxing his hold on the packages, then setting them down, "you will tell him no. You don't have to do anything you don't want to do." When she didn't respond, he said, "I'll talk to him if you like."

"There's no need."

"I don't mind."

"What I'm saying is that I mean to go."

He was mystified by this girl, almost fifteen years his junior. He was as much in love with her face as he was with her intelligence, her laugh, her tireless desire to learn everything about photography, and her happiness in the darkroom ("I grew up spending time in a photographer's darkroom," she said).

"I got all your favorites at the shops," he said, easing away from something he couldn't quite sort out. "I'll collage you a lunch," he said.

Alexander Van Pelt was quite tall and angular, and the gray in his hair, his English-made suit, and rounded spectacles made for an imposing man. Someone who looked like a success and knew it.

"So this is what a real Parisian artist's studio looks like," Mr. Van Pelt said, shaking Tin's hand, smiling in the direction of Lenny. "Hello, darling."

"Daddy," she said, smiling.

"Here," said Tin, taking Alexander's suitcase, raincoat, briefcase, and camera bag. "Please sit. I'll get us something to drink."

Tin had turned his back for a moment to grab the glasses and Pernod, and when he again faced their company, he witnessed Lenny, in her uncharacteristically traditional dress with the little white flowers on a dark blue background, curled up on her father's lap, the dark color of his suit matching the dark color of her dress. She leaned her head against his chest, her eyes closed. He looked so large, and Lenny, a child on his lap. A kind of Surrealist pietà.

Tin set down the glasses and liquor, picked up his camera, and, as if by agreement, the only movement was Alexander looking into the lens as he folded his hands on Lenny's hip.

The last thing that Tin thought before he snapped the photo was that she did not look unhappy.

————————

In Tin's photograph *Larmes,* a woman cries; her face is so closely cropped that all that really remain are her eyes, gazing upward ecstatically; the inky eyelashes are tipped with perfect, tiny orbs of mascara, while the tears that fall down her face are half circles of glass. The meaning of the tears, the emotion in the picture, is ambiguous.

————————

Alexander Van Pelt, amateur photographer, loved Tin's pictures, and Tin loved that Mr. Van Pelt loved them in the way he wished them to be loved, which is really every artist's dream when he thinks about an audience. They had a great deal in common, not the least of which was Lenny.

————————

The sole memento of that Swiss trip was a photograph taken from above: Lenny pressing her body, knees bent, into one end of the hotel bathtub. When Tin saw it, he stopped himself from asking if this bathtub was located in Lenny's room or her father's room, or if there was any difference between the two.

————————

It wasn't any one thing that brought the end; no one fell in love with anyone else. They could not even agree on what "being in love" looked like, and this caused Tin's worst self to emerge, colliding with Lenny's boredom. Nothing was duller than jealousy.

It was like a dream, Lenny would say of their years together, an extended game of pretend. The solarized pictures, the photographs of mannequins socializing at parties, reclining on divans, climbing fancy staircases. There were eyelids painted like eyes, and models with their features outlined in black paint. Heads appeared captured under bell jars casually placed on tables; white women wore African ivory bangles up to their elbows; a woman was painted like a violin with sound holes at her back, the picture title reflecting the idea of a woman as a hobby.

From Tin, Lenny learned to take pictures, use lights, touch up, develop; her vision, so in tune with the *modernisme* of the age, lined up perfectly with Surrealism. Is it the depiction of a dream, or is it the unedited subconscious made manifest? What did it mean when Lenny made a picture of a woman's hand (clearly a woman of wealth, evidenced by the size of the diamond in her ring) reaching out to open the glass door of an exclusive Paris jeweler, the extraordinary stone scratching the glass as so many other diamonds on the hands of so many other wealthy women had previously done? All those diamonds marking the glass so that, when the woman's hand was on the door, all those scratches gave the impression of her hand exploding?

The Girl in London, 1935

When Kristof Nash was invited to a small gallery showing of Lenny Van Pelt's pictures, he went thinking he would see her there. His new wife, Claire, had been Lenny's friend in New York. Though the young women had not stayed particularly close, they were still in touch from time to time, or they heard news of one another through the grapevine. Which was how Nash knew that Lenny was living in London, which was why he ended up looking her up when he came through the city to meet with the staff of British *BelleFille*.

Which was when, after basking in Nash's appreciation of her still considerable beauty, Lenny asked him to recommend her photography services to British *BelleFille*.

"I'm already in London," she said, "on my own steam, so it isn't like transferring someone here. I worked with Tin Type for three years, and I've been freelancing on my own for two. And"—she lowered her voice and leaned toward him across the table, with a hint of a smile, her gaze direct—"you and I both know that I can do this."

He appreciated the slight seduction in her approach, and, if he were a man given to seeing the humor in all things, he would've matched her smile, maybe said something flirtatious. But he wasn't, so he didn't, though he did give her the name of the primary photographer at *Belle-Fille,* saying, "It's up to Georges St. Georges."

———————————

"My God, you are like a beautiful golden goat boy of the Appian Way. Just like Mauritz and, frankly, just like me. Of course, we must work together and everything together."

Lenny had no idea who Mauritz was, but standing before Georges St. Georges was disconcerting, since it was very much like standing before a mirror, seeing her androgynous self in another person. That Georges St. Georges was fairly close in age to Lenny (in their late twenties, that sunset of youth) made the resemblance even more uncanny; that he was a man and a photographer made her feel twinned.

"I'm a photographer. I've recently worked with Tin Type and—"

"Then sometime we'll let you take pictures. What else can you do?" Georges St. Georges was very close, with both hands smoothing her hair away from her face. "I can see it, the angel and the vamp. The boy and the girl." Abruptly, he dropped his hands and walked over to his bag to retrieve a very thin brown cigarette, which he lit with a lighter of pure silver. "I shall talk to Mauritz."

"Should I be talking to Mauritz?" asked Lenny.

Georges St. Georges whirled around. "Is he here?"

"I don't think so," said Lenny, hesitant and looking over her shoulder toward the wide double doors leading into the cavernous studio space.

He held out a cigarette to Lenny, but she declined. "Do you know Mauritz?"

"No."

"Then—and I'm somewhat in the dark—why would you want to talk to him?"

"You said something about talking to Mauritz—"

"Yes."

"So, I thought—" She took a deep breath as Georges St. Georges calmly watched her, smoking his cigarette. "I want to work, and if this Mauritz is the person to talk to, then I want to talk to Mauritz."

Georges St. Georges pulled a small silver disk from his pocket. At first, Lenny thought it was a compact. In New York she had known a few men who powdered their noses, moistened their lips with lipstick, and accentuated their lashes with mascara. It had nothing to do with anything as far as she was concerned. But instead of powder, there were ashes. He then stubbed out his cigarette, dropped it inside, snapped the disk shut, and returned it to his pocket. "Did you think that I worked for Mauritz?"

Lenny said nothing.

"The day a photographer works for a model will be the apocalypse. Come around tomorrow at eleven."

When Lenny later thought about the moment she entered Georges St. Georges's studio, she thought about how much Tin Type would've appreciated its cavernous quality. Tin and all the other Surrealists, whom she suddenly missed very much (with the exception of Breton, the founding father of the movement, who could not have misunderstood women more if he tried), feeling especially soft toward Tin and glancing at her watch wondering what he was doing now—knowing his habits as she did—picturing him shopping and making her one of his assembled meals since, as he always said, "I cannot cook, but I can assemble." The English, she discovered, had not caught on to the dream-driven aesthetic as readily as the French.

If standing near Georges St. Georges was like standing in front of a mirror, then seeing Georges talking close and low to someone who was the mirror image of him, and therefore the mirror image of her, was akin to watching herself from herself. It was strange and surreal and familiar, given that she was already her brother's twin.

"Miss Van Pelt, please." Georges gestured for her to join him and the other young man. She moved toward them as if in a trance.

The other young man studied her, nodded, then said to Georges, "You're right. Again." Then to Lenny, "I'm Mauritz."

She almost wanted to say, "I'm Mauritz," they so resembled each other and, she believed, were even closer in age than she and Georges. "I assist Georges."

Georges had been showing Mauritz some sort of clothing when Lenny had walked into the studio, and now he gave one garment to Mauritz and the other to Lenny, saying, "If you want to go down the hall to change, there is a washroom on the left, or I can turn my back."

"Is this new modesty for the benefit of Miss Van Pelt?" Mauritz held Georges's glance just long enough for Lenny to understand the men. She wanted to protest that she was here not as a model but as an assistant photographer, but since Mauritz was also being asked to don the clothing and model, she said nothing.

"Perhaps we can locate a dressing room screen for our Miss Van Pelt," said Mauritz, watching her as he leaned into Georges so that their arms lightly touched. Georges seemed less aware of Mauritz than he was of her; she had enough experience with the territoriality that is a consequence of jealousy to know that the condescension in Mauritz's voice was a way of locking her out.

She pulled her shirt over her head, exposing her small breasts to the appreciative eyes of Georges and the less than pleased Mauritz—her shifting femininity was going to give him problems, she thought—before kicking off her shoes and stepping out of her trousers and undergarments. Pretending to examine the front and back of the bathing suit that dangled from her fingers, she casually stood before the men, completely comfortable in her nakedness. They had no idea where she was from when it came to her body. Object? Subject? She could turn it all off at will.

It was Georges who broke the silence, saying, "Mauritz, we don't have all day."

The resulting photograph, used to advertise a summer fragrance, was so successful than it ended up running for six months in *BelleFille*. The pair sat on the near the end of a dock so narrow it resembled a diving board, bleached white by the sun and seeming to be located on some deserted, pristine East Coast beach, with nothing before them but an endless expanse of the ocean. Though Mauritz sat closer to the end of the dock than did Lenny (she was closer to the camera lens), each with legs bent to the side, they appeared to be touching; their bodies were almost in profile and wearing identical one-piece swimsuits; their skin identically, wonderfully sun-kissed; their hair in the same careless, boyish style, golden and glossy.

The only thing the camera didn't pick up was their dislike of each other, fueled by distrust and their desire to win Georges, since neither was the least inclined to share, each wanting his attention as his or hers alone. They buried their mutual aversion beneath a veneer of professionalism and the need to please Georges. All this tension—their physical similarity to each other as well as to Georges, their artistic ambitions, their relationship to love, with one prone to jealousy and the other to indifference—translated into a period of superior work for Georges.

It wasn't romantic love that fueled Lenny; she wanted to take pictures. Mauritz desired Georges, *and* he wanted to take pictures. Georges also loved Mauritz but not only Mauritz, thus keeping Mauritz in a perpetual state of jealousy, a jealousy that almost eclipsed Mauritz's own photographic aspirations. Lenny was troubling for him because Mauritz didn't want to share Georges, either personally or professionally; it didn't help that she appeared somehow sexually mutable (her beautiful boy self, her siren self) and that Georges had an appetite for novelty and pretty things, compounded by his own sexuality that refused to stay fixed. The result was a difficult triangle where no one ever relaxed.

The studio was drafty and freezing, though it was only November. Mauritz and Lenny sat near each other, as close as they could to one of two fairly inadequate electric heaters, waiting for Georges, Mauritz seeming a little worn.

Lenny was wearing a cream-colored, heavy shirt made from a nubby fabric and cut almost like the shirt of an American sailor, with its V-neck and loose sleeves. It was nearly as long as her chocolate-colored short skirt with matching chocolate stockings. When she lifted her left arm, the sleeve fell back to reveal a pair of fourteen-karat gold handcuffs, both cuffs on the same arm and connected with a chain, that slid up and down.

"You must think I'm pathetic," said Mauritz.

"As a matter of fact, I don't think anything of the sort," said Lenny.

He sat there fighting back something: the tears, anger, despair that resulted from possessing the person you want without ever feeling as if you actually have him.

Mauritz reached over, traced a finger along the edge of one of the gold cuffs. "Georges wasn't with me last night," he said.

Lenny leaned back in her chair, extending her legs. "I just wish he'd get here."

"Those were a gift, weren't they?"

She shook her wrist, lightly knocking the cuffs against each other.

"And, I'm guessing, fully functional?"

"What would be the point otherwise?" She now leaned toward him. "Don't do this, Mauritz. Tell yourself that what he has with you is only with you. And here's something you know is true: Sex and love as a single thing doesn't really exist; it's more like a wish, a story that we tell ourselves when we're scared that someone will walk away with something that belongs to us."

"Where were you last night, Lenny?"

She sighed. "It doesn't matter."

"Then why not tell me?"

"Because it doesn't matter."

When Mauritz began to cry, Lenny stood and, using the long tail of her cream-colored shirt, gently wiped his face. "Mauritz. He wasn't with me." She knelt in front of his chair. "But it wouldn't matter anyway. Do you understand? Now, what shall we do?"

"Why not let me take your portrait?"

In her chair by the heater, she leaned back as she had during their conversation while he arranged the lights and set up the shot.

"Put your left arm—no—up—yes—behind your head—yes."

The sleeve fell back, the gold handcuffs exposed. When Mauritz looked through the lens, tightening the frame, he noticed what he hadn't seen when her arm was down: The inside of one cuff was engraved, in rather large script, *GSG*.

"Like this?" asked Lenny, gazing into the lens.

"No, tilt your head and glance to the side, as if you really can't figure out what it means to love someone."

The resulting picture was unusual in that it caught Lenny in an unguarded moment, with a wistfulness and a sweetness, as if she perpetually prowled the perimeters of love without ever stepping inside. When Georges saw it, he was moved by it. And when Lenny saw Georges's response, and Mauritz's pride, she laughed it off, mocking the sentimentality of the girl in the picture, saying, "Nice try."

––––––––––––––

All color had been leached from Georges's face when he finally arrived at the studio, interrupting Mauritz and Lenny after a single exposure.

"Where have you been?" asked Mauritz when Georges was scarcely in the door. "We've been waiting hours and—"

Georges dropped into one of the chairs.

"What?" asked Lenny. When Georges remained silent, she said, "You're scaring us."

"They've done it," he said.

"Who?" asked Mauritz.

"Two hundred synagogues destroyed. Every Jewish business looted. Vandals. Monsters. Thousands of people, thousands beaten, killed—I'm told that half the men have disappeared overnight." Georges held his head in his hands. "Where did they go? How do you make half the men of Berlin vanish in one night?"

Everyone knew about Germany's chancellor and the Nazis and their treatment of the Jews. Georges had family in Berlin, furriers to all the best people, and professors. One cousin was a civil servant, one of the few who had kept his position after 1933; Georges's family tried to tell themselves that, yes, things were bad if you were Jewish, but look,

Georges's cousin's job was spared; yet they couldn't quite believe it. They knew about the labor camps, the random violence and theft that German Jews faced every day. Once, Georges's fourteen-year-old niece was walking home from school when a German woman saw her from the window, came outside, and pulled her into her house to make the girl clean her kitchen.

There were laws affecting their professional lives, their education, their basic rights as citizens. But they still had the press, including one of the highest-circulating newspapers. And they were still German. Someone would see what was happening and stop it. This was Berlin, one of the largest, most worldly metropolises in the world. This was the middle of the twentieth century, for God's sake, how amok could everything run before someone stepped in and reminded the Germans that German was German? Hadn't they *all* suffered in the last war? Hadn't they all been punished since?

That Georges and Mauritz had felt reasonably safe as Jews living in London never altered the fact of what was happening in Germany and Austria. Berlin. Vienna. These daily events were shocking, but, against the sophistication of Berlin (and the recent tolerance of Weimar) and the grace of Vienna, they seemed an ugly hoax, an epic madness. It was huge. And it was Georges's cousin. It was his niece doing dishes for a stranger who forced her as she walked home from school. It was Mauritz's three sisters and his brother and their parents and grandparents.

And now it was this new thing, this unimaginable thing.

"They took apart the cemeteries. People watched people being beaten."

Lenny knew that Mauritz and Georges had been trying to convince their relatives to leave Germany but they had met a kind of hopeful resistance ("How can we have nothing when we've worked so hard?") or the excuse of someone's health ("She's too ill to travel") or the bureaucracy itself (Germany's emigration; England's immigration), and now it was dawning on everyone that (1) no one would save them—

"—people watched people being killed. In front of everyone"—

and (2) it just might be too late.

The Girl in London, 1939

In the same manner that Lenny in Elysium longed for Paris, with Paris setting off a longing for London, so was London creating the predictable (for Lenny) desire to be "anywhere but here." Then, on September 3, three things happened that changed everything: War was declared, a false-alarm air-raid siren sounded, and Lenny took up with Francis Walker.

It was impossible for Lenny to say which of the three things made London vital for her again, just when it had begun to feel tired and claustrophobic, but all three together renewed her in the most terrible, beautiful way. She ignored the advisory for all Americans to return home, keeping her studio in Knightsbridge while living almost full-time with Francis Walker at his Hampstead house.

That September, the month of the first air-raid siren, scattered many into basements, Anderson shelters in gardens, and Tube stations, though most people just slowed down, unsure where they wanted to be, and ending up nowhere special. It was also the month children were moved from London to the countryside. This seemed a continuation of children in transit that began with the *kindertransport* from Germany and Austria, those ten thousand Jewish children who were to be reunited with their parents after the war.

Then nothing more happened.

Lenny continued to work with Georges St. Georges; his distraction over his family, most of whom had emigrated to Paris, meant that she was doing more and more of the photographic work. No one knew the whereabouts of the civil servant cousin, but everyone hoped that he had reached safety after using every connection he had to get Georges's immediate and extended family to France.

Mauritz had called home one day to find a stranger answering his family's phone, demanding to know Mauritz's identity. The stranger said that Mauritz's family was "busy" and they would ring him. Would he be so kind as to leave a number?" Mauritz hung up, then rang the Italian neighbors he had known his entire life. What they told him made him despair, though they said not to, let them see what they could find out

and they would call. They also said that they had a number of possessions in safekeeping for the family, who had wisely been passing things
to them during the previous weeks.

Not long after Mauritz talked to them, the Italians, too, disappeared.

"As an American, maybe I can find something out? Maybe it's possible for me to travel to Berlin?" What Lenny didn't say was that she wasn't
scared by the prospect of going to Germany because she was fueled by
a sense of anger, and of risk. The hatred she felt for the Nazis was pure,
and the idea of hating them in person was, she knew, foolhardy; everyone she knew hated them, partly because most of the people she knew
and loved were Jewish, meaning that the news of what was happening
traveled at a different velocity in her world than it did in the press. Yet it
didn't fully illuminate her desire to be in a dangerous place.

Mauritz was so quiet that Lenny thought he was considering her
offer. The longer he said nothing, the more she committed to her plan,
until he said, "You aren't powerful enough to do any good," before turning and walking away.

Not being powerful enough touched something tender inside of her,
so raw and willfully ignored that her hands began to shake.

No one spoke anymore that day, except to say what needed to be
said to finish the pictures for *BelleFille*'s "The New Fashion" section ("A
gas mask that folds into a camera bag!" "Is khaki your color?" "This little
dickey doubles as a smoke blocker"), but when Mauritz went to leave for
the evening, he paused near Lenny and said, "What you said? It didn't go
unnoticed," before continuing out the door.

Lenny was in her Knightsbridge apartment, which was more of a spa-
cious, airy bed-sitter than a true flat. Along one wall was a tiny kitchen,
which Lenny used more often as a jury-rigged darkroom by hanging
heavy curtains, and a bathroom. Tall windows looked onto the street
two stories below. The plan was for her to spend more time in Hampstead with Francis Walker, and his estranged wife, Natasha, who had
made a reappearance since the night of the false alarm. His ex had raced

up to his house when the sirens sounded, then never went home. That was a year ago. Natasha was a high-strung woman in the best of times; Lenny didn't care that she lived with Francis, and often with Lenny. The unexpected result of their threesome was that Natasha seemed more attached to Lenny than she was to Francis, her devotion a shade oppressive and difficult for Lenny, driving her back to her bed-sit more often than not. Francis, too, spent more time at Lenny's place. Crazy for two people to remain in a single room while Natasha had all that luxury of space back at the house.

Lenny was alone in the apartment, the windows opened wide to the warm day, when she heard the planes. At first, she didn't think much of it because the sound of the engines was sluggish and grinding, the opposite of flight, nor was this the first instance of planes over London, often on their way to somewhere else. What forced her to the window was that the sound indicated so many planes, not just a few but a swarm (over 300 bombers. Over 600 fighters, she read later).

Then it began.

Lenny moved back from the windows, closing them softly. She sat on the edge of her bed.

For two hours bombs and artillery shells fell from the sky.

It was the quiet that stirred her from her spot. Checking the clock, she saw that it was nearly six, and she and Francis were having friends for dinner at eight thirty at his house. Why it didn't occur to her that the dinner might not come off said much about what Lenny did and did not consider an emergency. She was hurriedly packing some clothes and wine for Hampstead when her phone rang once, then was cut off by the most tremendous explosion, which shook the plaster off the ceiling and walls. It was only a moment later when she realized that the same droning planes had sounded just before the explosion.

Everything came unglued in this second air run. The clear skies of the day gave way to a clear night, with the fires of the bombs creating a tracery of flame that aided in the aim of the new planes. Lenny (dinner now definitely canceled) raced up to the roof, standing there as London shook and broke and burned in the night. The sky went darkly pink; she heard the crackle and felt the heat of the fires below. Or maybe she imagined feeling the heat. Billows of smoke rose, illuminated by the fires, before dissipating and leaving the blackness of a bombed build-ing or the miracle of an intact building. There were bursts of light and sound, fountains of sparks, and still the ever-present wave of planes. There was something terrible and gorgeous in all of this.

She should've been terrified—watching an air attack? *From a roof?* Why was novelty stronger than fear? The bombing didn't end until the small hours of the morning (that deafening noise). She should've run, or cowered, or tried to be less alone.

Instead, she felt exhilarated, calm, and not unhappy—all the emo-tions that she would never, ever, for the rest of her life, admit to anyone.

———————

After that first, big attack, Lenny's father sent her a telegram, demanding that she come home. She sent him a telegram with her London address, a reply both definitive and unmistakable.

———————

The attacks of the Luftwaffe went on for fifty-seven days and nights, with the worst fires, the most damage, the most casualties occurring in the following May. In between the fifty-seven consecutive raids and that unthinkable day in May, Lenny went on as did everyone else: working, falling in and out of love, arguing, making up, raising children, having children, going to school, going to the market, seeing friends, falling out with friends, being with family. People did not flock to the Tube stations. People did not rush to their Anderson shelters. People were so calm that a kind of weird boredom settled in. It was almost as if the planes over-head, the antiaircraft fire, and the enormous barrage balloons—which were just thin silver-tone material around gas, so insubstantial, yet effec-tively protecting the city and its inhabitants by forcing the planes to fly higher to avoid them—created an atmosphere that both provoked and negated fear. Though she understood them as a defensive measure, the barrage balloons only reminded Lenny of the lighting lessons of Tin Type, who'd explained that a silver object doesn't generate its own light.

An artist friend of Lenny's who'd fought in the Great War told her of the time he came upon dead farm animals suspended from the branches of a very old, very large tree, which struck him as an ideal Surrealist sculpture: the horse, the goat, the pony, all blown up into, then tangled among the branches, the very things that should not have been there yet seemed ordinary in the panic of the war.

She reflected on her Surrealist photographic tendencies as she donned a tin hat to go out amid the wreckage of the city, day after day, making pictures of the nightmare that now surrounded her: a tall old building, its entire center blown out, leaving the sides and the top floor, approximating Venice's Bridge of Sighs; the smashed typewriter; the waterfall of books that rushed from the windows of the library onto the street.

There were doors completely blocked with rubble; a classical statue of a woman lying on the ground in the embrace of another fallen statue. Still another statue, of a sixteenth-century king, wearing a gas mask and a flak jacket, with a sign around his neck saying, "All dressed up and nowhere to go."

The bombings democratically hit every borough of the city, bringing its citizens together in a way that hadn't happened before.

Lenny viewed the cityscape, with its vast holes where houses and businesses once stood, marveling at the random pattern of destruction, picking her way through little mountains of bricks, stones, mortar. She wanted to weep when she came upon a structure, centuries old, damaged beyond repair (often leveled altogether), thinking of all the men and the hundreds of years it took to construct this city, only to see it come to this in a historically scant fifty-seven days. Mostly, Surrealism kept away despair, except when she wondered as she walked in the wake of the bombs and fires, Is this Breton's convulsive beauty? Or, when she though of all those vacant Jewish houses, Is this de Chirico's empty city?

Francis Walker was away more and more working with the military. Lenny had no patience for Natasha and her needs and her fears; Natasha said that Lenny's coldness was due to jealousy, and Lenny allowed her to believe that because it was easier.

Mauritz had emigrated to America after begging Georges to come with him. But no amount of pleading or declarations of love could dissuade Georges from traveling to Paris to be with his family, despite the Vichy government, which surely sealed all their fates. It was always a mistake to think that, no matter how well you had done in the world, you would be seen as the exception.

Lenny went to A.W., the female editor in chief of British *BelleFille*, asking to be given war assignments. "I'll take pictures and I'll write," she said. As if anyone, let alone a high-fashion magazine, would send a woman to report the war. When she was told no, she continued photographing at home.

Then, after D-day, women in numbers so small everyone knew their names began reporting from France. This was how Lenny found herself on a transport plane, bumping and rolling through choppy air, to land on the French coast where the Americans believed the Germans had surrendered, only to find themselves fighting for territory. Lenny, excited and scared and brave, began shooting rolls of film, recording the battle from the vantage point of the soldiers, stopping only once to feel the love and elation of being back in France.

This was in 1944, when Francis Walker was in Italy and the Allies were ending the war and Lenny, in her custom-made soldier's uniform, boots, and bags of film; her camera, her typewriter, her cigarettes and gin, traveled with the American military, taking pictures of the surrender, with the exception of that first battle. She never would've been sent if the magazine had known it was a war zone; women weren't sent to photograph war. She was meant only to write and photograph the war's end.

Paris was not Paris. All her old friends, the ones who had somehow escaped the camps, or had been in the camps and survived, now seemed unhealthy and hollow and barely present. She was moved to fury and sadness as she held them in her arms. Prewar memories of masquerade balls, dinners that went deep into the night; art exhibitions, paintings traded for meals at La Coupole and Le Dôme and the occasional, awful American breakfast at Deux Magots because an American begged for it. All the love affairs and broken hearts and marriages. The manifestos. The feeling of promise. No one could think of it now. So seeing one another was a double-edged blade that couldn't help but cut when handled.

No one expected that a high-fashion magazine like *BelleFille*, with American, French, Italian, British editions, would pay Lenny to travel with the American troops as they moved through Europe in the waning days of the war that was all but formally over. But when Lenny happened into battle, the extraordinary A.W. saw the possibilities of her dispatches. It was an almost unimaginable pairing: Fortuny gowns and Cartier jewels and Hermès handbags with the wreckage of war. To that end, who better to photograph and write the dispatches than a former fashion model with Surrealist sensibilities and an attraction to risk?

"Here," said the young American soldier, a photographer for a U.S. paper, who had been assigned to drive Lenny, that is, when Lenny would allow him to drive. It was an ongoing argument between them.

She took the telegram and read it before lighting it with the same match she used to light her cigarette. She noticed Jack Fisher watching her. "Francis's wife. She's very needy."

Francis knew that Jack's involvement with Lenny wasn't limited to driving, and that they shared a bed on the road and a room at the Hôtel Scribe when in Paris—though the room reflected her more than it did Jack. All her belongings—typewriter, camera, film, prints, negatives, underwear, cigarettes, tins from her parents, along with the chocolates she loved so much, canteens, gin bottles—were scattered everywhere. The perpetually unmade bed, the crowded desktop, the filled ashtrays, and wastebaskets with tossed paper both inside and outside. Her uniforms, her leggings, her filthy boots.

Jack's gear, on the other hand, was limited to what could fit into a camera bag and a footlocker that he slipped under the bed.

Their nine-year age difference excited him. In college he'd studied art with the idea that he would one day make movies. He knew of Lenny before their introduction: She was the subject of work by Tin Type, Picasso, Cornell, and Cocteau, whose film, in which she starred as Venus, was said to be a "visual poem, made in a state of grace."

She said the reason she and Francis Walker got along so well was that he was crazy about her (Francis had his own aspirations to make art) and he didn't care about sexual exclusivity. "Thank God."

When thinking of Lenny as a lover, a companion, and a comrade, Jack found himself questioning the line that divides reckless from adventurous, until she languidly came over to where he was working across the room and unbuttoned his shirt, changing the direction of his inner debate completely.

So began their crisscrossing of Europe, a journey marked by drinking, smoking, sex, photography, reporting, the surprise of each day. It was an unpredictable vagabond life punctuated by the danger of a dwindling war. Lenny and Jack would venture out for weeks, then head back to the Scribe, then out again. They lived in suspended time that rendered everything weightless. They asked each other "What day is it?" so often that it became a running joke. Whether she was drunk or sober, Jack had never seen anyone more content or calm than Lenny.

As Lenny, Jack, and the American soldiers rolled through villages that reminded her of fairy tales, she found herself thinking of the lines of an e. e. cummings poem that she barely knew:

> *anyone lived in a pretty how town*
> *(with up so floating many bells down)*
> *spring summer autumn winter.*

These towns had her imagining the travelers and dogs and window boxes of roses that were there before the Nazi graffiti, pushing love for the Fatherland. She imagined the aroma of roasted chicken and cinnamon-scented apples in pastry, and the peal of bells. Lenny repeated those lines like a mantra to keep her focused when she saw the pretty, ruined towns in Alsace and France.

She went into a city where the inhabitants were nothing but refugees from the local zoo; a Western European town that resembled a jungle, with its zebras, chimpanzees, and birds with feathers of red, blue, yellow, and green.

Then there were the vacant German homes filled with little luxuries— a set of sheets, a silver gravy boat, a platinum-and-diamond locket— embroidered or engraved, and not matching the addressed mail on the hall table. And the other part of the poem she remembered,

women and men (both little and small)
cared for anyone not at all.

Lenny and Jack went to Eva Braun's house, with its phone lines marked Berlin and Berchtesgaden, and a gold bracelet of all the countries of Europe, studded with ruby swastikas, and engraved on the reverse was a single word, *Mine,* in each country's language.

In France, Lenny translated for French collaborators, with their shorn heads and shame. In Luxembourg, she took pictures of shapeless statues bound in rope and net to protect them from bombs. She saw villages smoldering, reduced to rubble with people sleeping and cooking in the open. Old castles and city walls were crumbled.

And then she entered Dachau.

Lenny's pictures of wartime celebrities (Chevalier, Dietrich, Crosby, Colette, Picasso) ran alongside her pictures of the lifeless twenty-year-old daughter of an SS officer, a suicide that looked made of ivory, lying beside her dead father and mother. There were camp guards hung, or floating in streams, beaten by their former prisoners; these deaths nothing next to the stacks of concentration camp bodies spilling out of abandoned boxcars. And more bodies, more carnage, among them the living so skeletal and still, almost impossible to distinguish from the dead.

No one could get a tight shot without getting close to the boxcars and the open graves and the barracks. Jack watched the men, soldiers and medics, who watched Lenny working precisely and methodically, as if she was indifferent to the images in her viewfinder, or the stench, and he knew that they knew their hands would not be so steady, or their stomachs so strong. A reminder that photography can be an intimate art.

Sometimes he thought he heard her murmuring the same four words, *spring summer autumn winter,* under her breath as she worked. *Spring summer autumn winter. Spring summer autumn winter.* He couldn't have known that sometimes these four words, repeated as she worked, were the reason she appeared so collected, when inside she was terrified of coming apart permanently. *Spring summer autumn winter.*

Once, while she was standing on a hill of dirt to get her shot, Lenny's foot broke the surface, which sent her sliding down the mound, taking the topsoil with her, revealing the mass grave beneath. She continued, unflinching.

The only thing she said to Jack as they drove away, past the lovely villas situated in the sumptuous, verdant landscape, was "They knew." She thought of Georges St. Georges joining his family in Paris, and of Mauritz's family, trapped in Berlin. "All of them knew."

And later, when in a German village that greeted the Americans as "liberators," an elderly German woman tripped, dropping her few possessions in the road near Lenny, Jack could see Lenny reflexively move to help, only to stop herself and step over the mess, her eyes straight ahead.

———

When Lenny and Jack entered Berlin, that damaged, cosmopolitan city, she said that, having seen the beautiful countryside and their modern buildings, she couldn't understand the Germans, why they wanted anything more. Lenny parked the jeep to allow them to walk and take pictures. On a corner near Potsdamer Platz was an enormous building, partially bombed and open to the sky. A broken name was still affixed to the facade: *Piccadilly*. They picked their way through the mess at the open door, discovering a massive, multilevel interior with torn velvets, upended and broken chairs and tables, smashed mirrors, and a half-filled man-made lake with one untouched swan boat, aimlessly floating along, the rest broken and half-capsized.

It was unsafe to try to climb the grand staircases, with their missing steps and lost handrails. So they left.

Lenny and Jack entered Hitler's apartment, where Jack took a picture of Lenny bathing in Hitler's tub, the dirt of Dachau darkening the water. Afterward, she took stock of the fairly modest flat that she thought looked like the charmless, middlebrow home of a bureaucrat. If anyone asked her to describe the place she would say that it lacked personality—from the kitsch sentimentality of the art to the fact that you could probably clear the place out for a new tenant in less than an hour. It didn't surprise her that someone who lived so practically, so prosaically could be so cruel.

When word of the final surrender reached Lenny, she was sitting under a tree in the middle of a field in Alsace with Jack Fisher. They were smoking cigarettes, her Rolleiflex on the grass nearby. Both of them were so dirty from being too long without access to a shower that every time they moved they seem to release a fine puff of dust. Lenny didn't care; she could remain unwashed forever.

It was the noise of celebration coming from a passing Allied convoy of four vehicles, the whooping and honking and the knowledge that the German army had been collapsing and giving up for days, that allowed them to sit quietly for a bit longer, having figured out what the commotion signified.

"I'm going to miss this," she said. "It's the first time something's been done with me before I was done with it."

"It'll be strange, our lives," he said.

"I will miss you too, but that isn't what I meant."

"Then what?"

She was quiet. "I'm not Cinderella. I can't force my foot into a glass slipper."

"Not with those boots on you can't." He smiled. He nudged her booted foot with his booted foot.

"It's like I've had this great adventure, as if I've found my truest self," she said. "I'm not really fit for a woman's life."

Jack straightened up. "Look. I don't know if you've never heard of you, but you weren't exactly living like a middle-class American wife and mother, with the kids and the husband commuting to the city. My old life in Brooklyn was a helluva lot less colorful than your old life in Paris, not to mention London."

She was weighing her words and choking back the tears she most definitely did not want to fall. How could she tell this young American soldier that she couldn't bear feeling estranged from herself again?

"You can't know how restless I would get. Everything would work for a few years and then—"

"Then what?"

"Then it would all go quiet. It was like, like the world would click into high gear when I changed lives or locations—you know, I was a wild one when I was younger, but then there was New York, then Paris, then London—the novelty accelerated everything—lovers, photography, art class, modeling, and all those New York parties, even the Blitz—until the routine set in, and with it life would adjust down to normal speed. Then this war, where every day was without precedent. Where uncertainty was normal—or, I guess, normal for me. You know what I mean because you've lived it too."

"Yeah, well, I wouldn't have signed up for any of this, especially some of what we saw that I fucking wish I'd never seen—"

Buchenwald. Dachau. *The pretty how towns. Spring summer autumn winter.*

"It's over now anyway," he said.

The tears she fought so hard, fell. He scooted over beside her, put his arm around her. "The world can't stay at war for you, Lenny."

"I've always been the one who had to keep moving, until the war, since it was now the one moving. I could stop without stopping."

He tenderly combed her hair with his fingers, smoothing it, though it was sticky with dried sweat and longer than its former, cropped cut.

"It was as if all my life was moving toward this experience, you know?"

Jack dropped his hand. "I'm ready to be done with it."

"Well, I'm thirty-eight years old. And a woman, and I'm broke. What am I going to do? Photograph shoes for *BelleFille*? If I'm lucky? Women and fashion and weight gain and marriage. What am I going to do?"

"You'll have a life, Lenny. And, if we're lucky, we'll forget. What we've been living isn't a life, Lenny, it's an interruption." He took a deep breath. "You'll go back to Francis, who loves you. You'll move into that big house of his, with that clinging wife who wants to be your best friend"—this got a smile from Lenny—"and Francis'll paint and you'll take pictures, and you'll have dinner parties with all your artist friends. It's not right that a war, any war, but especially one this shocking, should feel like home to you."

"You know, I only saw combat as a photographer by accident. Women reporters weren't exactly allowed. But then there were those Germans, holed up in that fortress like nothing was ending. . . . It was all an accident," she said. "I had no idea that I would love it so much."

"Listen, I don't know your deal, but I do know that, if you don't figure it out, sooner or later you're going to break all to pieces."

They said nothing, for a while, listening to distant sounds of celebration. They heard voices and horns and military vehicles speeding on dirt roads. The nearby trees rustled in the breeze.

"When I was seven," said Lenny, "my mother was sick. Some virus. She wanted my father to send me away while she recovered. She worried about contagion. And he didn't want to, but they both wanted to keep me safe. They had some friends who lived in the city—good friends whom we saw a lot, childless, and they loved me especially. They loved my brother too, but me most of all. So, I went to stay in their apartment at the same time that a nephew was there. He was young and had been in the war, in France, and he would start drinking first thing in the morning even though I don't think anyone ever saw him drunk. I liked him. We got along. And one day, when the couple had to be gone and had no one to watch me, they asked the nephew to keep an eye on me, just for an hour or so.

"We were alone and something happened, something so . . . terrible, and the couple were beside themselves, blaming themselves, and my parents blamed them too. And also blamed themselves. All those adults deep in their own misery. It was confusing, and I felt like I wasn't even a person to them anymore but a situation where everyone could feel bad. They did feel bad because they loved me.

"I went to a doctor—besides the medical doctor, though I had been to see him too, you know, afterward—a psychiatrist. My parents were always very modern, very forward-thinking, and the doctor they took me to explained what I needed was to be taught that love and sex are absolutely separate. And so I was, and I do."

"My God, you were just a little kid."

"My father took the first nude picture of me. I was almost eight years old and freezing in the snow . . ." Her voice trailed off. Her eyes looked into Jack's. "He was trying to fix things, telling me that doing this would help me 'reclaim my body,' but I was so young, I didn't understand that anyone thought my body wasn't my own anymore. Maybe he was just trying to understand how to love me.

"Anyway, it's not like I ever cried about it—oh, poor me or anything—and so when the war happened, it became the only time in my life where the unstable outside world matched the unmanageable inside me."

Then they gathered up their things, put them in the back of the jeep, and went to join the others in celebrating the end of the conflict.

SUCH ARE THE DREAMS OF THE EVERYDAY HOUSEWIFE
OR
ARTÍCULOS ELÉCTRICOS PARA EL HOGAR (ELECTRICAL APPLIANCES FOR THE HOME)

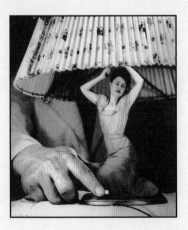

On a gray day in March 1927, Charlotte Blum stood back from the mannequins that she had been wrestling with all afternoon in the spotless display windows of Wertheim, one of the city's premier department stores, to take in the effect of her arrangement. The point was to sell sunglasses, items one usually saw on movie stars, so casually glamorous in the casually glamorous sunshine of California. The citizens of Berlin seldom found themselves wishing for a pair of dark glasses in their often overcast city, but if Charlotte had learned nothing else in her twenty-four years it was never to underestimate the lure of dreams.

Her department manager, Miss Schmidt, thought as long as they were selling the outrageously stylish glasses, perhaps they could add an evening dress? Maybe some high-heeled shoes with open toes, in silver metallic leather? What about sequins on pajama trousers? Oh, and even though it's early March, isn't there still time for someone to purchase a fur for the unpredictable weather of a German spring?

What Charlotte and her manager didn't discuss was the recent easing of the violently hard times that had come on the heels of the Great War, impoverishing so many Germans. Had Charlotte mentioned it, Miss Schmidt would have said, "But you aren't talking about *our* customers, Miss Blum."

It was true, there were still well-heeled shoppers who strolled the elegant Leipzigerstrasse; the manager's unspoken sentiment was a swipe at the young men and women crowding the streets. Especially the women, with their corsetless figures moving freely in their light garments: the short skirts, the loose blouses. Charlotte knew that her manager, a middle-aged woman who had known her place all her life, bore no affection for the New Woman, who was now—or so Charlotte felt—only a reminder of how devastating it can be to be born at the wrong time.

Miss Schmidt checked her wristwatch, a gorgeous object that

Mr. Wertheim himself had brought back from Geneva as a gift to her. It was still common to see women wearing small lapel watches on their blouses, or men relying on pocketwatches, so wearing a wristwatch immediately made the manager look modern. How Charlotte envied her that watch! For all Miss Schmidt's complaints about the "girls of today," the manager was aware that the watch gave her a certain contemporary cachet; it made her less easy to peg as the traditionalist that she really was, and Charlotte knew this sort of misrepresentation pleased her. It wasn't so she could pass herself off as something she wasn't; it was so she could, in some small way, be a part of the sexual revolution that was already leaving her behind.

There were so many ways for a woman to be frustrated, thought Charlotte. Even when you bestow a new life on young women, by definition you leave the older ones out. The truth was, this new Berlin didn't belong to all young women; it easily excluded the ones who were working-class or poor. Factory workers who considered themselves New Women still cleaned and cooked on their days off. Wives still had children to look after, along with the husbands. And then there were the secretaries, who could never hope to have positions equal to their bosses'. Women who had less opportunity to be New Women than those spirited, athletically built middle- and upper-class girls in summer dresses. Girls who smoked, openly took lovers, chose bohemian society, and pretty much did as they pleased because they, like the manager, were affected by the accident of birth. In their case, into money. Charlotte knew this because she was one of those girls who came from comfortable circumstances and privilege, though it didn't prevent her from observing the world around her.

Even her window-dressing job came as a consequence of studying typography, having spent two summers drawing advertisements for a design firm. Her education came because her parents could afford it, and because they, particularly her father, were progressive, never thinking to offer something to her brother that they would not offer to her.

It didn't occur to Charlotte that this was unusual parental behavior in those pre–Great War years, and when it did finally occur to her to ask about it, her father had laughed and said, "I never really thought about it, but I will say I made more of an effort after our Denmark holiday."

When Charlotte was nine years old, her parents had traveled with her and her brother to Denmark. In Copenhagen, placed all by itself on a rock in the harbor, sat a statue of Hans Christian Andersen's Little Mermaid. It wasn't very big, the size of a real girl actually, and Charlotte was entranced by this fishgirl, her lower body half legs, half fins, and the tragedy of her inability to win the love of her prince.

Nothing in the city enthralled her as much as the statue, who sat so close to the shore Charlotte felt she could march right out and touch her.

On the second day, her family indulged her request to visit the statue again; on the third day, her mother and brother refused to go. "Charlo, how can you keep coming back to this little tourist statue?" asked her father.

She didn't want to say because she was so beautiful, with her slim figure, her pretty, downturned face, her hair loosely gathered at the base of her neck. The mermaid seemed like a girl she could have gone to school with. So delicate, the sort of girl the other girls might have crushes on. Charlotte wouldn't have thought to say this to her father, because she wouldn't have articulated it in this way, but her feelings could be summed up as, What's the difference between my loving to look at this bronze girl, a creature of fantasy, and my friends who like the girls in the cinema?

"The story of this little mermaid?" her father said. "That's not your story. You will never fall in love with a prince you've rescued who isn't even smart enough to know that it was you who saved him. You will never sell your voice for legs that feel like a thousand knives every time you walk."

"I know," said Charlotte.

"It's a terrible story, you know."

Charlotte nodded.

Father and daughter gazed at the little statue. "Mr. Andersen," said her father, "never had a daughter."

Charlotte couldn't tell her father that the story of the Little Mermaid frightened and fascinated her.

"Come on, kid," he said. "Your mother and Trilby are meeting us at the Tivoli Gardens."

Reluctant to leave the bronze fishgirl, Charlotte followed her father to the amusement park.

"Miss Schmidt," said Charlotte, "would it be all right if I stepped out for a moment?"

Her manager looked at her watch and said, "Ten minutes." That Charlotte was being timed was a given, for productivity, and for Charlotte to be reminded of the beautiful watch that belonged to Miss Schmidt.

Being outside allowed Charlotte to get some fresh air, which she immediately polluted by lighting up a cigarette. She was raised to believe that women shouldn't smoke, and, if they did, smoking on the street was déclassé. Even Charlotte thought it lowbrow. So when she did it, it was because she was courting an image that no more represented her true self than Miss Schmidt's modern wristwatch represented her; it wasn't rebellion as much as it was a kind of game of pretend.

She stood across the street from the windows she was working on, her coat pulled tight against the wisps of snow as she held the cigarette she barely inhaled. Sunglasses. How to get passersby to look at the sunglasses? These same pedestrians bustled around her as she remained stationary.

Charlotte stubbed out her cigarette beneath one well-shod foot. The windows were shaping up, but something was missing, something that would catch the feminine eye. There was talk about making Charlotte a permanent window dresser, which meant more pay and job security in the union. It wasn't a completely unattractive prospect, since she believed the job carried a possibility for theatrics.

Until now Charlotte had not moved very far from the prim Wertheimer aesthetic—smartly dressed salesgirls, tasteful music, perfectly modulated lighting that fit the architecturally graceful arches at the entrance and the soaring atrium—but all at once she saw another direction for the windows. In her excitement, she hurried back across the street, arriving at her post with two minutes to spare and never noticing another young woman who had been watching Charlotte as Charlotte had been watching the storefront windows.

———————————

Charlotte Blum worked quickly. Three scenes: In the first window, a wife and mother cooks dinner in the kitchen. In the second window, a secretary sits at her typewriter, Dictaphone nearby as she transcribes a recording. In the third, a woman works in a factory.

———————————

"Do you find this job amusing? Do you think this is just for fun?"

Miss Schmidt was standing just outside one of Charlotte's tableaux, refusing to enter while still able to see the passersby who stopped to stare at the mannequins. "Am *I* amusing?" said Miss Schmidt, insensible to the crowd that was attracted to the windows but stayed on for the obvious reprimand Charlotte was receiving.

An arm of the mannequin in the kitchen caught Miss Schmidt's critical eye: On its rigid, skinny wrist was a beautiful watch. She stepped in and yanked the arm out of its pose to get a closer look, then shoved it into an opposite, awkward pose in disgust. "Is this what you think of . . . of . . . of all of us?" as she made a sweeping gesture with her own watch-adorned arm. "Our customers? They aren't secretaries. They are to be treated with respect, not like some burlesque."

"It wasn't meant as ridicule—" Charlotte began.

"Stop!"

It seemed Miss Schmidt had more to say, then thought better of it as she turned and left Charlotte in the kitchen scene, unsure of what was expected of her.

When Charlotte had examined the display windows from outside the store as she smoked her cigarette, the idea of women daydreaming came to her in full. The sunglasses, of course, they represented a life of sunshine, vacations, paradise, and moonlight. If she were to make tableaux depicting an expensive lakeside resort, or a midsummer's picnic in the heart of New York City, then where is the dream? Where is the unexpected? Where is the connection to the dreariness of life and the flight of fancy?

It was the juxtaposition of the two things that would draw the eye and stimulate the fantasy, then the desire to make it real, then the sale of the thing being sold, in this case, the sunglasses.

In the wake of Miss Schmidt's departure (and presumed march up to the floor supervisor), Charlotte remained motionless near the stove. The mannequin mother, intent on cooking dinner, wore a silk dress, a shimmer of pale blue ice that seemed the weight of a butterfly's wing. Delicate ropes of diamonds wound around her throat and wrists, with individual stones scattered in her upswept hair. A pair of black-framed sunglasses shielded her eyes from the harsh light of the display windows as she went about her task, her pose indicating that nothing was amiss in her hausfrau attire. Her children sat in the corner, constructing a tower from a metal Erector set. The message, Charlotte tried to explain to Miss Schmidt, was that her family may see her one way, but this glamorous costume was how she saw *herself*.

The secretary in the next window wore red-framed sunglasses with green lenses as she transcribed a business letter on her typewriter, a full-length mink coat casually flung over the back of her chair.

The final window was of a factory girl clad in ruby velvet overalls studded with rubies. Ruby and diamond cuffs sparkled on each wrist as she tightened a cog with a gold-painted wrench while peering through her sunglasses, sky blue lenses set in round tortoiseshell frames. Her high-heeled shoes were an intricate web of red satin and velvet ribbons.

If Charlotte was sure of nothing else, she knew that even women who didn't work in offices or factories or fix their own supper would recognize the lives in the window. They would recognize them and, in a passing fit of fantasy, imagine they were in their place, sentimentally perhaps, but that wouldn't stop them from responding to the daydreams of working girls. Desire, thought Charlotte, only unexpected desire can have any effect.

She wandered over to the secretary's window and dropped into the leather office sofa. It was hard to imagine that she'd be keeping her job, or that she'd want to keep her job if all it meant was dressing and undressing mannequins without doing anything more interesting than pretending they were guests at a party. Charlotte struggled to see the reasoning behind selling goods if you weren't selling the *ideas* behind the goods.

While she tried to muster up the energy to find Miss Schmidt and learn her fate, which she was fairly sure would be to dismantle everything, she noticed a young woman taking in the window displays. Some of the passing crowd still stopped to look, but not with the undivided interest of the young woman.

Charlotte watched her pause before the first scene, studying it, leaning a little to one side. The girl looked to be about Charlotte's age and was, not unlike Charlotte, dressed in a gamine outfit of a crisp white men's shirt tucked into pleated trousers topped with a wide, simple belt with a rhinestone dress clip attached just next to the buckle. Her navy blue wool overcoat was tailored, though unbuttoned; Charlotte noted the way it tucked in at the waist before flaring out again and stopping midcalf. Charlotte had spent enough time around luxury to recognize the very fine coat as easily the most expensive item the girl wore. But the trousers, the rhinestone pin, and the lack of a hat (in winter, no less), revealing her unfussed, bobbed hair, pulled Charlotte's attention. The young woman was, in short, adorable.

As this thought occurred to Charlotte, the girl wandered over to the secretary scene, breaking her concentration long enough to see Charlotte. At first, she seemed slightly startled to see a live girl keeping company with the imitation girl. Then she relaxed, smiling a smile so unexpectedly charming that Charlotte could not breathe.

It was decided that while the elder Blums were in England for an extended period, Charlotte and her brother, Trilby, would stay in their parents' modernist house of glass located on the edge of Berlin. The hard, reflecting surfaces stood in contrast to the garden of roses that surrounded the home. Climbing roses, wild roses, trees of roses. The large garden and glass house, designed by Charlotte's architect-father, Bruno, were bordered by a tall stone wall that hid both house and garden from the street.

The family loved this house to distraction. They loved it for the play of light through the walls of glass, loved how the walls slid away, transforming the large, undivided living space into a kind of industrial gazebo. They loved the extreme height of the ceilings, the kitchen, with its sleek cabinetry that ran almost unnoticed along one wall. The most expensive element of the house was the series of retractable skylights in all of the bedrooms, reduced in size so that more space could be given over to the public rooms and studios where Mr. and Mrs. Blum worked; he was an architect, she designed glassware, and together the family had a thriving glass-manufacturing firm, Blum GlasWerks. Trilby had a compact studio whose decor still reflected his student days at the Bauhaus, where he had taken classes on all manner of design—furniture, lighting, carpets, textiles, glass, and pottery. And Charlotte's tiny studio of colored pencils, pastels, watercolors, inks, and papers and was atop the garage, accessed by a sky bridge.

Inside the home, colorful carpets in geometric patterns sat on planked floors (the bedrooms) and concrete floors (the studios and living room). The furniture was leather and comfortable and avant-garde. Charlotte's parents had included touches of velvet and aged crystals, but so perfectly that the connection between glass and velvet, concrete and crystal was seamless. The success of her parents' company depended upon the Blums' love of the new.

Books lined the floor-to-ceiling shelves. There were tables of metal and mirror, lighting fixtures of aged metal and amber glass. The displayed art was spare and well-chosen—a small sculpture here, an oversize oil abstraction there—all of it personal, not simply decorative.

It would be safe to say that no house ever represented a family as this house did the Blums: their twentieth-century ideas, their intellect, their commitment to high and popular art, their unity. Their unwavering affection for each other.

———————————

In 1914, at the Cologne Werkbund Exhibition, Bruno Blum built what looked like a Turkish temple made of glass. The monumental dome, which swirled like a serving of whipped cream, was a multihued fantasy of diamond-shaped panes of wavy glass in paint-box colors ranging from indigo and rose at the base through deep green and grass, to lavender, to buttery yellow, pale orange, and back to an incandescent yellow that resembled pure light.

Etched lines of modernist poetry wrapped around the exterior walls.

Inside the temple were a pair of clear glass stairways that bordered an interior waterfall, the water mirroring the wavy glass in the dome.

This little pavilion of color, light, and glass honored the workers at Blum GlasWerks while announcing Bruno Blum's dream to make a "crystal world." Mr. Blum was not a religious man; he, along with his family, adhered to humanist values. Kindness and forgiveness were his moral compass, and a belief in the possibility for an earthly paradise found through glass.

Glass, he reasoned, allowed people to be seen, and loved. It invited light into people's lives, making it inevitable that transparency, and a banishing of the darkness, would naturally lead to a better world. If you called Bruno Blum a utopian, he would agree. "So I'm a little luft-mensch," he would say with a laugh. "There are worse things."

While Bruno Blum pursued his realization of livable glass buildings (his wonderful home being one example), his brother ran the factory, along with Trilby, who was being groomed to take over the entire operation. Blum GlasWerks made not only ordinary windows but also windows for churches and synagogues and department stores. It was the company that most of Europe looked to for municipal aquariums and flower conservatories. They made art glass for interior doors and windows. Every German who could afford it purchased a Blum greenhouse, or garden house.

The greenhouses further fueled Bruno Blum's ideas regarding glass structures that housed people instead of plants. His philosophy of glass led to the establishment of the Glass Chain—a series of letters among ten other architects who loved glass and steel as much as Bruno Blum. Eventually, the paper conversation became influential as close to home as the Bauhaus and as far away as the rest of Europe, and America.

In between his glass projects, Blum built public housing, fanciful and solid. Not pure glass, but full of windows and sunlight just the same, as he made the correlation between contentment and light.

Marcelle Blum, Charlotte's mother, was a designer of glass tiles, vases, smaller decorative windows, transoms, and light fixtures for a dedicated department of Blum GlasWerks. Mirrors. Floor screens. A collection of breakable animals that pleased adults as much as they did children. The waiting list for her chandeliers and floor lamps alone was impressive.

Rainier Ermler, the photographer, had been a friend of Bruno Blum since Charlotte was very young. He specialized in architectural and landscape photography. Not surprisingly, the several portraits he made were so saturated with light that the faces resembled the facades of buildings.

Mr. Blum and Rainier Ermler were involved with the architects at the Bauhaus in Dessau, who taught progressive ideas of form and function, looking at the construction of a thing as well the "nature" of an object. And the idea of beauty "doing something" and not just "being something" was meant to affect the lives of the common man too. The school held classes in painting and color theory and textiles, pottery, and wall coverings; typography and advertising and architecture, while photography came and went until Rainier Ermler and Laszlo Moholy-Nagy made it a more permanent fixture in 1929, around the time that Rainier was shooting Bruno Blum's Rainbow on the Rhine, an apartment complex meant to mimic the Royal Crescent in Bath while allowing maximum light to the interior. Its arc shape and pastel coloring had earned it the descriptive nickname. Mr. Blum didn't care what it was called as long as there were those who called it "home."

It could be said that Rainier Ermler cared more about painting with light than he did about psychological insight, or placing his unseen self in the photograph. Exercises in abstraction didn't interest him; his pictures always looked like what they were: a cup, a rose, a hand. A house of glass, an arc-shaped apartment complex of many hues. A face flooded with light. He wanted the building (the interior, the portrait, the cup, the rose, the hand) to be exactly what it was, yet presented in a new way.

He would say to Charlotte, "If I photograph you in the shadows, you become mysterious, perhaps unknowable. If I light you from above, so your eyelashes throw shadows on your cheeks, you could be a Hollywood film star. And if I fill the room with light, to an almost unforgiving degree, it will flatten your features, as if I am a public servant taking a passport photo."

"I like the idea of the passport photo," said Charlotte.

Rainier said, "That's because, in trying to hide nothing, it prompts the imagination. We ask, 'Where is this person going? Where is she from?'"

"But you said you wanted the thing to be 'what it is.'"

"Yes. And it is. It is a face, a portrait. We can all agree. Whereas we may not all agree when looking at an abstract picture—'oh,' we say, 'That's a mountain. No, it's a teapot.' But by not disguising the thing in the picture—in this case, the face—we are freed to move beyond what we see. We are past What is it? and on to What does it mean? What's the story?"

"All right then," asked Charlotte, "what is the difference between your passport picture and my snapshot? Is my snapshot as interesting?"

"Sometimes. The difference—and this is what I will teach you, okay? The difference is that if your interesting snapshot is an accident, you aren't controlling the outcome as much as something simply caught your eye and, snap, snap, there you are. This is why people are bored with most snapshots of someone's vacation to the spa or the seashore.

"But, when you learn about light, you learn that light is everything. Contrasts of white and gray and black. We photographers are lashed to light and time, and we must make the most of both. If I'm good, I can get a picture that looks like a snapshot but feels like mystery. Maybe even a masterpiece—a Vermeer!" He stopped, sighed. "The most important thing I can say is that you must be precise. You must be particular."

———————————

Charlotte was Rainier Ermler's sole pupil at the Berlin studio. No longer working at Wertheim, she would ride in on the train from the exclusive southwestern district of the city where her family's glass house was located near woods and lakes. It wasn't a long ride—no more than half an hour—yet it was a world apart from the crush of the city. Every day, without exception, Charlotte felt a rush of excitement when the train pulled into the station, as she exited the doors into the crazy, kinetic intersection of five boulevards at Potsdamer Platz. It was the surge of the crowd, and the streetcars, bicycles, buses, automobiles that sped about the crisscrossing streets, avoiding each other as if the traffic were choreographed. There were newsboys and flower sellers and the occasional horse-drawn cart. Tram bells and car horns. There were couples of every class and gender combination strolling arm in arm. It was a jolt: the noise, the smells, the buying and selling and rushing and strolling and conversing and meeting and parting amid all the enormous buildings housing offices, stores and shops, cafés, theaters, and packed restaurants, spilling people into the streets. It was the thrill of being in the congested center of such a metropolitan city, populated by shopgirls, workmen, noblemen with their formal manners and air of entitlement; students, local and foreign. Scientists, artists, musicians. Poets. Factory owners, department store owners, bankers, and purveyors of fine goods. People passing through; people without the means to move on.

There were artists, painters, street vendors, wives of the rich, mistresses of the same rich; businessmen everywhere. Professors, politicians, brownshirts, Nazis, communists, and those who hovered politically more to the center.

Everywhere were ads for goods, medicines, and party candidates.

One painter portrayed Berlin as a vortex of three groups: the veterans of the Great War, with their missing limbs and less visible war wounds, parked on the already crowded sidewalks; the capitalists, somehow surviving the cataclysmic cost of the war and the consequent reparations; and the prostitutes, whom one could spend the better part of an afternoon categorizing before even addressing all the sexual appetites they satisfied.

Among the women were Boot Girls, Fresh-Air Women, and T-Girls, who worked in pairs, sometimes as mother and daughter. Kontroll-Girls were registered with the government, *Nutten* were teenage girls who looked like boys. *Munzis* were pregnant women. Young "medicines" came with "doctors." *Minettes*, racehorses, and dominas. Five O'Clock Ladies, shopgirls, and secretaries worked the trade part-time, and their counterparts, Mannequins, were from good families and worked in the best brothels.

There was something for everyone: lesbian, gay, transvestite, transsexual, with every category of "characters" and amusements. Charlotte was reminded each morning as she observed people in late-night finery on their way home, looking a little worse for wear, that the current sex industry (both its economics and its scope) was a marker of a hollowed-out nation, something that seemed to move beyond human nature.

Berlin was the picture of a large metropolis on the losing end of a world war. The handfuls of marks to buy a loaf of bread, the wounded, the war debts, the people with money, the New Women with jobs, the modern buildings, the sexual commerce, the clubs and cafés, the ever-changing political dance in the wake of the deposition of the Kaiser.

The city never brought Charlotte down because every day was new. Even though Berlin itself was not as picturesque as London or Paris, and even though *charming* could never really be an appropriate adjective, Berlin was charismatic in the roguish way of a lover who, even as he (or she) is wooing you with kisses and whispered promises, and making you laugh, you know won't call in the morning. It was a lover who was a little dangerous in ways that didn't always show, keeping her a bit on edge, a bit in love and endlessly forgiving because it made her feel that she was exactly where she was meant to be.

That's what it was to be young and in Berlin in those years between the wars: Berlin made you like who you were when you were there, as if everything worth being a part of in the world—all those modern ideas about sex and art and women; all that possibility—was right there, in its dark, beating heart.

Charlotte had had eight months of Rainier's undivided attention. She had listened as he explained the relationship he made between photography and mathematics and philosophy. He was serious and exact, thought not completely without a sense of humor, as she soon discovered. The trouble was that their personalities were radically out of sync when it came to light social interaction, even as they meshed perfectly as teacher and pupil.

One day Charlotte entered the studio to see Rainier composing a still life of a rose on tiers of glass, with a piece of tin arranged behind and below the little glass shelves. There were three pale pink pearls near the white rose. A bit of silk ran through the arrangement. He was bent to his work, using tweezers to perfect the placement of the rose, the pearls, and the silk. He would make a minuscule adjustment, then step back and slightly redirect the lights. Then back at the still life, using the tweezers, then back at the lights. The window shades refused to be adjusted in such subtle ways, a fact that clearly frustrated him.

None of this obsessive activity caught Charlotte's attention: Rainier was being Rainier.

What did catch her eye was the other person in the room, with her back to Charlotte as she seemed absorbed in Rainier's activity.

Her sandy hair was a mass of loose curls cut in a bob, ending just below her ears. She wore a men's-style sweater, too long for her slight frame, trousers, and boots, but it was the way she was standing, leaning a little to the side, her arms crossed in front of her, that seemed familiar.

The girl quickly glanced over her shoulder when Charlotte entered the studio (not wanting to miss the glacial progress of Rainier's adjustments), then looked again, this time twisting her body to give her a small, waist-high wave and a smile before turning back to Rainier.

Charlotte would've known that smile anywhere.

It turned out that Rainier had taken Ines on as a student when she wrote him a letter about a picture she had seen in a magazine of an unmade bed, a pair of hairpins forgotten among the sheets, taken by a woman named Cymbeline Kelley.

"American," said Ines, "and a woman." She and Charlotte were sharing two pastries at Kuchenform café on Friedrichstrasse, the thousands of lights doubled in the slick, wet street. "I asked if he knew anything about her—he didn't—and said that I preferred a picture like Kelley's to those of someone like Morris Elliot, with all those vegetables that are cropped to look like something else. Same thing with Moholy-Nagy. I like things to look like what they are, I said, because then I can make up my own story. I don't like being dictated to."

"He must have loved to hear you say that," said Charlotte.

"Apparently," said Ines, her words a little sloppy from the bite of cake she'd just taken. She delicately wiped her mouth with her fingertips. "Sorry, my napkin's on the floor and—"

Charlotte held out her own napkin. Ines used it, then handed it back.

"So, you're not really Rainier's only student, are you?" she said.

"For the last several months, yes. I mean, that I know of."

"Hmmm."

"He doesn't really have time for students, and, well, I think he really took me on as a favor to my father." And when Charlotte said her father's name, Ines replied, "Rainbow on the Rhine! I know a family that lives in one of the flats. I love the meadow in the middle of the complex and, of course, all the light." She took another bite of cake, with Charlotte giving her the napkin before she even asked. "Isn't he also the glass architect?"

"You should see our house."

"Invite me. Or, if you don't want to be exclusive, invite everyone in our class."

Charlotte laughed.

"Are you still dressing windows at Wertheim's?"

"Fired. Mostly fired, I guess, since I went in to talk to them about my ideas with the intention of leaving if I had to keep doing what I was doing. Somehow the conversation never got around to what I wanted and more or less concentrated on what they wanted, which was 'someone who absolutely understood their clientele'—and I pointed out that actually I understood perfectly, making my windows seem like 'an act of rebellion'—"

"God, they think everyone is committing acts of rebellion these days. If you question the government, if you're a girl and want to do something else with your life besides kitchen, kids, and church—"

"Did you go to Hannah Höch's lecture where—"

"I love her photomontages—"

"Me too! I love them so much!"

"*Cut the Cake with a Knife*? Brilliant. All those mannequins as brides? Fantastic. Just aces, you know? The whole idea that even as modern as we think we are, women are never seen as complete in themselves."

"And marriage? Never mind marriage. She said that 'mannish women were both celebrated and castigated for breaking down traditional gender roles.' And what about when she talked about when working at magazines that catered to women and how the image and the reality are not even close to the being the same thing?"

"I liked when she read that list of images in her work: the 'fabulous beasts; fantastic planets; pretty, alienated girls.'

" 'The machines and cats, and newborn babies in starlike arrangements. A train, a girl with faraway eyes. At the end she said, 'my heart; your heart; my heart.' Remember how she said that even though she was the only woman allowed to be a Dadaist, the men still ordered her around and made her make them lunch?" Charlotte sighed. "I want to do what she did."

"Make lunch for a bunch of lazy Dadaists?"

"Photomontages." Charlotte laughed with Ines. "That's the main reason I'm learning from Rainer, you know; his whole approach is so disciplined and traditional, even though I think the result is almost surreal."

"What do you think about advertising?"

Charlotte smiled an enormous smile. "Are you kidding?"

"You know," said Ines, handing Charlotte's napkin back to her, "I think it's good we found each other."

The first time they decided to meet to take pictures, Ines traveled out to Zehlendorf to the Blums' glass house. When she took in the sense of play, the nothingness of the glass against the straight lines of the steel beams, and all surrounded by that uncontrolled garden of roses, Ines whispered, "I'm going to have to think about this." Not because it was the only contemporary house in the district, or because it looked like money, but because being in it was like stumbling into a story, as if it were less surrounded by the newly mechanized world and more like a place of enchantment. "The roses," said Ines as she stood before one of the walls of glass, "they seem almost sentimental."

After the girls left the house, Ines said, "I remember going to a place near here once when my family was visiting Berlin—some sort of island of peacocks?"

"Pfaueninsel," said Charlotte. "Peacock Island. My parents used to take us there because, in 1685, Frederick William I of Brandenburg gave a chemist, Johann Kunckel, the money to build a glass factory on the island, which was then destroyed in a fire."

"You know, my parents sometimes made me recite poems," teased Ines.

Charlotte laughed. "I know, but my father has this passion for glass. Anything to do with glass, and my family has a glass foundry."

"So even though the glass factory wasn't on the island anymore, you still had to make the Glass Pilgrimage?"

"Parents."

"Mine live in Heidelberg. Professors," said Ines.

"You grew up in Heidelberg?"

"We lived in France, Italy, and New York, so I really didn't grow up anywhere. You don't think the peacocks are still there, do you?"

This is how the girls found themselves on the ferry that traveled to and from the island, thinking that the gardens, the fake ruins, and the storybook castle would provide some photographic opportunities. But more than that was the unexpressed sense of wanting to revisit the place of their childhood as a way of deepening their connection; maybe they had toured the little island during the same summer, or even the same day, without knowing it? It would be as if they had been there together, establishing a makeshift shared history without either of them thinking through why the idea of already having a past with each other was so appealing.

They arrived at the Pfaueninsel and weren't disappointed: It was as ghostly and strange as it was in their memories. The inauthentic ruins came straight from a tale with jinn and magic carpets, with the palms, and the castle. The day was overcast, providing nicely diffused photographic light, though neither girl reached for her camera.

As they stood, side by side, looking at the castle, peacocks strutting around them amid the rustle of leaves, punctuated by the occasional far-off peacock cry, Charlotte said, "Let's get out of here."

———————————

The following Tuesday, the girls stood at the edge of a small lake not far from the Pfaueninsel.

"That's not someone's house, is it?" asked Charlotte of a large, plain structure situated on the far end of the field. It was almost like a meadow, except the grass and weeds were cut very close to the ground and there was no sign of a crop of any sort. Charlotte wandered a little, only to notice another, almost identical building behind the first.

Before Ines could answer, the noise of a plane engine filled the space between them as a biplane landed nearby and rolled to a stop. Ines smiled, walking toward it. "Marlene," she said softly.

The pilot, whose attire was quickly revealed as she lifted herself out of the cockpit with practiced precision, wore, in this order: a shiny chocolate leather helmet with goggles (being torn from her face), a long matching leather jacket that ended at the hips, where Charlotte could now see a pair of what looked like knee-length shorts that were rolled once. Her legs below the shorts were bare, until the ankles, where her laced-up boots began. The pilot and Ines embraced.

"No Moka Efti today?" asked the pilot.

"Wednesdays," said Ines.

"What's Moka Efti?" asked Charlotte.

With her arm still around Ines's shoulders, the pilot pulled off one leather glove with her teeth, stuffing it in a pocket before reaching out a hand to Charlotte. "Grete Grun."

"I thought your name was . . ." said Charlotte, confused but offering her hand. Grete's grip was firm and warm.

"This is Charlotte," said Ines.

"Charlotte," Grete said. She was no longer half-embracing Ines. Instead she was leaning against the fuselage.

"Café Moka Efti," said Ines to Charlotte. "On Friedrichstrasse. I work there on Wednesday afternoons."

"Oh," said Charlotte.

Grete Grun laughed. "Your friend thinks you're a barmaid."

"I work in the back," said Ines. "With the businessmen."

Grete said, "I think you explained that beautifully, dispelling the barmaid aspect and implying a career that pays by the hour."

"Moka Efti has a room where businessmen can work and drink their coffee. They hire people like me—stenographers—to take dictation so they can claim to be working and not hanging around a café. They even have telephones on the desks in case someone calls. It's a stupid job, but the pay isn't bad."

"So are you in or out for Wannsee this weekend?" asked Grete.

"In."

"And you, Charlotte, will you be coming too?"

"Yes, Charlotte, will you be coming too?" asked Ines.

"I don't know," said Charlotte, looking to Ines.

Grete shrugged her shoulders. "If I see you I see you." To Ines she said, "Gotta get this put away before dark." Grete turned her back as she pivoted the plane in the direction of the simple structures. Airplane hangars, thought Charlotte, not houses. "Saturday, Marlene," called Grete.

"Why did she say that?" asked Charlotte as they walked to the car.

"A group of us are meeting at Wannsee on Saturday, to swim and eat and spend the night on the beach. You really should come."

"Not that—Marlene."

Ines said nothing, then, "I'll be at your house at noon on Saturday."

Giselle Weiss worked in a film lab. Neile raced cars. Maria was interested in architecture and was a student at the Bauhaus; she was very excited to meet Charlotte, being an ardent admirer of Bruno Blum's public housing projects and his work with glass. She, too, wanted to construct great monolithic buildings of glass, the passing reflections of the clouds giving the illusion of walls of sky.

And then there was Grete Grun, who was a kind of informal organizer of their modest encampment by the lake. There were two small canvas tents, folded wooden stools with canvas seats. A large hamper of food and another of drinks.

But it was Ines who brought the record player.

The girls were all about the same age as Charlotte and Ines, mid-twenties, and all from families in business (with cultural affections) or education (with cultural affections), and they all typified the media image of the New Woman, with their bobbed hair—except for blond Giselle Weiss, who wore her curly hair in two short pigtails behind her ears—and their androgynous clothing—the tailored jackets and girlish, flat-heeled shoes. They wore trousers or long shorts, much as Grete Grun had worn that day at the airfield. One of the daily papers had taken to running weekly a feature that asked *"Bub oder Mädel?"* with half a dozen head shots of Berliners the readers were to identify as boy or girl. The girls laughed about it (there was something intoxicating about thinking you could be that close to having social power), but inside they could never fully decide who was insulted more.

As permissive and decadent as those days were—exhilaratingly so—being a homosexual man was illegal. It was dangerous and made more so by the fact that there were so few arrests, making gay men less guarded and thus more at risk. There was nothing worse than thinking yourself safe when you weren't.

But the girls who liked girls were never considered criminal. Grete Grun said it was because "if you don't count, then whomever you choose to sleep with doesn't count either. By association, if you will."

In truth, it was sometimes difficult to tell all the Berlin girls—the lesbian, the androgyne, the gamine, the New Woman—apart.

As the phonograph played that day by the lake, the girls danced, arms around each other's waists, no one resting a languid hand on someone's shoulder; everyone was the Girl, and no one the Fellow, the other hands clasped. Though they laughed and clowned and sometimes exaggerated their movements (a tango, a waltz, a fox trot), there were moments of quiet, a touch, a lingering kiss.

Charlotte lay on the grass next to the beautiful Giselle Weiss, her blond pigtails undone.

Later, the girls waded into the water near the shore where a flat-bottom boat with a striped cabana and gathered curtains, with the word *Eis* in white paint on its side, sold ice cream.

"Marlene," said Grete Grun as they sat in the soft summer evening, roasting sausages over the fire, "what were the Katz twins doing with Alice last week?"

"Marlene?" asked Charlotte.

"The Katz twins," said Neile, shaking her head. "They'll sleep with anyone as long as they have a trust fund."

"The Katz twins?" asked Charlotte.

Grete Grun, the pilot with her boots and rolled shorts, placed each cooked sausage in a roll with mustard and sauerkraut before handing it round. "Vivienne and Veronika Katz," said Grete, "frequent horse, car, and air races. They dress identically in men's suits with neckties and knee boots and hats, and always seem to be in the company of a woman with money who can't decide if she likes girls or not." She licked some mustard off her fingers before handing a roll to Maria. "In this case, it's one Miss Alice Ring, who, if I'm not mistaken, seemed more than a little uncomfortable sitting between the twins."

Maria said, laughing, "It was as if she just found herself flanked by those two."

"And her pearls," said Neile, "seriously."

"Opportunists," said Ines to Charlotte. "You wouldn't like them. No girl does."

"What about Alice Ring? She likes them?"

Ines tore off a piece of the sausage roll, popped it into her mouth. "That's another kind of girl."

It was then that Charlotte finally caught on to the utterance of Marlene. It made sense: the unabashedly bisexual Marlene Dietrich. It was a gay endearment. It also made Charlotte feel just a little jealous when Ines said it or, more so, when Grete Grun said it while looking at Ines, her voice not unlike the sexy rasp of Dietrich herself.

"If only they'd stop coming to my races," said Neile.

"Neile won twice last year," said Ines.

"And crashed four times," said Maria.

"Or stop acting like a pair of party boys," continued Neile.

"Yeah, or they'll find themselves in '*Bub oder Mädel?*' in the paper." Everyone laughed.

"I dislike his work," said Ines.

The girls were lying around the campfire, long after dinner, smoking cigarettes, Neile and Grete Grun smoking a little hash.

"I don't understand how you can't like it," said Giselle Weiss. "There isn't another novelist today taking on the complexities of modern Berlin. Okay, just the description of the 1918 demonstration of the war veterans? That image of a group of young men, marching down the boulevard with their missing arms and legs and eyes, as if it was a human collage of body parts? I remember that parade and I don't remember anyone saying anything half as true about it."

"Perhaps *dislike* is the wrong word, since it indicates a reaction, when, in fact, his books leave me indifferent."

The girls were talking about a recent literary reading given by an internationally known Berlin writer at one of the big department stores. Giselle Weiss, with her aspirations to be a film editor, loved books. Her parents, like Ines's, lived in Heidelberg, where her mother was a poet and professor, and her father a psychiatrist, which, claimed Giselle, doesn't exactly make for the most involved parents. "It was like growing up with housemates," said Giselle. "Very loving housemates."

Talk then turned to movies and the recent protest against the showing of *All Quiet on the Western Front,* which Carl von Ossietzky, pacifist and editor in chief of the cultural magazine *Die Weltbühne,* called Fascism's "first victory. Today it was a film, tomorrow it will be something else." This brought the conversation back to the Great War and its casualties, which had Giselle talking again about the internationally known writer.

They talked about photography, the New Objectivism and Expressionism and how its time was now officially over, as far as Charlotte was concerned. They talked about Surrealism and collage and Hannah Höch with her photomontages of women and politics, and someone said something about John Heartfield's photomontages as well. They talked about various magazines, politics; Grete and Giselle were Communists, while Charlotte and Ines demurred and said they chose art instead, prompting Maria and Neile to say that you can't parse one from the other.

Then it was time for bed and all the girls piled into the tents, where everyone fell immediately and blissfully asleep.

Rainier Ermler had moved his class to the Bauhaus in Dessau, where Charlotte and Ines would travel twice a week. He taught them how to judge a picture from a negative and how important it was to "be the eye of the camera," a statement so simple that it was radical.

Ines made a picture of Charlotte that prompted Rainier to grunt and say, "Who knows what you'll do with your life, but you should never give up photography."

"I was actually terrified when he said that," Ines told Charlotte, "because it suddenly seemed something too enormous in my life. What if I'm good only with this one picture?"

"Then you'll be one of those people who does one thing really well," said Charlotte, tucking a curl behind Ines's ear.

"We could open a studio where I sell only that one portrait of you."

"I could take one of you. You know, just to show our range," said Charlotte.

"Is that like 'less is more'?"

"It's more like 'less is less.'"

"I love you," said Ines.

"You're a great photographer. And I'm not just saying that because I love you too." Charlotte said, "Or because I'm copying Rainier."

In 1930, when Charlotte and Ines were twenty-six and twenty-seven, respectively, Rainier Ermler made a permanent move to Dessau, and Charlotte came into a small inheritance, giving her the means to move out of her parents' house, now solely occupied by Trilby, since their parents were in the Netherlands while her father collaborated on a Dutch project with another architect.

She purchased a large studio with living quarters upstairs, close off of Friedrichstrasse, with its array of city lights. Downstairs was outfitted with the photographic equipment she purchased from Rainier Ermler.

"I want us to be partners," said Charlotte to Ines one morning over coffee.

"Is this about the minimalist, less-is-less studio?"

For the past year, the girls had been studying with Rainier Ermler, and refining their ideas about photography, not to mention falling in love in a way that made Charlotte question the difference between having a best friend and having a girlfriend, only to tell herself that all love is mutable, only the love itself the stable element. They both believed that there was no more thrilling place to be than Berlin if you were young and eager for a world that made no distinction between art and commerce.

Advertising was their passion.

"We can open a photography studio specializing in advertising and, when we need to, portraits. Functional art," said Charlotte. "We can do this."

---

kitten + kohl was the name of their studio because it was young (they were young), the profession of advertising photography was young (nearly unheard of), because *kitten* was playful (they were playful) and *kohl* sexually suggestive (in the first flush of first love it was nearly impossible not to see the world in erotic terms).

In the window, and on their business cards, they used a double self-portrait: Charlotte—dressed in a sleeveless striped shirt, wide-legged white trousers, tucked into black leather boots—reclined nearly horizontal on a very small, wooden folding stool, her hair hidden under a scarf, with a long, fake black beard, and wearing black gloves that ended above her wrists. Ines, her curls held back by a gauzy bow, wore capris and an identical striped shirt, only with a pair of pale net angel wings affixed to her shoulders; she balanced on the stool, her foot planted between Charlotte's thighs, with her other leg angled behind her in an arabesque. Charlotte's gloved hands held Ines's bare fingers while both girls looked at the lens of the camera.

All of this was set before a white wall with a small rectangular black backdrop, so there was no mistaking the location as a photography studio.

The Strongman and the Flying Something was the title of the whimsical picture that said nearly everything there was to say about the girls and their work.

The Monkey Bar was Neile's suggestion.

The same group from that first camping trip to the Wannsee (Grete and Giselle, Maria, Neile, Ines and Charlotte) had gathered to celebrate three years of kitten + kohl and the fact that the studio had just won its first prize at the Deuxième Exposition Internationale de la Photographie et du Cinéma in Brussels for one of their advertising posters. The partners had been mentioned in various graphic arts magazines for their style of clean lines and collage, along with their images of women that often conveyed what seemed at first a slightly exaggerated female depiction in the service of self-mockery, except that the astute observer couldn't miss the political commentary beneath the joke. Sometimes their models were mannequins made to look like real women and, just as often, real women were made up to resemble mannequins. It was this duality, of the image seeming to be one thing when it was also another, that drew clients to their work.

The barrage of ads—on windows, walls, posts—thrilled Charlotte. Twenty-nine years old and she had her own studio, clients, a business partner and lover who shared her vision. Or maybe Charlotte shared Ines's vision. Advertising was still so new that kitten + kohl had the opportunity not only to be a part of it but to influence it as well. The newness of the profession allowed for a lot of creative space, colliding with the embrace of the modern. kitten + kohl moved past the "monumentalizing" of the thing being sold and went quietly ironic.

They posed female mannequins tending real children, offering them cough syrup and comfort.

A model faced away from the camera, her beautiful face and figure out of view, wearing a white evening gown that pooled around the legs of the tiny table she sat upon. Her skin was white, her short hair black, matching the one arm, encased in a black opera-length glove, that held on to the seat of the chair, while she faced the wall, gazing at her own shadow. Her shadow, more compelling than facing the camera.

Long legs dominated the frame in an ad for floor tile, while miniaturized businessmen looked on in anxiety and wonder.

A white cardboard cutout of a woman (a reverse of the shadow woman) enjoyed an evening out with friends, her inanimate figure placed among the laughing, live couples as they all drank a popular wine.

kitten + kohl's work appeared to exalt the dominant view of femininity while subtly undermining it with mannequins and collages.

New was the only way for Charlotte and Ines to get in; *established* would have locked them out. This was reason enough to believe in the possibilities offered by Berlin.

With her parents, Charlotte had spent months, sometimes years in other cities—primarily London—and each place had its own delights, but no place was like Berlin, with its slippery social groups, the enormity of its postwar problems, the consistently contentious politics, and a kind of sexual infinity. She loved the way the city turned on at night, a switch flipped that illuminated another Berlin entirely. A midnight place where nothing was fixed or forbidden, so everything was permitted. And the way the rain in the streets doubled the images of the city due to the effect of the lights illustrated the reality of two Berlins. No place she had ever been seemed to thrive so well on risk.

In Charlotte and Ines's prize-winning ad, a full, red-lipsticked, disembodied mouth drew on a sleek German pipe, the smoke an ethereal cloud against a pale blue background. The lipstick clued the mouth as belonging to a woman; the pipe suggested a man. In the lower section of the picture what appeared to be a pane of glass rested at an angle, as if it were leaning against the blue background. And written on the glass, in the typography of a typewriter, were the words "This is not a pipe."

On the way to the celebration at the Monkey Bar Charlotte and Ines couldn't stop talking about how much this prize would do for their studio, how they could cut back on portraits and maybe lessen the impact of the recent economic depression. The Great Depression in Germany had actually accelerated the advertising business, along with the use of photography.

Grete Grun was already seated when Charlotte and Ines arrived, soon to be followed by Maria, Neile, Giselle Weiss, and her new boyfriend. Giselle was the only girl in their group who wasn't lesbian or bisexual ("But we love you anyway," Grete Grun said). Grete Grun jumped up from her chair when Giselle came in with her boyfriend, greeting him as if he were hers and not Giselle's.

"Well," said Giselle, laughing, "are you just happy to see us or are you trying to pass?"

Grete Grun glanced around the room before abruptly releasing Giselle's beau, then dropping back into her chair.

Each of the guests at the table then put on a black mask, tied at the back of the head and coming across the eyes and the bridge of the nose. Grete Grun had already been masked when the other girls and Giselle's boyfriend arrived.

Every patron in the room was also masked, and because they were nearly all dressed alike in evening clothes—the women sparkled, the men in tuxes—it was nearly impossible to discern who was who. Between the hidden identities and the drinking and smoking, the audience was fairly inclined toward uninhibited behavior. That the audience was largely well-off and sexually straight made the evening twice as amusing for the girls in Charlotte's group, if only because the Monkey Bar had a reputation as a lesbian bar that tolerated men and occasional adventurous tourists. A female hostess, in a beautiful blue velvet frock coat, trousers, and no shirt, her breasts exposed, wandered the floor, a rhinestone choker around her neck and a delicate jeweled riding crop in her hand. In one corner sat butch *bubis,* little gamines on their laps, near another table of women in tuxedos and horned-rimmed eyeglasses, their faces powdered white.

The girls had considered going to one of the occult clubs, with their potent mix of drugs, sex, and magic, which served, among other intoxicants, white roses that had been dipped in a mixture of chloroform and ether, from which one bit off the frozen petals, but chose their old haunt instead.

"I can't remember the last time that we were here," said Maria.

"It's been two or three years," said Ines.

"The last time I was here, they did this thing where they reenacted Greek myths, except with goddesses pursuing and deceiving and violating mortal women," said Maria, who added, "I once dated Io and Persephone."

"At least it wasn't Ceres and Persephone," said Neile of the mother and daughter goddesses. She smelled of hash and was well into her second drink.

"Yeah," said Maria. "That's another bar."

As a single blue spotlight lit a man and a woman lying on a bare mattress on the stage, Charlotte rose to go to the ladies' room, but Grete Grun, again, her eyes scanning the room, placed a hand on her arm, holding her back.

"What?" whispered Charlotte.

Grete's eyes, peering through the holes in her mask, were almost pleading.

"What is it, Grete? You haven't been you all night," said Charlotte.

"Shhh!" whispered Grete Grun.

"I'm coming back," said Charlotte, "though who wouldn't prefer spending an evening in a ladies' room?"

Grete Grun shook her head. "Stay."

The naked couple onstage caressed each other as a scratchy record gave a clinical play-by-play of the sex act.

. . . *The man stimulates the woman's nipples and clitoris in an attempt to arouse the woman as well as himself. This is known as foreplay* . . .

Ines leaned in to the two women. "Didn't this used to be a girls' bar?"

"Maybe they're in the ladies' room," said Charlotte.

"What are we talking about?" asked Maria, noticing Grete's hand on Charlotte's wrist.

"Nothing," said Grete Grun.

. . . *When the woman is sufficiently lubricated the man will insert his penis as they lie, face-to-face, in the missionary position* . . .

"Grete, I really have to—" said Charlotte. She could see Grete trying to relax, which, paradoxically, had the effect of making her seem more agitated.

. . . They reach a climax simultaneously . . .

Neile laughed. "*Mädchen*, I haven't been with a man in a long time, but I know it can't have changed that much."

"Seriously," said Ines, "who is this show for?"

It was then the group at the table realized that, with the exception of the hostess, one or two couples, and themselves, the usual girls were in rather short supply.

Giselle announced that she and her boyfriend were going to leave, that it was late, and that the news about kitten + kohl's award was fantastic, and that one would think they, as the token straight couple, should enjoy this show, but what the hell? "I don't even think my parents do it like that," she remarked, causing Maria to say, "Please don't use the word *parents*." Ines said, "Speaking of straight sex," indicating the makeup of the audience, and Charlotte said, "Maybe they should post a sign," and Maria said, pointing to the postcoital stage couple, "I think they did." Grete Grun was too distracted to comment, and Neile too loaded.

As Giselle went to kiss everyone good-bye, Grete Grun stood, saying, a little too loudly, "Of course we'll go with you. I hope you have a friend for me," to Giselle's boyfriend.

The stage couple finished *copulating* with *sighs of satisfaction*. The narration stopped for a second, with only the sound of the scratching record, before the final words: *Heil, Hitler!* as the girls followed Grete Grun, who was hurrying after Giselle and her boyfriend. Neile swallowed the rest of her drink and the remains of the other drinks on the table. As she trailed behind the group now crossing to the door, she bumped into the table of two couples who seemed like well-to-do young marrieds. As Neile went to apologize, she held the edge of their table and she put her face close to one of the wives, but instead of saying anything, she kissed the young wife full on the mouth.

"What's wrong with you?" demanded Grete Grun, who had turned around in time to see the kiss. The girls, sans Giselle and her beau, were crowded into a cab, heading back to Charlotte's studio. Everyone had left her mask on the table except for Grete.

"Me?" asked Neile. "Nothing. Nothing at all." She stared out the window.

No one said anything. It had been nearly a month since Neile had been banned from racing cars. At the time she said she didn't know if it was because she was Jewish, female, or gay, with everyone half hoping it was because she was female—female being the preferable prejudice—though no one believed it.

As the cab moved down nighttime Friedrichstrasse, Charlotte thought about how much she loved Berlin. All the parties, and the nights when she and her friends would migrate from cafés and bars to the apartments of other friends, to country places and the lake, and how beautiful it was to go boating in the moonlight. These days it often seemed that everything in postrevolution Germany was up for grabs. It was riding out the good in post-Kaiser Germany—progressive policies like the eight-hour workday, trade unions, health insurance, the Bauhaus, the New Woman—with the bad—the dance of various political groups like the Communists, the Catholic Center Party, the Socialist Democratic Party, the German Democratic Party, the capitalists, the nobles; a slight increase in street violence; the Nazi speeches that were becoming more common. And the sexual variety, which was both good and bad, depending.

Charlotte knew that she should be afraid, but she wasn't; politics was politics, and, in truth, this flux inspired her. She was in the thick of a life she never could've had before the war, no matter how progressive her parents.

Then there were times when she thought maybe it was love that made everything burn so bright.

And then Maria reached over to untie Grete's mask.

When the streetlights illuminated Grete's face, no one was sure at first that the terrible bruise surrounding one eye, a smaller one on the inside of the other eye, along with the swelling at the bridge of her nose, weren't a series of shadows. But all the girls responding at once (a sharp intake of breath, a soft "Jesus Christ") confirmed that what they were seeing was what they were seeing.

"I had just walked into the hangar when I saw Michael and Hans doing something around my plane," Grete Grun told the girls when they arrived at the studio, ignoring the glass of water Ines had given her.

"Michael and Hans?" asked Maria.

"Sons of the caretaker of the airfield, who is also the mechanic. I didn't think much of it—I've know those boys since they were little, when I used to let them sit in the cockpit, sometimes take them up for rides. They're maybe fifteen or sixteen now. And I didn't think much of anything."

"You said that," said Maria gently.

"I did. But there was something different. It was the way they reacted to my coming into the shed. Like they had been caught.

"So I told them that they weren't to touch my plane when I wasn't around, and Michael, the older boy, came up to me and said, Who was I to tell him what he could and could not do? It wasn't until that moment that I realized I hadn't seen them around very much lately . . . You know, I didn't realize how much taller he was than I. He came very close to me and said quietly that I was a Jewish swine and a man—he knew I wasn't a 'natural woman'—and so he thought it was time that I took it like a man."

"You're not even Jewish," said Charlotte.

"What was the other kid doing?" asked Neile.

"Watching."

It was almost as unnerving to imagine Grete intimidated as it was to hear the menace of these boys, the way they thought they could bully her and the fact that the bullying came to them so easily, so naturally. Charlotte could not imagine Grete without her swagger.

"So I said, 'If I'm a man, then "giving it to me," as you say, makes you a poof.'

"Then the next thing I knew I was on the ground, my face almost numb from the blow." Grete Grun started sobbing. "I refuse to be scared," she said, then quietly added, "There was no warning."

"My God," said Ines.

"I said his name. 'Michael,' I said, 'you know me.' It affected him enough that he hesitated. In the stillness, the door opened and in walked a pair of Nazis. 'What's this?' they said, maybe not knowing I was a woman at first but helping me up anyway.

"I said it was nothing, a misunderstanding. Nobody moved. Then they walked to just outside the door, where they were waiting for a pilot friend of theirs."

Looking at the girls, Charlotte could see the anger and fear in their faces and bodies. A tension had so tightened up every muscle that Charlotte felt as if she might go faint with the stress of it, the enveloping rage of it, the breathtaking terror of it.

"Those boys," said Grete Grun, now composed, with a voice kissed by wonder, "acted as though nothing had happened. As if time had rewound."

When Grete left that night, she forgot her leather gloves, her lucky flying gloves, as she called them. When Charlotte and Ines called to tell her, she said, "Keep them."

They had never known her to fly without them, they said. To which she replied that all the gloves in the world couldn't keep her safe as long as her plane was housed at that airfield, and wasn't that precisely the point?

———————————

Charlotte and Ines didn't feel it too much at first, aside from the directive to deal only with Jewish businesses, which they mostly had done anyway. Then Giselle Weiss was fired from her job at the film lab, where she was informed that she would no longer be "taking" employment from "good" German men. She said, "When people start identifying some people as 'good,' you just know that 'bad' as a designation is coming right up." There was the burning of the Reichstag, with the Nazis blaming the

Communists, then using the incident as a way to justify book burning and other demonstrations and repressions. As Bruno Blum said of the Reichstag destruction, "Communists? No, you must look at who profits from the incident."

A brick through the window of kitten + kohl; someone calling Maria a Jewish whore as she boarded a train to Berlin from Dessau, almost daring her to try to sit in an empty seat. There were the gay men Charlotte and Ines knew from the Bauhaus and the neighborhood and the advertising companies, who quickly butched up, taking seriously for the first time the antihomosexual laws that had seldom been enforced before January 1933.

Some Jews remained in civil servant positions, along with some in the private sector, even though wives were begging husbands to consider leaving Germany. The husbands said, No, we're German. Our love for the poetry and music and beauty of Germany is inside us. And the wives said, I have to find a store that will sell groceries to me. Sometimes I spend all morning searching. And the husbands said, We're war veterans. We all fought, side by side, for the same country. And the wives said, The teachers make our children sit apart from the other children. And the husbands said, After the war, no one had any money and we all suffered, side by side. (One internationally known Jewish shipping magnate opened his own personally financed soup kitchen to feed impoverished Berliners, crushed under the demand for war reparations.) And the wives said, They humiliate your children. And the husbands said, You make it sound as if we are hated.

And the wives said nothing.

Charlotte's father and mother were still in the Netherlands when, on a day in July, she ran into her former classmate Ignacio Martín. They had first met when Charlotte was commuting to Dessau to study with Rainier Ermler. Like Charlotte and Ines's friend Maria, Ignacio was interested in architecture as well as glass work, though he lacked the religious zeal of Bruno Blum.

Through glass Ignacio Martín and Charlotte Blum became friends. They were close enough to enjoy animated, unguarded conversations when they would run into each other at the Bauhaus, or have coffee or lunch or take in a film. On occasion, Ignacio had supper at the Blums' when Charlotte's parents were in town and Bruno invited him.

Charlotte liked talking to Ignacio because conversation with him was so much less one-sided than it was with some of the men at the Bauhaus, even the ones who wanted to impress her enough to get close to her father. She thought maybe it was because Ignacio was from Argentina, and not Germany, making her think that she would like one day to see the country that had produced someone like him.

On that July day in 1933, Ignacio ran into Charlotte near the train station in Potsdamer Platz and said, "It's awful."

Charlotte could feel a freeze in her chest. By now everyone knew someone who had been sent to a camp (the ones who came back barely "came back" at all), so naturally her mind went to the worst place possible even as she tried to tell herself whatever she hadn't heard about couldn't be that bad or she wouldn't be hearing about it now, casually, on the street, from a sometime friend like Ignacio Martín.

"The Bauhaus," he said.

In April the Nazis had raided the Bauhaus, arresting students, confiscating what they called "incriminating material." Nearly everyone had been released in short order; it was harassment and nothing more, Ines said, though it was enough for Rainier Ermler to accept a permanent position at a Chicago university.

"They're just looking for something to do," said Charlotte to Ignacio, breathing a little easier.

"It's over," he said.

She slowly took him in her arms, there outside the train station in the busiest platz in the city, where five streets converge among the office buildings, department stores, cafés, restaurants, and news shops. There where the streets were mobbed with passersby, newspaper and flower vendors, strolling couples, nobles, capitalists, students, and working girls. There where the trams, buses, automobiles, horse carts, bicycles, trucks, and motor scooters raced in crazy disarray. Amid all this, Charlotte held Ignacio as he wept.

---

kitten + kohl shot an advertisement for face powder, the silver compact held in the empty fingers of Grete's beat-up leather gloves. Charlotte made a series of still lifes with flowers and milkweed; then she made a picture with ivy branches lying on a table, along with a seashell, a scattering of blouse buttons, two camera filters, two protractors, and a woman's hand mirror that held Ines's reflection. *My heart; your heart; my heart.*

Charlotte and Ines produced a series of pictures, *The Strongman and the Flying Something*, the two girls in their striped, sleeveless T-shirts; Ines in her wings, Charlotte in her black boots. They posed side by side; they sat in a prop rowboat and pretended to be rowing; they drew fake tattoos on their upper arms; they pretended to sleep on the floor in the sun flooding in through the window.

Hannah Höch was scheduled to have a retrospective at the Bauhaus in Dessau. Charlotte and Ines looked forward to the show and to meeting Hannah with all the enthusiasm and elation of being in the same room with someone whom you can hardly believe exists, you love her work so absolutely.

Only this was in July. Only this was in the New Germany, the one that had shut down the Bauhaus forever with all of Höch's fabulous images still leaning against the walls, waiting for all the people who would never see them.

"I don't know what I was thinking," said Maria, "even after the arrests in April, even when you still tell yourself that life will go on because life always goes on."

Charlotte and Ines were eating a picnic dinner with Maria in the Tiergarten as brave squirrels edged ever closer for a handout. Maria absentmindedly threw them pieces of her sandwich.

Neile was drinking too much these days, with rumors of opium balls and morphine vials, holed up in her Grunewald house. When Grete Grun went to check on her plane two weeks after the incident with the caretaker's sons, this time accompanied by Giselle's boyfriend, she saw that it had been defaced with antilesbian graffiti and Stars of David, along with more epithets. It didn't matter that she wasn't Jewish; in the New Germany it was the company she kept and the girls she loved. The propeller was missing, and someone had used the fuselage for target practice. Without packing she went straight to the train station and bought a ticket for Switzerland, a place where she said they didn't even speak "real German" but the people were nice, if a little dull, and she had met someone.

Giselle's non-Jewish boyfriend wanted to marry her, but Giselle said that marrying a Jewish girl might not be the wisest decision just now, and he said she was being overly cautious, not all Germans felt as the Nazis did, and it was too late anyway because her fate was his fate. Maria didn't have the money to leave, so she decided to hope for the best. She spent the better part of each day sketching houses she wanted to build and looking for work, even though she had recently had a job starring in a movie called *A Sunday in Berlin,* which followed two couples on what was meant to seem a usual Sunday, on which the couples have breakfast, go to the lake, sail on two tiny boats, fall asleep in the sun. Then, one of the girls wakes to find her boyfriend gone. She looks around their deserted beach area, until she hears a noise in the tall grass and stumbles upon the other girl, played by Maria, naked and engaged with the other girl's boyfriend. The first girl can't decide if she wants her presence known or if she should just return to the beach, prepare dinner, and act as if nothing has happened.

When the first girl returns to the beach, having decided on invisibility, the boyfriend of the girl played by Maria comes back from swimming to an early dinner of potato salad and schnitzel and wine. He asks her why she seems so sad. She says, "Because it was such a perfect day and now it's over."

Not all the neighbors were menacing, but it took only one. It took only a single neighbor, someone the girls had had no problems with during their time there, to begin to take an interest in kitten + kohl. The neighbor asked about the square footage of the studio, and how many bedrooms did it have, and it appeared the back of the building received a good amount of sun, or were there trees or other buildings obstructing it? Was it quiet? How was the hot water? The heat? A fireplace perhaps? And a garden, was there a garden? Overgrown or kept?

There was the day they returned to a kicked-in front door. Alarmed, though it was only late afternoon, the girls cautiously went inside. Nothing was missing. They pushed furniture up against the door until the locksmith came by, paying him double and agreeing that he could come after dark, so no one would see him doing anything for a Jew.

Their neighbor came by the day after the door incident. "Someone's temper getting the better of them?" he joked.

And then they knew. They knew that even the most neutral neighbors would be tempted to take what they had not even thought to covet until recent events had made them understand that possession was nine-tenths of a law that favored *them*. It was not uncommon for someone to show interest in your jewelry, your home, your job, your painting, maybe even your wife—it was as if the temptation was too much, the possibilities of possession too great to pass up. If you were Jewish, you began to spend all your time trying to go unnoticed. Or making your winter coat go unnoticed. Or your car, your garden. It was nearly impossible to have things and hide them at the same time. How could anyone fight what a Jew now represented to many Germans? It was as if they were walking catalogs of splendid goods and real estate and business and career openings. The trick was to disappear without disappearing.

And when Charlotte said to Ines, "I have relatives in London. We can pack it all up and move our studio. Just until everything gets sorted out," Ines agreed.

––––––––––––––––––––

"They can't make you go back there ["there" being Germany]. Who are you hurting by staying here? What space are you taking? What difference can one person make to them ["them" being the English]?" cried Charlotte.

Ines laughed a rueful little laugh. "It seems the entire equilibrium of the Empire rests on my residency."

It was 1934, almost 1935, and Charlotte and Ines had been living and working in London, making portraits of literary figures, film stars, and people with money who were fairly open-minded in their ideas about photography. Advertising jobs were few and far between and often consisted of working with hospitals or other public service professionals, none of whom were very interested in anything visually groundbreaking. Though their style and the client seldom made for a sympathetic matchup, they could make ends meet by cobbling together work in addition to the small monthly stipend from Charlotte's trust fund, the same one that had paid for Rainier Ermler's equipment in what now seemed ages ago.

"You know I've run out of visa options," said Ines. "I don't have family here. I don't have a history."

It was true that her extended family, and the years Charlotte had spent during her childhood in London, not to mention her money and career, had all made for an easy transition to this new country. Since it was growing evident that the casual cruelty of Berlin was becoming policy if you were Jewish, Communist, intellectual, or homosexual—and woe to the person who was all four—Germans who could leave were trying to leave.

But even as Germany demanded the exile of all of the above, it would allow them to take no property (so much of which had been confiscated or looted anyway) and almost no money. Countries like the United States and England were not interested in "penniless immigrants," falling back on the "immigration laws already in place that you cannot expect us to disregard." France was not much better.

Because Charlotte had left early enough to take her belongings and bank account with her, she was able to build something of a life in London. But she could not change the legal fact of Ines not being her family. They could not marry. How could England expect her to send Ines Wolff back to a place that hated her, would deny her a living, and was likely to ship her to a work camp?

As the days counted down, Charlotte had to stop herself from shoving all those safe and self-satisfied Brits off the sidewalks and into the gutters. She told herself that she never wanted to live in this country in the first place, but the truth is that she didn't want to live anywhere without Ines.

———

After Charlotte and Ines fell in love, Ines took a photograph of Charlotte applying lipstick, her eyes following her own reflection in the mirror, the fingers of her right hand lightly pressed against the glass; the ordinary moment that reveals the extraordinary. It's the smallness of life that quickens the heart. It's grocery shopping. It's picking up the laundry and repeating an overheard conversation or reporting on someone's hair, or clothing, who sat next to you in a café, or on a bus, knowing that you both see the hair, the clothing, the overheard conversation with the same lightness of life. So when Ines said of the photograph, "This isn't how I love you best, but it is how I love you," Charlotte knew what she meant. This mutual act of Ines taking the snapshot made Charlotte love Ines in much the same way that Ines loved the snapshot itself. Capturing the commonplace, the unremarked upon routine. *My heart; your heart; my heart.* Ines took the picture to Trilby at the Blum GlasWerks and asked him to fashion a glass cube, roughly the size of an ice cube, and place the little portrait inside.

———

The ship's captain was more than happy to marry Charlotte Blum and Ignacio Martín as they crossed the Atlantic on their way to Buenos Aires. "Everyone's a romantic," said Ignacio.

Ignacio Martín had been traveling through London on his way to his home. Once the Bauhaus closed, he remained in Berlin, waiting to see, hoping to see, if the school would relocate again. When it didn't, he decided to travel to Zurich, then Paris to see the Maison de Verre, a beautiful industrial house of glass by Chareau, Bijvoet, and Dalbet, a furniture and interior designer, architect, and metal worker, respectively. The tall house, with its glass blocks, moving screens, metal framework, had only been completed in 1932; when he visited it three years later, it was everything that Ignacio believed a house should be.

In London, he arrived at Charlotte's studio.

"Ignacio!" she cried, hugging him, thrilled at the pure joy of him, especially in the wake of Ines's departure. They walked and talked and ate lunch and dinner together. Then they talked some more. They went to gardens and parks and strolled along the Thames. They went to museums, studied statues and paintings in the spaces of silence in their ongoing conversation.

"You were right to leave Berlin," said Ignacio, which didn't make Charlotte miss it any less (her Berlin, not the existing Berlin). Nor did it make her any less anxious about Trilby, though she would tell herself that, because the Blum house was a short train ride from the city center, no one would notice it, meaning no one would notice him. No one would covet their beautiful glass house, so at odds with Nazi traditionalism, or Blum GlasWerks—how big was the factory really? Her parents were panicked over their boy, yet they comforted themselves by saying, The glassworks would be impossible to sell, and how devastating it would be to walk away from it in any case. No matter that walking away, as a rich man or a poor man (read rich Jew or poor Jew), had become increasingly difficult. It was unthinkable for them to admit that Trilby might not be able to get out at all, so it was better to think of everything in terms of the fate of the Blum GlasWerks, and not the fate of their son.

Charlotte was telling Ignacio that he wasn't the first old friend to come through the city, and how she and Ines made portraits of immigrants (often writers and architects) when he asked, "How is Ines?"

"Gone," said Charlotte.

He said nothing. Then, "Will you stay?"

She thought of how British immigration, along with the very slight influence of Bruno Blum, had taken scant pity on Ines, allowing her to emigrate to Palestine. When she secured passage on a ship, there was no suggestion of Charlotte coming along, since Charlotte's emigration would mean more red tape, more liquidation of assets, and leaving Mr. and Mrs. Blum, who were already struggling with the reality of Trilby being back in Berlin.

"I suppose," she said.

He talked about his home in Argentina (she too longed for home), extolling all the wonders of the place, ending with "I leave on Thursday." He kissed her. Then he spent the night, because suddenly the thought of Ignacio leaving was unbearable.

During her last hours in England, Ines had watched Charlotte from the ship's deck. The girls did not wave, only stood very still, gazing at each other. Charlotte recalled the experience of Ines's reading the denial of her visa request in England, and the sheer will it took to secure a visa for Palestine; the days leading up to Ines's departure, which were filled with the studio chores of making ads, cropping images, developing prints, taking photos (grateful for the gray light of London). The joke of calling each other "wife." Their memories were ordinary—there was no cinematic quality to their love affair of friendship, affection, passion, and an artistic sympathy that allowed them to see the world in ways that each other understood. Who would understand Ines now? Who would know Charlotte?

A last memory of Ines in her navy blue wool coat and tousled curls, a rhinestone pin played against the tailored coat, the men's-style white shirt and trousers as she smiled that first smile at Charlotte, who stood in the department store window in Berlin.

On the Tuesday before the Thursday when Ignacio Martin was setting sail for Buenos Aires, Charlotte walked out on a girl whose portrait she was taking. She returned her fee to the surprised parents, then gathered her things and called Ignacio.

———————————

He suggested marriage because it would simplify their lives. And because, he said, he was in love with her.

"This isn't a sailor-at-sea kind of love, is it?" she said.

"Is that a problem?"

She laughed.

"I don't expect you to be a wife. I expect you to be, well, you."

Later, she would say that maybe it was the sea air and feeling the disconnection that one feels in the middle of a lengthy ocean passage, with no land in sight, no way to fix your location, that led her to say yes.

———————————

Ignacio Martin's family were *porteño*. They were a lively, intellectually restless bunch, looking, examining, questioning, and telling. There was no shortage of opinions, or tenderness. Ignacio's father caressed the bearded cheek of the grown-up Ignacio as if he were still a boy. All the men kissed their children, as if time could not alter adult affection. The women held hands, sometimes as they strolled, sometimes when they were sitting near each other. All of this touching was easy and unforced and not too much, but more than Charlotte was accustomed to seeing in Germany.

"My family is mostly Italian," said Ignacio. "Most of Buenos Aires is of Italian or Spanish descent. We can't help it," he said, laughing, "we're lovers, not fighters."

She liked the easy manner of his family, their easy acceptance of her; she liked the intellectual clamor. It made her miss her own warm-hearted, smart family.

On a piece of land not too far from the city center, Ignacio designed a glass box house for them. Twenty-foot ceilings, matching studios, a sky bridge and rooftop terrace. He constructed a center courtyard—a mixing of traditional with the new—that had a spectacular garden and bathing fountain. The newspapers wrote about this "prodigal son architect" who "spent his time in Germany mastering the art of the office building" and has now "moved into one." It was hard not to notice that sharp contrast between slow, sunny, romantically traditional Buenos Aires (as Catholic as Berlin was Christian and Jewish, and not too devout on any front) and the cosmopolitan, morally fluid, glittering Berlin, its glitter diamond-hard.

These differences expanded to a dismissal of Charlotte's photographic style as well: Her portraits were thought to be too direct, too unsparing, her critics missing the obvious (she thought) beauty in the unadorned, unable to see how realism can be so precise as to seem almost surreal. For Charlotte, Ines, and Ignacio, the tension in their art was often located in that place between the actual and the dream.

The paradox of Charlotte's life was having the time and support to make the pictures she wanted to make but no place to show them. Nor did she have a clientele receptive to them. It seemed the *porteño* (and the Argentine in general), as she had been told more than once, preferred work that was a bit less demanding. Couldn't they agree on what was beautiful? Surely that was a universal; a sentiment that wasn't entirely encouraging.

Ignacio found a job with an architecture firm that made municipal buildings, hoping for eventual commissions for public housing. He said, "Change must begin somewhere," and one of the partners did seem to like him.

Charlotte found herself making little photomontages, or walking the city, studying the handbills, billboards, and other advertising, which she found provincial and uninspiring. In the midst of a mild spring day, while inhaling the scent of flowers from window boxes, she would dream of snow. The sound of traffic would suddenly intensify in her memory as she saw herself immersed in the surging crowds of Potsdamer Platz, the smell of car exhaust, the grind of trolley wheels, the bus and car horns, the deep buzz of motor scooters. At night, she would see the starlight of an Argentine sky melt into the reflections of city lights on wet, Berliner streets.

Sometimes her waking dreams of Berlin gave way to nighttime rendezvous with friends and family and Ines, Ines often enough to prevent her heart from healing but not so frequently that Charlotte couldn't find a kind of contentment and pleasure in her new life. Ignacio was a good man. He liked her as much as he loved her and lived without the expectation that she would be an Argentine wife. It was common enough, Charlotte thought, the middle-class wife with her maid and her children, willful ignorance of the mistress, her bridge and her secret boredom. And the ones who weren't bored were a brittle bunch who cared too much and pushed too hard to hang on to the life they had. The difference between Buenos Aires and Berlin was the Church, which dictated to these wives, seeming to pick up where their husbands' demands of feminine behavior left off.

On the other hand, Charlotte was mesmerized by the icons and art of the Church; whether opulent or plain, it was all tears and blood and gold and silver. Stars and stained glass and saints whose various tortured deaths bordered on the pornographic. The processions, with their carried statues, and penitents on their bare knees, sometimes dragging chains, were like grand street theater. "You are not supposed to enjoy it in that way," Ignacio said.

"Oh," said Charlotte, nudging him. "But I am supposed to enjoy it?"

And confession seemed to her the best invention of all. Sin on Saturday, repent on Sunday. Debauch then fast; demand then beg. It was a faith of extremes.

All in all the days ran apace until Charlotte got a letter from Ines. *My exile has ended! Will be arriving in London three weeks. Wish you were there. Ines.*

Ignacio wasn't entirely happy about Charlotte's plan to sail to London to visit Ines, but he wouldn't think to tell her that she couldn't go because he loved her. "But I'll be back," said Charlotte, to which he replied, "Yes, but it's the part before you get back that I'm not looking forward to." "Then it will make the part where I return so much better," she said.

She touched his cheek. "Is that your brave smile?" she said. And he said, "I know that Ines is your friend."

He gave her a gruff, affectionate kiss at the dock, then waved good-bye.

If someone asked Charlotte if 1937 London was different from 1936 London, she would say, "Not really, except that it was alive and beautiful again because Ines was there."

"You look different," said Ines.

"Perhaps it's the Argentine effect. Do I seem languorous?"

"Maybe. Whatever it is, it's working for you."

"The crossing didn't exactly agree with me—I was either sleeping or throwing up. I couldn't quite get my sea legs, I guess."

And when Ines asked, as they embraced, "Would Argentina make you feel different too? Charlotte?"

Because all color had drained from Charlotte's face just before she raced over to vomit into the bathroom sink.

Charlotte's daughter, Barrie, was born in London, five months after Charlotte arrived. At first Charlotte had ascribed her nausea to a rough passage, then the loss of her period to upheavals personal and political in nature, as well as to the rigors of travel. But in the end, a doctor said that it wasn't flu, or travel, or the seismic shifts of her worlds (interior and exterior): it was simply pregnancy.

The first letter she received after she wired Ignacio was joyful: *I can't believe our good luck!* The second, arriving two weeks later, was confused: *When did you say you're returning?* And the third was an example of lost patience: *You are my wife. That is our child. We all belong together.*

Charlotte deflected Ignacio's requests for her return by saying that the pregnancy had progressed to the point where she couldn't stand the thought of being tossed around at sea, since she was now "seasick" all the time. She also was "pregnancy clumsy," as she called it. These statements were true.

What her letters left out was her happiness with Ines. She neglected to mention that she had reopened her old studio—her equipment exactly as she had left it the day she walked out, almost two years prior. And she said nothing about her and Ines contacting old clients and pursuing new ones.

They had fewer émigrés than before, having heard that the Nazis were making it impossible to stay but also impossible to go. A Jew was permitted to deal only with other Jews—except there were no Jewish-owned businesses anymore. On the fashionable Kurfurstendamm, signs everywhere blocked Jews from entering. One émigré told them that all you saw, on every door, every window was "JewJewJewJew. Like it's one long refrain, this 'Jew' that appears everywhere. I can live without the luxuries," said the émigré, "but not without bread and meat and coal."

They were told that in Berlin all Jews had to add "Israel" or "Sarah" to their names. Stars lost all their meaning of dreams and aspirations when affixed to clothing.

Jews were being told not to bother looking for apartments. Possessions were sold for nothing, and even those who could get permission to leave were not allowed to depart with any money, guaranteeing their impoverishment and being turned back by various countries. It was a desperate, confusing state of affairs to be so unwanted and so unable to go.

Ignacio was getting impatient. Barrie was three months old, and he wanted his daughter and his wife home, with him. Charlotte and Ines had fallen back into their easy "wife" routine, now expanded as a small family. Charlotte's life was doubled as a legal, conventional wife and an emotional, unrecognized "wife."

Bruno and Marcelle Blum were in Toronto, having left London just as Charlotte arrived. Though her parents said nothing about Charlotte returning to her husband, she knew them well enough to know that this omission was their way of saying Ignacio was her husband; he was Barrie's father. Their empathy for Ignacio ran high in light of their separation from their son, daughter, and now granddaughter. So many families they knew were being involuntarily torn apart.

The tension of living day to day without making any sorts of long-range plans wore on the young women. Charlotte and Ines pulled a little away from each other in anticipation of Charlotte's inevitable, they thought, but did not voice aloud, departure. They really weren't each other's wives; they would never be seen as a family. Words like *wife, family,* and *mommy* would always be in quotes for them, and they knew it.

Charlotte thought about the meaning of *wife*; she thought about the brokenness of her life without Ines. She thought about Ignacio, and she thought about Barrie's little smile, which looked nothing like Ines's or Charlotte's.

———————

On an otherwise unremarkable day in November 1938, Charlotte and Ines received word of *Kristallnacht*, the Night of Broken Glass. Synagogues looted and burned; homes looted and burned; women and children brutalized. Countless Jewish men sent to camps, tortured and killed. The entire city smashed to shards of jagged and crushed glass. Someone neglected to tell the thugs who demolished the Blum Glas-Werks that it was no longer a Jewish-owned business; it had been owned by Aryans for over a year. They were idiots destroying their own property.

Charlotte remembered her brother's office, previously her uncle's office, and the fragile glass models of houses and windows and sculptures. She thought of the little glass ice cube with her portrait, taken by Ines, one of the only things she had brought to her Buenos Aires studio.

Charlotte thought about her father and his passion for glass, his belief that glass was the way to utopia, the best possible world for all men, the spiritual possibilities of glass. The Glass Chain. Bruno Blum and the other architects would never think of the glass chain again without hearing it shatter. The smashing of the Blum GlasWerks. The smashing of the family's glass house. Charlotte covered her face with her hands as she stood in her London studio, whispering, "Trilby."

———————

218

And then it was time to go.

This time it was Charlotte who stood on the ship's deck, holding little Barrie in her arms, gazing down at Ines. This time Ines and Charlotte didn't watch each other, not daring to move; this time Ines, on the dock, mugged for Charlotte. She blew kisses, threw her arms wide, then settled her hands back over her heart in romantic exaggeration. She fluttered her eyes, waved wildly, mouthing the words "Don't forget me."

Charlotte watched her lover's antics with amusement; Ines had always been the more expressive of the two girls. She's the one who should be living in Argentina, thought Charlotte.

When the ship pulled away from the dock, Charlotte stood there, watching Ines grow smaller and smaller until she was lost in the crowd.

There was relief in knowing that Ines made it to America. London no longer felt like a refuge; Europe felt precarious enough for Charlotte to book passage back to Buenos Aires and for Ines to marry a young New Yorker she had known for six months. When Ines arrived in the States, she picked up her camera and began taking portraits and art shots, making a small living but a living nonetheless. She no longer shot advertisements. *My heart is not in it*, she wrote to Charlotte, though she didn't have to say as much.

The war came and still no word of Trilby Blum. Charlotte's parents stayed in Toronto and their relatives in England weathered the Blitz. It was strange being in another country because you could no longer stay in your own. Hannah Arendt wrote that it isn't enough to enter a new country and willingly and happily take on its nationality, because you will never be French, or Swiss, or English, or Czech, you'll only ever be a Jew. Patriotism, you learn, isn't an option. She said of Hitler that no one wanted to know that these times had formed a "new kind of human being," found in concentration camps, and in internment camps—sent to each by enemies (the former) and friends (the latter).

Persecution erased all the differences of nationality, social class, religious or secular beliefs. Your social alignment was no longer your own;

you became Them. And immigration wiped away your professional identity. If you can't practice law, are you a lawyer? To go from "somebody" to "nobody" takes its toll.

Somebody who, at a very young age, had her own photography studio, kitten + kohl; somebody who made avant-garde advertisements and won a prize; somebody who had friends who worked in films, flew planes, and raced cars; somebody who fell in love, lost that love, regained it, then had to surrender it. Somebody whose famous father believed so absolutely in the spiritual and utopian properties of living in glass that he began an ongoing epistolary conversation called the Glass Chain among ten brilliant, like-minded men.

Steady yourself.

Then break the chain.

Charlotte stepped onto the dock in the sunlight of Buenos Aires's January summer, still a little disconcerted by the reversal of seasons. The jacarandas were in full bloom, dropping their papery purple blossoms all over the sidewalks to be crushed underfoot, often attached to the soles of shoes.

Charlotte used her time at sea getting over Ines, trying to reconnect to the life around her. Little Barrie forced her to move outside of herself and her sadness, except for the nights when she was unable to stop thinking. Then she arrived in Buenos Aires, Ignacio meeting them at the dock, his smile meaning even more to her now that it was reproduced in the loved face of their daughter. Their mirrored smiles made Charlotte reconsider (again) being a wife and mother.

In the three months that she had been back, the only times Charlotte picked up her Rolleiflex was to take the infrequent picture of Barrie, sometimes Ignacio with Barrie; the two were like a mutual admiration society, which pleased Charlotte more than it gave her feelings of exclusion.

She cooked, oversaw the maid who cleaned the house. She made a halfhearted stab at gardening before hiring someone for that too. All around her she saw untaken pictures, which still didn't move her to pick up her camera. Ignacio rather liked Charlotte's devotion to their family; though he didn't say it, she could tell. There was a shadow of formality between them now, a bit of distance that she tried to bridge by supporting his work, and spending her energy being domestic. In this way they were almost normal by Argentine standards. No one seemed to notice that she wasn't making pictures anymore.

If anyone had, she would've told them that she'd lost her voice. She was so derailed by news of the war, her friend Maria's death (she never got to build her houses), and the imprisonment of Giselle Weiss (who was Jewish) and her husband (who wasn't). She heard a rumor that mentioned a baby; Charlotte hoped it was just a rumor.

Still no word of Trilby.

Ines wrote that she liked New York because it was so eager to please and guileless. *Charlotte,* she said, *we would be great here.*

In 1948, with the war behind the world (Trilby living in Zurich with Bruno and Marcelle Blum, too broken by his years at Dachau to live alone), Argentina had become the unlikely destination for Germans. Charlotte imagined that most expatriates, upon hearing their native language, sought out the speaker, just to talk to someone with a shared knowledge of a lost place. Not so in Argentina, where the German voice could be Jewish or it could be Nazi, and so the expats lived side by side as if the other didn't exist at all.

Charlotte still wasn't seriously taking pictures, even though Barrie was getting older and more independent. What no one tells you about having children is that it isn't the physical demand they make in your life that affects your art, it's the emotional space they fill, crowding out your art. So even when you have the time to work, you're still mentally occupied.

She referred to herself as the Dilettante, something that she could see irritated Ignacio, who said it was just a way of feeling sorry for herself.

"You have everything," she would say. "A career you want, a child, a wife. I think we can all agree that I am the Perfect Wife."

"No," said Ignacio, before storming from the room, "you're the Dilettante."

———————————————

A dinner party at Ignacio and Charlotte's could include architects, a magazine editor, two college professors, and all their wives, along with one professor who had a wife and mistress in attendance, though one knew about the other while the other remained in ignorance. Charlotte liked these parties made up of colleagues and intellectuals, people they knew mostly through Ignacio. Some were people he had known in school; others he'd met professionally. The women always ended up together near the kitchen, even when none of them were cooking. And no matter if they had professions of their own, it was always understood that their careers came second. No one questioned this arrangement, not even the women.

When they were together one-on-one, or if there was enough wine and the men were out of earshot, the conversation made enough turns to arrive at locations of discontent. This, it must be said, didn't mean that a wife didn't love her husband, especially since some of their husbands (and lovers, as it sometimes happened) were far more broad-minded than society at large. Then again, these were the sorts of men who would be drawn to women who wanted more than domesticity even when they made no significant move to change the status quo.

Then everyone would thank the Martíns for a lovely evening and life would continue accordingly.

Charlotte wasn't unhappy with Ignacio, and their arguments were infrequent. Then one night she dreamt about Ines; it wasn't only the particulars but also the quality of the dream. They were in Berlin, before the war, surrounded by Neile, Grete Grun, Giselle Weiss, and Maria at the Wannsee. The sunlight hit the water of the lake. Then they were in New York, and Charlotte had been living there for months.

When Charlotte woke up she was crying.

And all because she had received a letter from Ines that said, Charlotte, *we would be great here.*

Charlotte sent a letter to Ines while she was out shopping for the dinner party that night, that read, *Anything is better than this lonely fate. I love you and I miss you and I'm leaving him.*

On this particular night, her decision to leave had the effect of making her more relaxed than she had been in years, and also more energized by happiness. What was the point of surviving Germany if it was to settle for a life marked by an absence? Barrie was old enough to spend summers with Ignacio, and she would love New York; the Martins were lucky enough to have an adaptable, curious child who enjoyed novelty.

It was in the spirit of the relief (and anticipation) of her decision that, when the magazine editor casually asked to see some of Charlotte's pictures she took him to her studio, where he quietly studied the kitten + kohl work—portraits and advertisements, some photomontages—as well as some of what they had made in London.

"How old were you?" asked the editor.

"A mere child," said Charlotte.

"And the other photographer?"

"Also a child."

"This work," he said, "it's new, I think, and exciting."

As they returned to the party, the editor said, "May I call on you next week? I have an idea that I've been wanting to do for some time, and you may be just the person I've been looking for."

Charlotte agreed to meet, since she still had some months to figure everything out before she could arrange her journey to New York.

Idylls of the Queen, edited by Charlotte's dinner guest, was a magazine for the middle-class Argentine housewife, the one who had aspirations and longings but who could use practical tips on cooking, cleaning, dressing, taking care of her husband, and child rearing. The editor wanted to run a column called "Psychoanalysis Will Help You."

"I want to get someone who knows something about the subconscious—we'll call him a psychiatrist, even though he won't technically be a psychiatrist. We'll ask our readers to send in their dreams, and our 'doctor' will offer analyses of the dreams."

"Am I the psychiatrist?" asked Charlotte.

"No. You're the photographer. Your pictures already have that strangeness, that feeling of the fantastic."

"Whose dreams?"

"Those of our readers. You know, the 'typical Argentine housewife'—you'll show her her own dream."

The title of the magazine section was

> *"Tales Son los Sueños Diarios de una Ama de Casa"* (Such Are the Dreams of the Everyday Housewife)

The stars can line up for an artist in ways she could never have imagined; Charlotte Blum's assignment at *Idylls of the Queen* was such a celestial occurrence. Her photomontages were the visual embodiments of all the anxieties and fears of the middle-class Argentine housewife: the lack of identity, the loss of autonomy, no control over one's fate, the confinement that is home, husband, and child. The worry over society's reaction to a woman who isn't happy being married, who may never have desired marriage, who may not want children, or think she is a good wife or mother, or maybe she loves other women. Maybe she wants something other than this life, even if it is a very good life; wrestling those feelings of acting on the stage of another's life. Imagine going through your day thinking, *This is not me.*

Charlotte made photomontages of miniature women putting giant keys in giant doors that opened on deserted, winding mountain roads. A woman gazes at herself in a hand mirror, only to see her husband looking back at her. A baby lives in an enormous lily held by his mother's oversize hand, with horses in the background, calmly grazing. A kneeling woman is the base of a lamp (a lampshade held over her head as if to cover her) while a man's hand turns her light on and off. A secretary is shocked to look away from her typewriter and see that her legs have turned into trees, her feet roots sunk into the floor. Another woman kneels inside her own gigantic open mouth, her hands resting on her teeth.

A woman is stung by a huge wasp. A married couple skate on top of crashing ocean waves. A woman is tied to a chair by a web of string.

Women beseech ancient Greek statues, or try to play a violin with a broom instead of a bow, or try to escape a vat of soap suds, climbing a washboard as if it were a ladder and unable to get traction.

Women in birdcages, sitting on living room chairs. Women window-shopping for husbands posing with price tags dangling from their wrists. A biplane crashes and burns in a garden. A paper boat holds a woman sailing out to sea. The salon drapes are made up of a dozen eyes. A ladder going up leads only to a ladder going down.

There are recurring images of the solar system, boulders, mountains, roads, mirrors, musical instruments, men, violent seas, flying, and falling.

Anselm Cooper was the real name of magazine's "psychiatrist," a sociologist called Dr. Roberto Obermann. He was the man who told the women what their dreams meant—it was as if the editor of the women's magazine still didn't quite understand that a man interpreting a woman's subconscious was not that different from the liberal-minded husbands of Charlotte's friends allowing their wives' careers as long as they didn't interfere with their wifely duties. The real dream interpretation was Charlotte's. Only her photographs captured the experience with whimsy and a wink and a touch of sadness for anyone looking closely enough; it all comes tumbling out.

And the readers of the magazine loved them.

Six months passed in which Charlotte had the success she didn't even know she wanted until it finally found her. The column was renewed for another year, announced at a party given in honor of Charlotte Blum and Anselm "Dr. Roberto Obermann" Cooper. The upper-class women readers were clamoring for Charlotte to take their portraits. A handful of companies, looking to change their images, came calling. Charlotte spent her days taking pictures to cut and paste into her montages, as well as searching for images in newspapers and magazines. She thought of Hannah Höch, the artist she and Ines loved, as she looked and cut and looked and cut.

She wondered why it was that a woman's life—whether it's a single life or a general experience—could so effortlessly be told using collage. As if women could never be anything but the sum of their parts. The products of their many desires.

––––––––––––––––

"Are you going to New York?" Ignacio asked, holding what Charlotte knew was a letter from Ines, the one where she told Charlotte that she had found the perfect studio. Maybe they could even live there, like in Berlin, like in London (the first and second times). Rainier Ermler would envy the natural light. Seeing Ignacio with the letter was a relief. It also scared her. "God, don't make me ask you a second time," he said.

Charlotte said nothing as she thought about the previous six months and the unexpected collision of her decision to be with Ines in New York and her national fame in Argentina. She knew that she loved Ines, but she also loved making her photomontages of female fears and fantasies. She liked being known, liked being taken seriously as an artist, and to leave Buenos Aires would be to leave the demand for her work and start all over. She had known what it felt like to have zero interest in her work, she knew the silence of the telephone—and now she knew the thrill of the flip side of that silence. Could she go back to that place where no one called and no one cared?

"Have you thought about Barrie?" asked Ignacio, still clutching the letter. "Have you thought about me?"

She thought about them more than she thought about her photography, but only slightly. It was her secret shame that, once she was a wife and mother, those roles didn't eclipse her passion for her work. Who can say why we love the things, or the people, that we love? At a point very early in her life—before Ignacio, Barrie, Ines—she fell in love with the camera, and everything since then had been a way of integrating her love of Ignacio, Barrie, Ines with that original love. And guilt? Always guilt.

"Ignacio," said Charlotte.

He opened his hand, the letter fluttering to the floor. "You'll think me slow, but I didn't know always about you and Ines."

She went to him. Placed her hand on his arm.

"You'd think I'd stop loving you, knowing that you didn't love me."

"You're wrong."

"Even without Barrie, I still want you. Even with the other women, I've still wanted you."

Theirs was never a grand love affair, but that didn't mean there wasn't love. And she appreciated his discretion when it came to his other women—not many, not serious, not yet—often hoping that he would find what he didn't have with her and also dreading that he would find it.

"I thought you knew," she said.

"I don't even know my own heart, so how am I supposed to know yours?" he asked her. "I know you hate being a wife."

But she didn't hate being a wife. If she hated it, she would've hated it with Ines too. She didn't hate being a wife any more than she hated being a mother. What she hated was the way that wife, mother, and photographer created an unsolvable equation. What she hated was trying to solve the mathematics of her various roles. Factoring in her love and artistic connection to Ines was nearly impossible. Factor in fame and success, and she was no longer certain about anything.

She saw Ines on the deck of the ship as she left London. She saw Ines standing on the dock as Charlotte gazed down at her from the ship taking her to Buenos Aires. She imagined leaving Barrie, or Barrie leaving Ignacio. She imagined herself leaving Ignacio, realizing how much she would miss him. She imagined leaving the photography career she'd always wanted only to realize that she knew what it was like to be without Ines, just as she knew what it was like to be away from Ignacio, but she never knew what it was like to walk away from the thing she had most wanted. Years later she would say, "Photography allowed me to make the world and be in the world."

"You still haven't answered my question: Are you going to New York?"

Ines Ines Ines, she thought, will understand better than anyone that a woman always has to choose.

A WORLD THROUGH MY WINDOW
OR
EARLY SKYLINE

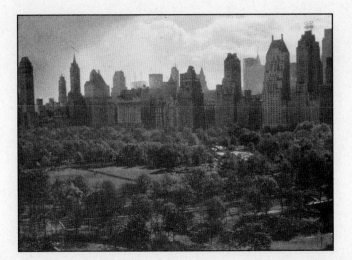

The Morning Was Marked by the Reappearance

The eighth morning of Miri Marx's stay in Rome was marked by the reappearance of a young woman with whom she had shared the hotel bar that doubled as a breakfast room for the first four mornings, before the girl's absence on the fifth. Miri's breakfast companion had caught her attention for a couple of reasons, not the least of which was the young woman's complete lack of interest in anyone, or anything in the room as she sat, for four mornings in a row, reading the paper and drinking her coffee. From time to time, Miri glanced over at the girl as she drank her own espresso, tearing off little bites of her breakfast roll and working the crossword puzzle from an English-language newspaper, her Leica another object on the morning table, with the girl never glancing back. A tourist, Miri reasoned, would not be so completely disengaged from her surroundings.

Miri noticed her because she was new to Rome, and curious about the guests in this rather small hotel, with its twelve floors, rooftop terrace of tables and chairs, and, of course, the cozy breakfast room–bar, with its marble fireplace, formal chairs, and crystal chandelier that could use a good polish. She had initially been attracted to the hotel's intimate size, wedged in between other old buildings and cafés, as well as its excellent proximity to everything in Rome.

The Hotel Locarno was located on a narrow street several hundred feet from the Piazza del Popolo, not too far from the Tiber River, the Borghese Gardens, and the Via Condotti, which led to the Spanish Steps, and which became a kind of touchstone for Miri's explorations around the city. She liked the constant crowd that gathered around the base of the wide stairways. She liked her evening walks, because she liked the nighttime lights of Rome—shop windows full of beautiful shoes, sweaters, suits, and jewelry; illuminated fountains and statues; the lit apartment windows, cafés, the streetlamps that spilled light onto the Spanish Steps.

Miri Marx was traveling Europe without an itinerary. Her only plan was to keep going as long as she could, wherever she could, but since arriving in Rome she'd had no immediate desire to be anywhere else. There was something about the city that was high-voltage and leisurely all at once. Rome was bustle and long meals; excited voices and measured arias; lazy afternoons in the sun and restless nighttime forays to clubs and restaurants. She had been living a rather restless life herself, and the paradoxes of energy and stillness, an inclination toward art and music, and the complex elevation of women combined with their second-class status made a kind of sense to Miri, whose vagabonding in foreign countries, and taking pictures, was not the usual life for a bright, educated twenty-nine-year-old woman in 1951.

On the fifth morning, when Miri had come to expect the young woman, she never showed. Miri briefly wondered why it was that they never ran into each other beyond breakfast in the bar, especially in a hotel this small, where the chances of seeing other guests dropping off room keys, or sharing the compact cage elevator that slid up and down the center of the twisting staircase, were pretty good. It baffled Miri that the girl was nowhere to be found; she assumed that she had checked out, almost immediately regretting that she hadn't tried to speak to her, if for no other reason than that the young woman was beautiful, tall with wavy, dark hair whose smooth surface caught the light. Her face was a perfect arrangement of lines and angles—the high forehead, the straight, strong nose, with the equally strong chin, a mouth with full lips—perfect for the camera.

Now, seeing the young woman back in her customary morning spot in the bar after her absence of three days felt so comforting that Miri had to remind herself they were strangers.

But it wasn't only seeing her for four mornings, then missing her for three, then Miri's feelings of familiarity upon her return; it was that there was something about beautiful girls denied their privacy, as if, by being blessed with such physical good fortune, they had entered some informal, weird visual public domain where their beauty belonged to everyone. A funny little contract between the admirers and the admired. Miri wondered where the girl had gone for the past three days, then wondered why she should care. Then conceded that maybe she just wanted to talk to someone who seemed a little like her: young and traveling and here.

Miri Marx Grew Up

Miri Marx grew up in Los Angeles, in the Valley, to be precise, the sort of sweet, precocious only child who seemed more like a roommate living with her happily married parents. Though Mr. and Mrs. Marx could not have adored her more, it wasn't in them to monitor her every move. They valued her independence. If pressed they would sum up their parenting by saying, "We simply didn't need her to be the embodiment of our dreams."

And they were dreamers: her father, with his exquisite mechanical toys (ships, airplanes, trains, cars) and enamel birds, and her mother, a movie wardrobe mistress who quickly advanced to becoming Esme Esme of Hollywood and a head costume designer just when movies stopped asking the actresses themselves what they had at home in their closets, and, by the way, could they sew?

Between the glamour gowns of her mother and the intricate transportation machines of her father—the adult dresses ideal for the dress-up games of the most imaginative child, the children's toys collected by adults who paid handsomely for each perfect object—it was no surprise that Miri Marx found photography, inheriting her father's love of machines (cameras) and her mother's sense of glamour (the image that heightens life). She eventually came to believe that a portrait should read like a story.

When Miri was seven years old, her parents told her that by age eight they would like her to begin to pursue a creative discipline, so she might give it some thought between now and then. Exactly one week later Miri said that she had given it some thought and had concluded that she liked the cello, thought watercolors were pretty, didn't think dance or acting was for her, and had ultimately decided on photography. That year Hanukkah brought her a used Vest Pocket Kodak Model B with a compact folding lens and "autograph" feature that allowed Miri to write on the paper of the film, three rolls of 127 film, a small camera bag, a fountain pen, and a little leather-bound book for notes. Mr. and Mrs. Marx were neither pleased nor displeased with their daughter's choice because the only thing that mattered to them was that she liked what she chose.

By the time she was twenty-five years old, through multiple jobs, Miri had purchased the Leica. She would never know if her view of the world was shaped by her love of photography, or if photography encouraged her to see the world as potential pictures: People's faces were angles and planes. Palaces, skyscrapers, mosques, ripples on a lake were contrasts of shadows and light. A portrait wasn't a single picture but a series of shots, a collection of events, a story.

Which is why when Miri Marx walked the inner perimeter of the Pantheon later on her eighth day in Rome and spied the girl from the hotel bar standing just far enough from the oculus to avoid the last drops of afternoon rain (disappearing into nearly invisible holes in the marble floor), the broken sunlight reflecting on her smooth, dark hair pulled back in a bun, her beautiful face tilted upward, eyes closed, Miri thought, What's her story? Miri's interest increased by the unusual occurrence of seeing the young woman outside the hotel bar, and for a second time in a single day.

The girl lowered her face, opened her eyes, and looked around the shadowed interior of the Pantheon, with its seven niches for seven gods and goddesses. Miri could see that the girl was adjusting to the darkness of the enormous circular room, exactly as wide as it was tall, the perfect symmetry noted by anyone who entered. The girl didn't notice Miri, who (again) realized that she half expected the girl to greet her since she felt she almost knew her.

The girl remained motionless in the middle of the Pantheon, smiling a half smile as a young man came striding toward her. He placed a crown of flowers in her hair, then took her face in both his hands to kiss her. A long kiss spotlit by the slow moving disk of sunlight provided by the oculus. A kiss interrupted by the girl's purse, which slipped off her forearm, landing at her feet.

The Oculus

The oculus was a thirty-foot-wide circular opening located at the apex of the Pantheon's domed, coffered ceiling, inviting light where the only other light source was the huge entry. Considering the age of the structure (nineteen centuries), its geometric elegance, and its historical significance, the idea of cutting a hole in the ceiling, exposing the interior to the elements, seemed utterly odd to Miri.

The ray of light provided by the oculus circled the interior of the temple, much in the manner of an inverted sundial, defining the time of day, the year, the solstice, the equinox, the seasons, the weather.

When Miri was a child, her parents took her to San Francisco, where they rode the Muni out to the edge of the Pacific Ocean to a camera obscura—a tiny, squat structure with a miniature tower set in the middle of its roof. The darkened room they entered barely fit six people and had a large, white circle on a table in the center. A lens on the outside tower rotated 360 degrees, "photographing" everything, then projecting it, like an endless, unedited film, onto the white circle. Now, years later, in the Pantheon, as she watched the progress of the disk of light, Miri was reminded of the camera obscura and the white disk that brought pictures of the outside world into the darkness.

The more pictures Miri took inside the Pantheon, the more she wanted to take, as the circular window, opening the roof to the vagaries of the sky, changed the interior of the temple hourly. How different was the temple at night? Or in the winter? She patiently shot the light, the statues, the visitors, which was how she happened to see the young woman from the hotel, now wearing a crown of flowers that had Miri thinking, What's her story?

Very Early the Next Morning

It was very early the next morning that Miri decided to take her coffee and aeroposts and pen up to the roof terrace. The day was already shaping up to be hot, but the morning was still manageable, fresh and clear. As she wrote her letters, she found herself thinking about the Pantheon, wondering if she could find someone who could get her inside for a series of night shots; this distracted thinking led her to lose interest in the letters she hadn't had much interest in writing anyway.

She gathered her things and was pulling on the hotel roof door when it came at her with a great deal more force than she was exerting.

"Oh!" said Miri.

The person pushing on the other side seemed as surprised as Miri, as she awkwardly pitched forward.

"Mi scusi," said the young woman whom Miri recognized from the breakfast room–bar, and the Pantheon. In a way, having the young woman speak directly to her was a little like being addressed by an actor on a stage while sitting quietly in a theater.

The two smiled at each other as Miri stepped back to allow the other woman onto the terrace before Miri went inside.

Miri was only a few steps down the staircase when the door again opened, the young woman half in, half out, holding a palm-size book in the same hand that held the door.

"Um, sigorina, ah, mi scusi, were you, um, *lei e stato solo qui?"*

"I'm sorry," said Miri, looking back at the woman, "I don't speak Italian."

"Neither do I. Clearly. I was asking—attempting to ask—if you were alone." The girl was American.

"You mean just now? Or in general?"

"When you were outside."

"Yes."

"No one was there when you went outside? Or, happened by, or anything?"

"No."

The American girl hesitated. She then stepped forward, letting the door fall closed behind her.

Miri was unsure whether to continue down the spiraling stairs without saying something more. It seemed rude to simply turn and go, so she said, "Are you alone?"

"How do you mean?" The girl was walking toward Miri, and when she reached her they naturally fell in step, the stairs barely wide enough to accommodate them.

"Are you traveling by yourself?" asked Miri.

"Oh, I see. Yes. I was supposed to meet someone . . ." she said. Then, "What are you doing today?"

"I'd like to see the Colosseum."

"It's filled with cats, you know."

"I love cats."

"Well, I wouldn't love those cats if I were you."

They said nothing more as they descended the last stairs into the lobby, Miri handing the receptionist her room key.

"I guess I can go with you," said the girl.

Though Miri hadn't thought to invite her along, she felt completely comfortable with the arrangement.

Out in the bright summer sun, the American girl took a pair of sunglasses from her leather bag with its unusual drawstring closure—the bag that Miri recognized from the day before in the Pantheon, when she had seen the girl kissing the young man.

"Aren't you meeting someone?" asked Miri, hesitating at the hotel's entrance.

The girl smiled, and Miri was struck anew by her looks.

They walked toward the Via Condotti, with the girl stopping every so often to admire something in one of the shop windows. Miri enjoyed stopping along with her; it had been a while since she'd spent time with anyone.

The American girl leaned against the wall of one of the stores as she fumbled in her bag, extracting a cigarette and lighter, holding the pack out to Miri, who shook her head. Miri waited while the girl lit the cigarette, inhaling and dropping the pack and lighter back into her bag in one fluid motion. The girl's eyes closed briefly as she savored the smoke. When she exhaled, she opened her eyes and said, "I'm thinking we *should* go to the Colosseum. You'll see that I'm right about the cats. And I'll be awed all over again by the place, which really is remarkable. Then we can grab a bite at a nothing place I know nearby. Have you been to the Sistine Chapel yet? Oh, of course you have. It was on the first day, wasn't it? What about . . . let's see . . . not the Catacombe di San Callisto which is a four-story burial ground that is creepy in every language . . . unless?"

Miri shook her head.

"I didn't think so. You strike me more like someone who has three things on her List of Things to See but really likes to wander? You like to stumble upon some sort of adventure? Sort of see where the day takes you? Am I close?"

"You mean, given that I'm sightseeing with a stranger?"

"I've become unused to using names," she said. "A consequence of traveling alone for an extended period."

"Miri," said Miri, offering her hand.

"Daisy," said Daisy, smiling, shaking Miri's hand.

Miri said, "So who were you meeting this morning?"

"A Colosseum cat."

Then the girls continued on their way.

Miri was a cute girl who looked younger than her twenty-nine years; her youth, and her being a woman alone in postwar Rome was enough to garner male attention, but it was nothing like being by the side of the tall, beautiful American girl, who brought out an aggressive appreciation in the loitering men. With few cars on the streets, most people walked or rode little Lambrettas, and there were a number of people, mainly men, evidently unemployed, whiling away the hours, smoking cigarettes, drinking coffee, playing chess, and talking. Always talking. Miri noticed that one often saw very young Italian girls, or women on the rather far side of middle age, usually dressed in black, but the women in Miri's age-group, that is in their early twenties, were seldom in public. Rome was a decidedly male world in one respect and, in another, as sensitive and mysteriously female as one could imagine. All that art, all those worshiped, beautiful male statues; female statues in states of undress, the opera, the food, the gorgeous indolence of the place.

Even paintings and sculptures of women saints, their heads thrown back, with their closed eyes to heaven in states of ecstasy, underscored the moment of physical female rapture.

Rome was a church, a garden, a piazza, a palazzo, a ruin, an Egyptian obelisk, a café, a street, the Spanish Steps, an elaborate fountain where the coins you threw determined your fate, the Colosseum.

She liked observing the mix of Romans and tourists, the permanent and the transitory, mimicked in the architecture as well, and the places where they intersected. She believed that one of the pleasures of travel was the opportunity to either act unlike yourself or, just as often, act *more* like yourself, uncensored by family or friends. She wondered how much of the tourist's unguarded behavior rubbed off on the locals.

"Don't you just love this city," said Daisy, leaning back with her long legs stretched out in front of her, the girls now just two more people idling on the Spanish Steps. "It's positively postcoital half the time."

They had spent the better part of the afternoon at the Colosseum, with Miri experiencing the momentary disconnection that comes in the presence of such a famous landmark. There it is, right in front of you, and yet your brain can't stop thinking about full-color posters or films. And then the collision of images gets compounded as you stand inside the arena, able to imagine—and finding it hard to imagine—what the Colosseum must have been like before it was quarried for building materials, with time picking up where the scavengers and thieves left off. Could anyone really regret the glory of a structure that was used for such violent entertainments?

The interior was nothing like what Miri had pictured, since she'd expected the center to be flat and dusty, like a bullfighting ring. Men in twos and threes trailed the girls at a distance, trying to catch the attention the girls never gave. Miri had to resist petting the many feral cats that ran around or basked in the sun or seemed to be stalking some prey; Daisy hadn't exaggerated about the cats.

The warm day turned into a warm night as the girls headed back toward the Hotel Locarno. When they were still several blocks away, Daisy leaned over to give Miri a European-style kiss on each cheek, saying, as she was already walking away, "I'll see you tomorrow! In the lobby." Miri realized that she expected they would return to the hotel together and was a little disappointed—she'd forgotten how fun a foreign city could be with the right company, as much as she liked traveling on her own. If asked, she could tell someone that they visited the Colosseum, but the rest of their day would sound uneventful—no more landmarks, or museums, or fabulous food. It would sound as if they did nothing, when in fact they laughed and walked and talked, moving about the parks and piazzas on impulse and nothing more. She couldn't even tell you the name of a church they went into, or a statue they saw. It wasn't that kind of a day.

She watched the American girl take her thin scarf from her shoulders and tie it three times around her slim waist as she walked off into the hot, airless night.

Where was she going? Miri wondered. But before turning back on her own way, she caught the distant sight of the American girl, standing still, placing a cigarette in her mouth as a man walked up to her, his hand holding out a lighter, the American girl's hand reaching to bring his closer to the cigarette.

The American Girl Was Already Waiting

The American girl was already waiting when Miri entered the little hotel lobby. It was nine a.m., so while the time wasn't particularly early, it was if you lived life late at night. When the girls had parted the night before, it had been midnight.

"I need coffee," said Daisy.

They walked to a small café where they stood at the counter drinking espresso. They ordered chocolate croissants that they wrapped in napkins and took with them.

"This is the best croissant I've ever eaten, and I've eaten them all over Europe," said Daisy as they crossed the Tiber on their way to see the Basilica di Santa Maria, said to be the first church dedicated to Mary, a claim, of course, disputed as such claims tend to be. "Supposedly, the Santa Maria Maggiore boasts the same thing." The melted chocolate filling, resembling chocolate pudding, dripped down her chin and fingers, which she promptly wiped and licked, respectively. "If you get to Paris, you must go to this place by the Tuileries, very worn-elegant, you know, silvered framed mirrors, marble tables, and ladies who lunch. They serve a hot chocolate in little pitchers with a bowl of whipped cream. *L'Africain*," she said. "It'll knock your socks off."

"Is that the name of the place?" asked Miri, feeling the combined energizing effects of the espresso and the rich chocolate pastry.

"Uh-uh. The chocolate drink."

They were in Trastevere, a district of cobblestone streets and students from the many universities. As they came out into the piazza belonging to the old church, Miri asked, "How long have you been in Rome?"

"Let's see . . . I arrived on July twenty-fourth, no, twenty-fifth, and . . . I've been here one month." Daisy seemed a little amazed herself.

The inside of the Basilica di Santa Maria was resplendent. The apse, a perfect dome, held a gold-inflected, thirteenth-century mosaic so intricate and ornate that the thing Miri most remembered when she thought about it later was the row of sheep, lining up from the right and the left and meeting in the middle, beneath a figure resembling Mary, though Miri couldn't make out if Mary was sitting with apostles or saints, popes, and Jesus.

Outside the church was another grouping of figures, this time girls—maidens she assumed—twelve in all and holding lamps, though she couldn't tell if all the lamps were lit. Not being Christian, Miri knew what twelve men meant in religious art, but twelve young girls? Who were they? Why did they carry lamps? Maybe they were dates for the twelve guys. You know, one met somebody, then was asked if she had eleven friends.

"See those twenty-two columns?" whispered Daisy of the heavy pillars that marched like soldiers up the nave to the apse. "They're from the ruined Baths of Caracalla. Before they were sacked, they housed public baths and two libraries—one in Greek and one in Latin—"

"So is that where the habit of reading in the bath was born?"

"That, and buggering little boys. Anyway, Penn Station is modeled on those baths. Just some trivia for your diary."

"How do you know I keep a diary?" asked Miri.

"We all do, because it's the only way to know that being here, away from America, was real."

"Are you going home soon?" asked Miri, as they sat in a Trastevere cafe, two tables of men, maybe students by their ages, openly staring with appreciation at Daisy and her very cute friend, the one with the Leica taking pictures.

The American girl held the gaze of one particularly handsome boy a little too long for modesty before turning back to Miri and biting into an anisette biscuit. "I think I am home."

Later Daisy asked Miri if she could find her own way across the river and back to the hotel since she thought she'd stay in Trastevere a little longer. They would meet in the morning in the bar.

The next morning Daisy didn't show. Miri waited in the hotel bar and thought about questioning the clerk at the front desk about the girl, only to remember that she didn't know her last name. In the end it didn't stop her from asking the woman behind the reception counter if she knew the *camera* where the *bella signorina* slept? "You know, my friend?" Miri attempted an elaborate miming of what their friendship might look like to others: laughing together, pretending to be drinking coffee in the morning at two separate tables, raising her hand to indicate the height of the American girl, taller than Miri by several inches.

The woman tried to understand; she tried in her own pleasant way to explain something to Miri, until she gave up, shaking her head, No. No woman, she said, with Miri insisting, There is a woman, a *bella signorina*, and so it went, in the sort of language circle that Miri was used to from not speaking any language but English in foreign countries.

Miri decided to return to the Pantheon, to take more pictures and dream of the oculus allowing a light snow into the temple. She crossed the river to visit the Basilica di Santa Maria in Trastevere again; it also had an oculus, though smaller than the one in the Pantheon. The church oculus was more ornate, with its four putti hovering at the edge of the opening and holding aloft what looked like a ring with columns and windows above, letting in the light. This opening, with its layers of light and four decorative sculpted figures, lacked the purity of the window in the Pantheon, making it less intriguing to her. The oculus in the Pantheon, with her series of photographs, was a story; the one in the church in Trastevere was not.

As she stood in the church she realized that she was half searching the laughing, hushed groups of tourists and Romans for the American girl.

The next morning, Miri entered the lobby to see her new American friend, sitting in a chair, reading the newspaper.

"Here you are," said Miri. "You had me a little worried yesterday. I mean, I wasn't sure if we had plans or not and I don't know your room number, or your last name—"

The girl stood up, dropping the folded paper onto the seat of the chair she'd just vacated, and stretched almost imperceptibly, saying, "I guess I'm not used to having anyone miss me."

"I thought maybe you were sick or something," Miri said, which caused her friend to laugh.

"Yes. I had a case of Roman fever."

Miri laughed with her.

As they walked toward the Trevi Fountain, Miri moving faster than the American girl, who was hesitating to adjust the scarf thrown over her shoulders, Miri turned to see her friend walking alone through a gauntlet of men: old, young, and middle-aged, leaning against the heavy, historical facades of buildings, or sitting in twos on parked Lambrettas, or at the tables of a little corner café. They smoked cigarettes, and wore jackets, some with the jackets thrown across their shoulders like capes. Miri saw the look of appreciation and appraisal at the beautiful American girl, tall and leggy with that healthy American stride, as if nothing could touch her unless she allowed it.

And then Miri saw the story: An American girl in Italy in 1951, her travels and discoveries no different from those of every other American girl who has traveled to Europe since there was an America. Privileged, young, eager for experience, sophistication, art, and freedom; alive to the moment, the desire for adventure outweighing fear or trepidation. Miri responded to the timelessness of the tale, in some ways amplified by the stifling of women in postwar America; marriage, kids, the concerns of the house, all those quasi-exotic recipes without the pleasure of food, the Puritanism of America that permeated every ordinary activity, the difficulty of a career, or of keeping a career once you almost had one. Miri never really had to ask what Daisy was doing, traveling alone, in Europe; she already knew because it was her story too.

When Miri was a teen, she knew that she wanted still photography to tell stories much in the way of movies. She knew, too, that she would one day want to tell her story, though she wasn't quite sure how to do so when she was the one holding the camera.

"Stop," said Miri when Daisy passed the men. "Go back and walk it again, only can you ask the men not to look at me when I take the picture?"

They spent the rest of the day with Miri setting up and taking pictures of the American girl drinking coffee in a café, standing in the center of a piazza, studying statues and paintings, struggling with the money, the language, asking for directions. She sat on a Lambretta, in a sports car (that an all-too-accommodating man allowed), on the Spanish Steps, at the edge of a small fountain. The citizens, nearly all men, that the girls asked to assist in the shots were natural actors, good-natured and amused, but serious when the picture was made. What man wouldn't be flattered when asked to pose with such a beautiful young woman, dressed in a loose black summer shirt and skirt, cinched with a brown leather belt, her flat sandals reducing her height to that of most, but not all the men? Her wavy, dark hair held back in a tortoiseshell clip, tiny gold earrings, her scarf always over her shoulders or tied to her funny little leather bag.

"I was born in Los Angeles, an only child. My father makes mechanical toys that no one ever buys for their children because they are extraordinary, so much so that adults collect them like art. And they're not wrong, by the way. They move and make noise and are as delicate as Swiss watches."

Daisy was tossing her orange peel toward the pigeons in the Borghese Gardens, where the girls sat in the shade, eating a late lunch. They were too hot to do much of anything, and spent by all the pictures and posing. "What type of toys?"

"Birds. Every sort of bird you can imagine."

"With feathers?"

"Painted metal and enamel work. Also, transportation conveyances—boats, ships, airplanes, trains, cars." Miri ate a slice of orange. "And my mother's career—"

"Your mother?"

"My parents have some different ideas about a girl's life. Independence being one of them."

"Then what are you doing here?"

"As you know, the rest of the country hasn't caught up."

The girl placed her head in Miri's lap as she finished off her orange. "My mother's life would be ruined if anything changed for women. She's the mistress of the house, the lady of fund-raisers, a deb who went to Vassar, coming out to the world only to go back in. She may as well live in a tower with servants."

"Where is her tower?"

"Greenwich, Connecticut. And she's fine with her gilded cage, except when she's sober, which is nearly never."

Miri's family had enough money but were never rich, she said.

"Oh, so your people decided to be happy instead."

"As romantic a view as that is, no, but they are happy."

"And your mother's not a Los Angeles housewife?"

Miri said, "She started out sewing the occasional costume for the silent movies. Then she began dress and costume design, and everyone loved her work. Esme Esme of Hollywood. She's won two Oscars and has been nominated for four."

"I can't tell you how impossibly glamorous it all sounds."

"Having a socialite for a mother isn't exactly being invisible."

"Did I mention that my mother modeled during college?"

"My parents gave me my first camera when I was a kid, and I would go with my mother and take pictures of the actors and actresses. I even went to a few movie star funerals."

"Taking pictures?"

Miri shrugged. "I know. What a ghoul."

"I went to art school. Where I had an ill-advised thing with my professor."

"An ill-advised thing?"

"A misunderstanding. It was never what it appeared to be, though that didn't seem to matter when I got thrown out. He, on the other hand, kept his job. Of course."

"Of course."

"Did I care?" said Daisy. "No. I did not. I was happy to be out of that mausoleum. Then my aunt died and left me enough to travel on and, *voilà*, as they say."

"What kind of art?"

"I was mostly a muse. A confession. It wasn't only my professor who got me into trouble. I wanted to be an Abstract Expressionist, but I think I'm more of an architectural watercolorist. I like patterns. Crazy, huh?"

"And you like traveling alone."

Daisy smiled.

"You know, I went from Los Angeles to San Francisco on my bicycle the summer I turned seventeen. I took pictures every day."

"Geez, now I'm impressed. I've been knocking around Europe since April, but it's a little different to be a twenty-four-year-old woman with a trust fund than to be a kid on a bike."

"Yeah, but don't you think the impulse and the pleasure are the same?" said Miri.

"What are you doing in Rome?"

"I was returning from Jerusalem, where I was doing a magazine assignment, and was thinking of stopping in Paris, only I came to Rome first and haven't wanted to leave. So here I am."

"And you like to see where the day takes you."

"And you?"

Daisy got up, smoothed her summer skirt. "I'll be here until I'm not." The girls collected their things to head back to the hotel.

Miri asked for her key and waited for her friend to ask for hers. When she didn't, Miri said, "Aren't you going to your room?"

"I don't stay here."

"But . . . I saw you . . ."

"Oh. *Mon petit chou.*"

When Miri said nothing, Daisy continued, "It's a French endearment. He's my little French endearment who likes meeting me here."

"And at the Pantheon," said Miri, "about a week or so ago? The day before we met."

"Maybe," said Daisy. "It's possible."

Miri remembered the day in Trastevere and the handsome boy. And the day Daisy stood her up. She admired the American girl's unapologetic romantic life, which lacked the coyness and artifice of popular girls back home.

The girl smiled. "I think you got some good pictures today. You'll have to let me know how they turned out."

"Wait," said Miri as Daisy headed for the door. "I don't know your last name."

The girl turned slightly to face her, still moving a little. "You first."

"Miriam Marx."

"Like the brothers."

"Well, you know, without the horn and double entendres."

Daisy said, "You'll think it's invented."

"Is it?"

"Let's just say my very educated mother had a sense of humor." The girl now stood perfectly still. "Miller."

"Oh, God, Daisy Miller? Let's hope your mother didn't have the gift of prophecy as well," said Miri, laughing.

"Isn't it a kick in the pants? Years from now you can tell your friends that you went to the Colosseum with an American girl named Daisy Miller who had Roman fever, and no one will believe you."

Miri, unlike Daisy with her trust fund and time on her hands, was a working girl. She'd told the truth about the magazine assignment in Jerusalem but neglected to mention that her leisurely trip home had a purpose other than recreation and his name was David Rose.

She'd met David at an impromptu exhibition of student work held in a New York gallery of no importance to the larger art world. Every month, a group of students of various ages, who shared a largely unloved brownstone in the Village, cleared all the furnishings out of the high-ceilinged living room–parlor–dining room, slapped a fresh coat of white paint on the walls, and hung an art show. Someone played cello at the opening. Or a kind of jazz drum solo with brushes. No normal adult would be able, even as part of a group, to pull together any sort of art show this often, but they were young and enthused and had it down to a science. The art was usually the work of someone who would never be great, with the occasional appearance of work that would one day be great; work with a glimmer, a spark, a line, a color, a form that could give the game away, but for that you must have the other half of the art equation, which is a discerning audience. One cannot be its best without the other.

These art shows were as much rent parties (asking for donations at the door) as they were exhibitions. The spirit of the enterprise (along with music, the cello eventually giving way to records; alcohol being accompanied by reefer) often had the effect of people meeting and believing themselves, even if just for one night, "in love."

It was in this art-scented atmosphere that Miri met David Rose, an aspiring filmmaker. Mutual love of movies drew them together, prompting them to speak in the shorthand of the film-besotted. It was kismet that David should meet someone with a mother who had distinguished herself in wardrobe design and was on speaking terms with almost everyone (especially the stars whom she measured and draped and knew intimately), and who saw the world as a story. It was kismet that Miri would meet a young man who loved movies and filmed stories as much as she and saw in her a kindred spirit who, by the end of their first night together, wanted to make movies with her.

Meeting one's mate, Miri thought, was really a problem when one really liked traveling alone.

Their courtshipfriendshipcourtshipfriendship was exactly that: a thing that bounced from one sort of attachment to another then back again. Sometimes it was work that took over and pushed love aside, taking up all available space in each of their lives. It didn't always happen in perfect symmetry; sometimes Miri was more caught up in work than David, and sometimes it went the other way. Often it made Miri happy to have both David and work, not to mention a man who understood her work. Other times, she was happier to have him as a friend, the romantic momentum stalled. Sometimes there was someone else. After all, she was twenty-seven when they met, and she had been on her own for a decade. During those years she had had the occasional encounter without anything blossoming into something more profound, everyone parting amicably. When she thought of what she loved, it was her work. People, too, but also her work, as if it was another lover she barely had enough time for.

Then came the Jerusalem assignment. Then came her decision to stop in Rome and Paris, just to make sure that she still liked traveling alone as much as she always had.

There had been no sustaining drama during the two years of their life of courtshipfriendshipcourtshipfriendship, and what Miri wanted to know was if there was sustaining love.

The day she left Israel, there, in her hotel mailbox, was a sterling silver charm bracelet of four sterling silver cameras, each with a tiny hinged back where one would load the camera, and a note that said,

> *Oh! kangaroos, sequins, chocolate sodas!*
> *You really are beautiful! Pearls,*
> *harmonicas, jujubes, aspirins!*

She recognized the opening lines from the Frank O'Hara poem "Today," which David would recite to her—not the entire poem, which was only two verses—sticking only to the opening, which struck him as silly and joyous and because, as he said, he thought her beautiful.

The other lines he would recite to her were

> *(i do not know what it is about you that closes*
> *and opens;only something in me that understands*
> *the voice of your eyes is deeper than all roses)*
> *nobody,not even the rain,has such small hands.*

1959, New York City, Central Park West

Miri Marx was positioned at her dining room window, her Leica in hand, the camera trained on the Sheep Meadow of Central Park, across the street from her apartment. At fifteen stories up, Miri could shoot straight across, capturing the panorama of park and city skyline; or she could concentrate on the immediate view below, a section of street and sidewalk. On this day, it was the panorama of sky, structures, trees, and field.

It was a spring afternoon, with rain clouds gathering and bouncing light above and below, reminding her of the English countryside. The fullness of the leafy trees contrasted with the clean, angular geometry of city buildings crowding behind. The expanse of the empty meadow spread out in front of the buildings and the greenery. Miri waited for the sun to shift ever so slightly before making three exposures.

Two months after Miri's return from Rome she and David Rose quietly married, then spent their honeymoon in England, driving around the country, laughing more than she thought she could laugh, each in love with the other, and writing their first movie. It was the story of a nine-year-old boy who gets into a fight with some other boys on the street. As he miraculously pins one of them, the pinned boy blurts out that the first boy's father has a girlfriend. The boy is shocked and disbelieving, except he realizes that he doesn't really know his father's life outside of their home.

The next day, Saturday, he follows his father all over New York City— jewelry store, flower shop, barbershop, ending up at the Plaza—beginning to believe that his father does have a girlfriend, only to discover his father rendezvousing with the boy's mother. "Oh, my God, we're already planning our escape from our own children," joked David.

In England they had traveled on a budget, staying in guesthouses, eating plowman's lunches in pubs, sometimes driving through the night to save on lodging. Though the landscape was gorgeous and the long walks they took led them from one picturesque place to another (evocative Hardy country, the Cobb at Lyme Regis, the lush Lake District, the ugly duckling beauty of the Brontës' moors), the mark of the war could still be found. Not just in London but in Coventry, where they stayed one night, marked by new construction, the consequence of Luftwaffe bombings that had destroyed the historical city center.

Mostly, Miri loved her walks with David and the way the sky could go from cloudy to sunny to golden to purpleblue. It was the same quality of light and weather that she was looking at on this day in New York.

Miri and David's movie about the nine-year-old boy garnered praise and awards at home and in Europe, inspiring young directors like Truffaut, influencing the New Wave, showing how a smaller story over the course of ninety minutes could be transformed into a love letter to a city. Miri believed her life to be so ideal it seemed one more Hollywood confection.

As Miri gazed out her window, she saw four teenagers, dressed up as if they were on a double date. She leaned out a little, her knee on the chair pushed up to the sill, framing the shot as the teens stopped to awkwardly light cigarettes, so desperate for adulthood and sophistication; she had just focused, when—

"Mommy?" Their almost-four-year old, Teddy, who had been occupied with a set of colored blocks, stood next to her. She climbed onto the chair that Miri used to steady her camera, the high back acting as a guard. Miri could see that the four teens were no longer in the position she wanted, too far apart to be captured in a single frame and carrying too little tension individually, these kids who wanted to be anything but kids. Miri looked down at Teddy, who told her that she was hungry. With one final glance out the window, she gently set her camera down next to her other camera, a Contax, and the rolls of film she always kept on the unused end of the dining room table, before lacing her fingers through Teddy's dark curls. She picked up her daughter's soft little hand and kissed her perfect fingers.

Their first daughter was born in 1955 while David was in Venice for a showing of their film. The baby arrived a month early, otherwise David never would've gone. Unlike many fathers-to-be, he wanted to be with his wife. Though Miri was happy about the baby, she was worried that having one would change everything; that is, she couldn't quite picture how she would take care of the baby, the apartment, and still work. And for someone who had taken pictures since she herself was a child, and been working and on her own since age seventeen, Miri simply couldn't imagine not working. Not taking pictures. Additionally, she and David had a second film lined up just before Miri discovered she was pregnant. David assured her that a baby was only *a* change in their lives and nothing more.

But she hadn't counted on being as tired as she was (or having a first child at thirty-four years old), nor could she have known how much she would love being with Teddy. She loved her company, her smell, her toothless smile and smooth little feet without feeling particularly maternal or, at least, what she imagined maternal was meant to feel like.

Elizabeth came along in 1957.

Between Teddy and Elizabeth, David began his second movie, coming home or calling (depending on the length of the shoot) to check in with Miri and keep her informed as if she were there, since they had developed the story together. Miri knew that he missed working with her; their shared professional life added a dimension to their attachment. He wanted her there, but she couldn't be there because someone had to be here.

And this was her paradox: She wanted to be in two places at once, to be two people at the same time. If she could split herself, one Miri would be happy spending all day with her toddling children with no thought about doing anything else. They would play with toys on the floor, or she would enthusiastically read to them. Nap when they napped. Eat when they ate. Her other self would be making movies with David. Or possibly taking pictures on her own, with no lingering regret about not having children, or not being home with her children. She wondered if she felt this constant, low-grade conflict because she'd had a childless life, a profession prior to motherhood, only to discover too late that you cannot replace one life with the other, and now she often lived in a place of suspension where she loved two things too much.

It was hard not to feel resentment that men weren't forced into these choices. Some days she felt that she would spend all her time trying to forget her life before children because she loved them too much to be reminded of the heat of Rome in the summer and a beautiful girl who turned heads as she walked down an Italian *strada*.

So she told herself that she'd never had coffee in the piazza outside the Pantheon, never watched the changing light within; there was never a confection of a fountain where tossed coins could tell her future. The art of forgetting, she believed, could be learned.

Some days it shamed her to want to be anywhere but home making jelly sandwiches and reading the same books that she had read a thousand times and using nap time to pick up the house, only to find herself drawn to the dining room window overlooking the park. She would watch the pedestrians and the sky, the trees, and the way the countless windows lit up, wondering what was going on behind them. Up to that spring afternoon, Miri had taken the occasional picture of people below on the sidewalk, or a horse-drawn carriage; an event in the meadow, lazily leaving her cameras and film on the dining room table.

She loved Teddy and Elizabeth, and her marriage to David—she adored him and he was good to her; they were both products of their time and nothing more. But the fact was that she couldn't square the force of her love, the sheer monumental quality of it, with her nostalgia for her former life. She was a puzzle of miscut pieces.

———————

A postcard from Daisy Miller: *I have the most marvelous all-over tan, courtesy of Mykonos, Santorini, Thassos, and Chios. Have you ever been to Corfu? Did you know the people are named for the love child of Poseidon and some nymph he abducted? Hope all is well. Kisses.*

Miri placed the postcard of the unbelievable blue of the sea in her desk drawer.

1961, New York City, Central Park West

Sometimes when she sat, chin in hand, gazing out the window at the park, the expanse of the meadow empty or crowded, depending on the weather and the season, Miri was joined by Teddy or Elizabeth, six years old and four years old, respectively. It occasionally troubled Miri to see them in imitation of herself, her wistful expression as she took in the world outside her window. It wasn't always easy being a woman of forty with young children. She realized it was both good to have had a life before having children (which, in all truth, was simply a different sort of life) and hard to have had a life before children. Like a variety of phantom limb syndrome, you would wake some mornings not quite rested for having two small kids, and in your sleepy state believe yourself to have the unplanned day spreading before you, only to hear the voice of your four-year-old daughter.

Elizabeth looked out the window, then called her mother over to show her something: The Central Park horses were all done up with pastel-colored streamers, their manes and tails brushed, or braided. The drivers were in jewel-toned velvets and silks. "Mommy," Elizabeth said, "you need your camera."

This wasn't the first time that Elizabeth or Teddy had called Miri to the window to see something, along with the insistence to bring her camera. In no time at all, taking daily pictures from her window became as integrated into Miri's home life as making the beds, doing the laundry, or cooking dinner.

She went so far as to set perimeters for her pictures: two cameras, three lenses, no filters.

She still missed some shots because Elizabeth was in the bath, or Teddy had fallen down, or someone wanted something from a high shelf, or a squabble had to be mediated. But at some point, her day began to revolve around life outside the window as she recorded dawn, and dusk, day and night. Winter, spring, summer, and fall. And every imaginable event, from weddings to picnics, to concerts, to sunbathing, to lovers' trysts and lovers' quarrels. Protests and parades. And the ever-changing skyline of New York City.

Much later in her life she would write of the window pictures:

> My situation was ideal, I suppose (although I don't remember thinking of it quite that way at the time). My children, of course, were also there on a twenty-four-hour-a-day basis, so they got photographed, too, just like the view. 6:00 a.m.: mist/feedings . . . 2:00 p.m.: view/ playpen time . . . 5:00 p.m.: dusk scene/baths . . . 10:00 p.m.: night shot/baby asleep.
>
> Now that I think about it, I don't see how anyone but a housewife could have got all this done.
>
> In retrospect, it seems one of the main things I did was wait.

———————

Another postcard from Daisy: *Cairo is shockingly great. Beirut is romantica. Fez is like a dream—not a dream, but like a dream—a distinction I know you understand. Kisses.*

Miri placed the postcard of the casbah in her desk drawer, then went to change the sheets on the beds.

1963, New York City, Central Park West

The women's magazine that had originally published Miri Marx's portrait of Daisy Miller, titled *An American Girl in Italy, 1951,* as she walked the gauntlet of men in Rome, decided to run it again, as part of a travel piece. Many women readers remembered it from the first time it ran, when it had been part of Miri's photo essay about a girl happily traveling alone. The mail that poured in to the magazine in 1951 expressed a pleasure in seeing this daydream of a lazy day in Rome as a beautiful, unfettered girl followed her heart's desire; they particularly liked the picture of Daisy strolling down the Roman street with all male eyes upon her.

But everything had changed in the wake of *The Feminine Mystique* and civil rights and the publicly expressed discontent of women.

So when the photo ran a second time in a spread on women photographers, young women took exception. "Look at her face," they cried, "and tell us that she isn't feeling fear! The men are menacing!"

"'The men are menacing'?" said Miri to David, laughing and baffled. "It was a lark," she said. "It was fun."

This was before feminism took another odd turn, when sex became something that oppressed *and* liberated women, depending; when it seemed that women were being encouraged to pursue who they really were, unless that included being a housewife, which, somehow, was no longer a politically acceptable choice. Women sometimes turned against women, as time and perceived societal roles churned and lurched forward. Change is seldom one smooth, uninterrupted process, and most women remained in the house whether they wanted to be there or not. Miri was frustrated because she had been raised as if women were already equal, with no expectations that she would stay at home, yet there she was, willingly, and still knowing what it cost her.

Another postcard from Daisy: *Romania, Russia, caviar, and men. The sort of diffused lighting that you like. Can't wait for London and Paris. Kisses.*

Miri ate the rest of Teddy's leftover tuna salad sandwich, then placed the postcard of a man lying on the ground with a bear sitting on his back in her desk drawer.

1965, New York City

In the catalog copy for an exhibition of works by Miriam Marx called "A World from My Window/ Oculus" Miri wrote:

> If you want to know what it's like to be a housewife, I can show you:
> Reddish yellow sunrises behind buildings with the park lights still dotting the darkness of the park, a lavender haze of sky, and buildings, a green foreground, billowing clouds skidding in the sky, rainy streets marked with yellow lines, a horse-drawn carriage, hot-air balloon, a purple sky, a thousand released balloons, cars, a parade, a red sky with black smokestacks, more snow, more ice, crowds of people in the sun, at a wedding, in protest, at a concert, winter, spring, summer, fall. Fireworks, political rallies, a presidential motorcade, the sun, the rain, the heat, the cold, the fog, the fog, the fog. Red, purple, blue, white, yellow, lilac, gray, black, pink. Geometry and movement. Buildings and cars. Helicopters and horses. Three people and a dog looking straight up at me.

Cymbeline Kelley was one of many who made the trip uptown to the photography center to see the window pictures. As she moved slowly from picture to picture, she thought about how perfect they were, with this housewife showing the patience of a field photographer, waiting. She understood Miri Marx as a modern Rapunzel, high above, watching the outside world.

There was no mistaking that Miri Marx's serial portrait of her New York City neighborhood was as much a portrait of Miri as a wife and mother as Cymbeline's garden pictures were of her life as a wife and mother. Cymbeline thought, We abstract the experience and the men only see what we do as sweet, sentimental, missing the meaning entirely as they view us as women who make photographs in our spare time. They don't take our subject seriously because they cannot see it—even when Miri Marx writes, *If you want to know what it's like to be a housewife, I can show you.* Nor do they consider the steel it takes to raise the kids, run the household, be a wife, and still keep alive the artist part of you. Picasso, thought Cymbeline, could show the many angles of a woman's face simultaneously; try showing the many angles of a woman's life simultaneously.

Before she left the show, Cymbeline marveled that, in its way, so little had changed since her own garden–domesticity pictures, forty years earlier. (And men wonder why women are "impatient" and short-tempered.) Still, Cymbeline was in New York to shoot a glittering luncheon to be attended by a famous modern dancer, a famous movie star, a celebrated painter, and two well-known musicians (one classical, one jazz) for a popular magazine. We must take our victories where we find them, she thought, then went on her way.

———————

On an early summer day with a morning shining like a new dime, Miri dressed in the bedroom as she listened to David making breakfast for the kids. He was trying to tell them about dinosaurs and how the animals at the Natural History Museum weren't alive, a concept that both kids understood, but with which Teddy, nine years old, struggled. Elizabeth, at seven, sometimes called the museum "the zoo," because of the hall of taxidermic African animals, with the man who had originally collected and stuffed many of the specimens buried in the gorilla diorama. As young as she was, she didn't have a problem seeing the "standing still animals at the zoo" along with the "bone lizard," as Teddy had called the dinosaur skeletons when she was younger. Miri had never liked the stuffed animals; they were in a hall of dead things, and she could barely abide being there, something Teddy shared with her mother.

The first time Teddy saw the stuffed animals, she was satisfied, with no need to ever see them again, much to Miri's relief. No, her girl preferred the starry heavens of the planetarium. Like her mother, Teddy loved looking at the sky, always different and changing; she especially adored the stars. David had bought some glow paint and carefully and accurately reproduced a winter sky of constellations on the ceiling of Teddy's room, complete with a Milky Way made by running his thumb across the bristles of an old toothbrush loaded with glow paint, and stars tumbling from the ceiling down her room's walls.

Being in Teddy's room was almost like being under a rural night sky.

Miri heard David telling the kids that he couldn't take them to the museum today because he had to work.

Imagine, thought Miri, having the luxury to work. To tell your own children that their needs come second to your work.

He and his editor were putting the finishing touches on his new (third) film; she knew the process. She knew it was a little of this, a little of that, and mostly fighting off the fatigue and perfectionism that come with being done with something yet unable to concede the end of the project. They would talk, laugh, eat a leisurely lunch, and enjoy that perfect moment that comes between finishing your project and showing it to an audience. The pleasure in that time space was one she knew well, relief and anticipation colliding. When had she last felt that? When had raising kids and tending a home—even on its best day—ever replicated that fine exhaustion?

Love—for her children, for her husband, for her photography—had that way of opening and closing her life; the possibilities evident, and elusive. Her window exhibition was wonderful, but it was more like an interlude than a life-changing event, or so she believed.

When David came home, during the shooting of the second movie, he always shared his day with Miri. "Today we shot at St. John the Divine." Then he would relate some funny story about the actors (they were playing a photographer and his assistant specializing in weddings), followed by some filming foul-up. There were shots at the photographer's studio (shooting children); a street fair in Little Italy; a cemetery on Long

Island. The Bronx Zoo, Playland, and Brooklyn. All accompanied by
David's anecdotes, funny and frustrating, and all of them sounding like
heaven to the woman who once had a career taking pictures and made a
film that someone said was like a series of moving art shots.

Miri liked being a part of David's work even if it was secondhand.
"Could you help me with this dialogue?" he would ask, and she would
say, "Just let me get the kids to bed first." Or he would ask about a shot
that had him undecided: "What would you do?" And she would say, "Let
me look at it after I put the dishes away." He didn't notice her domestic
life because he wasn't raised to notice it. Miri, on the other hand, who
was not raised for this life, knew that someone had to stay home and
someone had to be the breadwinner. As a couple, they didn't really fit
into anyone's idea of "arty," so they used to joke, "We're closet bohemi-
ans," as a way of explaining the ordinary appearance of their lives. They
laughed that the kids were just one more way of disguising their hidden
bohemian selves, you know, on a good day.

———

A postcard from Daisy: *You'll never guess where I am—Rome. The cats
still follow. Made me miss you, American girl. Love and kisses and wish you
were here.*

Miri placed the postcard of the Colosseum in her desk drawer before
taking the kids to the Penguin House in the park.

———

It began with burning the roast. Smoke billowing out of the oven as
Elizabeth called "Mommy!" with Teddy echoing in imitation of her sis-
ter's tone of alarm, "Mommy!" causing her sister to turn to her and say,
"You don't even know what's going on."

"Do, too!" cried Teddy, prompting a shove from Elizabeth, a matching
shove from Teddy, then tears all around, Miri immediately feeling guilty
that she'd gotten distracted by a cloud formation outside her window.
She set the camera on the table, not knowing whether to attend to the
kids or the fire first.

There was the damp underwear in everyone's dresser drawers. The toothpaste no longer found its cap, oozing out on the inside shelf of the medicine cabinet. Dry cleaning was hooked onto the open closet door. Toys seemed to always be underfoot, or under sofa cushions, and sticky fingers had left little smears of jelly in unexpected places. It's nearly impossible to keep a home neat with two young children, but this was something new in the Marx-Rose house.

"I don't expect much" was the way David began his complaint about the untended state of their home, with Miri responding with a mirthless little laugh. David, annoyed, said, "If you don't care then—"

"Then what?" asked Miri, genuinely curious.

"Then I don't know!"

"Is that your idea of a threat?" said Miri, and they both began laughing, the kids running in and tumbling around them.

After the incident with the burning roast, Miri couldn't say for certain what happened, but she knew that it started when she took her large camera bag from where it hung on the bedroom door, noticing that it was the size of a travel satchel. Against the background sounds of her family in the other room, she dropped a toothbrush, toothpaste, a hairbrush, hand lotion, and a lipstick into the bag. She heard David promise Elizabeth that they could go to the observatory this weekend as Miri stuffed underwear, a pair of slacks, two shirts, and a sweater into the bag. She imagined telling David and the kids that she was dropping off some laundry (should they ask), but when she picked up her keys as she went out the front door, no one asked.

As she cut into the edge of the park, she wondered if there was someone like her watching from *her* window, envying her the luxury of free time. Walking along the paths to the east side, she tried not to think about anything. To live without a plan. As she considered where she'd go once she left the park, she realized how long it had been since she thought only about what *she* wanted, not what someone else wanted. She almost didn't know what to do with this realization.

It had been a long time since she walked at street level with a camera, and all the sights, and smells, and people rushing around her seemed chaotic; even if she had had her camera, she would have been unable to concentrate enough to find a picture. She stopped in the park, people and dogs running around her, and thought how isolated she still felt; the perspective on all this activity was wrong, a distant memory of another life. At one point in her life she'd thought, How lucky, how grand, to have the chance to place your art at the center of your life, for it to be your profession. This feeling of good fortune was never commonplace for Miri; it was always extraordinary. Now she wondered if those riches were meant to be hers for only a short while, whereas she had misunderstood and thought they would last a lifetime.

She stood below her building looking up at her apartment and, for a moment, thought she saw someone moving in her family's window, before deciding that it was her imagination.

Somehow she found herself uptown at the photography center. Her name was painted in large white letters on the window, framing a reproduction of one of her park vistas. The show had gotten a couple of notices—good ones—and she had the fleeting thought that she didn't want her window pictures to be thought to be good because she didn't want them used as a justification for keeping a woman artist at home. There should be no possibility that women would be thought to do their "best work" in the "domestic sphere" and not in the larger world. It wasn't as if, living in New York City, Miri was unaware of the avalanche of criticism piled on women painters who "neglected" their children because they chose to divide their time between family and work, while their male counterparts (artist-fathers) could be as absentee as they liked, almost romantically so.

Mostly what she thought, as she entered the gallery and studied her own pictures, was that they may have represented her family (she could remember the exact circumstance of each shot—the whereabouts of Teddy, the involvement of Elizabeth, the warmth of David's voice as he stood behind her, telling her she had a "good eye"), but they were also documents of her conflicted love. She thought about when she'd walked out the door that morning with her packed bag and how no one had said anything, not because they didn't care but because they trusted her. And that sometimes their trust just killed her because she trusted them too. Even with conflicted love the operative word is *love*.

That night she quietly let herself back into the apartment. It was very late. She placed her camera bag on the floor, next to the front door and the little table that held the keys and mail and the occasional toy. In the darkness, she saw David, with his back to her, sitting and smoking in the chair pushed up to the dining room window, only now it faced the park.

"You forgot your cameras," he said without turning around.

She crossed over to him, took the cigarette from his fingers, and placed it in an ashtray. She climbed into his lap, her arms around his neck as she kissed him on the mouth, a very long, deep kiss, before pulling back and nestling her head in the spot beneath his chin. His embrace tightened around her, and she felt how afraid he had been; all the worry and love and loss of the day was conveyed in the muscle tension of that embrace.

JESSIE BERLIN
OR
PHOENIX ON HER SIDE

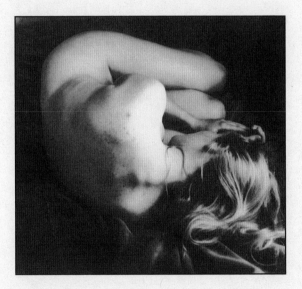

Jessie Berlin checked and rechecked her watch as she waited on the sidewalk, cursing her imagination (so easily accessed and advantageous when making art, so wretched when applied to other areas of her life). No one belongs to anyone in this scenario, she reminded herself, that was part of the deal. Emile had a way of getting her to agree to nearly every proposal, convincing her that what he wanted was also what she wanted. This manner of persuasion had the added benefit of making her believe that their mirrored desires were proof that they were meant for each other. It was only later when she felt forgotten, or taken for granted or that she could be any other girl to him, that she realized she didn't want what Emile wanted—she only wanted Emile.

But everything became complicated when they decided to do this photography series called the BelleFemme Project, born out of a dinner party that went too late into the night with too much talk, too much wine, too much smoke. The women at the table turned strident (how she'd come to hate that word!) as the men argued in favor of the difference between the sexes, with the women countering that there was no provable difference and claiming this "difference" was just more rationalizing for men to do as they pleased.

The debate moved on to gender-influenced worldviews, making a philosophical stop at art and professionalism before arriving at infidelity; because all conversations, debates, and fights these days seemed to find their way to who was fucking whom and what it all meant. Really, thought Jessie, wasn't it really all about who was left crying, and who felt guilty, and who was and was not sorry?

It seemed that if the 1960s had been about political and cultural idealism, then the early 1970s were shaping up to be about sex. And on the subject of fucking, where the fuck was Emile?

She yanked open an oversize satchel holding her Nikon, wallet, house keys, a sterling silver brooch that she kept on hand in case she lost a button, a roll of Scotch tape in case her hem came loose, duct tape, three pens, a pad, film, a light meter, and the thing she was searching for: a lollipop. Suckers were her way of trying to quit smoking. Tearing the wrapper was slightly similar to ripping the cellophane off a package of cigarettes, and the thin, rolled white paper stick was, if she used her imagination, a distant cousin to a Marlboro. Maybe she should have waited until she and Emile were truly over before giving up the one legal thing that could calm her down when she felt this irritated and anxious.

She stepped off the curb as far as she dared during a pause in traffic, taking one final visual sweep of the well-traveled San Francisco street that fronted Cymbeline Kelley's 1920s cottage, searching for Emile's BMW. He had the Rolleiflex, the tripod, the strobes, the Polaroid, and the umbrellas. She was certain she'd told him 9:30.

When Jessie turned her attention back to the cottage, she noticed the front door standing wide open. A very small, rather old woman was staring out from the doorway, her eyes magnified by the lenses of her clear plastic eyeglass frames, which dominated her face. As Jessie waited on the street side of the gate, Cymbeline Kelley said in a surprisingly strong voice, "Oh, don't make me come to you."

"I thought I might be early," said Jessie, knowing it was an unbelievable excuse for not coming to the door sooner.

The elderly woman's cloud of white hair was partially secured by a wide blue scarf, her bangs grazing the top of the invisible-framed eyeglasses. Though the day was warm, Cymbeline seemed dressed for much cooler climes in her black, long-sleeved dress, belted at the waist and falling below her knees. As if in concession to the bright heat of the day, her legs were bare, her feet in short socks and leather sandals. She also had a length of fabric, imprinted with peace signs, wrapped multiple times around her wrist. Her activism was becoming well-known, as she was one of the first photographers to attend peace rallies, snapping away as she protested the war. In 1971, protesters were many, except in Cymbeline's age-group, where they were nearly nonexistent. A sharp divide had occurred in the country over this Southeast Asian war, and, more often than not, the fissure ran along generational lines.

When interviewed in the *San Francisco Chronicle,* Cymbeline Kelley said, "I've never understood why most people don't become more liberal in their ideas, more open-minded, less judgmental as they age—what have you got to lose? Why not allow life to interest you? This is why there are more young people in my life than contemporaries. Well, that and, you know, death."

"Okay," said Cymbeline. Jessie knew when she was being humored.

The cottage was architecturally and situationally incongruous for San Francisco. It was not vertical, or Victorian, or located in a quieter, more residential pocket of the city. Instead, it sat between the sprawling offices of a department store chain and a compact multiuse professional building that mostly rented to lawyers. It was also three miles from downtown; Jessie had walked from the Powell Street station, taking advantage of the balmy and beautiful summer day. The house had a garden, quite wild, though it seemed that its overgrowth was more a result of nature than of neglect. A concrete driveway ran the length of the left edge of the garden, ending at a wide gate belonging to a tall wooden fence.

The inside of the house was larger than it appeared from the outside, loft-like, with sun spilling in all around (with the exception of the side with an archway leading to the bedroom). Jessie briefly wondered how Cymbeline worked with the light that came through the many windows, since she was the founder, along with Angel Andrs and Morris Elliot, of a group called f/64, that believed in "natural" photography. No arty tricks that created "painterly" effects, no contrived lighting. Photography was its own art form, not some poor substitute for the real thing. Which was why Jessie was thinking about the light.

Across from the archway was a perfectly proportioned, slate-colored marble fireplace, accented in white. The twin columns on either side of the firebox were beautiful nymphs, their slender arms holding the marble mantel aloft. Facing the fireplace was a kind of lovely, well-used deep green sofa that looked like it belonged in a hotel lobby; next to the sofa was a midnight blue velvet chaise longue, also a little worse for wear, and a much less lived-in matching midnight blue velvet armchair. In the midst of the seating arrangement was a low midcentury coffee table, all polished atomic-age angles in blond wood.

A dining room table held a collection of photographic objects—camera, film canisters, used film, negatives and contact sheets, a shoulder bag, a light meter. Spanning most of the shared rear wall of the dining area and kitchen were a pair of glass doors allowing access to the outside. Not only was it possible to see into the back garden from the front door but one could walk a straight, unobstructed path door to door as well.

Jessie's first impression when she entered the modest home was that it felt more like someone was staying here indefinitely than actually living here; maybe because the personal touches were few and gave the impression of a traveler in a rented room who had chanced across a souvenir or two, displaying them in her temporary lodgings.

Her second impression was that this someone lived alone.

Cymbeline's Rolleiflex 3.5E, the leather case undone, the viewfinder snapped open with the magnifying glass flipped up was next to a white bisque rose and a palm-size, hand-painted metal zebra, and a pile of loose change.

In the main room, a box of light-sensitive paper and a bottle of fixer sat outside a closed door beside the archway, which Jessie assumed to lead to the darkroom. Only a person who doesn't have to consider another person's comfort would be so unconcerned with her work materials lying around; only a traveler would (most likely) treasure the wonderful little zebra.

Jessie examined the four pictures in the room. They struck her as particular and a bit cryptic; then again, there wasn't too much wall space, so maybe the choices weren't coded at all, just a recognition of limited space. There was a framed rectangle of black wool stitched with worn, early-twentieth-century silver milagros from Spain, and two paintings: one of a gray barn that Jessie believed to be a minor

O'Keeffe. Cymbeline had met Georgia O'Keeffe, and this little picture was a gift. Later, after Cymbeline had shown her tightly cropped flower photos, O'Keeffe had made some close-cropped flower pictures of her own.

The second painting had a background of pale blue with a grid pattern that looked applied with graphite pencil. The nearly uniform lines resembled men's suit fabric, or a visual meditation. Jessie instantly recognized the picture as being by a reclusive woman painter named Daisy Miller, who called her work Abstract Expressionism even though others called it Minimalist. Cymbeline said, "I have the most unexpected affection for her work."

Jessie approached the fourth picture on the living room wall. It was a photograph of a beautiful, young, naked woman with multicolored artificial flowers in her hair, a stuffed songbird in a golden cage hung so close to the top of the picture that it was almost out of the frame. The woman sat at a sewing machine, running through yards of billowing tulle in lavender, pale blue, and pale pink, though it didn't look as though she was actually making anything to wear.

"It's called *Machine Worker in Summer, 1937*. Madame Amadora. British," said Cymbeline, standing near Jessie. "Not my style at all— quite the opposite, with all that garish color and artifice. Fake flowers. Fake bird. Fake industry."

"Who is she again?" Jessie moved closer to study the print, which was fairly large, the colors as dreamy as a watercolor.

"Madame Amadora. Amadora Allesbury. Her best work was between the wars—her color work; it's what she's most known for"—Cymbeline gave a small laugh—"except here, of course, where no one knows her at all, which is how I could buy this print. She did advertising work, too, but then who can run a studio without doing advertising? Or portraits," she added, "one can only do certain portraits for pay. But then you already know that."

The importance of the aging photographer and the awkwardness of the acknowledgment that Cymbeline was Jessie's assignment left scant room for Jessie to say what she had wanted to say ever since she arrived, which was that she may never have fallen for photography if it hadn't been for Cymbeline Kelley. Now it seemed too late, too pandering.

"But I'll tell you where we're alike," said Cymbeline, and for a moment she thought Cymbeline meant she and Jessie. "Madame Amadora and I were both suffragettes—you can see where she stands on women's issues in her work. In this picture, for example." Cymbeline stepped closer to the picture, closer to Jessie, who was almost hulking next to the diminutive photographer. She waited for Cymbeline to continue, but, instead, after studying the picture, the older woman smiled to herself.

Whatever made Cymbeline smile, or however this Madame Amadora, with her fake this and fake that, was anything like the woman who had cofounded a photographic society based on absolute naturalism, Jessie couldn't quite grasp. What Cymbeline saw that indicated "women's suffrage," Jessie's youth, and the radicalism of this current, second wave of feminism blinded her to the political underpinnings of the picture. She peered more closely at the photograph of the beautiful naked woman at her sewing machine wrestling with all that cool, pastel tulle.

Cymbeline sighed. "One thing one misses in one's contemporaries is humor."

A young man, his dark hair falling over his forehead and skimming the collar of his shirt, came in from the back garden carrying a metal strainer of strawberries and asparagus, leaving one glass door open and opening the other. The fragrant breeze moved lightly about the kitchen that ran along the back wall of the main room.

"Sam Tsukiyama, Jessie Berlin; Jessie, Sam," said Cymbeline.

Jessie held out her hand to him.

Sam wiped his hands on his jeans before taking her hand. "May I say how very cool it is to meet you."

Cymbeline said, "Sam is my lifeline."

"As if she needs anyone," he said to Jessie.

"It's true. But only with the heavy lifting. And the printing. The shows. The appointments. The correspondence. The garden. The cooking."

There was affection between the two.

"I've seen your work in Berkeley, in that group show," said Sam. "The lady in the Chinese pajamas with the sable cuffs? Man, that picture just kills me."

"In his real life, Sam is a photography student. And a very good cook."

"Yes, as long as it's something, like, without too many moving parts," he said. "You know, it really is great to meet you." He pulled out a dining room chair for each woman, settling Cymbeline in without drawing attention, before moving into the kitchen.

The Rolleiflex camera that sat amid the jumble on the end of the table was classic and nostalgic and beautiful all at once. A compact box of metal and ground glass with wheels and hand-crank film advance moved in a backward and forward motion. The back of the camera had a metal inset chart of f-stops. There were tiny silvered numbers and concentric circles that resembled a target and a reflective double lens cap that was tossed to the side of the camera.

"Go ahead," said Cymbeline.

Jessie loved the weight and scale of the Rolleiflex in her hand. She gazed down into the viewfinder to scan the room, finding, as she expected, the image perfectly clear yet reversed. The image was true (this is the room, no doubt) and not true (everything is backward). It was hard for Jessie not to love a camera that told the truth and lied.

"I'm sure it's unnatural to adore cameras as much as I adore Rolleis," said Jessie, returning the camera to its original spot, then gently collapsing the magnifying glass and viewfinder.

"My second one," said Cymbeline. "I've had that since 'fifty-seven, though the screen's been replaced. My eyes," she said. "I bought my first one for portraits."

"Did you have a studio in San Francisco?"

"No." She smiled. "I didn't have a studio at all—I had a family. Two kids and a husband who taught art at Mallory."

"I'm a Mallory girl," said Jessie.

"Had you been there from 1920 to 1934 our paths may have crossed."

Mallory College was a pleasantly situated girls' college, nestled in greenery, not far from San Francisco. There was something insular about it; the girls used to call it Brigadoon, in reference to the enchanted Scottish town surrounded by a mist that separated it from the real world. The town was accessible only once every hundred years, and anyone who entered believed they had traveled back in time, for each Brigadoon day was the equivalent of a real-world century. None of the townsfolk could leave the village, lest the place vanish forever.

Other people referred to the college (predictably, Jessie felt, insultingly) as the Nunnery, in part because of its architecture, which resembled cloisters. The verdant grounds that were perfect for meditation. And partly because it was a women only institution.

"I graduated in 'sixty-five."

"Nineteen sixty-five," Cymbeline said wistfully. "Living at a college was almost like living in suspended time-space where you girls never changed while I just got older."

"But—" Jessie caught herself before insisting that Cymbeline "wasn't old" when she realized that her meaning could be mistaken. In truth, Cymbeline seemed physically very old (she was in her late eighties), but she also had that air of amusement that touched her facial expressions without coming into full view, the intelligence in her eyes, and that sort of playful timelessness that often attaches itself to artists. It isn't that they refuse to age; it's their connection to nearly everything around them (how else to have grist for the mill?), seldom missing a thing, that keeps them contemporary even when the body is clearly breaking down.

Sam set glasses of lemonade before them.

"I've applied for grant money to print up a barrel of glass plates that I've had in storage since I moved to California, in 1917. That's the real reason for Sam. That he does all the rest is my good luck." She sighed. "All those glass plates—I wonder if I was any good."

"The Mallory portraits were good," said Jessie.

"They weren't mine." Cymbeline took a sip. Her face, for the first time, lost some of its softness. "They were made by Angel Andrs," she added quietly, "that pompous ass."

"I thought you were friends. Didn't you start f/64 together?"

"F/64 was before all those ridiculous commercials he's starring in these days. God, even when I was younger, Kodak tried to sell to young women. Now they use an old man who likes young women. He's a good photographer, and I don't care about the girls—but it's an affectation that I keep telling him he may want to rethink." She took another sip of lemonade.

"Even years ago at Mallory, people were falling all over themselves over him. You see, Leroy taught painting at the college—I was the faculty wife with the kids. That's how they saw me—not as someone with a university degree in chemistry, or a professional photographer who once had her own studio. I had already been to New York, even took a picture of Stieglitz—and it was a girls' college after all. I tried to keep up, but it was hard with a husband and kids and all those students always coming over for dinners.

"So, I got my first Rollei and starting asking the girls to sit for me. I couldn't pay them anything—living on a teacher's pay—but I did their portraits for three years. Just to keep my hand in, as they say.

"One day the dean called me to ask if I had a phone number for Angel Andrs. I didn't think anything of it until they hired him to take portraits of the girls." Cymbeline's face relaxed, her lightness returned. "As I said, Mallory was a timeless place. Even my resentment is timeless."

Though they laughed, Jessie could imagine the disappointment Cymbeline must have felt. The anger that she'd had to tamp down, lest she be labeled ungracious or, worse, envious. Watching a man hired to do the job that you were already doing, then having your reaction called jealousy would've been too much.

"You know," said Jessie, "I didn't want to say it before, but I did feel that the Mallory pictures weren't your best work."

Jessie asked if she could use Cymbeline's phone. She called Emile's apartment, which was more like a catchall for his things since he, for all intents and purposes, lived with Jessie. No answer. She called her studio. When he failed to pick up, she told herself that he must be on

275

his way and that traffic from the East Bay could sometimes be tricky, even if you were only coming over from Berkeley; she told herself that he was coming from Berkeley and not somewhere else, and who knew if there was an accident or bridge problem or some other mishap. As difficult as it would be for her if he forgot, she allowed that possibility on her mental list.

When she returned to the table, Cymbeline said, "Let's get this done before lunch."

"Could we wait a bit longer?"

"For what?"

"Emile Pasqua. The photographer?"

Cymbeline said, "Are you asking me or telling me?"

"He's the photographer."

"Then who are you?" Irritation colored Cymbeline's voice.

"I'll also be taking your picture." Jessie wanted to add that Emile had the other cameras and their equipment, except she suspected that Cymbeline, with her naturalist approach to portraits, wouldn't understand why Jessie couldn't take the photo anyway.

Cymbeline reached out to Jessie, bringing her wrist with its wristwatch closer to her face. Her touch was dry and cool. She released her. "I'm not much good later in the day."

"I thought he'd be here by now."

"It's my age," said Cymbeline. "Mornings are better. You graduated college in 1965, so I don't expect you to understand."

Her sharp comment made Jessie realize how much she looked up to her. All the women in her women's art collective loved Diane Arbus, and the other young women coming up who were photographing street kids, or making self-portraits in which they impersonated men, or movie stars. Jessie liked them, too, but they didn't influence her the way Cymbeline did.

And here is the funny thing about artistic influences: They don't always come from the person whose work you love best. For example, Jessie very much liked Cymbeline's pictures, but they weren't her overall favorites. The importance of Cymbeline, for Jessie, was that she was the one who made photography possible for Jessie, both in her own mind and in the external world. She influenced her. And someone that important, that meaningful is not someone you want to think less of you. Again, she cursed Emile.

"I'm sure he'll be here soon."

"What is this for again?"

"It's called the BelleFemme Project, which is a reference to the fashion magazine *BelleFille*. Also a critique—"

"Beautiful Woman instead of Beautiful Girl. I'm already starting to see where this is going."

Jessie caught something that she couldn't quite grasp, partly because she spent time in Berkeley and was used to the uncontested feminism of her women's art collective, and to the men who claimed to be supportive of equal rights, though it wasn't unusual for them to proclaim one thing and expect something else entirely, making them suspect when push came to shove, as it were. Women were breaking in all over the media, with the culture quickly catching up. So to hear even the slightest sound of cynicism—especially from someone like Cymbeline Kelley—was perplexing.

But Jessie pushed that aside as she explained the BelleFemme Project, born at that dinner party.

"The idea is for Emile and me to photograph the exact same women, either on the same day or within the same week. The gender of the photographer kept secret."

"Hmm," said Cymbeline.

At the dinner, everyone had expressed admiration for the "conceptual purity" of the project, so simple, so straightforward. And who better to do it than Jessie and Emile, who had been a couple for a little more than two years, were within the same generational boundaries (she twenty-eight years to his thirty-four years), and were both photographers who enjoyed portraiture? And that they were lovers would only add, they were sure, to "self-discovery." There was the ensuing talk about "the male gaze, and the female muse." Jessie said that she agreed to this project to prove the audience couldn't tell the difference between the male and the female hand on the shutter, and to finally lay to rest this infuriating idea that men were serious artists while women were hobbyists. The idea that *only* men are willing to sacrifice everything, accepting solitude and silence for their art, as if women wouldn't give almost anything for the same solitude and silence to do their work. This, predictably, set off a round of vocal affirmation by the women, accompanied by what seemed like agreement on the part of the men until they began their equally predictable qualifications and rationalizations.

Jessie could have added that women were too busy keeping house, tending to the garden, and the children, and trying so hard not be branded "selfish" to fight for their need for aloneness to create. Selfishness is the crime of anyone who isn't supposed to think of herself first: women, mothers, wives, childless women, women, career women, women, women with only one child. Women. Women with messy living rooms. Women who didn't get to the market or the dry cleaner. Women who wanted to work. All selfish. But Jessie wasn't at a point where she said everything on her mind in mixed company.

She did say to Cymbeline, "I guess it's to show that a woman photographer can be indistinguishable from a male photographer. Or, well, maybe it's the opposite." She really hadn't worked out if she was after difference or similarity because she hadn't worked out which would cause men to value her as an artist.

The women in her collective would say that she cared too much about a man's approval.

Sam placed sandwiches on the table, along with a cold asparagus salad. Jessie knew he had been listening as he worked, and she admired his silence; no man she knew would've allowed this conversation to continue without offering his two cents' worth. No man she knew would be making lunch either, not without some applause for his efforts. Sam not weighing in was the most intriguing comment of all. Maybe it was his youth. He looked to be twenty.

"I gotta jam. I'll be back this evening," he said to Cymbeline.

They ate in silence after Sam left.

"I'm so sorry," said Jessie. "Emile isn't usually like this."

"What's he usually like, then?" Cymbeline looked at Jessie, who felt judged with those magnified eyes upon her.

"On time. Mostly."

"Yes. But what's he really like?"

It felt as if she would open a floodgate if she were to honestly answer Cymbeline's question, What's he really like? *He's like a habit you don't remember developing. He's like a fever, and the best day you ever had.*

"He's a good photographer," said Jessie.

"As good as you?"

"Well, I suppose that's subjective." Her answer was reflexive; anything else was too risky. Not that Jessie was often asked, but to say "Yes" or even "No, I'm better," would be to knock the earth off its axis—no woman could stay with a man less accomplished than she, and if she did stay it would be almost impossible to freely admit it. It was pressure from within and without. The women Jessie knew might complain about all the ways in which their men's careers superseded theirs, but secretly they were all a little relieved. Weren't they all raised in families where everyone depended on the earning skill of the man in the house?

More than that, wasn't it just a tad emasculating for the woman to be more talented than the man? And, if she was, wasn't it just so gauche to allow it into the open? And what did it say about her willingness to take a backseat to his pursuits? *Yes* made her feel bad and *No* made him feel bad. It was a creative woman's problem, a battle she could not win.

Cymbeline placed her napkin next to her partially finished lunch. "You can tell me later."

Jessie left the dishes next to the sink without washing them, something she intuited would be a mistake on any number of levels. She could sense Cymbeline's displeasure, boredom, and, oddly enough, bemusement in equal measure. She couldn't tell if this sort of situation (Waiting for Emile) was amusing or annoying, and not knowing was making Jessie all the more tense.

"So," said Jessie, as she glanced around the main room. "Perhaps we should begin." Cymbeline sat unmoving at the dining room table as Jessie retrieved her satchel from the floor near the front door. She pulled out the Nikon as she circled the room, hoping that she looked as if she were studying the various photographic possibilities; she understood that wanting to appear to be doing what she was actually doing meant she was really in a bad way. That is to say, she was trying to focus on the setups and not on the whereabouts of Emile. It was 12:30 already.

The room, being relatively spare in its furnishings, did offer some advantages, and Cymbeline's black clothing and white hair would look quite graphic on the midnight blue chaise. The deep green sofa and slate gray fireplace with the white walls could also be good, though the idea of posing Cymbeline on the blue velvet chaise in the manner of an odalisque seemed humorous for a woman who'd once said "I invented the male nude" and all the flak she took for those pictures. The blocks of color in the room made Jessie sorry not to be shooting in color.

Jessie had called Emile once before and once immediately after lunch, so that, when the phone rang, she almost jumped to answer before remembering that it wasn't her phone. She listened to Cymbeline listening to someone on the other end of the line and hoped that it was Emile, working his Emile-ness. He had the kind of charm that women could see through, and that he knew women could see through, so everyone ended up laughing and he was forgiven in the end; it was like a fun house of charm, full of infinity mirrors of charm. Then Cymbeline laughed, and, for the smallest moment, Jessie could clearly see the girl in the old woman. Everything about Cymbeline shifted with that wonderful laugh. She heard her say, "Bring two, would you, dear? I can't thank you enough." Then she hung up without saying good-bye.

Jessie remembered the times that she had spoken on the phone with Cymbeline, setting up this appointment, and how the woman didn't say good-bye then either. The first time she thought they had been cut off, and the second time that the older woman was rude.

She was too shy and too proud to ask if that was Emile; asking, she felt, made her seem lovelorn and incompetent and unprofessional. She might be lovelorn, but she wasn't unprofessional. As weird as it felt not having her strobes and umbrellas, Jessie told herself that photographing Cymbeline according to the photographic principles of Cymbeline's f/64 group carried a kind of correctness. Cymbeline wouldn't be out of her element in the light of her own living room.

With this in mind, Jessie photographed Cymbeline as she had photographed: in natural light, sharp contrast, no planned manipulation in the darkroom, no intention of cropping the image. The picture representing the reality of that day. Who ever would've thought that being tethered to reality in photography would present such a challenge?

Of course, the reality for Jessie would be that she would always see in this picture the absence of Emile.

Emile Pasqua was sitting in the little backstreet San Francisco bar in North Beach called the Youki Singe Tea Room. It was a funny place, with eccentric decor devoted to all things Japanese and French without having a coherent idea of what either meant. In the back was a traditional teahouse, where the clientele (a mix of poets, grad students, secretaries, and longshoremen) smoked weed.

Jessie was twenty-four and newly returned from Morocco, where she had fallen in love with an ex-architecture student who dreamed of growing Cara Cara oranges, which led to a romance with an American expat living in a stucco room above the bluest sea, followed by a brief interlude with a disenchanted stockbroker trying to "find himself," which led to a thing with a traveling radical from Berkeley who explained that one was either "on the bus or off the bus." She decided to get on, and followed him home. They eventually parted, and she allowed him to think that their breakup left her sad, when she was really only relieved. It was a lot of work being his handmaiden, and once the lust burned to ash, there was no real reason to stay.

Throughout her life, on family and solo vacations, Jessie would visit the known homes of artistic women—Georgia O'Keeffe, Emily Dickinson, Dorothy Parker, the Brontës, Lee Miller. Isadora Duncan proved particularly difficult since her Bay Area family was constantly evicted, leaving their belongings as they stole away in the dark of night. Some-times she could go inside, other times she saw their homes from the sidewalk; either way she documented all these visits on film, which were eventually assembled into a show at a Berkeley gallery, catching the attention of the women's art collective who loved her "Women-centric journeys that celebrated the Portrait of the Artist as a Young Woman."

It actually was "empowering" to be with a group of politicized, cre-ative women, even if Jessie existed more on the fringe. Her sense of humor kept her from being as radical as some of the women, and her belief in the fairness of equal rights kept her in their company. Or, to put it another way, she wouldn't call her work the product of "Women-centric journeys"—her photographs were more like "cut-rate side trips"; the collective's assessment gave her work a larger import when her moti-vation wasn't political at all but a personal combination of curiosity and affection. Still, with the way things were going in the movement, if you weren't "on the bus," you were "off the bus."

It was around this time that Jessie was introduced to Emile in the Youki Singe Tea Room. A small gallery in the City had decided to show her "Side Trip Series," and friends and friends of friends were meeting at the Youki Singe after the opening. At some point in the evening, talk turned to Weegee, and Emile (whom Jessie would describe as "easy on the eyes") said, "If you like crime scenes, you should check out the Bal-timore Medical Examiner's Office." When Jessie pressed him for more information, he said, "I don't want to ruin it for you."

The next day, an envelope was delivered with a plane ticket to Bal-timore and a note that said, *Congratulations again. Call me when you get back. Emile.* Her first impulse was to send it back, saying, I can buy my own plane tickets, but then again, it was the perfect overture: the intrigue of whatever it was at the Baltimore Medical Examiner's Office; the right amount of imagination; the celebration that could prompt a gift; the right amount of distance (he didn't ask her to go with him); the ideal excuse for a date ("Tell me what you think"); the fact that he was even interested in what she thought. The confidence that she would use the ticket. More to the point, it was also the most ingenious test to see what sort of girl she was, because if she was someone who would fly three thousand miles to see she didn't-know-what, then she could be the girl for him. And, true to what she learned about him later, he probably expected her to see through this *romantica* gesture, and he knew that she knew that he knew that she did. Geez, thought Jessie, this guy is good.

The Nutshell Studies of Unexplained Death was a series of eighteen doll-house dioramas set into the wall on the third floor of the Baltimore Medical Examiner's Office, and made by a grandmotherly millionaire with an unsavory obsession for unexplained violent crime. The attention to detail in these tiny tableaux was staggering: a silk stocking that had been knit using sewing needles with the width of a human hair, rooms furnished down to the dust on the furniture, imitation food painted with such care that it was hard to accept it as imitation, perfectly fashioned cigarette butts littering bisque ashtrays.

It wasn't enough to people and furnish her idealized rooms; she placed within each one a corpse or two who had met their demise by accident, murder, or suicide. The deaths were as exquisitely rendered as the settings and props, right down to the rope around the neck, the blood that gushed from a well-placed wound, the fracturing of limbs and skulls, the bloat from drowning in one's own bathtub. There were rigor mortis and busted furniture and glass, an icebox left open next to the dead housewife. There were flowered wallpaper, pink slippers, an ironing board, a gun, a knife, a struggle, a murder. Jessie learned that Mrs. Glessner Lee used them for her forensics lectures, being an amateur, three-dimensional Weegee, albeit one who wasn't content to report the crime. She wanted to re-create the crime. Solve the crime. Then talk about how she solved the crime. They were, in short, exquisite little horror shows. Jessie couldn't tear herself away, even as she battled revulsion. This was exactly the sort of thing—this little cultural footnote, this odd little feminine detour—that she loved.

Jessie photographed the miniatures, discarded any writings of

Mrs. Glessner Lee, replacing them with her own stories of the scenes accompanying her photos. Each one a love affair gone wrong, illustrating the physicality of the loss of love. It was her most conflicted project and one that she hadn't planned to show until a friend ended up at her studio (still mostly just a room in her enormous and very cheap South of Market loft), returned to New York, told another friend, who then asked for transparencies, which she was hesitant to send. At the time, Jessie worried that this strange series would define her. Sometimes she thinks the works of an artist are like slots on a roulette wheel; you make one project or picture after another until the wheel stops and you are "discovered," never knowing if the discovery is going to be the project that most represents you.

A few months after Jessie's return and the news about New York, the same group was back at the Youki Singe Tea Room, again with Emile. It should have been awkward since she hadn't bothered calling him upon her return, but he seemed genuinely unconcerned. When she tried to apologize in a semiprivate moment during the evening, he said, "Really, you don't have to. The dioramas were just something I thought you'd find interesting."

How did you know? she wanted to ask. She had been with other men who, even after several months, knew nothing about her. Yet she spent one evening with Emile and ended up with a photography show in New York. Sometimes, Jessie found it challenging not to believe in Fate, or past lives, or rays of light or whatever the fuck when it came to love.

As the evening progressed, Jessie and Emile joined the others in the little teahouse, only to have the power fail in the bar twice in the space of five minutes. Amid the flickering light, the music that blared, then went silent, then blared, then went silent, then back on, and that jump of one's pulse, Jessie began to fall into the most delicious love of her life. As Emile walked her back to her loft that night, they passed a shallow alley where he pulled into the shadows, pressing her against the uneven brick wall, kissing her so hard that she experienced an erotic suspension of time and place that, heretofore, she had never believed in. "My god," she said, barely catching her breath, "if you make me laugh when I'm not wrecked, I'm marrying you."

In many respects, it was the depth of her feeling for Emile, that heedless plunge (and he did make her laugh), combined with a photography career that kept her in the women's art collective. Without her independence, she would end up following Emile to the ends of the earth; without Emile, her independence would turn to dust. She needed both things—love and independence; photography and Emile. She laid her concerns before Emile, who agreed that it was a new age, when it was possible to have everything. "Your photography is one of the things I love best about you." That's what he said. That's what he told her as he unbuttoned her blouse.

Two years and they *almost* live together, they joke. Emile has a place in Berkeley that they *mostly* share, when he isn't *mostly* sharing her studio in the City. After the show in New York, Jessie won a Guggenheim Fellowship, had a catalog published, had another show of her *Violent Rooms of Love* series, got another small grant, enough to photograph statues in France for a month, resulting in a show called *Women on Pedestals*. She received a trio of honors, including an artist-in-residence at a college in Rhode Island that she hadn't yet decided to accept.

They didn't officially live together, much less marry, because "no right-thinking radical feminist would buy into the current cultural hegemony of marriage," which did nothing for women but expect them to accept and submit. However, living together wasn't far off from marriage, and while Jessie and Emile never rejected the idea of an open relationship, they never agreed on it either. Maybe this was why she was hesitant to bring up his recent behavior, which included not always being where he said he would be. She wasn't the kind of person to keep track of anyone, and now she wondered if her trust was just naïveté. The confusion for her was that he was still the same Emile. Loving. Supportive. Making her laugh.

They also never discussed the possibility of one of them having the greater success, and that one not being Emile.

———————————

"Is Berlin your given name?"

Jessie had been struggling with distraction, taking a few frames of Cymbeline on the blue chaise.

"It's Saltman." It was sometimes odd to have a camera to your eye as you were talking to someone.

"Were you married?"

Jessie gave a little laugh. "Never. Um, maybe tilt your face, to catch the light—there." Working with the glare off eyeglasses is always a bit of a trick.

"*Warum heißt du Berlin?*"

"Sorry? I don't speak German."

"I asked why you're called Berlin."

"Why should I continue the patriarchal theft of my identity by keeping my father's name?"

Cymbeline shifted on the chaise, placing her feet on the floor.

"Besides, most of the women I know have rechristened themselves: Chicago, London, Shanghai, Cairo—"

Cymbeline burst out laughing. "You all sound like an atlas."

Jessie laughed along with her.

"So, you aren't close to your father."

"You know, he supported everything I ever wanted to do. He never once said that I had to marry and have children."

"We sound as if we had the same father," said Cymbeline.

"It's a conflict for me because I don't care if a man opens the door for me. I mean, I don't see it as patronizing. My consciousness-raising group? Forget it. All that talk about men crying, and the Masturbation Issue, and the Good Girl Tradition, the Orgasm Issue, and there is no way that I will ever be down enough to taste my own menstrual blood like Germaine Greer."

"I'm still thinking about the men crying."

"Yeah, they're only 'good' men because they're 'in touch with their emotions.'" Jessie dropped into the chair next to the chaise.

"I thought it was because they were being asked to partake in the menstrual part of your program."

"Can I tell you something? My father is a thousand times better to women than those men who cry, but I won't even bring him up with the other women because I don't want to hear how I have false consciousness when all I know is my dad is a great dad. I'm not a feminist because of my father. It's the larger world. Geez, if society followed my father's example, the women I know wouldn't even be having these conversations. I believe absolutely in equal rights—it's the other stuff—"

"The blood and the orgasms?"

"Yes! That I don't care about. I think I changed my name so the other women would know how deeply I feel about legal abortion and equal pay and employment . . ." She fell silent.

Cymbeline touched her hand. "Sometimes I don't understand how you young women can get it so right and so wrong at the same time."

When Cymbeline said she needed a break from posing, Jessie knew the older woman understood that Jessie's concentration was shot. Jessie followed Cymbeline out to the garden, where every so often the summer air revealed the nearness of the sea.

When Jessie mentioned that she recognized some of the plants from Cymbeline's pictures, Cymbeline said, a touch of tension in her voice, "Tell me that this day isn't about some lovers' quarrel."

"Actually, we rarely fight," said Jessie.

"I'm not one of your feminist friends," said Cymbeline.

"It's true."

"Then why don't you tell me what else is true?"

So Jessie said, Emile is so good at his profession he makes it seem effortless. He can be funny without strenuously trying to entertain, and he understands the art of flirting and self-deprecation. He isn't petulant or prone to silent fits of ill temper. One of his most winning characteristics is his endless interest in everything.

And his most dangerous trait is his interest in everyone.

And that there is no drug like the moment he discovers you.

She said that when she fell in love with Emile she believed she had found that mythical love of equals, thinking, Oh, we'll travel and takes pictures, side by side. He didn't care if they had children—odd fact: He was great with kids—or if she knew how to cook. He was a bit of a neatnik and accustomed to cleaning the kitchen or doing laundry.

"You know what I love?" she said. "To watch him iron."

It was Emile's blurring of traditional roles that bolstered Jessie's confidence in their chances to make it work, though it also distanced her from the women's art collective, all those women with their complaints that began with the words "He never—" The women seldom noticed that Jessie didn't join in when their talk turned to the angry weariness at the physical caring for another human being over the age of consent.

Once or twice she tried to defend Emile, only to have her group say that she was a victim of "double-consciousness," W. E. B. DuBois's idea that one is always looking at oneself through the eyes of others. You are an insider and an outsider, politically and socially speaking, all of which has the effect of keeping you from your own true identity.

Only sometimes she wondered if her true identity was Lover of Emile. The lover, not the loved. Though, she added, she was loved. He made her feel loved.

"I heard of you before I met you," said Cymbeline. "I hadn't heard of Emile."

"I know."

"Is that the reason for your joint women's project?"

"No. No. As I said, the BelleFemme Project is about showing that art can be without gender, you know."

When Cymbeline didn't say anything, Jessie could feel her throat start to constrict; ashamed if she should dissolve into tears, turning this bad day into a dreadful day. She said softly, "I don't always know where he goes."

Cymbeline sighed. "You think that offering up these women—these women that you are sharing with him, will fix things."

"I don't know what I think. I only know that I love him and I can't lose him and I can't say that to anyone." Jessie caught her tears before they fell. "You must think I'm foolish."

"I was married for nineteen years. I don't think anyone in love is foolish."

The bedroom was as modestly furnished as the rest of the house. As Cymbeline sat on her bed and pulled a worn copy of Dawn Powell's novel *The Wicked Pavilion* from the lower shelf of her bedside table, folded papers stuck between the pages, she said, "I was offered an assignment at *Vanity Fair* in New York City. Our kids were gone, and I had been a faculty wife for so long I almost forgot I ever had a life before wife and mother. I was forty-nine years old.

"So, here I was with my heart's desire and Leroy wanted me to wait until the term was finished—another fifteen days—before coming to New York with me. I told him they wanted me now, and he could meet me later, but they wouldn't wait. He said that if I left, our marriage was over," she said. "It wasn't my choice to have to choose.

"This is what I wrote him from the train to New York," she said, handing one of the pages to Jessie.

She read, in bits and pieces:

> *Why in the world would you think that it puts you in a ridiculous position for me to go away for a time on a working job. . . . I am sure you are bitter about my methods of working my exit, but with your attitude nothing else was physically possible for me. I begged too many times for co-operation and permission. . . . I cannot get myself straightened out through idleness—I have never really learned to play—and if I did want to play, I could not afford to. . . . I assure you I do not value myself so highly as a photographer as you seem to think, but neither could I venture afield unless I had some confidence in my ability. Only by putting myself thru it, as it*

were, can I really think that I am worth anything to you or the family. . . .
Try not to forget that I have always really done the essentials, have always
been at home after school, when the children came, that my work has not
been as distracting as most wives' occupational bridge, that I had always
had the hope that in place of going down in the scale of worthwhileness and
achievement as most hausfraus do that I was going up. . . . I really thought
I had the right of an adult to undertake an obligation. I never thought for a
moment that a person so liberal in all else would deny me this.

Cymbeline said to Jessie, "I never think anyone in love is foolish. We do the best we can."

Jessie handed the letter back to Cymbeline.

She said, "But you must know that this project is your affection's swan song."

They had just returned to the backyard when the women heard a car pull into the driveway. The seven-foot wooden fence that divided the driveway from the back garden obscured the identity of the car, but Jessie recognized the radio station and the funny little wheeze that accompanied the cutting of the engine. She felt the thrill she always felt at the prospect of Emile: something she thought would lessen over time but continued nonetheless, and mixed in with relief.

The car's back door opened, and Jessie could hear their camera gear being dragged across the leather seats before the door of the BMW was slammed shut.

It wasn't until she heard the soft footsteps of the driver walking to the front door that Jessie knew it wasn't Emile. There was no aural evidence of a passenger.

"Hello? Hello?" The woman's voice was slightly husky, the vocal equivalent of an unmade bed.

"In the back," said Jessie, standing with Cymbeline near the fence.

The gate opened to reveal a barefoot girl in a thin cotton sundress that didn't cover much territory, more youthful and fresher than the quality of her voice suggested, struggling with the assorted bags that Jessie recognized as belonging to Emile: the camera, the tripod, the strobes, the umbrellas. Upon seeing Jessie at the gate, the young woman said, "Thank God," and handed off the bulkiest, heaviest bag.

"She's a little gorgeous, isn't she?" whispered Cymbeline, as the girl moved past the women, dropping everything else on a lawn chair. The appearance of this girl unexpectedly altered the entire relationship of Jessie to Cymbeline. Whereas they had spent the first half of the day in a conversational thrust and parry, trying to find the common ground that so many women seem determined to find when meeting other women for the first time (in this case complicated by the shy hero worship of Jessie for Cymbeline), they now had feelings of long friendship, a kind of connection, summed up by the word *we,* when Cymbeline whispered to Jessie, "Do we know her?"

"So, I drove over here," said the girl, "in Emile's car? He wanted me to bring his stuff, you know, to meet him here?" Her voice trailed off as she took in her surroundings, searching for him at the same time. "He said he'd be here?"

Without warning, she swooped down on Cymbeline, giving the elderly woman a hug of such spontaneous affection that Cymbeline was startled into hugging her back. The photographer's stature seemed that of a child next to this tall, willowy girl who commanded attention with the sheer force of her Nordic beauty. "I hate to ask, but can I get a drink of water? I'm parched."

"Inside," said Cymbeline, whose eyes followed the sylphlike girl as she went into the house.

"Jesus," said Cymbeline. "She's like something out of Greek mythology. The sort of being that lives in a stream or a wood and has Hera turning everyone into livestock. Who is she?"

Jessie shrugged.

The girl called out to ask if she could use Cymbeline's phone, and Cymbeline told her to help herself, then said under her breath, "Just don't expect Emile to be on the other end," which caused Jessie to laugh. Which caused Cymbeline to laugh.

The women were sitting on the painted metal slider; Jessie closed her eyes, enjoying the sun for a moment.

Then they heard the girl on the phone laughing.

"You know," said Cymbeline, "I sometimes think things are harder for young women now than they were in my time. Oh, we could also be shamed into doing things that didn't really benefit us in the name of modernity."

"No one's forcing me to do this project." Jessie shifted her position, sitting up just a little straighter.

"Yes, well, maybe that's the true burden for women—progress—the thing that appears as liberation when it's really just another way for men to get what they want. Not what you want."

"I do want to photograph all the different women," said Jessie.

"Except the women aren't all that different, are they?"

Before Jessie could think this through, or argue with Cymbeline, they were joined by the girl, hurrying into the garden, her beautiful body collapsing next to Cymbeline in a pose of forceful exhaustion, setting the slider in motion.

"I'm Ibis," she said to Cymbeline, whose smile said everything about the girl's name being Ibis. "Short for Scarlet Ibis. Like the firebird." These days, everyone seemed to be rechristening themselves with names like Zephyr or Free or Love Butterfly—as if everyone under twenty-five was engaged in a child's game of pretend. It seemed no one wanted to be an adult. As much as Jessie wanted to comment on "Ibis," she knew that her own self-chosen name of Berlin more or less disallowed commentary. Then again, when Cymbeline was young, what about all those Italian and Eastern European names that entered Ellis Island and came out anglicized? Sometimes, Jessie thought, only in America is identity a choice and reinvention an imperative.

"I'm Jessie," said Jessie to Ibis.

Ibis laughed her wonderful, throaty laugh. "I *know* who you *are*."

Of course, thought Jessie, Emile.

"Your house is really cool," said Ibis. "I could live here really easily."

"Did you talk to Emile?" asked Jessie.

"Not exactly," said Ibis, her eyes now closed and her lovely face tilted toward the sun, light mirroring light, much in the manner of Jessie moments before. Except for the light mirroring light.

"And?" said Jessie.

"Oh, he'll be here," said Ibis. She smiled a wide smile, lowered her face.

"Fuck," said Jessie softly, then, louder, "We're losing the light."

Cymbeline struggled from the swing with help from Jessie and Ibis.

Jessie noticed that Ibis's bright mood had seemed to darken slightly when the two women were left alone, Cymbeline in the house.

"He *did* say to meet him here," said Ibis, her tone a little wounded.

The childlike moue of disappointment, the posture of a gangling adolescent. *Except the women aren't all that different, are they?* That's what she meant, thought Jessie, those women, they're all young.

"He wants to take my picture," said Ibis. "I'm supposed to be part of a project he's doing."

A bruise, already beginning to yellow, showed on the tender underside of the young woman's upper arm as she stretched in the sun, her long legs dangling over the arm of the swing. Catlike is such a cliché, but even more cliché, thought Jessie, is the colorful bite mark on the sweet softness of the girl's outstretched arm. She's very young, this girl, maybe (maybe) twenty. Maybe.

Cymbeline had correctly guessed Jessie's reasoning when she'd agreed to this dual photography experiment: It would allow her to keep Emile to herself. It wasn't about gender, or the male gaze, or who can better read a woman; no, it was knowing Emile's charms and history, and trusting that, if she encouraged him to take pictures of all the girls he wanted—all those nude girls, or girls in diaphanous hippie garb; girls in bedrooms and sitting rooms and sunrooms and gardens. In the bath, in a pool, sleeping in the tall grass—then he would be satisfied. It would be all the possession he would need.

Look, she was saying, I won't be like those other women you've left brokenhearted with your wandering.

Here, she was saying, I'll go those brokenhearted women one better and stay by your side. I'll admire the girls you admire and see what you see and want what you want. It'll still be you and me, babe.

She remembered the first lines of Frank O'Hara's "Meditations in an Emergency":

Am I to become profligate as if I were a blonde? Or religious as if I were French?

Each time my heart is broken it makes me feel more adventurous (and how the same names keep recurring on that interminable list!), but one of these days there'll be nothing left with which to venture forth.

Why should I share you? Why don't you get rid of someone else for a change?

I am the least difficult of men. All I want is boundless love.

Even trees understand me! Good heavens, I lie under them, too, don't I? I'm just like a pile of leaves.

Jessie turned toward the house to see Cymbeline coming outside, the Rollei dangling from its leather strap. Cymbeline dropped the camera in Jessie's lap, saying, "You don't need him. You just think you do."

———————————

Jessie found Ibis sitting on the concrete stairs leading up to the cottage. She looked distressed, as if she had begun to cry, then stopped herself. Turning toward Jessie, she said, "He's not coming, is he?"

"I honestly don't know."

Ibis said nothing as Jessie, moved by the young woman, this (maybe) nineteen-year-old girl, nearly a decade younger than Jessie, who foolishly fell for an older, involved man. Jessie sat close to her, their bodies brushing against each other, and the sweet, floral scent of the girl mingled with the jasmine and roses of the garden, punctuated by the exhaust and stray cigarette smoke of a passerby, and that elusive whiff of ocean. An embrace was more than Jessie could manage; sitting side by side on the narrow stairs as they watched the street was her limit.

"C'mon," she said after they'd sat quietly for several minutes. "Let's take your picture." She lightly patted the girl's back—barely touching her really, the memory of the bruised love bite still fresh in Jessie's mind. "You're too lovely to waste."

"Sometimes it bums me out to be so pretty."

Earlier, such a comment would've sent Jessie into a dark mood. Now it simply seemed silly that her attempt at comforting her lover's mistress should be met with such undisguised self-love; the girl was very pretty.

"I'm serious," said Ibis. "You don't know what it's like."

This made Jessie laugh to the point where she found herself reclining on the sharp little steps. "No," she said between breaths, "I guess I don't."

The girl blushed slightly. "God, that sounded terrible. And you've been so nice and, God, I mean, I think you're very attractive, you know, for your age."

"Oh, Ibis, you must stop before I turn on you." She stood, extending her hand to the girl.

Beauty was something that the feminists in the women's art collective didn't like to talk about, unless it was to disparage men who liked "that sort of thing," implying that the attraction to beauty was just another failing. But Jessie wanted to say, If you're an artist, all you think about is beauty. Yes, it was possible to have a more personal definition of what you found exquisite, but there were some beautiful things that most people agreed upon: a cathedral, a house, a bridge, a nature vista, a necklace, a garden, a gown, a girl.

You couldn't politicize beauty, no matter how much you wanted to; and you couldn't shame people for being entranced.

It was understandable how a pretty girl could be taken up, then dropped, or not listened to, or accepted into something for all the wrong reasons, or be perceived as being something she wasn't, or treated as purely ornamental, and that must carry its own class of loneliness.

Then again, thought Jessie, it's like the I've-been-rich-and-I've-been-poor-and-rich-is-better problem. Who cries for the pretty girl? Isn't that why she has to cry for herself?

"Let's go find Cymbeline," she said.

As they walked back through the cottage, to the garden where Cymbeline waited, Ibis said, "I'm sorry," though Jessie didn't have to ask why. In the same way she didn't have to ask if Emile slept with Ibis. She knew that Emile was sleeping with Ibis; Emile slept with them all.

The photograph was playful. Ibis, a happy nudist, stood in beautiful contrast with the dark-clothed Cymbeline, her beloved Rollei dangling from her neck, her white hair escaping her bandanna, her sandals and socks and surprise at coming upon such a lovely creature, a nymph in her unkempt garden, the girl as surprised and curious to see Cymbeline as Cymbeline is to see her.

One was short, one was tall, one was a photographer, one was a model, one was old, one was young, one was clothed, one was nude. Jessie used Emile's Rolleiflex, speaking to the women as she peered down into the viewing screen, the camera no longer between her and her subjects. For the first time, Jessie felt not only calm but content. It was one of those moments of perfect happiness, all the more wonderful because it was unexpected.

It was so perfect, in fact, that when Emile's knock on the front door broke into the flawless choreography of the afternoon, no one was moved to answer it.

GOOD NIGHT KISS
OR
CRESCENT MOON #4

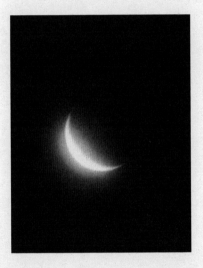

Stellamare was the sort of small town that wasn't exactly charming unless you considered pushing against any kind of encroachment of late-twentieth-century modernity "charming." Mostly, it was inconvenient, slightly eccentric, often insular. It was nestled in the wine country of Northern California, in the midst of other, more promising towns, which is why Stellamare wasn't anyone's destination. Paradoxically, it was this general lack of interest that transformed it into a kind of travel trophy for the wine tourist always on the search for a "discovery." By the early 1980s the wine country above San Francisco was so overrun by visitors who glamorized agriculture according to its crop (grapes = sexy; cabbage = not), and fetishized enology and viticulture, that a casual mention of any "out-of-the-way village" at a dinner party was the perfect little conversational bagatelle, a souvenir if you will, that set you apart from your fellow winophiles.

None of this changed the basic fact that Stellamare was a rural, dual-class region of weekenders and workers, with the workers being mostly Hispanic and the weekenders being mostly not-Hispanic. The townspeople shared traits with both groups.

Everyone in and outside of Stellamare knew the local banker, Wallace Westerbrooke Lux, a graduate of Stanford and Yale who'd served in World War II and had the world at his feet upon obtaining his degrees in economics and finance (with lucrative job offers in San Francisco and New York) but chose to open up a farmers' bank in Stellamare.

His business sense was unerring, even though at times his practices seemed counterintuitive and unorthodox. However, the people with whom he dealt felt him to be a reliable and honorable man. When asked why he'd settled so far from the financial thick of things, he said that money had its charms but his heart belonged to gardening. And to the construction of the occasional odd little assemblage (bones, claws, jewels), often under a glass dome or arranged inside a box.

Summerplace, Wallace Westerbrooke Lux's farm (or garden—it was referred to as both), was extravagant by anyone's standards, with its mix of trees imported from China and India, Japan and Italy, the Middle East and the American South. There were native palms. A rare East African tree. There were an orange grove and fountains and wild strawberries. A garden of blue flowers (lilies, delphiniums, plumbagos, violets, Johnny-jump-ups, musk sage, lavender) and foliage plants (*Agave americana, Agave franzosinii, Brahea armata,* the atlas cedar). Thousands of pieces of luminous blue sea glass, their edges worn by tides, marked the paths.

There was a white garden of such strong perfume it felt enchanted, and a silver garden of dusty miller. Bougainvillea, climbing roses, cacti. Ornamental plums and cherries; lotuses the size of tabletops floating on pools large enough for swimming. An enormous working clock, planted in patterns of the zodiac. A Japanese garden with an orange moon bridge; a stepped, grassy amphitheater where the Lux children performed plays and concerts and poetry recitations.

Cycads, ancient, rare, and as expensive as emerald bracelets, composed a garden that looked prehistoric ("the dinosaur place," said the Lux children); it was next to a bromeliad garden that was like a mysterious jungle, the sun dappling the dirt floor.

There was a natural pool. And a pool to swim in and a pool to sit beside and a shallow pool the color of a summer sky surrounded by a sandy beach and studded with giant clamshells.

The air of Summerplace was fragrant with the smells of eucalyptus, jasmine, orange blossom, roses, cut grass, and earth. Scents that always brought Jenny Lux, Wallace's only daughter, back to her youth.

At night, without the interference of the reflected city lights, the sky spilled diamonds. Late summer was a show of shooting stars, a million wishes made through Jenny's life on those falling stars.

As the beauty and artistic reach of Mr. Lux's garden increased, so did his reputation as an eccentric. No one could understand a money-man with compassion, nor could they fathom why someone with a keen understanding of the bottom line would choose to turn an expensive California wine country parcel into thirty-nine acres of sheer folly.

Over time, the idiosyncrasies of the garden attached themselves to whoever lived at Summerplace, pegging the entire family as eccentric, and no one more so than Jenny, the youngest of the six children. She was a pretty girl who never behaved like a pretty girl, with her marvelous hazel eyes, luminous really, and clear skin that never quite tanned beyond a slightly darkened cream, despite her outdoor pursuits. Her bobbed hair was an adequate shade of brown, its thick, springy texture responsible for its attractiveness. All the Luxes had the same build: average height and lithe. Jenny's five brothers, her mother, her father almost seemed "too related," her parents appearing nearly as members of the same biological family. Their loving and devoted marriage was also cause for suspicion. This, naturally, gave rise to more speculation and gossip, which was countered only by the general gratitude the townspeople felt toward Mr. Lux and Mrs. Lux, who always seemed generous with their business expertise (Mr. Lux) or time (Mrs. Lux) or money (Mr. and Mrs. Lux).

The natural beauty of their daughter drew the boys; then, when they got to know her a little, baffled the boys. Their expectations, such as they were at that age, went unmet, with the boys too unworldly (yet) to readjust them with regard to this splendid, slightly wild girl.

Her wildness was more animal in nature and not limited to sexuality. Her father had not raised her to "be a girl," which is how Jenny Lux would've put it had she thought of it in those terms. That is, Mr. Lux obviously raised her as he thought a girl should be raised, but his parenting style was clearly not in accord with either their community or the times. When feminism came to the fore in her late teens, early twenties, Jenny quite honestly didn't know what to think about it. Had she been treated differently from her brothers, had her ambitions been calibrated to account for her female lot in life, had she been told that there were limits, or somehow taught that women were more effective when they used charm, a little subterfuge, feminine wiles, then perhaps she wouldn't have confused her suitors. In short, she didn't know what she didn't know.

Another thing that set her apart: She meant what she said and said it plainly and without a lilt in her voice; there was no trace of that girlish, self-questioning speech pattern. Even the boys who were most captivated by her would not have described her as charming. It's a fallacy that no one wants to "play games" or that they wish for someone to dispense with guile, because the truth is that they live for the game. Someone who doesn't "play games" is someone who doesn't know the rules. It was this lack that made her not only different but suspect.

If she liked a boy, she told him. If they went out, she often made the first move, and, when she didn't, she was a willing participant. Not if she didn't like the boy, but then she rarely went out with someone she didn't already like a little.

The unpredictable aspect of all this was that Jenny didn't gain the reputation of an easy girl. If she was involved with someone—even casually—there was no bragging, no smearing of her name around school. It wouldn't occur to her that anyone would want to do that, to anyone. Social mores, by the time she was in high school, in the mid-1960s, were changing so quickly that it was change as much as a cataclysm, but the small American towns lagged years behind. In some of those towns it wasn't 1967, it was 1957 and all that went with that. Girls still wanted to be cheerleaders to the boys who wanted to be football heroes.

Jenny was unconsciously liberated enough to know that she didn't know what she wanted to be. And that was the most dangerous thing of all.

———————

Nothing Jenny Lux did was much of an issue because the townspeople (weekenders and workers) liked having Summerplace to talk about as something that gave their little village distinction. Every town had vineyards and wineries and tasting rooms and at least one restaurant that served wild, grape-fed boar on couscous, but none of them had Summerplace.

The weekenders and the townspeople told and retold stories of the six Lux children, unsupervised, shoeless, often in shorts and nothing else, including Jenny, who spent much of her childhood running wild through the fanciful landscape her father created. Her companions were rarely her brothers—a quintet of pragmatists less dream-driven than their sister—instead she could be found keeping company with the family's four Portuguese water dogs and a lone blond cairn terrier, a male dog with a mercurial personality (five stand-ins for her five brothers). The dogs had individual names, but because they were a fairly insepa- rable pack, they all answered to the each other's names, which is to say, they all answered to the same name. Eventually, the family dispensed with all but one name, Linus, and it worked out very well. Even the one female in the group was Linus. It wasn't until Jenny was in kindergarten that she learned the breed of the dog was Portuguese water dog and not Linus.

The townspeople thought Jenny was feral.

She thought she was feral too.

Sometimes she waded in the sky blue water of a pool while the dogs lazed on the white sand beach with its giant clamshells. Other days she could be seen napping among them under a live oak. Or they would walk the perimeter of the property together, Jenny in the midst of the pack. Her father, they said, indulged her every whim, including allowing her to stay home from school two days a week to explore "art." The school principal said, "It's always unacceptable to keep children home if they aren't ill. Some parents"—she sniffed—"think they know best." Never mind that Jenny was at the top of her class, well-read, and whip smart in science and math. Never mind that she was a thought- ful, observant child who loved nature in the best possible way, that is to say that she allowed it to be what it was without imposing her will upon it. She seemed more interested in watching people or animals or events than in interacting with them, or controlling them. Never mind her natural curiosity.

When she was older, it wasn't uncommon to see Jenny setting up her father's 1956 Rolleiflex 2.8D camera, sometimes with a tripod, sometimes using the light meter she often had in her pocket, studying her surroundings until something caught her attention. Always checking the watch she was never without, gazing up at the sky. She would ask people of Stellamare to pose, or train the old camera on plants or structures. All the other kids had new Kodak Instamatics, not expensive ten-year-old cameras meant for serious photography, asking more of the photographer than to point and shoot, making it seem that Wallace Westerbrooke Lux was simply forcing his brand of unusual onto his daughter.

The thing was, when the Luxes opened up their gardens one week a year for the public to tour (at the request of a women's society that Mrs. Lux sometimes met with for charitable work; they were mostly affluent housewives, and seven days of being allowed into Summerplace proved quite lucrative), Wallace Westerbrooke Lux set up a tent displaying Jenny's pictures, and everyone had to agree that you couldn't quite take your eyes off of them.

When Mr. Lux died, and Mrs. Lux moved to live closer to her eldest son, in Florida, the beautiful, singular Jenny inherited the gardens and the animals of Summerplace. This turn of events pleased the townspeople, since nearly everyone had met Jenny Lux, giving their tales about Summerplace a little more authority when they spoke to tourists. They spoke with the tones of insiders, their stories touched with a kind of awe and a sniff of condescension.

And when she married Abner Huxley, the townspeople simply folded him into their stories of Summerplace. In certain circumstances, they could also be protective toward Jenny and Summerplace, that is, until Sam Tsukiyama and *those photographs*. Suddenly, it was if Jenny had hoodwinked them into believing her harmless when she was a viper in their midst all along. Once the attention fell on Jenny Lux and her photographs, Summerplace suddenly seemed like a facade, a diversion from the activities within, masking something sinister.

Jenny hadn't had a lot of lovers by the time she met Abner Huxley, during the summer following her junior year at Stanford. Once she and Abner took up together, there was no one else for her. She would say, "I knew I wanted to be an artist and that I had to choose: I could have lovers with all my energy going into them, or I could use my time and attention in other ways. I chose other ways."

She replaced the Rolleiflex 2.8D that so puzzled the townspeople with an even older camera, a Seneca from 1909.

"I look for imperfection," she would say later, explaining why she would even bother to use such an old camera, let alone one that had clearly sustained some unusual damage. "Everything that moves me, or captivates me, can often be found in the space where things go wrong, or fall short."

The five-by-seven Seneca No. 9 was a camera that Mr. Lux had picked up in a used camera store called Schonneker's Camera Emporium, located near Union Square, on a warm San Francisco day of intermittent clouds. When Wallace Westerbrooke Lux found himself with time on his hands between business meetings, he strolled in and around the square until he came to a funny little store with a Seneca Black Beauty displayed in its window. Inside he saw another Seneca, a No. 9, the leather a little singed, looking as if there was some damage to the lens, which the shopkeeper, Ed Schonneker, assured him would still take decent pictures. "Not perfect, you understand. After all, the camera is older than I am."

Ed Schonneker showed Mr. Lux how the bellows extended beyond the camera bed; he showed him the spirit level, the detailed industrial metal fittings, the revolving camera back along with the leather flap that opened like a door to reveal the ground glass viewfinder, showing the image upside down ("Laws of optics," said Mr. Schonneker). "It can hold two glass plates," he said, then demonstrated the use of the dark slide for exposures. The camera closed up into an elegant, little boxlike package, "for travel," said Mr. Schonneker, "very compact dimensions." He offered the closed camera to Mr. Lux to test the weight. "And," he said, "you can make full-size prints, or postcard size. Of course, you do have to have an understanding of dry plates and dry-plate printing, but when you make a picture from one of these cameras, you *are* making a picture."

It was the chemistry of the plates and the promise of imperfection that swayed Mr. Lux. In his mind he saw Jenny, now fifteen and still enamored with the Rolleiflex, and understood that the mechanics and complexity of the Seneca would intrigue her. He wasn't sure what she wanted from photography, but he knew that whatever it was there was a greater chance of finding it in this anachronistic camera store than in a place lined with new Nikons. Nothing about that girl was predictable; he supposed that he would never know if it was nature or nurture, and so decided to simply accept it as *what is.* "Okay," he said.

As Ed Schonneker was writing up the ticket, he stopped. "Wait, I do have something else," he said, and with that he disappeared into a back room.

Mr. Lux wandered about the crowded store, studying the array of cameras. One was a massive old plate camera on a stand making it nearly as tall as he, with a lens the size of his hand. The box was a reddish hued wood, marred and dulled in spots. And then there were the handsome vintage wooden cameras looking impossibly new, their brass fittings as polished as the natural stained wood.

There were Graflex cameras, black boxes with tall, black leather hoods that sprang up like jack-in-the-boxes. And newer Graflex Speed Graphics with round flashes, which he had seen in every vintage movie that showed a newspaper reporter. There were Rolleiflexes, so visually and mechanically flawless. Rolleicords, Kodak Retina Big and Small Cs that reminded him of family road trips through the Grand Canyon; Contessas, Contaxes, and Leicas of every vintage, in every imaginable condition. Panorama and pinhole cameras. There were strobes and leather camera bags, and lenses. Tripods and glass plates and film backs for sheet film. Sets of lens filters in green, red, yellow, and blue.

All these cameras, these tiny "rooms" of light and shadow; these beautiful machines that produced the stuff of dreams. They were so appealing in their construction and appearance that Mr. Lux realized he desired them in the same way he coveted a painting or a sculpture.

Many of the store's wares were on shelves behind the counters, or in the vitrine, or lying about—an indication that the owner either trusted his clientele or didn't care what disappeared from his vast collection.

"Look, let me just give you this." Ed set a smallish, substantial black leather case with a hinged lid on top of the glass counter. It was taller than it was wide and opened from the top, as if it were meant to hold business files. "It's a carry case for the camera. Obviously, whoever owned it didn't use the case too often." It was in remarkably good condition compared to the camera, which isn't to say it looked unused—only that it appeared less used. The unlatched and opened lid revealed two compartments, neatly divided by a leather-covered divider. Mr. Lux slid the closed camera into the larger section; the other section held six glass plates.

"Let me pay you for it," said Mr. Lux, who really wasn't all that interested in the carrying case.

Ed Schonneker put up his hands. "What am I going to do with it?"

After he latched the case with the camera inside, Mr. Lux paid the bill, then stepped out into a San Francisco afternoon cooled by incoming fog.

The camera that Mr. Lux bought for Jenny that day in San Francisco sat on her dresser, while the carrying case was shoved in a closet.

"I got you this camera because it's an elegant machine, and the way it takes pictures is with a great deal of stillness and contemplation. This characteristic will force you to think about what you see. It will slow you down," he told her. (Jenny, at fifteen, was carrying on a love affair with speed: she ran with the dogs, she rode a ten-speed racing bike, she gunned around the gardens in a ratty Jeep. She was the one who kissed the boys who asked her out first—not that there were too many—rushing into everything. She ran up the stairs in her parents' very modern, very spare house; she ran to the bus that she took to school.) "A blur is just a blur," he said.

But Jenny was more interested in other things, like the cycle of life on Summerplace, which offered ideal examples of birth and decay, growth and decline. She was impulsive, hurried in her curiosity about the wheel of life—always about life. The abstract world, the fantastic, the dreamy and intangible didn't enthrall her—with the exception of Summerplace, sprung from Mr. Lux's imagination—and for this reason she was as bored by religion as she was excited by science.

Her parents would say it was because, unlike the majority of the townspeople, they didn't attend church. When asked why he eschewed the church, her father said, "I don't need the business contacts and I don't need a lecture."

Her mother was less absolute but, in the end, gave in to her husband, as she did in most matters. Their marriage, like so many, was one of negotiation, with their particular summits deciding that he would do what he wanted to do, while she would find her own hobbies; she would influence the boys, and Jenny would be his charge. Not that it mattered; Jenny and her father were so simpatico that her mother never would've had any sway regardless. Jenny was her father's favorite. Not as surrogate son (he had five sons) but as the child who shared his interests.

The summer after Jenny's junior year, Abner Huxley, a senior in the landscape architectural program at Berkeley, had contacted Mr. Lux to ask if he ever hired interns to work at Summerplace. Mr. Lux had laughed over dinner at the idea of having an "intern," since his fabulous garden, despite people's curiosity, was still a private home.

But over the next few days, whenever he had to do something like retrieve the mail, Mr. Lux would sigh, "If only I had an intern." When Mrs. Lux asked him to move a chair, he replied, "Why not wait until the intern arrives?" Suddenly, all manner of household chores and errands became the responsibilities of the Mythical Intern, so that when Mr. Lux did end up meeting, and "interning," Abner, it was as if the younger man had been around forever. His normality, his laugh and easygoing nature meshed nicely with the Luxes. And Abner fell in love with Mr. Lux's exotic gardens, his affection for arts, and with Jenny most of all.

For Jenny, meeting Abner was feeling that she had known him all her life. For once, she didn't rush into anything, and when she saw him walking the path lined with pieces of blue sea glass winding through the blue foliage and flowers, she only knew that she didn't want him to simply pass through her life, but she was too inexperienced to know how to express it. So she said, "Wait here," while she ran back to the house to get her father's Rolleiflex 2.8D, to take his picture.

It was during this same visit that Mr. Lux, observing Abner's enthusiasm for the garden, asked him if, upon graduation in June, he would like to work for him. "My sons have their own homes," he said. While this job offer was almost tailor-made for Abner, his attraction to Jenny made him hesitate; he was the least opportunistic of men, sometimes to his detriment, and he didn't want to suddenly seem like an opportunist. Mr. Lux, unaware of the spark between Abner and Jenny, insisted, saying, "This is what you studied for the last four years, isn't it?"

Jenny's happiness was so pure that it felt like a distillation of happiness. Maybe it was being in love along with being in lust (instead of just lust), but her parents' home had now become a romantic landscape, a dressed stage, a cinematic backdrop for the man she loved. Strange to think that the thing before her (the wonders of Summerplace) was the very thing she could not see until there was a shift in perspective. Later, Jenny would say that she seldom knew what she would take a picture of when she picked up the camera, that she only knew once she peered through the viewfinder, as if the photograph had finally found her.

———————

She recited this to him:

> *And she would quote Cocteau*
> *'I feel there is an angel in me' she'd say*
> *'whom I am constantly shocking'*

"Ferlinghetti," she said. "But it could be me."
And he replied, answering in Ferlinghetti:

I once started out
to walk around the world
but ended up in Brooklyn

And then she went back to Stanford in the fall, while he stayed with her father and mother.

———————————

The Luxes were surprised though not completely displeased when Jenny announced that she and Abner were getting married. Nothing fancy, they said. The wedding, they said, was only a starting point and nothing more. Someone mentioned their youth (twenty-one and twenty-two, respectively, barely out of college, Jenny having graduated only a week earlier), and Jenny countered that they had known each other for a year and, besides, how lucky is it to meet the person you know you want to know your entire life at an early age? "Youth and love," Jenny said, "are not gasoline and matches."

Her mother was about to protest, "That's exactly what they are!" when Jenny's father lightly placed his hand on his wife's wrist.

———————————

Jenny and Abner traveled to London, Berlin, Madrid, and Rome. They loved Rome. Berlin was a divided city, the Brandenburg Gate a sad, grand monument that was the location of an August protest that summer in 1971, commemorating the ten-year anniversary of a similar protest. Abner and Jenny could understand only that the East was shutting itself off from the West "until further notice." Spain belonged to Franco, London was still getting over the war.

Not Rome. Rome felt indolent and indulgent, its famous timelessness a consequence of knowing that one day you're an empire and the next you're nothing; it's simply the way of life. A living thing, by definition, is unfixed, rising or falling. It was this very characteristic that reminded Jenny of Summerplace: the births of the dogs and cats, a family of ducks, the gardens in bloom, the quickening of spring, the fading of fall.

They walked and walked in Rome until they had to purchase new shoes, then they walked some more. Jenny bought handfuls of postcards that she pasted into a travel journal.

When Abner asked her why she didn't take photographs instead, she said that all she wanted was an illustrated record of their trip, and that she didn't bring a camera because she didn't want to spend their trip looking through a viewfinder. The postcards would remind her of where they had been. Besides, it was wonderful here, but it wasn't home. What she meant was, there was nothing she wanted to say about the places they saw that hadn't already been said a million times in postcards.

About a month into their extended honeymoon, Jenny and Abner spent the day at a centuries-old garden called Bomarzo outside of Rome. It was a strange, overgrown, contradictory place that a duke had once used for trysts *and* to honor his adored wife. There were peculiar statues of sea monsters rising from the ground, and of bizarre, double-finned mermen; a two-story house that was built to lean for no discernible reason; there were inscribed messages that were as cryptic as some of the statues. They agreed it was almost a kind of spectacular roadside attraction; nothing about it explained itself. What did this structure mean? How to decipher an arrangement of statues in an expanse of lawn? What would Mr. Lux make of it? What about all the mysterious messages carved into the stone figures? Jenny was taken with the atmosphere of mortality and time, Abner with the landscaping, both with its sheer mystery.

They heard a classical trio play in a church in Venice.

They stayed in a cheap hotel that smelled like someone's basement in a tourist town on the Adriatic, the two of them, alone, holding hands, wading out into the sea for what seemed like miles, the water never rising above their ankles.

They spent two days at the Uffizi in Florence. They visited the imitation David in the Piazza della Signoria. And then they saw the real thing at the Galleria dell'Accademia; the contrast between the fake David in an enormous, open-air space and the genuine David in a room was startling in that the locations so radically changed the scale of a human to him.

They climbed to the top of the Spanish Steps, along with all the other visitors to Rome.

When they split up for the day, each wanting (and needing) a little time alone, there were five postcards waiting for Jenny at their room:

1. A mythical stone girl lay on her back creating a makeshift bench, the Latin words etched on her side worn away by age. The message read: *Having a Coke with you is even more fun than being freaked out by Bomarzo.*

2. The Bridge of Sighs: *I can't believe I ever thought this was romantic. And yet, it was romantic being there with you.*

3. A picture of the sea with a distant shore: *I think if we kept walking we could've made it there.*

4. A picture of Botticelli's *Venus*:

   *and the portrait show seems to have no faces in it at all, just paint
   you suddenly wonder why in the world anyone ever did them
   I look
   at you and I would rather look at you than all the portraits in the
     world
   except for possibly* The Polish Rider *occasionally*

5. A picture of the Trevi Fountain:

   *I once started out
   to walk around the world
   but ended up with you.*

   Thank God.

For twenty years the Seneca sat on a shelf in Jenny's studio, a reminder of her father, now deceased, her mother, relocated. Jenny and Abner had moved to Summerplace upon their return from nearly two years of travel.

Their residency was meant to be temporary, but Mr. Lux liked having Abner around to help with the gardens, now quite grown and established, the men carrying on a continuous conversation about the plantings and pools. Abner was also a part-time professor at a local college that specialized in enology. He taught landscape architecture, his ambition to strike out on his own supplanted by caring for the living art of Summerplace.

Jenny was restless, aimless. She didn't know what she wanted, except that she wanted, in many respects, exactly what she had: Abner, their three girls, her father's botanical dream. Once they came home from their travels, she was sated; whatever is the opposite of wanderlust, that was what she had. Her disquiet was not about domesticity—it was about photography.

She occasionally picked up a photography assignment (a property for a real estate agent or homeowner; a high school tennis team; a wedding) using her father's old Rolleiflex, telling herself it was good to "work the creative muscle." However, working the muscle implied that this sort of photography was an exercise that affected what she really wanted to shoot when, in truth, the pictures were throwaways. They had as much to do with making pictures (for her) as mucking out a horse stall. It was not arrogance that brought her to that conclusion as much as uncomplicated fact: There was almost nothing that she felt "too good for," but she was aiming and shooting without saying anything. It was like "mute photography," and that was why each job was ultimately useless to her.

And she loved being home because there every day was new. It was her inspiration and her world. In Rome she had discovered that she could love being there and not be moved to take a single photo. She intuited that she had something to say about the pleasures of domesticity, she just didn't know what it would be, or if anyone would care.

As a modern woman, she had nothing stopping her from pursuing a career outside the home. It was encouraged if one was to be taken seriously. For a girl who wasn't raised traditionally or expected to live traditionally, it wasn't that surprising that the contentments of home seemed extraordinary and marvelous.

In 1986 the girls were seven, five, and three years old, respectively.

Babe, Bunny, and Agnes, respectively. As Jenny's mother once said of Jenny as a mother, "When I'm with you and the children, I always get the sense that you're not really raising them. It's more like you're *observing* them."

There was truth to that statement; Jenny was not the sort of parent who liked arranging the lives and hobbies of her kids. Instead, she enjoyed being around them, watching them, or listening to them. They had the same freedoms on the farm that Jenny had had in her youth. Their hours were their own as they played with the dogs and other animals, often in states of undress (usually for, but not limited to, swimming), or partial dress, or (Jenny's favorite observation) playing dress-up. The kids in costumes gave way to various forms of playacting. Because Jenny would rather watch than interfere, the children often forgot about her presence. "I'm like the Jane Goodall of my own offspring," Jenny would say with a laugh to Abner.

One day, when Abner came into Jenny's darkroom to see a series of photos of a recent wine event hanging up, he turned to his wife and said, "I can take time off from work."

"For what?"

"You can't keep doing this."

"I know."

"You could go somewhere. See something."

She slid her arms around his waist, her cheek against his back. "I would miss you. And the children. And Summerplace. I don't think the answer is leaving—I think it's staying."

Jenny could never say what inspired her to pull the old Seneca off the shelf in her office. If she so desired, she could probably trace a sequence of thoughts that looked something like this: wife-parent-children–the future–love-identity-love-art–her father–her father–her father–missing him–the five-by-seven glass-plate camera he bought for her at Schonneker's Camera Emporium in San Francisco, where he exited the shop to be greeted by a late-afternoon fog rolling in.

Maybe it was curiosity. Maybe she was remembering taking those first pictures of Abner. Maybe it was the fantastic thinking of Summerplace as an isolated wildlife science station in Africa. Maybe it was the thought of shooting one more high school sports team, or staff at a local bank, or wine party that made her consider never picking up a camera again and then panicking at the very idea. Maybe it was the magical notion of thinking it could bring her father back to her when he said that the Seneca, with its glass plates, was a camera made to slow the world down. "A blur is just a blur," he said. There were moments when she felt lonely in her eccentricity, even though she couldn't have asked for a better companion than Abner, or a more fitting home. Later she would say, "My art was not elsewhere."

On a whim, with the kids being watched by the housekeeper, Jenny tossed the Seneca in the car and headed for the city. Not stopping to wonder if the camera store was still there, off Union Square, or if it had become a victim of dislocating high rents over the course of the past twenty years. This wasn't the sort of endeavor where one thought it through, or called ahead; to hesitate would be to be ensnared by the doubt of a forming idea (as well as missing her father), and that would be too much to risk.

———————————

Schonneker's Camera Emporium. Like the Tadich Grill, the City of Paris, Schroeder's, Magnin's—it remained. The place was still a jumble of cameras, ranging from the nineteenth century through the seventies. "Yes?" said a man of such advanced age she was sure he was the same Ed Schonneker who'd sold her father the Seneca. The realization that he was, in all likelihood, the same Ed who'd spent part of an afternoon with her father unexpectedly moved her.

"A Seneca Number Nine," he said, when she set the camera on the counter. "The man who bought this was trying to decide between it and a Seneca Black Beauty."

Now the image of her father trying to think of which camera her fifteen-year-old self would prefer was threatening to undo her completely. But she managed to say, "There is a glass plate in the back, and I don't quite know what to do with it."

The man made no move to touch the camera. Instead, he slowly walked to a desk near the counter, pulling a bit of pencil from a drawer along with a notepad with a logo for a local cab company. In perfect school-taught penmanship, he wrote a name and address. "Sam's young," he said, "but he knows what he's doing."

"Young" Sam Tsukiyama turned out to be a thirty-five-year-old man, the same age as Jenny, though he was a youthful thirty-five, much like Jenny. Everyone must seem young when you're nearing ninety years old, she reasoned of Ed's description.

Jenny showed up at Sam Tsukiyama's Victorian, on Twentieth, half a block from busy Mission Street, with its mix of taquerias, dime stores, and markets. Other shops selling elaborate quinceañero dresses, religious objects, kitschy Vegas-style furniture, and inexpensive clothing lined the street. A blast of exhaust from a barbecue restaurant hit her as she approached the house, weaving through the sidewalk shoppers.

Two kids sat on the terrazzo stairs leading to the front door. They seemed unfazed as Jenny stepped between them.

One of the kids said, "You can just walk in, lady. He don't care. Here." He jumped up, pushed opened one of the two identical tall, narrow doors with carved wooden angels and inset with high, stained-glass windows.

The boy left her on the threshold to go back to his friend on the stoop.

"Hello?" said Jenny.

No reply.

"Um, anybody?"

She walked into the shadowy, high-ceilinged entry, almost as long as it was tall. Unwilling to close the door behind her, yet nervous to leave it open, she glanced down the hall and up the stairs to the left. She could see a living room, part of a dining room, and into a very large kitchen, all with the same fourteen-foot ceilings.

Very little light came into the house because of the close-set houses on either side, and what light there was came from the still-open front door and, Jenny could see, the other opened door next to a wall of windows at the back of the kitchen.

Closing the front door, she walked a straight line past the living room, through the dining room, into the kitchen, then out the back door and onto a wooden landing. Below the landing she saw a young man in the garden. He was hacking some sort of resistant vine with a hoe.

"Excuse me," she called over the chop-chop of the hoe as it hit stem and ground. He stopped without looking up, as if he were listening, then resumed.

"Hello?"

This time he looked up. "I thought I heard someone," he said, seemingly unsurprised at seeing a stranger newly emerged from his house. His dark, straight hair fell to the base of his tanned neck, damp with perspiration; suntans were unusual for San Franciscans, leading her to surmise that he spent quite a bit of time in his garden. He was of medium height and slender, with a pleasing face and smile, a nice-looking man. There was an ease about him, almost as if her appearance on his wooden deck was usual and ordinary. He wasn't, in some respects, unlike Abner.

"Ed sent me? From Schonneker's Camera Emporium?"

He held his hand to the side of his eyes, blocking the lingering sun. "Oh, Ed. Look, I'm a little"—his hand fell from his face as he indicated the stubborn foliage—"uh, could you come back another time?"

"Sure," she said.

He waved as he returned to his labors; a handsome Siamese cat with her dark chocolate and cocoa-colored markings accented by sections of bright, white fur marched over to him, then sat down nearby like a one-cat audience. Jenny saw him stop, turn toward the cat, and smile.

She drove to Green Apple Books on Clement Street. It was the sort of inviting store that probably made half its income by tapping into the natural curiosity of the reader, banking on spontaneous purchases; the more one browsed, the more one wanted to read (and to buy). She bought one novel, one short story collection, one biography, and four books on photographers.

She crossed the street to buy cheap dim sum that she ate while leaning against a building and watching the commuters jumping off the Muni, heading home or ducking into a market or take-out place.

She got into her car and drove back to Sam Tsukiyama's. This time he answered her knock, dinner napkin still in hand as he said, "You again."

"You said to come back another time."

He laughed. "I guess this is another time."

"I have children, so my time isn't strictly my own."

"Then you better come inside."

Sam showed Jenny how to tilt the lens using the camera bed; to check for pinholes that allowed light in the bellows. "You'll have to replace them if this happens," he said. He talked about the No. 9 and told her that it was one of the Seneca models that produced "postcard prints." He demonstrated the revolving back for horizontal and vertical photographs. "And this," he said, opening a hinged flap, also in the rear of the camera, "is where you see the image." She tried to see what he was talking about, but the image was barely visible on the ground-glass screen.

"You'll need to wear a black cloth over your head if you want decent resolution. Here." He handed her a sweatshirt that was tossed on a nearby dining room chair.

As she scanned the dining room, she saw the Siamese cat now sitting on the table with the same audience demeanor she'd noticed when it was in the garden; she saw pens (including a fountain pen), a notebook, a short stack of books, a partially complete *New York Times* crossword, and, finally, Sam. The screen was large enough to offset the disorientation she felt at the images being upside down and reversed.

"You have a tripod, right?"

"Somewhere," she said.

"You may want to use it, though the camera is light enough to hold it steady. Just check the spirit level," said Sam. "Once upon a time you could buy prepared dry plates, but now—I mean if you really want to pursue this—you'll have to do it yourself. It takes practice and patience."

He explained the process of preparing the plates (gelatin, silver nitrate, potassium bromide, and a tool to spread the emulsion). He said that they could stay sensitive for months, unused. He said there was a chemical shortcut of ready-made emulsion, but it was up to her. He said she could dispense with the plates and go to paper. Or film. "And by the way, what are you using now?"

"My father's old Rolleiflex."

"I had a very good friend who used a Rollei." He seemed to leave her for a moment before saying, "Okay, then, you've got to get the stillness down, because you'll need it with glass plates. So, be still. Mind the dark slide."

———————————

"You'll have to come out to my house," said Jenny to Sam on the phone, canceling their session; this time it was Agnes who needed her. Again. Since that first meeting, Jenny had gone two more times to Sam Tsuki-yama's for instruction in dry-plate photography. She needed help with glass-plate preparation and printing. Using the Seneca proved fairly easy once she understood it. "I can't always come to you, as I explained, and I have a studio and darkroom and all the chemicals anyone could need." She hesitated, as if trying hard to remember something, then brightened. "Please," she said.

"I can do it in the late spring and summer. You have children, I have students."

"I'll make a room for you in the Little House," she said. "It's near a fountain and the zodiac clock."

"Zodiac clock?"

"You'll see when you get here."

"I didn't say that I would come and stay for the spring and summer."

"You could bring your cat?" she offered. "We have a jungle garden."

Sam started laughing. "I don't think Kali's been pining away for a jungle all her life."

"As if you'd know the innermost workings of the mind of a house cat."

"Didn't Montaigne say something about not knowing if he was playing with his cat or if his cat was playing with him?" he said.

"Then I'll invite your cat and you can come with her."

––––––––––

The first photograph was of Bunny, Jenny's second child, who was all of five years old, mosquito bites up and down her bare arms, like metal studs on the sleeves of a leather jacket. In her underwear, she looked slightly miserable at the grouping of bites.

"I know they itch, sweetie, but I just need you to stay still for a few minutes," said Jenny, adjusting the camera on its tripod. Checking the upside-down, reversed image in the ground glass at the back, alternating between checking while under the black head cloth and coming back out to reassure her daughter. "Almost, almost," she said.

Sam sat nearby smoking a cigarette. He was reading *The Great Gatsby* for the tenth time; he read it every other summer and only in summer. Kali stretched out asleep on the patio of the Little House, a one-bedroom, stucco, Spanish-style place that Sam had to admit he rather loved. ("You weren't kidding about the zodiac clock," he said to Jenny as he stood near the working clock of flowers and star signs, which dwarfed him with its size.) Wonderful, too, was spending a summer outside the city, with its fitful days of sun and fog and cool nights that rarely felt like summer. Summerplace was short-sleeve evenings, restless sleep from the heat, and access to any one of the pools, even if the floating lilies were a little creepy. There was the collision of fragrances from the flowers and plants; a breeze carried something sweet, followed by something with more bite that smelled like one might imagine dust to smell, then back to perfume.

He took his meals in the main house with the Huxley-Luxes.

It was his living there for so many months that got people talking.

And it was the resulting photographs that made people believe they were justified in what they said. Judgment, innuendo, accusation.

It wasn't unusual for the Luxes to have a stream of guests out to their property; the Little House wasn't the sole outbuilding. There was a shingled place, two stories and built in 1901. It had an open first floor with a decent-size kitchen and a second floor with the rooms on one side of a hallway—the wall on the other side collapsed like shutters to turn the second floor into a porch. The lack of insulation, making it fairly frigid in the winter, showed that it was only ever meant to be a summerhouse.

The main house, where the Luxes lived, was the one where Jenny grew up, all glass and post and beam and disappearing walls. When all the sliding doors and windows were opened, the place became a kind of tropical covered patio, with worn concrete floors.

The nudity or partial nudity of Babe, Bunny, and Agnes, witnessed by various townspeople who made their way to Summerplace for work or deliveries, seldom went unremarked. It was often the precursor to criticizing Jenny Lux. "It's sheer laziness not to clothe your kids," they said. "And it's plain wrong." "This isn't France," said people who had never been to France but had heard stories about topless beaches and sexual permissiveness. Never mind that the adults were always clothed.

The guests who came and went were one thing. Abner teaching at the college (his long commute adding to his absence) was another thing. But the last thing, the hushed thing, was Sam Tsukiyama living out there at that pagan paradise, where children ran naked and undomesticated. Who knew what went on there?

When Jenny had first shown interest in the Seneca, she'd found two glass plates already in the holder. She thought nothing when she removed them, leaving them on the counter in her darkroom. Sam asked about them, was told they came with the camera, and he, too, ignored them until the day they developed some of Jenny's shots—Babe in sundress and pearls, leveling her clear-eyed gaze at the camera, a candy cigarette in her hand. She held it as if she were a socialite who had been smoking since prep school.

Sam accidentally picked up the old plates, placing the unexposed plate in the developer and then, realizing his mistake, immersing the other one. The image that came up showed a toddler, a little boy, nude and squatting in the dry dust of what looked like a California landscape, among the native plants of someone's garden. The boy had a spider or an insect between his fingers in that way of very young children who haven't quite learned how to calibrate the physical pressure when holding a living thing. His expression was rapt. A decomposed shoe lay nearby, along with a discarded dinner fork.

Jenny couldn't decide if the picture was pleasing or disturbing (the crushed bug, the rotting shoe, the dinner fork, the naked child in the semiarid environment). Despite the fact that there were no real markers of an era, not even the length of the boy's hair, the picture looked decades old. She said without thinking, "His mother was the photographer."

And everything that she had been searching for was found.

The picture left nothing out: The composition, and the capture of the right moment, no simple task with the Seneca, said that the photographer knew what she was doing (and, perhaps, had gotten the child to comply). The age of the picture, and the nudity of the child in the unkempt garden said that she was at home and used to being at home. But the picture was not a snapshot of her child exactly—it was a picture of childhood, and it was this distinction that revealed the reach for art in the photograph.

No one except another woman with children of her own could read that conflict between motherhood and the constant push to create. Was this picture of the boy in dirt the picture she wanted to take, or the picture she ended up taking? There was the art-mother problem in that children and art asked for the same things: your undivided attention. Art required solitude, a disengaged mind, free to sort through the inconsequential and the profound, sifting through the mess in the mind until it found what it sought.

But kids interrupted this process at every turn, whether it was because they needed you or because you needed them.

Jenny adored her children so deeply that she could hardly stand it, because the world was as rough as it was wondrous, and being a parent threw that knowledge out of balance much of the time.

She was the least mystical person she knew. Life was right now, and when it was over, well, it was over. But when she saw the picture of this woman's child, it was like being handed a key.

"How do you know the father didn't take the picture?" asked Sam.

"It's too intimate. It's too ordinary. This is a picture of the everyday; there are limitations."

Sam clipped the print to the slender line that spanned the darkroom.

———————————

Jenny's pictures of her girls were of bruises and scraps, of roller skates and pets, candy cigarettes, pearls, and gloves, games played, swimming and hair wet and tangled from the pool. They were of napping on the fake beach, on an old mattress, in the grass. Playing dress-up, playing with lipstick, blush, and nail polish. Rhinestone barrettes, and felt-pen pictures drawn on tanned skin like little tattoos. Acting in the garden's terraced amphitheater. The girls were streaked with chocolate or circus-colored melted Popsicle sugar, standing around in bathing suit bottoms or cross-backed sundresses. There was blood, and tears, childhood mishaps, and ice cream. Dogs and birds and Sam Tsukiyama's bemused cat pictured stretched beside Agnes, both fast asleep on the green canvas of a garden chaise longue; tiny twigs and grasses along with dirt gathered in the tufts and folds of the pad.

Every so often, clothed adults were pictured in the periphery of the children's lives, talking among themselves, eating or drinking, paying no attention to the unfolding of childhood.

———————————

"I've never cared about things," said Jenny. It was one of the aspects of her that Abner most loved; she genuinely wasn't interested in clothes or jewelry or furniture. She cared about the ephemeral: images, her dogs, love. Summerplace. All the things you can enjoy but never really possess.

The summer of 1986, Sam and Jenny appeared inseparable; everyone saw them everywhere. When they came to town to pick up ordered chemicals from the post office; purchased glass plates from Acme Glass and Windows; went marketing, or filled Jenny's Scout with gas, it was even more damning that these activities were domestic. Errands were a married activity.

So when they were seen eating lunch on the patio of a café, or stopping for ice cream, their laughter, their intense conversations, the way they were unaware of the world moving about them made everyone feel sorry for Abner. There he was, teaching summer school, in the weird freeze of an air-conditioned classroom, or meeting with students and other faculty, when he'd rather be outside (they believed) while his wife and her "friend" were acting so "familiar."

Those poor kids—already too free by half—who knew what they saw out there in that "garden."

If only Jenny would explain herself. Not that anyone would believe her, which was the paradox of explaining herself; the weekenders and workers were convinced she must have something to hide. Her hands were always stained with chemicals; she didn't even bother fixing herself up for her poor husband.

"We should just rig a tiny camera onto her collar," whispered Jenny to Sam as they tried to track Kali on one of her daily rounds.

They were following the cat to settle a bet about her daytime activities. Sam said she preferred the patio next to the Huxley house, and Jenny said that she snuck off to the cycad garden.

Instead, Kali turned and walked toward them, greeting them with her tail in the air, as if she wanted to join in on whatever they were stalking.

Here was the part that confused the question of What Goes On Out There for the people of Stellamare: Abner and Sam could sometimes be seen together, at the nursery, or engaged in hours-long conversation following a leisurely lunch on the deck of a local restaurant. Instead of defusing speculation regarding the relationship of Jenny Lux and Sam Tsukiyama, seeing Sam with Abner made it more volatile.

———————————

The girls were playing cards. Seven-year-old Babe was wearing a rhinestone brooch in her messy hair and a green plaid sundress. Bunny wore pearls around her neck and wrists and was in an old vest of Abner's, no shirt, and a pair of underwear. Little three-year-old Agnes had just cut her own bangs, gouging out an uneven swath from the otherwise thick, brown hair that she'd inherited from her mother. She'd even nicked her left eyebrow in the process.

Jenny set up her camera, peering through the viewfinder and waiting for the right moment, then calling out "Freeze!" The girls were natural models, knowing not to alter a thing, yet making their inaction appear unforced. They had mastered the art of behaving as if no one was watching them.

Sam was nearby, alternately talking to Abner and another guest while loading glass plates for Jenny and handling the exposed slides.

"How did you learn to work with glass plates?" asked the guest, a colleague of Abner's at the college who taught composition and frankly hated doing it.

"I was a photography student, and I heard that Cymbeline Kelley was looking for an assistant."

"You're kidding," said the professor.

Jenny turned her attention from the girls. "Why didn't I know this?"

Sam said, "She got a Guggenheim and needed someone to help her print a barrel of glass plates."

"A barrel?" asked the professor.

"I was really just one of the boys who helped her."

"What kind of camera did she use?" asked Jenny. "For the plates, I mean."

"I don't know. When I knew her she only had the Rolleiflex."

"When was this?" asked Jenny.

"I must have been twenty, twenty-one. The project took a couple of years. She really couldn't do it herself, so once she taught me, I became pretty proficient. The fact that I became the 'print guy' was really one of timing."

"She must have been close to ninety," said the professor. "What was she like?"

It was then that Bunny took all the cards, laughing, and threw them into the air, making Babe furious (she was winning) and Agnes sigh in imitation of adult exasperation, which pretty much ended the conversation.

"What was she like?" asked Jenny later that evening, when she and Sam sat on the porch, looking at the stars and sharing a cigarette. Abner was getting the girls to bed while the professor was settling into the large shingled guesthouse.

"Tiny."

"Everything I think about her has always been influenced by that photograph with that beautiful naked girl. You know, the Rollei around her neck—"

"—in her garden," he said. "The Jessie Berlin."

"It's a great picture."

"Cymbeline was kind of a great person but, you know, not perfect or anything. She could be kind of tart."

"Was she mean?"

"Oh no. But you didn't want to bore her. Not that she expected to be entertained, but she did think everyone should bring something to the proceedings, as she used to say. It was really about being a good conversationalist. She didn't have a lot of patience, I guess."

"And not married?"

"She was, once. She said their friendship began only when they were no longer married. Leroy had passed by the time I knew her, but I had the feeling that she always cared about him."

"What else did she talk about?"

"She hated the Vietnam War, and got along well with people younger than her grandchildren. I wouldn't call her maternal, exactly. We were friends. Loved her own children, though she wasn't one of those people who seemed to live through them, you know? She took pictures of them"—he hesitated—"like that one you found. In your camera. Weird, right?"

"It was probably just in the style of the time."

"Probably."

"Most likely," said Jenny. "It wasn't as if San Francisco was a tiny backwater with one camera, and one woman taking pictures."

"True. Anyway, when I was helping her with the printing project, I made a print of a portrait of Cymbeline. She was so young I didn't recognize her at first, and she was standing in front of some kind of outside wall with a sort of gray, ornate etching on it. I knew that she had made some self-portraits when she was young, but this one didn't look like she was alone, if you know what I mean. You could see it in her expression. You know, there's such a fine line between being conversational and being intrusive, so I didn't say anything and just put it in with the other pictures I printed that day.

"As she was leafing through the pictures, she stopped when she saw herself. I thought I heard her say, 'Julius,' but so softly I couldn't be sure. She slipped the picture from the others and went and sat in the garden. She just wasn't there, you know?"

"Who's Julius?"

Sam shrugged and shook his head.

"She never said anything?" asked Jenny.

"I just left her alone. Then the next day, when I came to work, I could see that she had been going through all the plates. The place looked frantic, plates everywhere. She must have dropped a few, which didn't surprise me because she wasn't very steady later in the day, and I can only imagine her at night. I just started cleaning up and reorganizing and acting like everything was normal and she didn't look as old as she looked that day. I mean, Cymbeline didn't really seem old, generally speaking.

"She wanted to know where I had found that plate and I told her it was in with the others and she said that she thought they were gone."

Jenny and Sam said nothing. Stared at the stars.

"Do you think she meant 'I thought they were gone' as in 'I thought I'd gotten rid of these?' Or like 'I thought they were gone' and was relieved that they weren't?"

"She said there had been a fire in the house she shared with her family in Seattle, so there's that. It was clear to me that the plates she was asking about may have been kept apart from the others—or were meant to be kept apart? I don't know. I asked if maybe they were with some plates that she had already printed, and she said, no, that she always meant to print them, when the time was right, but somehow the time was never right."

"What do you think was on those other glass plates?"

"Maybe she had a secret life," said Sam.

"Yeah, maybe she was like Catherine Deneuve in *Belle de Jour*," said Jenny.

Once Jenny had recorded the days of her daughters, she wanted to record their nights. One photo has them sleeping, tangled up in the sheets and each other, three exhausted Greek muses. Another is of Bunny, in her cotton nightdress, the pearls around her neck and wrist reflecting in the moonlight as she reclines upon tossed pillows, her only companion a cat; she is a girl in her room who is expected to spend the night spinning straw into gold. In another, the moon contours Babe's thin shoulders and face; the oldest girl, also in her nightclothes, seems to be waiting for something, or someone, as she gazes toward the open door. Agnes, topless in underwear, her chest draped with necklaces of pop-beads and rhinestones, in the moonlit garden, with a silver paper crown, joyful and regal as if patrolling her kingdom.

Jenny made a picture of two of her girls kissing each other good night. It was chaste, and blurred from the action of the kiss. But it was at night. It was also on the mouth.

"Jen," said Abner, studying the collection of photographs of their three girls taken over three summers, beginning in 1986, soon to be published in a book called *Summer Studies,* "I love these."

"Do you?" Her happiness was leaving her a little breathless.

"I do. All these seemingly unimportant moments when you rush around, not even thinking about them. God, look at Babe, when she just had to touch the center of that broken car window. The blood. The crying. I remember that day."

The accompanying essay by Sam Tsukiyama talked about Jenny "locating the darkness, the complexity of childhood and parenthood." He used words like *authentic* when describing the scenes of Babe, Bunny, and Agnes holding Kali the cat too tightly, or imitating adults by pretending to drink coffee and smoking, or displaying stitches on a knee from an unfortunate experience with the concrete patio. He wrote about her night pictures, and how they were "little fairy tales," slightly mysterious and otherworldly, and how the darkness and the moon are different experiences for a child than they are for an adult. Sam wrote about life and death and Freud's pleasure principle, and growing up, and how childhood is sometimes more like a kind of parallel universe that adults can see but cannot quite enter.

He wrote about the natural, eccentric beauty of Summerplace, and how Jenny Lux recorded her children's lives without sentimentality and with an avalanche of affection. It was a risk, he said, for a female photographer to take pictures of her children because doing so made it easier to dismiss her, to treat her pictures as a vanity project. Cymbeline Kelley took nudes of her children, but she is known for her flowers and plants and celebrities. Miri Marx's most recognized pictures are of an American girl in Italy and a series taken from her apartment window, but not of the children she raised. If a woman must take photographs of children, then they must not be *her* children. It's too easy to label these women's family photos unprofessional, unlike male photographers, who are praised for the shots, often nude, of their wives and lovers. *Loved ones,* it seems, has many meanings.

And he wrote about how, in postfeminist America, Jenny Lux was a woman who not only chose to be home but found her great subject in the home, which somehow was the most radical thing of all.

———————

The first copies of *Summer Studies* were confiscated in two independent bookstores in Ohio. Mississippi followed suit, then Indiana. Then the rest of the South, with the exception of Florida (not quite the South) and New Orleans (immune to being puritanically bossed). Those feral children; those night pictures.

Libraries weren't easily bullied; they'd seen all this before, but even they couldn't stop people from borrowing the books and then never returning them.

Claiming to be the New Voice of the New America, there were those who made it their mission to attack artists like Mapplethorpe, Serrano, and Sturges. It didn't matter that they weren't in a majority, or that they could choose not to look at the work of Mapplethorpe, Serrano, and Sturges; they knew what they didn't like, and that was enough for them to decide that if they didn't want to see it, no one should see it.

They justified their grievances by talking about "public money" or "graphic sex acts on film" or "child pornography," but what they really meant was: no support for the arts, no homosexuality, and no attempting to record a human life from the cradle to the grave.

The stores that kept *Summer Studies* did so from back rooms. You had to request it.

———————

Many of the weekenders and townspeople, as if to prove that Stella-mare really was a small (and small-minded) American town, used this opportunity to express their opinions regarding Jenny, Abner, and the three summers Sam Tsukiyama spent at Summerplace. Of course, Sam was there when the girls were being photographed, they said (and those night pictures, why they could just imagine an adult creeping into their room, rousing them from their sleep, then photographing them in their subdued state). Of course, Abner was off, working. Of course, Jenny Lux was never like your usual girl, and wasn't she rather exceptional and wild in high school? And who knew what really went on at Summerplace? All this criticism, they felt, was not mean-spirited because people followed up by saying that it wasn't Babe, Bunny, and Agnes's fault; some people went so far as to intimate that the Huxley girls needed rescuing.

The criticism would've been easier to brush off had it come only from the right, but there were also those on the left, many of them women, who took exception to the photographs, which they found objectionable for the same "pornography" reasons.

"At least I'm a uniter," said Jenny to Abner.

"Yes, you're like Gandhi," said Abner.

And all of this was before anyone weighed in on the artistic merits of the work. "The silver lining," as Jenny called it, "as if anything they can say would be worse than being accused of exploiting my own children."

Jenny retreated into Summerplace. She didn't know that success—and there were those who loved the pictures for so many of the reasons she hoped they would be loved—could feel like a chair being kicked out from under her. She began following Abner around, asking questions about her work:

"Did you like the pictures?" (interrupting him as he replanted the garden).

"Did I reveal too much?" (interrupting him while he read students' papers).

"Am I terrible mother?" (interrupting him as he wrote an article about unusual European gardens).

Abner turned away from his desk to face his wife, who sat on the love seat in his office. "I love the pictures. I think they're the best things you've ever done. You know and I know that there's no point in making art unless you try to say something, and that you may fall short of your vision, sometimes the best work you can do exists in that grand misstep.

"When they say things about you being a mother, what they're doing is ignoring the fact that you're an artist. It's insulting, because you stay home and are happy to stay home and out of this experience you attempt to render the depth in domestic life. No one attacks Vermeer for spying on the women in his household. No one comments on his parenting. Seriously, are your photographs any more homebound than his paintings? At least you weren't tiptoeing around and peeking through keyholes, freaking out over all the letters being written, read, and passed around.

"Baby, you're punished if you make your art outside the home, and dismissed if you make it *about* the home. My God, you make the choice to *be* home, and it isn't enough. It wasn't just that you made people think about the complexity of childhood—you forced them to look at the complexity of motherhood. They wanted pretty, and you went for grace."

Sam Tsukiyama called her. "Cymbeline Kelley used to say that men ban women from the battlefield, then tell them that the only important pictures are taken on the battlefield. She said that women were kept at home because the men needed them at home, yet when they make art reflecting, or inspired by, the only life they were allowed, the result is dismissed as trifling.

"When she was first married to Leroy, she took a number of nude pictures of him—this was during the same time that male photographers were photographing nudes of women. She took so much shit for those pictures that she didn't show them again for fifty years. You make me miss her."

In the early fall, after all the noise about *Summer Studies,* offers came in for shows and lectures. The negative attention was starting to compete with a great deal of positive attention, but all Jenny wanted was quiet. She wanted to work on a new project (as did her publisher), but she was empty of ideas. The girls were not as willing to be photographed because it meant being home more and they were at ages when anyone else's house was so much more intriguing than their own. Jenny also realized that it was childhood, more golden and fugitive than she'd ever imagined, that was her subject.

She was cleaning out her studio and darkroom as both preparation and, she hoped, inspiration when she came across the black leather case that her father had given her along with the Seneca No. 9. As she moved it to free up the space it was occupying, she thought she should consider using it when she took landscape pictures. Or architectural pictures. Opening the long-ignored, never-used (by her) case, she found six exposed glass plates.

The next day, Jenny pulled the glass plates out of the black leather case thinking (hoping) that engagement in one activity could lead to that rare moment when an idea—one that hadn't even yet occurred to her—would catch. The sort of situation where if you *appear* to be working, then you will find yourself actually working. Proficient enough now to print without Sam's guidance, Jenny began the task of printing the exposed glass plates that had been stored in the black leather camera carrying case that Ed Schonneker had given to Mr. Lux when he bought the Seneca.

PICTURES OF BERLIN, 1910

1. *Waiting Room, Anhalter Bahnhof*
   (A cavernous train station of four waiting rooms, including one used exclusively by the Hohenzollerns)
2. *Mathematics & Love*
   ("I'm going to do a mathematical problem in my mind, and when you think I've come to the point of the greatest intensity of thought, take the picture.")

3. *Tulips*
   (A crown of tulips in his hair)
4. *Late at Night, the Brandenburg Gate*
   (Avoiding the awkwardness of a shared room)
5. *Something to Want*
   (Julius looking up at Cymbeline from the crowded Berlin sidewalk where all she could see was him)
6. *The Unmade Bed*
   (Two confessions of love)

But Jenny saw only a railway station waiting room with passengers dressed in turn-of-the-century clothing and signs in German; a nice-looking man of about forty, wearing wire-rimmed glasses, lost in concentration; the same man with tulips in his hair, maybe sitting in a park. She recognized Berlin's best-known landmark, the Brandenburg Gate (briefly thinking of her own visit there with Abner on their two-year European honeymoon in 1971). She saw another picture of the same man, previously lost in thought, and with tulips, only now he looked up from the street at the photographer. She saw the unmade bed with the slept-on sheets and a woman's hairpins.

Jenny strung the pictures across the darkroom and examined the prints as if they were a story unfolding, one that she thought she grasped, only to lose the meaning. Even when she was sure that these were Cymbeline Kelley's misplaced pictures, the ones she "couldn't bring herself to print," and the man was quite possibly Julius, she still couldn't say with certainty what it all meant. The images enhanced, then negated each other. Nothing was fixed. Nothing is any one thing really, and isn't that the beauty of it all?

AUTHOR'S NOTE

This book is a work of fiction inspired by several real women photographers whose lives and work have influenced my own. Those real women include Imogen Cunningham, Madame Yevonde, Tina Modotti, Lee Miller, Grete Stern, and Ruth Orkin. I should say that while I'm fascinated by photography—in its almost perfect intersection of machine, chemicals, and art—I've never considered becoming a professional photographer. The work of these particular women happens to coincide with how I see the world; the "stories" present in their pictures have meaning for me.

My treatment of the lives of these photographers is imaginative. For example, it's a fact that Imogen Cunningham spent a year in Dresden studying photochemistry. The invention is everything else. I don't know the exact nature of Madame Yevonde's marriage; I only know that she mourned her husband when he died. Grete Stern and Ellen Auerbach opened a studio in Berlin specializing in advertising photography, but I know nothing of their personal lives beyond the fact of their friendship. And Ruth Orkin's model for *American Girl in Italy, 1951*—a woman named Ninalee Craig who went by the name Jinx Allen—was not a privileged girl traveling on an aunt's largess, but an adventurous former nursery school teacher who saved up for her six-month holiday in Europe.

Like any novel, this book can be considered both an interpretation of real life and a portrayal of invented lives. I think of it as portraits rendered with words instead of paints—or as a series of photographs. When a photographer takes a picture, she is photographing an actual person, place or object. While there is some play in taking the picture (the use of filters, various lenses, camera speeds, flashes), making the picture doesn't end there. Many photographers will say that so much more happens in the darkroom or on the computer than a nonphotographer can imagine. There is the manipulation of the printing, of contrast, of color. There is hand-coloring, cropping, touching. Photomontage and collage are still another way to create meaning, using pieces of pictures to make a single photograph. One can also take a series of whole pictures and juxtapose them to create a narrative, allowing the photographer to make her own interpretation of the images. The photographers in my book had film; I have words.

This novel is my love letter, my mash note, my valentine to these women photographers, whom I have loved for most of my adult life. It is a fictional, sentimental history; it is not a biography of these women. It would be a mistake for any reader to skip their biographies and monographs if this novel sparks any interest in their pictures and their lives.

In writing this book, I consulted several important nonfiction accounts of the lives of these photographers and the time period. I am listing them here so that curious readers can read the real stories of these women's lives on their own.

SELECT BIBLIOGRAPHY

Albers, Patricia. *Shadows, Fire, Snow: The Life of Tina Modotti* (Clarkson N. Potter, 1999).

Anderson, Mark M., ed. *Hitler's Exiles* (The New Press, 1998).

Burke, Carolyn. *Lee Miller: A Life* (Alfred A. Knopf, 2005).

Calvocoressi, Richard. *Portraits from a Life: Lee Miller* (Thames & Hudson, 2002).

Chadwick, Whitney. *Women Artists and the Surrealist Movement* (Thames & Hudson, 1985).

Constantine, Mildred. *Tina Modotti: A Fragile Life* (Rizzoli, 1983).

Cunningham, Imogen. *Imogen! Imogen Cunningham Photographs 1910–1973*, Margery Mann, ed. (University of Washington Press, 1974).

Dater, Judy. *Imogen Cunningham: A Portrait* (Boston: New York Graphic Society Books, 1979).

Dater, Judy, and Jack Welpott. *Women and Other Visions* (Morgan & Morgan, 1975).

Engel, Mary. *Ruth Orkin* (Mary Engel, The Estate of Ruth Orkin, 1995).

———. *Ruth Orkin: Frames of Life* (documentary, 1995).

Gibson, Robin, and Pam Roberts. *Madame Yevonde: Colour, Fantasy and Myth* (National Portrait Gallery Publications, 1990).

Gordon, Mel. *Voluptuous Panic: The Erotic World of Weimar Berlin* (Feral House, 2000).

Haworth-Booth, Mark. *The Art of Lee Miller* (Yale University Press, 2007).

Hole, Lawrence N. *The Goddesses: Portraits by Madame Yevonde* (Darling & Co., 2000).

Hooks, Margaret. *Tina Modotti: Photographer and Revolutionary* (Pandora, 1993).

Lorenz, Richard. *Imogen Cunningham: Ideas Without End* (Chronicle Books, 1993).

———. *Imogen Cunningham: Flora* (Bulfinch Press, 1996).

Lottman, Herbert R. *Man Ray's Montparnasse* (Harry N. Abrams, 2001).

Lowe, Sarah M. *Tina Modotti: Photographs* (Harry N. Abrams/The Philadelphia Museum of Art, 1995).

———. *Tina Modotti and Edward Weston: The Mexico Years* (Merrell, 2004).

Mann, Sally. *Immediate Family* (Aperture, 1992).

Metzger, Rainer, and Christian Brandstätter. *Berlin: The Twenties* (Harry N. Abrams, 2007).

Obra Fotográfica en la Argentina: Grete Stern (Fondo Nacional de las Artes, 1995).

Orkin, Ruth. *A World Through My Window* (photographs). Text assembled by Arno Karlen (Harper & Row, 1978).

Penrose, Antony. *The Lives of Lee Miller* (Holt, Rinehart and Winston, 1985).

Penrose, Antony, ed. *Lee Miller's War* (Bulfinch Press, 1992).

The Photomontages of Hannah Hoch (Walker Art Center, Minneapolis, 1996).

Prose, Francine. *The Live of the Muses* (HarperCollins, 2002).

Rodgers, Brett, and Adam Lowe. *Madame Yevonde: Be Original or Die* (The British Council, 1998).

Ruth Orkin: American Girl in Italy, The Making of a Classic, introduction by Mary Engel (Howard Greenberg Gallery and the Ruth Orkin Photo Archive, 2005).

Salway, Kate. *Goddesses and Others: Yevonde: A Portrait* (Balcony Books, 1990).

Stern, Grete. *Sueños* (Institut Valencià d'Art Modern, 1995).

Weitz, Eric D. *Weimar Germany: Promise and Tragedy* (Princeton University Press, 2007).

Letters exchanged by Imogen Cunningham and Roi Partridge can be found in the Imogen Cunningham Papers at the Smithsonian Archives of American Art. For more information, please contact the Imogen Cunningham Trust at trust@imogencunningham.com. I quoted from the following letters:

Roi Partridge to Imogen Cunningham, July 24, 1917
Roi Partridge to Imogen Cunningham, May 28, 1914
Roi Partridge to Imogen Cunningham, August 13, 1914
Imogen Cunningham to Roi Partridge, July 6, 1917
Imogen Cunningham to Roi Partridge, April 8, 1934

ACKNOWLEDGMENTS

Writing is a solitary business, but it takes a crack team of finely trained experts to make a book. I could not ask for a better agent (or friend) than Joy Harris, as well as everyone at the Joy Harris Literary Agency. Thank you, Susan Moldow, for traveling to Barcelona. And thank you, thank you, thank you to my editor, the wonderful Whitney Frick, whose intelligence, insight, and impressively hard work have made this book better every step of the way. This may sound like hyperbole but, trust me, it's not.

I am deeply grateful to the writers of the biographies I consulted and of the monographs I studied (please see the Select Bibliography).

Along those same lines, I'd like to thank Meg Partridge for her incredible generosity in allowing me to use Imogen Cunningham's letters (and for copies of archival material), and likewise to Mary Engel for her support in the Ruth Orkin chapter.

A huge thank-you to Sandra Phillips and Erin O'Toole at the San Francisco Museum of Modern Art, who kindly answered every last one of my million questions.

There are eight images in this book, and a number of people were involved with securing those pictures. In addition to Meg Partridge, Mary Engel, and Lawrence N. Hole—all of whom graciously allowed use of their respective archives' images—I'd like to thank Chelsea Rhadigan at ARS/NY. It was my great good luck that led me to Jorge Mara and to Camille Solyagua, photographer extraordinaire (www.camillesolyagua .com), for their picture contributions.

In Portland, I want to thank Ed Schonneker for patiently instructing me in the intricacies of twentieth-century cameras, some almost one hundred years old. And to Jake, Zeb, and Faulkner at Blue Moon Camera & Machine for allowing me to get my hands on *their* vintage cameras. Also to Brian and Rebecca Newell, Kiyomi Shimada, and Aimee Albrecht.

In other areas of my professional life, I am indebted to everyone at *Tin House* magazine for their support over the years. And to Elissa Shappell, Gail Tsukiyama, Diana Abu-Jaber, Aimee Bender, Michael Chabon, David Shields, Carolyn See, David Leavitt, and the fabulous Peter Rock. And to the excellent editor Peggy McMullen at *The Oregonian*. And to Lisa Steinman, Jay Dickson, and Peter Steinberger. And Jane Anderson and Jesús Carles de Vilallonga. And finally, to Katherine Slusher, for sharing her knowledge of photography, her time and, most important, her friendship.

Thank you to Richard Riley, who has earned his own line.

Thank you to my mother, Constance Yambert, my brother, Bill Otto, and sister, Sloane Lowell. Also, Antoinette Sedoux; Michael Brod; Jan Novotny; Simone Sedoux; Ana Castaneda; and Tullio di Nunzio (Mr. Nordstrom). And to Bill and Jo Dean for the vacations and brunches and friendship, even if their mantra is too much, too late, and too far.

And thank you to the marvelous John San Agustin, one of the kindest people I know.

Last, but never least, the twin loves of my life, John and Sam Morganfield Riley. The apt metaphor here would be that life is a plane flight and no matter how neurotic I am as a seatmate, they would never sit anywhere but by my side.

PHOTO CREDITS

341

TEXT PERMISSIONS

BOOK CLUBS: MAKE
EIGHT GIRLS TAKING PICTURES
YOUR NEXT GREAT READ

This kit contains everything you will need for an evening dedicated to *Eight Girls Taking Pictures*:

A deluxe Reading Group Guide with topics and questions for discussion

Suggestions for ways to enhance your book club experience

An interview with author Whitney Otto

An interview with Mary Engel, director of the Ruth Orkin Photo Archive

Eight Girls Taking Pictures is sure to spark meaningful discussion!

Author Whitney Otto is available to call or Skype in to your next book club event. For more information, please e-mail BookClubs@Simonand Schuster.com.

EIGHT GIRLS TAKING PICTURES

READING GROUP GUIDE

INTRODUCTION

This mesmerizing novel reimagines the public and private lives of eight groundbreaking female photographers. Set in San Francisco, New York, London, Paris, Berlin, and Buenos Aires, *Eight Girls Taking Pictures* offers a lush portrait gallery of adventurous, restless women, moving across time and against the backdrop of some of the twentieth century's most momentous events. Fueled by the desire for experience and art and love, *Eight Girls Taking Pictures* examines the life that lies between public and private personae; love and passion; children and domesticity; and obligation and freedom.

TOPICS & QUESTIONS FOR DISCUSSION

1. *Eight Girls Taking Pictures* spans the greater part of the twentieth century. How did the roles of women in society change during this time? How about women artists specifically? What might twenty-first-century women be able to learn from the novel's main characters?

2. Describe Cymbeline and Leroy's relationship. How much responsibility does she bear for her unhappy—and unfulfilling—marriage? Taking into consideration the fact that the book opens in the early twentieth century, was Cymbeline, as she says, naïve to think she could have both a creative life and children? Why or why not? Which of the other characters struggle with this same conflict? How do their struggles reflect the changing times in which they lived?

3. Although some of the featured photographers casually cross paths, Cymbeline is the one who most interacts with the seven other women. Why do you suppose the author chose to have her as the central link in the novel? What is the significance of Jenny finding the glass plates from Cymbeline's time in Berlin?

4. What are the different characters' motivations for pursuing photography? In what ways is the art form more than a livelihood to them? How do they use photography to resolve personal problems, confront social issues, and support political causes?

5. Discuss how the characters' upbringings impact the directions of their lives. What similarities are there in the ways they were raised and in their parents' attitudes and beliefs? Which of the women were aided or influenced by their fathers in particular?

6. "Amazing to think that her life could completely change course in the space of a single encounter; then again, the impact of chance encounters was something that she had known about for a very long time" (page 131), thinks Lenny after meeting magazine owner Kristof Nash on the street. What other chance encounters have momentous outcomes for the characters?

7. What was your initial perception of Lenny? What elements of the story did you see in a new way after the traumatic incident in her past was revealed? Why does Lenny believe she finds her "truest self" (page 165) during her time as a World War II photojournalist?

8. Charlotte believes that Ines "will understand better than anyone that a woman always has to choose" (page 228). Why does Charlotte decide to remain in Buenos Aires? Is her decision more of a choice between Ignacio and Ines, or between creative fulfillment and a romantic relationship?

9. Discuss how marriage is presented in *Eight Girls Taking Pictures*, from Clara and Laurent's charade to Madame Amadora acquiescing to her husband's request that they not have children. Who would you say has the most fulfilling marriage, and why?

10. "Persecution erased all the differences of nationality, social class, religious or secular beliefs. Your social alignment was no longer your own; you became Them. And immigration wiped away your professional identity. If you can't practice law, are you a lawyer? To go from 'somebody' to 'nobody' takes its toll" (pages 219–20), ruminates Charlotte after being forced to leave Berlin. How might this idea also apply to women who are expected to give up their careers after marrying and having children?

11. What similarities does Cymbeline see between her own garden pictures and Miri's cityscape images taken from a high-rise window? Miri's other famous photos, featuring Daisy in Italy, were published twice, first in the 1950s and then again in the 1960s. Why do the

exact same photos elicit vastly different reactions a decade apart? How do they reflect the cultural changes of the times?

12. "This was before feminism took another odd turn . . . when it seemed that women were being encouraged to pursue who they really were, unless that included being a housewife, which, somehow, was no longer a politically acceptable choice" (page 256), muses Miri. How does this relate to her situation in the 1960s? How about to Jenny's circumstances two decades later? What, overall, does the novel have to say about feminism?

13. What does Jessie learn from Cymbeline about photography, as well as about life and relationships, during the day they spend together? Do you think Jessie stays with Emile after this? Why or why not?

14. How do you interpret Cymbeline's remark to Jessie that she doesn't understand how "young women can get it so right and so wrong at the same time" (page 287)? Why does she believe things are harder for contemporary women than they were in her time?

15. Which character's story resonated with you the most, and why? If any of the women could go back and undo some of the choices they made, which ones do you think would do so? What would they do differently?

16. Consider our current obsession with posting photos on Facebook and Tumblr and pinning photos on Pinterest. What do these contemporary photo essays say about our desire to document and be seen?

ENHANCE YOUR BOOK CLUB

1. In keeping with the theme of the novel, visit a photography exhibit at a local museum or gallery. Or have each member bring an interesting or unusual photo to your group's discussion of *Eight Girls Taking Pictures* and share what it is they find captivating about the image.

2. Have one or more members bring a camera to your book club gathering and document the evening's festivities; get creative and dress fancifully like some of the characters and their subjects do in the story.

3. One of Jessie's favorite pastimes is visiting the homes of female artists and writers. Check out www.LiteraryTourist.com to see what houses or museums are closest to your town and take a road trip with your group.

4. Author Whitney Otto was recently interviewed by bookseller and book blogger extraordinaire C. P. Farley for the Powell's Books blog—a blog affiliated with the legendary Portland, Oregon, bookstore. To read that interview and discover much more about the story behind *Eight Girls Taking Pictures,* please visit http://www .powells.com/blog/interviews/whitney-otto-the-powells-com-inter view-by-chrisfar/.

5. Have each member research one of the real-life artworks or photographers mentioned in the novel, such as "Distributing Arms" (www.Diego-Rivera.com; Diego Rivera Murals tab), the mural featuring artist Frida Kahlo, or Tina Modotti, who is the photographer who inspired Otto's character Clara Argento. Or Ruth Orkin, who inspired the character of Miri Marx; her famous photograph, "An American Girl in Italy, 1951," can be seen here: www.orkinphoto .com/photographs/american-girl. Do these photographs look the way you imagined them while reading the novel? How has Whitney Otto's novel influenced the way you see the pictures?

INTERVIEW WITH AUTHOR
WHITNEY OTTO

Author Whitney Otto was interviewed by Allison Frost for an episode of Oregon Public Broadcasting's *Think Out Loud* radio program, which originally aired January 28, 2013. A selection of that interview has been reprinted below with permission from Oregon Public Broadcasting, and has been slightly revised by Scribner.

To listen to the complete program, please visit www.obp.org, or go to http://www.opb.org/thinkoutloud/shows/whitney-ottos-portraits-eight-girls-taking-pictures/.

Allison Frost: What first got you interested in photography? I read that you were an amateur photographer of sorts.

Whitney Otto: Actually I'm a terrible photographer, as anyone who's had their picture taken by me can attest. I really just loved these pictures—the work by these women—from the time I was very young, and then as I got older I got interested in their lives.

Frost: How did you decide to write a fictional account of six historical woman photographers?

Otto: It wasn't even so much that I wanted to write about photographers as much as I was thinking about the artists (male and female) who inspired me, began to narrow it down to women, and then realized that so many of them were photographers. I was thinking about their work, and I just sort of thought about the larger thing I wanted to say, but filtered through them and their lives.

Frost: So it's six women—there are eight characters, and there are six of them who are roughly based on the lives of real women and then two are made up pretty much entirely. The six women are: Imogen Cunningham, Madame Yevonde, Tina Modotti, Lee Miller, Grete Stern, and Ruth Orkin. A lot of these names weren't even familiar names to me, and I just wonder, can you tell me some of the corresponding male artists who were contemporaries that we would know?

Otto: You would know Man Ray, in terms of Lee Miller. That's how I came to Lee Miller, through his photographs of her. She was his lover and muse and studio assistant. You would know Edward Weston, who was with Tina Modotti. Again, she was his lover, his muse, his assistant, and then became a photographer in her own right. With Imogen Cunningham, she was very involved with Ansel Adams and also working for Edward Curtis for a while. Edward Weston also was in the group that Imogen Cunningham began with Ansel Adams.

Frost: Tell me how you structured the narrative, which includes all these women and sort of starts in the early part of the twentieth century and moves toward the end.

Otto: Well, it's almost like this lucky accident. I knew the women I wanted to write about, and I knew that I didn't want to do biographies; I wanted to portraits. I knew that there were aspects of their lives and their work that I was interested in without being interested in their entire life—and a couple of them have extraordinary lives that deserve books on their own. So I needed a starting point. I started with Imogen, because she just seemed to work the best. Also, fortunately, she lived almost a century. So I began with her. It was also geographic in a way. I began in the West and as I moved east, I moved to Europe and then down to South America, and it naturally sort of configured, I have to say. So they each may begin wherever it begins, but each chapter ends farther along in the twentieth century; that's the sort of impetus that pushes you along.

Frost: Did their lives—obviously there are two fictional characters— did the lives of the six real characters really intersect, or did you have to fictionalize some of that intersection?

Otto: Sometimes they did. Imogen Cunningham met Tina Modotti and actually bought one of her photographs. Tina Modotti is the Clara Argento character in my book, who was involved with Edward Weston, who is the Morris Elliot character in my book. So they did sort of intersect in that way. I don't know if she was at the suffragette rally in London that Amadora is at, the Madame Yevonde character. They didn't really intersect that much with each other. She was kind of a huge figure of twentieth-century photography. People would see her work and know her, though.

Frost: How would you describe the relationship between Cymbeline Kelley (your character) and Imogen Cunningham (the real woman)?

Otto: They're very close. I took some liberties. I edited out a lot. As I said, I think of it as a portrait in the same way, say, you take someone like Picasso. Many photographers have taken pictures of Picasso, but each photographer brings his or her own idea of Picasso. I want you sitting, I want you painting, I want you smiling, I want you, you know, running around. When the photographer does that, they're interpreting Picasso in a sense, the image that they're grasping.

That's kind of what I felt I was doing. I would change Imogen Cunningham's life as I wanted to or needed to—that's why it's fiction. The other thing I should mention is, foremost in that first chapter, there is a young housemaid who lives with Imogen—Cymbeline Kelley, I should say, and her husband, Leroy—who keeps setting the house on fire. In Imogen Cunningham's life, that housemaid did exist, but she's a footnote. There's no name, there's no reason, there's no motivation; it's just . . . she tried to set the house on fire a couple of times. She finally succeeded, and that was the impetus that got them moving to California.

Frost: In terms of creating more of the details of the narrative—for instance, the housekeeper who sets the place on fire—obviously this is such a rich element of her early story. Do you have a sense of how far is too far? How far can you go with the embellishments, the fictionalizing, before . . . there's some line there?

Otto: If you go too far, it ceases to be that character, that real-life person whom you're pulling from and inspired by. And if you stick too closely, it can read too much like biography. There are great biographies already written about all these women. So I didn't want to do another biography, I really wanted to think about themes and stories.

Frost: You say that some of these women had interesting fathers. I believe you use the words "jaw-dropping and astonishing" to describe these fathers. Which of these real women had a father that stuck out the most, in terms of his progressive nature?

Otto: In terms of that progressive nature, interestingly, Imogen Cunningham's father was into mysticism; he was vegetarian, and they had a farm. But he was not necessarily progressive toward his own wife or women in general, which was true of more of their fathers. It was really just with their daughters. Imogen was from a very large family, and the first one to get a college education. She went to the University of Washington; she got a degree in chemistry and botany. She ended up winning a scholarship where she could study in Germany for a year with a photochemist.

Frost: There was no such thing as a degree in photography at that time?

Otto: No. Photography was very chemistry-based. But her father built her a little darkroom on the farm, so she was developing pictures then. As I said, the fathers tended to be forward-thinkers; almost to a one they had darkrooms for their daughters, or were inventors, or were just mechanically inclined for their girls.

Frost: The one that sticks out the most to me is perhaps the Lenny Van Pelt character, which is apparently based on Lee Miller.

Otto: Which is the jaw-dropper.

Frost: Spoiler alert—it sounds to me like she was abused, perhaps by her father, perhaps not, certainly by someone else, maybe her father. It was so riveting. This is one of the ones where I really wanted to know how much was based on reality and how much was invented.

Otto: The relationship she had with her father was really complicated, and no one really knows the absolute truth of how far it went.

Frost: He photographed her naked in the snow at seven or eight years old?

Otto: Yes. And even when she was in high school. He would photograph her naked, and her friends. Like I said, there's a terrific biography, very extensive, about her that talks about this. This has been talked about a lot, even on Wikipedia. She was raped when she was eight years old. Her parents, being progressive, sent her to a psychiatrist in New York City, who said that the way to help this girl was to teach her to separate sex and love, and never the two shall meet. And so that really sets up her life. Additionally—but I don't deal with this at all in the book—she also contracted venereal disease from this person. The treatment at that time was invasive, extensive, and lasted about a year. One of her brothers said that he remembered the sounds of her screaming in the bathroom when her mother, who had been a trained nurse, was treating her. So she was pretty traumatized by this. I don't go into that.

Frost: You don't go into that. That was just very briefly referenced, but it is toward the end and sort of explains a lot: how it seems that the character of Lenny Van Pelt is very distant from her own life, like she's not very emotionally involved, even with the people she is emotionally or physically involved with. She was trained to separate sex and love, so that does make sense. I thought one of the most dramatic moments really came when she was sort of on assignment photographing the end of World War II.

Otto: Lee Miller was one of the first people to go into Dachau when the war was winding down, and so my Lenny character is sort of pulled from this. Those images [for example, the scene in which Lenny steps on the mass grave] are very true to Lee Miller's life. The thing that I have my character repeating is actually from an e. e. cummings poem. I wanted to have something that she could anchor to, and so she sort of anchors to these couplets. But the interesting thing, too, about Lee Miller is that she was doing these postwar dispatches and photographs that were very, very graphic for British *Vogue,* which would be inconceivable today. And even then British *Vogue* was *Vogue,* it wasn't a different kind of magazine. But there was an editor there, Audrey Withers, who's again, just a different sort of person, and she ran concentration camp photos, which are so graphic, you can barely look at them today.

Frost: None of the other real-life women had anything quite as disturbing (at least, not in your book) happen to them either as a child or in their professional world. But there is a general sense of going on—not exactly disassociating, but certainly pursuing their art through adversity of various kinds. What were you drawing on, if not real people, when you wrote the two characters who were not based on real people? Jesse Berlin, for instance.

Otto: For Jesse Berlin's story, she's in her late twenties in 1971, and I was younger than that in 1971, but I also came of age during the second wave of feminism. What interested me about Jesse Berlin was that idea of a woman who was getting some success but in love with this very charming roué who's also a photographer. And I also wanted to talk about that time, because when we look back at historical events such as feminism, everyone thinks it's an unbroken trajectory, and it isn't. There are a lot of other things that happen. And we really come from the generation that came before us, because we're raised by the generation before us. So it's not like she would arrive in 1971 and think, "Oh, I'm this hard-core feminist, and I'm going to do this and this and this and this." She really is a feminist— she is part of this women's art collective—but she is in love with this man whom she doesn't want to distress by being more successful than he is. Because at that time, there really was the feeling that he's the man, he needs to be the success.

Frost: Bringing it full circle, bringing it back to motherhood and professionalism, with which you start the Cymbeline Kelley/Imogen Cunningham chapter: briefly, Jenny Lux is who you end up with, the last photographer, who brings us almost to current day. Briefly, who was/is she?

Otto: She's a woman who, you know, is a little bit eccentric in her own way. She adores her husband, she adores her children, and she adores the place where she was raised, and she embraces being at home. That's what she wants—whereas Cymbeline did not embrace that. But Cymbeline also loved her husband and loved her children. So it's a different approach to home life, but they're both still sort of raked over for it. So you kind of end with, "What do you actually want?"

Frost: It does seem that what you set up for her, being sort of criticized, she's in a damned-if-you-do, damned-if-you-don't situation. I wondered if that was a conscious way that you ended the piece.

Otto: It seemed right, and I also needed to end Imogen's/Cymbeline's story, and it seemed to naturally sort of move in a certain direction for me. I wanted to have these women who were very conflicted about their artistic lives and all the love they feel for the men and women and children in their lives.

INTERVIEW WITH MARY ENGEL

Mary Engel is an award-winning filmmaker and the director of the Ruth Orkin Photo Archive. She is also the daughter of Ruth Orkin, one of America's most famous female photographers. Orkin is the artist who inspired the Miri Marx character in Whitney Otto's novel *Eight Girls Taking Pictures*. Ms. Engel recently had an opportunity to discuss her work at the Ruth Orkin Photo Archive and her mother's influence on her life with a Scribner editor. Here is a snapshot of that conversation.

Scribner: Whitney Otto's character Miri Marx was inspired by your mother, Ruth Orkin. In *Eight Girls Taking Pictures,* Otto describes Miri photographing her friend Daisy Miller walking down a street in Italy, a scene that is loosely based on your mother's famous photograph "An American Girl in Italy, 1951." In real life, how did that photo come to be? Was it posed?

Mary Engel: The story of the photograph "An American Girl in Italy, 1951," is that it sort of just happened, as Ninalee (the woman in the photograph, who is also known as Jinx) and my mom walked toward the Piazza della Repubblica in Florence. Any woman who has been to Italy will confirm that Italian men often stare down and flirt with women on the streets. My mom had the idea of a picture about a woman traveling alone. She had met Jinx in her hotel and asked her to be a model for it. So they went out together and did what they were there doing anyway, which was being American tourists. This being just a few years after World War II, it wasn't common for American women to be traveling overseas. When she took this photograph, my mom stood in the middle of the street and asked Ninalee to walk down the sidewalk, and told the man on the Lambretta to ask everyone not to look at the camera. However, I don't think my mom's request meant very much; these men just did what they wanted, and they looked at the girl! It made for a great photograph.

Scribner: Do you remember your mother taking pictures while you were growing up?

Engel: Yes, my mother was always shooting, but she wasn't intrusive. She rarely asked us to repeat actions or tasks or to look at the camera. She always shot candids. She had five-hundred-watt floodlights in every room, which she would turn on when she shot, so she had better light. People laugh when I tell them this now. The wonderful result of all of this is that I have tons of fabulous photos from my childhood, which she put in these great scrapbooks that I love to look through and can now share with my son, who is twelve years old. So one of the beautiful things about my mother's photography is that it is being passed down through the generations of our family.

Scribner: When did you come to realize that your mother was a famous photographer?

Engel: I think probably when I was a teenager, and one of her books came out. She also started having exhibits. It was always pretty special going to one of her openings, and then going out with friends afterward. I have wonderful memories from those evenings. I was also always as proud and excited as she was when she was in the press or had received a positive review. She wanted people to learn who she was and about her life, and she especially wanted people to see her photos. I think she did an incredible job as her own press agent at the time. I don't know what she would have felt about social media these days, but it would have made things much easier.

Scribner: In *Eight Girls Taking Pictures,* Miri feels torn between her love for her family and her love for her career: "She wanted to be in two places at once, to be two people at the same time" (page 253). What was your mother like when you were growing up? Did she ever speak to you about her photography, or did you sense that she saw her work and her family as two separate pieces of her life, as Whitney Otto has imagined?

Engel: Actually, because my mother's office was in her bedroom, her work was a huge part of our whole family's life; it was all-encompassing. She adored us and was a wonderful mother, in part *because* she was so smart and passionate about life; she exposed me to the worlds of film, music, travel, and many of her other passions. However, she also was torn: she wanted to be with us, but she always had work to do on her photos, publicizing them, and getting shows and books published. I'm sure it was a constant balancing act for her. I used to help her file her papers and went on trips with her occasionally to different cities for shows, which was a nice time for us to be together.

Scribner: You have been a producer, director, and filmmaker yourself. Tell us a little about how the arts have played a role in your life. Were you inspired by your parents?

Engel: The arts have definitely played a role in my life. I always tell people that film was our family's religion. The Oscars were the most important holiday in our household. We are Jewish, but formal religion played more of a cultural role, and my mom was always interested in pointing out who the Jewish directors were in Hollywood. Also, I acted in commercials at a very early age, so I was exposed to that world, most of which I enjoyed. It was hard work sometimes, but I always felt it helped make me more outspoken, and the exposure became important throughout my lifetime. In terms of photography, my mom always wanted me to document where I went. I became photo editor of my high school yearbook primarily because people assumed I knew what I was doing and knew about photography because of my mother. I hope I did a good job. I certainly learned a lot from that experience.

Scribner: You are now the director of the Orkin/Engel Film and Photo Archive. Tell us a little about the work you do. Who is most interested in your mother's photographs today?

Engel: I work every day at the archive, and I love the freedom of it. It is hard to work alone sometimes, but the Internet has certainly helped tremendously in terms of connecting with people. I answer e-mails and deal with day-to-day requests, but also have long-term projects I am trying to pursue, such as books and shows. One of my biggest tasks is to create a complete inventory of all my mother's photographs. Remember, these were taken before digital files and archives, so a lot of what I do involves tracking down my mother's work. I am constantly looking for things—a particular photo, a negative, a magazine, an interview my mom gave, or some piece of paperwork. When you inherit an archive, it is not always in order, with lists and instruction manuals, so you spend a lot of time just trying to figure out what you have.

Scribner: What do your mother's photographs mean to you? Are there certain themes she returned to again and again? What were they?

Engel: Handling my mom's photographs has obviously been an incredible and unique way to keep her alive. It can be emotionally difficult, but the positive aspects definitely outweigh the tougher moments. I feel lucky that I have such a wonderful legacy to continue for her, and people seem to love her work, which is deeply satisfying. I know she would have appreciated the work that I do.